Redemption

Boys for Sale,
Book 2

By

Marc Finks

To all of those children,
Who don't have the love and support
That every child longs for and deserves.

Chapter 1

It had to be a dream.

Once again, Tavi was home and his brothers were crawling on him and wrestling with him. His mind knew it was a dream and yet he fought the urge to wake from it. If he could just hold onto this moment, this time when he was with his family again, then it could be his reality for as long as he could grasp it.

He heard his mother walking closer and he turned his head to catch a glimpse of her. But the light was too bright, and suddenly, in his dream, one of his brothers bit him on the ankle.

Tavi yelled and opened his eyes. He quickly reached for his stinging ankle, and he felt a soft, warm, hairy body twist under his hand.

Flinching away for a second, Tavi screamed again and jumped up. He kicked at the rat that was scurrying away from him, and then froze in surprise when he saw three older boys at the other end of the alley.

"Hey!" one of them shouted. "Someone's in our alley!"

All three boys immediately sprinted towards Tavi.

Tavi spun around and scooped up his bag, running away as quickly as he could. This had been Tavi's life for the past two days.

As he turned corner after corner and weaved in between the people walking along the sidewalk, the words that were spoken two days before echoed through his mind.

"We can't."

"What? Why not?" Tavi had asked in disbelief.

"We don't…" Kurt had hesitated as he glanced around at the others.

Byron was the one who had filled the interminable silence that followed. "Trust," he said quietly. "We don't trust each other that much."

"But that's stupid," Tavi protested. "Kurt and Kyle sleep together and they have no problems!"

Kurt held up his hands in objection. "Whoa. We don't SLEEP TOGETHER! We just watch out for each other." He smiled and looked at the others. "Come on. That was funny."

"Listen, Tavi," Kyle explained, shooting Kurt a dirty look. "These ARE my friends. But it's hard to find a place for five or six people to sleep safely every night. And we can't get caught. I would kill myself if I ever had to go back. It's just safer this way."

The others nodded their heads in agreement as Byron added, "But...I mean, we can help you try and find a safe place. We can show you which streets aren't claimed by any of the gangs. We have all day."

"Forget it!" Tavi shouted and stomped off. "If you guys don't trust me, then I don't need you." He had planned on spending the rest of the day exploring and finding a safe place to stash his bag and sleep, but Pablo's story about him and Yuri getting caught haunted him, and Tavi soon huddled up next to a dumpster for the rest of the day, too afraid that he might be seen.

Hunger finally drove him back onto the streets, but after buying a sausage at a food cart, he had immediately begun looking around for a safe place to hide for the night. Between two tall buildings, he could see a glimpse of the bridge that he had first seen long ago. Thinking that it would at least keep him dry, Tavi carefully made his way there, staying in the alleys, and running towards the busy streets whenever anyone took notice of him.

After forty-five minutes, Tavi arrived exhausted at the bridge. He carefully studied the dim underworld in front of him and could see several small fires burning throughout the area. A rank odor of mildew and dirt made him pause for a second, but knowing that he wouldn't be able to find the perfect home, Tavi trudged inside and sat down against a concrete pillar, not too far from the outside.

Within seconds, Tavi heard laughter and voices getting closer. Pulling his knees to his chest, Tavi tried to make himself as unnoticeable as possible.

"Hey, guy," a friendly voice to his right said.

Tavi looked up and saw a tall boy with a dirty face smiling down at him. He looked to be a couple of years older, and he was eyeing every inch of Tavi.

Tavi gripped his bag tighter in his lap as the boy's eyes rested on it for a couple of heartbeats. Flicking his gaze back towards Tavi's face, he smiled once again and said, "Who are you with?" Two more boys appeared behind him, and Tavi heard footsteps to his left as well.

"I'm with myself," Tavi replied.

"Oh." The boy's smile turned sad and he said, "You don't belong here then."

Tavi looked around quickly, feeling surrounded and claustrophobic. "Look," he said frantically, "I just need a place to sleep. Just…just please leave me alone."

"Aww. He said 'please', Jack," one of the boys said laughingly.

The spokesperson for the group – Jack, Tavi surmised – grimaced slightly and replied, "Shut up. Take his bag and kick him out."

Tavi wrapped the strap from the bag around one of his wrists and stood up slowly. In his right hand, he held a small piece of concrete that he had found lying next to him. It's worked before, he thought, when a flashlight to his left was suddenly turned on, blinding him. He raised the hand that was holding the rock to shield his eyes and he heard someone shout, "Watch out for that little rock he's holding!"

"Turn that off," Jack hissed. The light clicked off and Tavi blinked his eyes in the ensuing darkness. "I already saw it, and now because of you, we have to hurry before everyone else shows up."

A deep voice behind Jack announced, "You mean us, Jack?" The white flashes slowly dissipated and Tavi could see the outlines of people again.

Jack stepped back from Tavi and turned around, holding his arms out in a protective gesture. "Hey, come on, Momo. We found him first. And he's on our side of the bridge."

Momo stepped forward, and Tavi saw a tall, dark-skinned boy, even taller than Pablo. Behind him were several other boys were who about the same size. "He's ours now."

The children who had been scattered around Tavi quickly joined together into a group behind Jack. Jack glanced behind him quickly and shook his head. "Not this time. We have more people than you."

Tavi couldn't see what happened, but he heard a sickening thud, and then the two groups jumped together and began punching and kicking each other. Without a moment's hesitation, Tavi dashed out from under the bridge and ran until a cramp in his side made him bend over in agony. He leaned against the nearest building and checked to see if anyone was following him. Wincing at the pain, Tavi couldn't see anyone nearby. His eyes scanned the area around him and he saw a rectangular cube directly across from him. Tavi ran over to the port-a-potty, put the seat down, locked the door, and spent the night there, trying to sleep despite the nauseating fumes and the occasional knocking on the door.

The following day hadn't been much better. He had made his way back to the playground, but his pride and his anger wouldn't let him talk to his friends, and so he had burrowed his way into a giant bush and watched them while they relaxed on the jungle gym.

Hunger got the better of him, though, and when they split up and went their separate ways, Tavi went looking for some food, conscious of how much dirtier and smellier he was than normal. He considered trying to find Pastor Mike and asking him for help since Kurt and Kyle spoke so highly of him, but something about Pablo's story tickled at the back of his mind, and he decided that he would be better off on his own.

Remembering that Kurt and Kyle had made a home behind a dumpster, Tavi burrowed behind the first one he could find, covered himself with trash bags, and drifted off into an uneasy sleep. Until the rat had bitten him.

We'll see if you're really my friends, he thought as he turned one last corner and ran into the park. He glanced back and saw that all three of the boys had managed to keep up and were only a few seconds behind him.

The boys saw the exhaustion and fear written upon Tavi's face and began jeering and calling to him as they steadily closed the gap between him and them.

Tavi burst through the final wall of bushes that surrounded the area where the others usually hung out. "HEY!" he called out, only to hear his voice echo through an empty playground. He faltered for a second and the boys closed to within ten feet of him.

Breathing heavily, Tavi ran past the playground equipment and into the street beyond. Seeing the sign for Clarence's shop directly ahead of him, Tavi said a silent prayer and focused his gaze on the handle of the door. Summoning his last bit of energy, Tavi sped up, intent on getting into the store before the boys could catch him.

Twenty feet away. Tavi could hear one of the boys panting only a few steps behind.

Ten feet away. His left foot stumbled slightly and Tavi felt the passing of a hand as the boy tried to grab him.

Tavi grabbed the handle of the door without slowing down. Holding it tight, he checked his momentum as the boy who was right behind him collided into him. The boy bounced off of Tavi and fell to the ground as Tavi gripped the handle tightly.

Relieved that he had made it, Tavi shoved against the handle, knowing in his heart that Clarence would save him.

The door was locked. Tavi just had time to see that the lights were off inside when a fist collided with the side of his face.

Chapter 2

The first punch was the worst. The unexpected pain which exploded through his head helped lessen the following punches. When Tavi collapsed to the ground, he instinctively curled into a ball, gripping his bag tightly as he held it against his body.

A kick to his back. "Think you can come into our alleyway?!?"

"What's in your bag?" A stomp on the ribs. "Give it to us!"

"HEY!" A faraway voice shouted. Another kick to his back.

Tavi sensed movement around him as someone kicked his upper thigh. "Shut up, you red-headed dwarf!"

"Yah!" Someone else laughed. "Red hair and a dwarf. He's like the unluckiest person in the world!"

The sound of running footsteps got louder. "Get away from him!" the voice shouted again, as Tavi was kicked in the ribs for the last time.

The three boys surrounding Tavi laughed, and one of them shouted, "What are you going to do about it?"

As Tavi curled into a tighter ball to protect himself from the next kick, he heard the voice warn softly, "This," and then the boys were yelling as one of them tripped backwards over Tavi's body. He heard another one thrown into the side of the building, and a cry of pain and a loud smack as one of the boys got hit in the face.

"Get out of here now before I call the police!"

Tavi heard the boys scrambling around him and he slowly opened his left eye and watched them run away down the street. The tallest one turned around and shouted, "This isn't over, dwarf!" and then disappeared into the park.

Gentle hands touched his arm and for an instant, Tavi saw an image of his father. "You okay, boy?" a worried voice asked.

Tavi slowly straightened out and looked up at the man squatting next to him. He gave a weak smile and said, "Hey, Clarence."

Clarence's eyes widened in recognition. "Tavi," he said, helping Tavi sit up. "What happened?" As Tavi opened his mouth to respond, Clarence shook his head. "Never mind that. Let's just get you into the store." He helped Tavi stand up, and as Tavi leaned against the side of the building, Clarence unlocked the door and held it open for Tavi to enter.

Clarence hurried into the back room and brought back an ice pack for Tavi. "Here," he said, motioning to the chair behind the counter. "Sit here and put that on your head."

Tavi limped his way to the chair, already feeling less pain that he had a couple of minutes before. He eased into the chair and pressed the ice pack to his eye. Clarence came back a couple of seconds later with a glass of water and three pills in his hand.

"Take these," he commanded. "It'll help with the pain."

Tavi accepted the glass of water with his free hand. He lowered the ice pack to set in his lap, but then shook his head and raised it back up to his face. "No pills," he replied. "I don't want any more drugs – ever."

"It's just aspirin," Clarence protested, still holding his hand out.

Tavi shook his head and then leaned back with his eyes closed. "No, thank you."

Clarence studied Tavi's face for an instant before shrugging his shoulders. He set the pills on the counter and sat down on the stool next to Tavi. "So, what happened?" he asked.

Without opening his eyes, Tavi said simply, "I ran away."

If his eyes had been open, Tavi would have seen a wide range of emotions flow across Clarence's face. Surprise. Joy. Concern. Curiosity. "Good," he finally responded. "When?"

Tavi stopped to think. Had it only been two days since he had stabbed the customer with a screwdriver? "Two days ago."

"Good for you, Tavi. Um..what...or..." Clarence stumbled for a second before finally deciding on a safe question. "What about your friend? Mac, right? Did he leave too?"

In a voice devoid of any emotion, Tavi said, "Mac is dead. He took too many of those pills they were giving us and killed himself."

"Oh, Tavi," Clarence began, as tears filled his eyes. "I'm so sorry. Are you okay?"

"And then when I ran away," Tavi continued in the same voice, "those guys – Kurt and Kyle and them – told me that I had to find my own place to sleep. That they couldn't help me."

Clarence sighed as he studied the boy in front of him. He wished there was something...anything that he could do to help. "What did you do?" he asked softly.

Tavi shook his head. "I ran away and tried to find my own place. But I was too scared and I just hid next to a dumpster all day." He paused and let out a quivering breath. "My school is going to be looking for me. And when they find me, they're going to break my arm or kill me." Tavi's voice broke down into gasping breaths on the last word and he put his head on the counter and sobbed into his arms. Clarence hesitated for a moment, and then patted Tavi on the back to console him. Tavi recoiled at the touch of his hand and cried, "DON'T TOUCH ME!"

Clarence jerked back and watched helplessly as Tavi continued to sob on his counter.

Chapter 3

After listening to Billy plead and then threaten Javier with undefined consequences, Javier finally relented and allowed Billy to skip school for part of the morning so that he could help his father find his knife.

"What's going to happen?" Billy repeatedly asked. When Javier failed to reassure him, Billy followed up with, "What happens if someone found the knife? What if it has my fingerprints on it?!?"

"It's going to be okay, Billy," Javier promised. Inside, he had the same worries as Billy, but he could never allow his son to see anything less than complete confidence. "I'm sure it's not a very common place to visit. And they would probably have to be searching really hard to find your knife and…" He hesitated for a brief second. "…the body."

Billy became less and less talkative as they approached the turnoff. When they were only a few minutes away, he surprised Javier with his next question. "Do you still want to coach us in that tournament that's coming up?"

"Um…sure, Billy. Of course. I wasn't sure if…" Javier trailed off, reluctant to mention Tom again.

"Yeah, well, my friends still want to play. And Coach Tom didn't show up for practice for the last two days. I think everyone is wondering where he is."

"And what did you say?"

"Nothing. I just said that maybe he had a family problem or something, but that you could still coach us."

Javier glanced over and smiled proudly at his son. "Of course I'll coach you guys." Inside, though, he was begging

Billy to forgive him for putting him in this situation, and asking him if he was okay, and promising that nothing like this would ever happen again. "It'll be fun," he finished, as he put on his blinker for the turnoff.

As they drove slowly down the dirt road, Billy looked around with interest. "It doesn't look like any other cars have been here, does it, Dad?"

"Nope."

"It looks different in the daylight. Not as scary, I think."

"Good. I agree."

"Do you think his body is still there?"

Javier sighed. "I hope so, Billy," he muttered. "I really hope so."

He stopped his car at the edge of the clearing, and they just sat there and stared at the ground in front of them for a few seconds. "I don't see it," Billy said.

Javier opened his car door and stepped out. "Don't worry. It's so small that it's probably just hidden by some grass or something. We'll find it."

They wouldn't find it.

Javier instructed Billy to start looking on the ground near the car, while he would look where the killing had taken place. When Billy protested that it wouldn't be so close to the edge of the glade, Javier replied angrily, "You can either look there or wait in the car! You are not to go to the middle of the clearing."

Billy reluctantly agreed and kicked at the grass near the car. Javier strode to the center of the glade and began carefully searching every square inch of grass. He had expected to find it within the first few moments, and his sense of foreboding grew with each passing minute.

Javier glanced occasionally at Billy to make sure he was obeying him. He had obviously finished searching near the car, and was now moving his way around the edge of the grove, staying away from where Javier was.

Javier easily spotted some blood stains on the grass, and he could discern between the different footsteps left in the dirt, but he couldn't find the knife anywhere. He was positive that if Billy had left it there, then the metal would be easy to see. There was no way it could have been pushed so far into the ground that he wouldn't be able to see it.

Letting out a sigh, Javier dropped to his knees once more, convinced that he would find it this time. As he started checking the grass around him with his hand, Billy suddenly cried out, "Dad! Hey, Dad!"

Javier looked behind him and saw Billy standing at the edge of the forest where they had put the body. Hopping up, he hurried towards his son. "Billy, what the hell are you doing? Get away from there!"

"I didn't mean to come over here," Billy protested. "I was just following the edge of the trees, and then I realized where I was and I just had to see." He pointed into the undergrowth near his feet. "Look!"

"Billy! Now! I don't want to see it and neither should you!"

"No! Dad…there's nothing there!"

Javier rushed to his son's side and looked into the woods beyond. He could clearly see where the body had been. The leaves were still disturbed. There was a bit of blood. And yet, as Billy had said, there was nothing else there.

Javier spun around and quickly scanned the clearing. He glanced at his son who was still looking around for the body. "We have to go, Billy," he said urgently. "Now!"

Billy looked up at his dad in surprise, nodded his head, and then sprinted for their car with Javier right behind him.

On the way to his school, Billy only asked one question. "What does it mean?"

"I don't know. Let me talk to some people and find out."

They rode the rest of the way in silence. Javier tried to go over the possibilities in his mind. Either someone had found it. Or Tom wasn't really dead. Or animals had dragged it away. Or Giovanni…

The knife, though, that was a problem. Did it have Billy's prints on it? Did it have Tom's blood? Maybe Billy had lost it somewhere else? Maybes...what ifs...Javier silently cursed, frustrated and angry about how this was playing out.

When they got to Billy's school, Javier quickly wrote a note for Billy stating that he'd had a doctor's appointment earlier that morning. When Billy took it and just sat there, staring blindly at it, Javier gazed at his son worriedly and waited for him to speak.

"Dad?"

"Yeah, Billy?"

"What if we get caught?"

"Billy, I promise you. I swear on everything I love and hold dear. Nothing bad will happen to you."

A pause. "What about you?"

Javier grabbed his son and hugged him roughly. "I'll be fine," he whispered. "Go to class. Send me a message if your friends want to practice after school."

Javier tried to let go, but Billy squeezed him even tighter. "I love you, Dad."

"Me too, Billy. Me too." Billy released him and grabbed his backpack from the floor in front of him. Without looking back, he hopped out of the car, backpack in one hand, note clutched in the other, and trudged into his school.

Javier didn't move as he watched Billy disappear into the building. When the school door closed behind him, Javier reluctantly reached down and picked up his phone. As he searched for Officer Frost's number, his phone suddenly rang, startling him.

Giovanni

Javier immediately answered it. "Hey, Giovanni. I was going to call you soon."

"Hello, Javier. Is something wrong?"

Javier vacillated for a few seconds about how much he should tell Giovanni. "It's about that problem you helped me deal with."

"Funny coincidence," Giovanni said. "I'm calling about the same thing."

"What about it?" Javier asked warily, sensing something sinister about Giovanni's tone.

"I heard a rumor that, acting upon a tip from an anonymous source, the police found the body yesterday."

"What anonymous source?"

"And," Giovanni continued as if Javier hadn't spoken, "Sitting on my desk in a plastic baggie, I just happen to have a knife that I found. And it's covered with bloody fingerprints."

Javier ran his hand through his hair anxiously as he tried to keep his voice steady. "I don't understand, Giovanni. Why are you doing this?"

"We should meet tonight and discuss this," Giovanni replied in the same maddeningly calm voice. "If not for your sake, then do it for Billy."

Setting the phone on the floor, Javier pounded on the console between the front seats with his fist. The plastic split after the third hit, but Javier continued to beat it for the next twenty seconds as he struggled to control his rage. When he had enough self-control back, Javier picked up the phone. He glanced out of the passenger side window and saw a woman watching him in fear.

"Fine," he said calmly. "I'll come to your place at ten o'clock tonight."

"I'll see you then, my friend," Giovanni replied. "Ciao!"

Javier tossed his phone onto the seat next to him and tried to figure out what was going on.

Chapter 4

Tavi was startled awake by the sound of loud voices arguing near him.

"Listen, Candyman, you have no idea what our lives are like!"

Hopping to his feet, Tavi peered around the corner of the storage room where Clarence had told him he could sleep for the day. Wincing slightly at the sharp pain in his lower back, Tavi saw Clarence arguing with Kurt, Kyle, Pablo, and Chloe.

"I'm not saying you have an easy life, Kurt," Clarence replied. "I just don't understand why you guys wouldn't help Tavi."

"Help him how?" Pablo asked. "Honestly, I like him more now than I did before, but what can we do? We don't have houses or money or anything to give him."

"What about the money I give you for finding stuff?"

Kurt laughed. "Food. Sometimes new clothes or a new bag. Some more food. And the rest of it, well…me and Kyle want to start a food stand someday, and we need money for that." He shook his head in disappointment. "What did you think? We're like Peter Pan and his boys and we just have fun and play all day?"

"No. I mean, I didn't really think about it." Clarence looked so lost and bewildered that Tavi felt sorry for him. "I thought I was helping you guys have a better life."

"You are," Kyle said immediately, and the others nodded in agreement. "At least we don't need to steal everything we eat like a lot of the other kids."

"I still don't understand. Why can't you guys go home to your families?"

The four children exchanged glances and finally Chloe explained. "My parents sold me the first time and they probably would again if I came home. Byron's parents are dead. And for them…" she said, motioning at the boys, "Their families can't afford them and do you know how embarrassing it would be to tell them that they had sex with men for money?"

Clarence opened his mouth to reply, but slowly closed it as he thought about what Chloe had said. After a few moments, he said in a quiet voice, "And so none of you want to go home again?"

The others once again looked at each other before Kyle said softly, "Clarence…we have no homes."

Everyone spun around and looked at the door as the bell above it tinkled. Byron sauntered in, a big smile upon his face. When he saw how the others were standing and felt the tension in the air, the smile ran away from his face.

"What's up?" he asked with concern.

Clarence stepped past him and locked the door behind him. "Good. Everyone's here. Let's talk some more."

Exhaling loudly, Pablo complained, "Talk about what? We know what we have to do to survive. Just because you want to know…why does that matter to us?"

"I don't know yet," Clarence said. "But I feel like this does matter. You guys grab what you want and we'll have a shop lunch."

"Really?!?" Kurt asked with excitement.

"Will someone please tell me what's going on?" Byron said to the room.

"Go find something to eat and we'll talk while you're filling your bellies," Clarence responded. Looking directly at Tavi, he said, "You too, Tavi. Get some food and let's talk."

After they had all grabbed food to match their tastes – Chloe was eating yogurt and fruit, while Kurt was eating a box of cereal loaded with sugar – Clarence invited them to make themselves comfortable in his ample storage room.

"Okay," he said, swallowing the last bite of his granola bar, "let's start over."

"Good," Byron exclaimed. He was sitting on a box near Clarence's head, and his swinging legs were coming dangerously close to kicking him in the ear. "Since I never knew what you guys were talking about in the first place, that would be helpful for me."

"Man, whatever. Fine," Kurt said, from his perch next to Byron. "But you'll never understand."

Tavi looked at the others and tried to see them from a stranger's eyes. They were all so young. Frustration grew into anger as he thought about the boujies and how all of his friends should've been in school right now, and then afterwards, going home to their families for dinner and warmth and safety. He made a fist and gently punched his other hand.

"Easy, Tavi," Kyle whispered, pulling Tavi's fist away. "We all feel that sometimes."

"It's not fair!" Tavi exclaimed loud enough for the others to look at him. "Why can't we have normal lives?" He felt his eyes brimming with tears and quickly wiped them with his arm. "I just want to..." He couldn't express the anger and impotence and hatred that he felt at that moment.

"You see, Clarence?" Pablo asked softly. "That's what you can't understand."

Clarence watched Tavi for a few seconds before looking around at the rest of the kids. "Do you guys trust each other?"

"What do you mean?" Byron asked.

Clarence thought about what Tavi had told him earlier. "Do you trust each other? Not to rat on you? To help you? To fight for you?"

The others stared at the ground for a few seconds as Tavi's snuffles diminished. Timidly, they slowly looked around at one another and nodded. "Yeah," Chloe said.

"Then how can you not let Tavi stay with you?" Clarence asked angrily.

The quiet mood was broken and Pablo said irritably, "What are you talking about? Do you think we live in houses and we won't let him stay in the spare room?"

Clarence didn't reply as Pablo continued, "Fine. I'll trust you guys. Chloe and I sleep on the roofs of different buildings, but we have to move every couple of nights. There are others up there, and it's hard to find room for two people. It would be almost impossible to do that for three people."

"And we sleep behind a dumpster," Kyle said, surprising Tavi with his vehemence. "We try to make it look like no one is there, but do you know how little room there is? And we're sleeping in trash every day!"

Clarence was stunned and tried to think of the correct thing to say. "I'm sorry. I didn't know it was so bad."

"Again...what did you imagine our lives to be?" Kurt asked, all cheerfulness gone from his voice.

"I have a room," Byron said loudly. In a quieter voice, he added, "I mean, since we're sharing now and everything."

"What? How can you afford a room?" Chloe asked.

"I found it one time during a huge rain storm. I saw a basement window, and it was unlocked. I climbed through it and found a dirty basement."

"Doesn't anyone live there?" Clarence asked.

"Yeah. But they only come down once a month or so. I don't go there until night time, and I leave in the morning. The first thing I do every day when I get there is I take out the light bulb and shake it until the filament breaks. That way, I can be warned if they're coming since they have to go get a new light bulb. By the time they come down the stairs in the dark, I'm out the window."

"Is there a lot of room?" Kurt asked.

Byron looked around the room at his friends and shook his head. "No, not really. Maybe enough space for two more. But Pablo wouldn't fit through the window and..." He hesitated before continuing, "I'm sorry. But if there are too many people, we couldn't get out in time."

"Could Chloe fit?" Pablo asked.

Before Byron could respond, Chloe replied, "Forget it. You need someone to watch your back. I'm staying with you."

Clarence looked around at the group of kids. "You guys," he said softly, "I wish I could help you and even let you stay here. But this isn't a place where you can stay forever either. And I really don't have that much extra money."

"It's okay," Byron said, his cheerfulness belying the situation. "Tavi can stay with me. We can think up ideas together and I can help show him how to live."

Tavi perked up and stared at Byron. "Really? You would trust me that much?"

Byron shrugged and glanced at the others. "Sure. Why not? If you can't trust your friends, then you don't really have much left." He hopped down from the box and walked towards Tavi. Holding his hand out, he said, "Welcome home, roomie."

Tavi's eyes brimmed with tears, but this time, he didn't wipe them away. Smiling joyfully, Tavi reached out and shook Byron's hand. "Thanks, roomie."

Chapter 5

When Javier parked in front of Jasmine's school at two-thirty to pick her up, he couldn't remember what he had been doing since he had dropped off Billy. He had had a longing desire to spend as much time with his children as he could, and he remembered calling Laura and letting her know that he would take Jasmine to her horseback riding lesson, and that he would bring both children home for dinner after he met with Billy and his friends.

As the school bell rang, signifying the end of the school day, Javier went to stand by the door and stood with a couple of other mothers as they waited for their children to appear.

"Hi, Javier," Wendy, the blonde mother, said with a huge smile. "Where's your wife today?"

"She's on her way home right now to get ready for our fifteenth anniversary dinner." Javier gave her a bland stare. "Why?"

"Oh…never mind," Wendy replied, appearing flustered as she looked towards the students who had just begun exiting the school. "I was just asking. Congratulations."

"Thanks." Javier turned his back on Wendy and tried to catch a glimpse of Jasmine through the door as it opened and closed.

"DADDY!" Javier heard her a few seconds before he could pick her out from among the throng of rapidly moving children, all pushing and rushing to escape from the school. He finally saw her weaving her way through the other children, and as she burst through the door, she leaped into his hands. He caught her and raised her high into the air until slowly lowering her down and giving her a hug.

"Are you ready to go ride Puppy?" Javier asked, setting her down.

Jasmine grabbed her father's hand and began leading him towards the car. "Yep! Are you going to watch me?"

Javier laughed and said, "Of course I am. Let's go!" He made sure she was buckled safely in her seat, and then he drove to the stables as quickly as he could.

Watching Jasmine ride around on her pony, proudly showing off everything she had learned over the last year, made Javier wish that he had spent more time out there. Jasmine seemed to be a natural equestrian, and he could see why Laura was already talking about entering her into competitions.

After Jasmine had finished and was leading Puppy back to the barn, Javier walked up to Jenny, who was just standing there and watching her student with pride.

"She's doing pretty well, huh?" Javier asked. They could see Jasmine taking the saddle off of Puppy in the stable.

Jenny grinned and nodded her head. "She is. She rides like she's been doing it for years." She pointed towards Jasmine. "And look at her. Most of my students complain when I ask them to take care of their horses after lessons, but Jasmine does it with a smile."

Javier beamed and thought about what Laura had said earlier that week. "My wife was talking about a competition or something that we could enter her in. Do you think it'd be a good idea?"

"Definitely. Actually, I'm the one who brought it up with your wife." Jenny paused for a second before continuing. "However, there is one small issue."

"What's that?"

"Jasmine is growing pretty quickly. It may be time for her to get a bigger horse that she can grow into and ride for years to come. At the longest, she could probably ride Puppy comfortably for the next eighteen months or so."

All of Javier's problems came crashing back to his mind, and he wondered where he would be eighteen months from then. "I see," he finally said. "Um…what would we do with Puppy?"

"Well, Jasmine loves him, so if money isn't an issue, you could keep him here. Horses are social animals and it would be less lonely for the new horse if Puppy were here as well."

"Right. Let me talk it over with my wife and we'll get back to you soon. I'm going to…um…go help Jasmine," Javier finished weakly.

"Okay! And I'll give you or your wife a list of horses that I know are for sale, and if you need some advice, I can help you pick one out."

"Thanks," Javier said, walking away towards the barn. Sighing, he wondered if his family would even be able to afford one horse within the next six months.

After helping Jasmine brush down Puppy and fill his feedbag, Javier and Jasmine drove to Billy's school to meet his baseball team. When they arrived, half of the boys were playing catch, while the rest of the team were sitting in the grass under a tree.

"What's up?" Javier called as he walked towards the field.

The boys who were sitting under the tree all scrambled to their feet as Billy ran over from where he'd been playing catch in the outfield. "These guys won't do anything," Billy complained.

"Shut up, Billy," one of his friends, Tyrone, said. "We're just waiting for a coach."

"Well, I'm here, so let's get started!" He motioned towards his car. "The equipment is in the back of the car. Those of you who have been sitting, go get it. If you don't bring anything back, then you have to run five laps."

"Yes, sir!" a number of boys yelled as they raced to his car.

Billy looked up at his dad, a concerned expression upon his face. "Is everything okay, Dad?"

"Of course, Billy," Javier said, putting his arm around Billy's shoulders. "Everything's fine. Don't worry about it right now." As the boys who were carrying the equipment sprinted past them, Javier gave Billy a little push and said, "Go warm up. We're going to scrimmage in a little bit."

Billy flashed his father a huge grin and ran back to where Assaf was waiting for him. Javier smiled as he watched his son play pepper with his friend, and then he looked down at his daughter.

"Jasmine?" he said seriously.

"Yes, Daddy?"

"I'm making you the assistant coach. If you see anyone not hustling, you blow your whistle."

Jasmine's eyes opened wide and she shrugged her shoulders in confusion. "I don't have a whistle," she replied just as seriously.

Javier reached into his pocket and pulled out the whistle he had shoved in there earlier that day. "You do now!" He grinned and handed it to her.

Beaming, Jasmine draped the whistle around her neck, shoved it into her mouth, and blew as loud as she could. "Like that?" she asked, the piercing shrill still ringing in Javier's ears.

"Exactly like that," Javier said, stroking her hair for a second before she ran onto the field.

That night, Javier lingered over dinner longer than usual. At times, he was loud and excited and interested in everything anyone had to say. There were moments, though, when he would switch off and become withdrawn and inattentive to what was going on around him. This happened enough times that Laura finally declared that dinner was finished, and as the children scampered into the living room, she asked her husband, "Is everything okay?"

Javier almost broke down right there. He wanted to tell her about Giovanni, and the knife, and Tom Jackson, and what he had done to their son, and Javier's own life and the things that he had done. But when he saw the concern in her eyes and felt the overwhelming love, he wanted her feelings for him to survive for as long as possible. Knowing that his future with his wife and family was in jeopardy, Javier simply shook his head and said, "No. Not really. Just some work stuff I have to deal with later."

"Oh." Her disappointment was obvious. "So you have to go into work tonight?"

Javier felt a huge lump in his throat, and he had to swallow a few times to speak in a normal voice. "Yes, but it should be one of the last times I have to go in at night." He stood up and offered her his hand. "Go relax. You cooked dinner and so I'll do the dishes. I'll come join you guys in a few minutes."

Laura's smile was so filled with love that Javier felt his heart breaking. "You're the best husband," she whispered, standing on her toes to give him a kiss. He watched her walk away, his mind racing to find a solution to the mess he was in.

Later, as Javier walked through the door to the garage, he could still hear his family laughing about the game they had just finished playing. These are the nights that make us realize how wonderful life can be, he thought.

He climbed into his car and pulled the door shut. He stared at the steering wheel and then gripped it with both hands, squeezing it as hard as he could. Javier tried to summon the anger that he knew he would need to deal with Giovanni, but all he felt was remorse for how things had happened, and fear for the unknown future.

Javier turned the keys in the ignition, and slowly backed down the driveway. He put the car in park and made the phone call that he had been dreading all day.

"Sergeant Frost," said the man on the other end of the call.

"Hi, James," Javier said calmly, "This is Javier Lopez. I was hoping you could check something out for me."

"Sure, Mr. Lopez. What do you need?"

"Was there a dead body brought in today or yesterday? Probably found near the highway east of the city?"

A pause. "Um...let me check. Hold on."

Javier only had to wait five seconds before Sergeant Frost was back with the information. "Ah..yeah. Some guy was murdered. Multiple stab wounds. Genital mutilation. No identification on him. Do you know anything about him?"

Javier carefully thought about his next words and weighed them against what he thought his relationship with Sergeant Frost was. "He may have been a customer. I heard a vague rumor. If it turns out that the murder happened because of this man's...predilections...that could affect how the case would be prosecuted, right?"

"I'm not really sure what you want to hear, Mr. Lopez. There could be self-defense, or temporary insanity, or cold-blooded murder. But that's a bit beyond my expertise."

"Okay, I understand. Thanks for the information. If I find out anything, you're the man I'll bring it to."

"Sounds good, Mr. Lopez." Javier heard the click of Sergeant Frost disconnecting the call and wondered if he would be on his side.

Tossing his phone onto the seat next to him, Javier quickly pulled out of his driveway and drove to work. He parked in his usual spot and gave the boy who was sitting there one talent. Javier kept his gaze focused on Bangarang as he walked past The School House. Upon entering, his eyes coldly moved around the room, flicking past the men and their young paramours for the night, ignoring the cages filled with angelic pre-pubescent youths, and concentrated on a spot behind the bar.

"Mr. Delvecchio is expecting you," the massive bartender rumbled. "Please go up the stairs."

Javier nodded slightly and slowly made his way up the stairs. He paused for a second at the top to knock twice.

"Come in," Giovanni shouted.

The door opened into an immense office. Giovanni sat at a large, oak desk with a wall of CCTV monitors behind him. Reclining in his leather chair, he motioned for Javier to sit down across from him. "Have a seat," he commanded. "We were just wondering if you were going to show up tonight."

Javier glanced to his left and saw a familiar figure staring out of the huge bay window. He turned around slowly and Javier's voice was filled with disappointment as he whispered, "Vikram."

Chapter 6

"What are you doing here?" Javier asked as Vikram strolled over and sat down in one of the chairs facing Giovanni.

Before Vikram could answer, Giovanni said, "He's here because I asked him to be here, Javier. Just as you are. Now, please, sit down."

Javier reluctantly sat down in the chair next to Vikram. Only when he was completely settled did he turn his eyes from his employee to the man sitting behind the desk. He was a large man, bigger than Javier, and his eyes usually radiated a cheerful malevolence. Javier had never seen them as expressionless at they were that night.

Refusing to speak first, Javier blinked and slowly let his eyes roam around the room, taking in the books that lined the redwood shelves, the copies of famous paintings on the walls, and a number of large vases from a time and place that Javier didn't care about.

After a couple of minutes of silence, Vikram shuffled restlessly in his chair and said, "Well...can we do this?"

Giovanni shook his head in disappointment at Vikram and met Javier's gaze. "He gets impatient, doesn't he?" When Javier didn't respond, Giovanni continued, "And that's one reason why we're here right now."

"Explain." Giovanni smiled slightly at the tone of Javier's voice, the commanding ring that filled the room.

Vikram turned in his chair and tried to apologize to Javier. "Boss…I mean, Javier. I didn't want it to be like this." He hesitated a few seconds as Javier continued to stare at Giovanni. "I mean, I liked working for you. But now you have these new ideas…"

"Shut up," Javier ordered quietly, deigning to glance at Vikram. Returning his attention back towards Giovanni, he said, "Why don't you tell me what's happening right now?"

Giovanni leaned back in his chair and reached down to open a drawer from the right side of the desk. He pulled out a plastic baggie and held it up for Javier to observe. The bloody knife inside of the bag was clear to see, as were the fingerprints stamped into the blood upon the handle. Giovanni casually dropped the bag back into the drawer and reached down to close and lock it.

"I saw Billy's knife next to that pedo's stuff on the grass. I just grabbed everything – carefully, of course – and put it in my car. At that time, I had every intention of cleaning and returning it to you."

"But…?"

"But I've been speaking to Vikram here about your ideas and, to be honest, they scare me."

"It wouldn't affect you," Javier said with certainty.

"It wouldn't affect me? Are you serious? You really think they wouldn't affect me?!?" Giovanni raised his voice, showing emotion for the first time that night. "What happens when you change your place into a happy home? What happens to my boys? When would you start looking at my boys and start thinking to yourself that they should be saved as well?!?"

Javier thought about it for a second before shaking his head. "I don't think it would come to that."

"You don't think? As soon as you decided to try and "fix" things, you became my enemy. It doesn't make sense for you to just stop and try to only help the boys that you have now. Eventually, you would want to help all of them."

"Do you understand what we do, Giovanni?" Javier asked.

"Yes. We are providing a service that someone must provide. If we didn't do it, then someone else would. These little village rats that we sell to these men…what else would they do with their lives? They see more money working here than they ever would in their tiny dirty villages."

Javier refused to reply. He knew everything that Giovanni could say because he believed the same things not too long ago. He turned to Vikram and asked softly, "Do you agree with him?"

"I do," Vikram said, meeting Javier's gaze for a couple of heartbeats.

Javier pinched the bridge of his nose as he thought of a solution. "You were both there that night," he began.

"Maybe we were and maybe we weren't," Giovanni answered. "But there is a bloody knife with Billy's fingerprints on it."

"But…" Javier licked his lips and swallowed.

"But Billy will be implicated no matter what. And then what will happen to your perfect family life?" Giovanni asked softly.

Javier closed his eyes, knowing that he had to do anything he could so that Billy would not be a part of this. Ah, he thought. I see what they want. "You want me to take the fall, don't you? And then give The School House to Vikram." He glanced at Vikram, who refused to look at Javier.

"Well, actually, Vikram and I will share The School House," Giovanni admitted. "Fifty-fifty partners for the first couple of years, and then after he's learned everything he can from me, it's his to run as he pleases…within certain guidelines of course."

"Or…"

"Or I give this knife to the police and Billy gets accused of murdering his baseball coach. And most likely, your wife will have a lot of questions about what you really do."

"And if I take the fall?"

"What is that expression…'Mum's the word'?" Giovanni smiled cheerfully at Javier.

"I could fight you on this."

Giovanni tilted his head in acknowledgement. "You could, but again, it's your family that's involved."

Javier ran through the options in his mind. They were extremely limited, and everyone in the room knew it. "I have another proposition."

"What?"

"I sign The School House over to Vikram, you give me the knife, and everyone is happy."

Giovanni appeared to think about it for a second. "But then you're still around, and you'll probably stir up some trouble"

Javier fought down the desire to punch Giovanni in the face. "What do you think I would do?"

Giovanni shrugged apologetically and said, "I'm trusting my instinct, Javier, and my instinct says I can't trust you. And that's the end of that."

Swallowing his fury and frustration, Javier said, "Fine. I'll admit I killed him – alone. But there are several things we must agree to first."

"Of course," Giovanni replied. "Go on."

"First, Vikram is in charge of the knife. Once I admit to the crime, then he destroys the evidence against Billy."

"I'm not sure…" Giovanni began.

"You're a snake, Giovanni," Javier retorted. "At least Vikram has…or had…a shred of honor."

"Okay. I agree." Vikram pronounced loudly. He looked Javier and said in a softer voice, "I promise."

Javier nodded his head. "Next, I can say whatever I want about what happened, as long as I never mention anyone else who may have been involved."

"Explain what you mean," Giovanni ordered.

"For example, if I want to claim self-defense, then I can."

"Okay. And after we hear what you've been charged with, only then will Vikram get rid of the knife."

"Fine." Javier took a deep breath and warned, "My family stays out of this. My business life and anything to do with you or The School House is never mentioned to anyone."

Giovanni nodded his head in agreement.

"I promise you, Giovanni, that if my family is affected in any way outside of what I plan, then I will personally kill you the day I get out of jail." He looked at Vikram. "And you…if you fuck me over again, then I'll make sure that what happened to Tom Jackson looks like a picnic in the park compared to what my associates will do to you. Do you understand?"

Giovanni nodded his head once more as Vikram stuttered, "Yes..yes, sir!"

Javier stood up abruptly. "Tomorrow morning I'll sign The School House over to Vikram. After that, I need to talk to my family and explain what's happening. I'll go down to the police station tomorrow evening or the next day."

As Javier marched towards the door, Giovanni called after him, "Good luck, my friend."

Javier paused at the top of the stairs, one foot poised to step down. He hesitated for only the briefest of moments before continuing down the stairs.

"Well, that was easy," Giovanni said to Vikram, as he reclined back in his chair.

"Give me the knife," Vikram demanded.

"Come now, Vikram," Giovanni chided. "That's no way to start a healthy business relationship."

"Give it to me now or I leave right now and help Javier out of this mess."

Giovanni's eyes grew cold. Giving a small, emotionless smile, he bent down and quickly retrieved the plastic baggie. "Of course. You did give your word." He tossed the bag across the desk and Vikram caught it with both hands. "Satisfied?"

"Yes."

"Good. Now go find that boy who ran away the other day. He's an embarrassment to you and it's giving the other boys the wrong idea. And tomorrow, I'm going to show you how to make your boys work harder. Javier has been a bit too easy on The School House boys from what I've heard."

"Yes, sir," Vikram said. Standing up, he asked, "What should we do with the boy if we catch him?"

As his words filled the air, Vikram already knew how Giovanni would respond.

"Bring him back and kill him in front of the other boys. And you'll never have that problem again. You do want to make lots of money, right?"

Vikram swallowed before nodding his head. "Yes, sir," he said.

"Good. Now go find him before it's too late." Giovanni watched Vikram trudge out of his office and smiled at the thought of owning The School House.

Chapter 7

Tavi curled up into an even smaller ball as someone tried to shake him awake. Burrowing under the blanket, he tried to ignore the hand that was gently nudging him.

"Tavi, wake up. We have to get out of here soon."

Tavi lay there for a few more seconds before throwing back the blanket and opening his eyes to find Byron hovering above him. The small, dusty basement was barely visible in the early morning sunlight which filtered through the dirty window on the other side of the room.

"What time is it?" Tavi asked as he stretched and gave a slight moan.

Byron studied his watch, turning it so that he could read it in the dim light. "Five forty-five or so. We have to go."

Tavi attempted to pull the blanket back over his head, but Byron yanked it off of him, his face angrier than Tavi had ever seen him. "Why so early?" Tavi grumbled as he got to his feet. He looked around the basement which had been hidden in the dark. Besides a few boxes and a couple of old chairs, there wasn't much down there. Byron had moved some of the boxes near the boiler to hide behind while he slept.

"Because they could see us now if they came down. If you want to stay here, then you have to do what I say."

"Fine."

Byron rolled up their blankets and stuffed them deep behind the boiler. Stepping around the boxes, he hurried over and pulled open the window. Glancing cautiously at the door at the top of the wooden stairs, he whispered, "Hurry up. Stand on this box and climb out."

As they walked down the quiet street in the early morning light, Byron asked, "Do you know what would happen if they caught us?"

Tavi thought about it for a second before shaking his head. "No? I don't know. Call the police?"

"And then what happens?"

Tavi struggled to think of a response as Byron answered for him. "Remember Pablo's story? Those were cops that took Yuri back to your bar. And so, I don't know if all of them are bad or just some of them, but even if they weren't dirty, what would they do with us? We have no homes or parents."

"I get it," Tavi replied. He stopped walking and looked Byron in the eye. "Really, I understand."

Byron flashed him his usual smile. "Good. Let's go have some fun." The sound of laughter broke the silence as someone began beating on a metal trashcan lid at the end of the street. Byron looked around in distress and pulled Tavi down the nearest alleyway. "Let's go," he commanded, and began jogging in the direction away from the noise.

Tavi froze for a second in confusion before sprinting after Byron. As soon as he caught up, he matched his pace with Byron's and asked, "What are we doing?"

"We have to be careful in other people's territories," Byron said, breathing easily as they ran. "You can usually pass through, but if they have more people or if they're in the wrong mood, it could be bad for us."

"What? And how do you learn who has each area?"

Byron laughed as he slowed down to a walk. "If someone tries to beat you up for being in their territory, then you know that it belongs to them."

"And what territory is ours?" Tavi asked, imagining a large area from the night markets to the train station, and most definitely including the park.

"Um....the playground."

"You mean the park, right?"

"No." Byron stopped walking and squatted against the brick wall of a building. "Listen, Tavi. We aren't very strong. We are smaller than a lot of the kids out here, and we don't have as many people. And, to be honest, a lot of the kids out here are crazy. You don't want to mess with them."

"But at least we have the playground."

"Well, yes. But that's only because no one else has wanted it."

A wave of hopelessness washed over Tavi. "Why do things never seem to get better? I thought that once I ran away and found you guys that things would be okay, but it's just a different kind of bad."

Byron shrugged, a hurt expression upon his face. "Sorry...I guess. We didn't mean to disappoint you."

"No. That's not what I meant," Tavi insisted. "I owe you so much for letting me sleep with you. I just...There has to be a way to make things better."

Byron hopped to his feet and reached down to help Tavi up. "Well, if you think of a way, let us know. But right now we have to meet the others."

"Really? Why?"

"It's boujie time!" Byron laughed and began jogging again, headed towards the train station. "We try to find some rich kid walking alone and then we beat him up and take his shit!"

The feeling that life was unfair was still bouncing around inside of Tavi's mind, and so he laughed with Byron, excited about the chance to help balance things out.

They got off at a station that was unfamiliar to Tavi. As they walked down the stairs, he could smell a variety of aromas from the numerous food stands set up near the station. "So, what now?" he asked Byron as they jumped down the stairs.

Byron pointed to where Pablo, Chloe, Kurt, and Kyle were standing. Their mouths were stuffed with food, and they were trying to chew quickly as they threw the food wrappers into the nearby trashcan.

"Sweet! Breakfast. I'm starving," Tavi said as he checked out the different foods being sold.

"Afterwards," Byron told him, pulling Tavi after the others who were already walking away. "We were late today."

Tavi's stomach rumbled in protest. Kurt looked back with a smile and swallowed his last bite. "The banana pancakes were good today. I hope she doesn't run out." He laughed and turned to tell the others what he had just said.

After a few minutes of aimless wandering, Tavi finally asked, "Okay. So, what's the plan?"

Kyle replied, "We walk around until we find a boujie who's walking alone. And then we quickly jump him and run away before we get caught."

"That's it?" Tavi asked in disbelief. "That's your whole plan?"

Pablo rolled his eyes and stopped walking. "Fine, Mr. Know-it-all. What's your genius plan?"

Tavi thought for a second before asking, "Are we at least near a school?"

Byron nodded. "Three blocks away."

"And does anyone have a knife or something?"

The sound of five knives flicking open answered his question.

"Fine. I have a plan."

Twenty minutes later, Tavi was leaning against a brick wall, one block from the school. As a boy about their age passed them, Tavi took note of his private school uniform, glanced quickly around, and waved his hand above his head. Letting the student get ten feet ahead of them, Byron and Tavi eased their way off of the wall and quietly began trailing him.

The boy was unconcernedly passing a narrow alleyway when Kyle stepped out from a doorway directly in front of him. Flicking open his knife, he ordered softly, "Drop your bag!"

The boy's eyes widened in shock and he looked around wildly. Kurt suddenly materialized from the boy's left and stepped towards him. "Hurry up!"

Taking one step back, the boy glanced behind him and saw Tavi and Byron only a few feet behind him. Despair filled his face and the boy bolted into the alleyway to his right. The four boys followed at a slower pace. They knew what the boy was going to find waiting for him.

"Hurry up! Give us your bag!" Pablo was saying as Tavi got within hearing distance.

The boy glanced behind him and he sagged for an instant when he saw Tavi and his friends approaching behind him. "Fine," he said, surrendering to the inevitable. He slipped his bag off of his back, reached in through the top where it wasn't zippered, and pulled something out.

Turning quickly, the boy threw the baseball as hard as he could. It smashed into Pablo's forehead, who cried out in pain and dropped his knife. The boy slung the bag back over his shoulder and ran at Chloe, who had fallen back in surprise when Pablo had been hit.

Tavi was an instant too quick. He had already begun moving when the boy threw the ball, and before the boy was able to take more than three steps, Tavi had tackled him from behind and was punching him in the head.

He felt a kick to his stomach as the boy tried to get him off, but after a couple of seconds of stunned silence, the others were there to help him. They punched and kicked the boy until he stopped resisting, and then Kurt ripped away his bag and Kyle dug through his pockets. He gave a small cheer when he found a cell phone and money, and when he was finished, they all stepped away from the boy.

"Please," he moaned, sitting up. "Please don't take my laptop. My parents just bought it for me."

"What?" Kurt looked into the bag and then smiled broadly at everyone. "It IS a laptop. Do you guys know how much this is worth?"

Pablo stepped forward, still rubbing the spot where the baseball had hit him. "What's your name?" he asked.

"Assaf."

"Listen, Assaf. Your family is rich. They can just buy you a new one."

Assaf looked around him in anger. His eyes burning with pride, he snapped, "My family isn't rich! My parents saved money for a year to buy me that."

Pablo nudged Assaf with his knee and made him fall sideways. "At least you have parents," he said. Speaking to the others, who were all staring at Assaf with bemused expressions, he ordered, "Let's go before we get caught." He spun around and jogged down the alleyway. As Kyle passed by Assaf, he casually let the cell phone slip from his hand and fall into the boy's lap. Within seconds, Assaf was alone in the alleyway, weeping silently, and wondering how he would be able to explain to his parents what had happened to his one week old birthday present.

Chapter 8

Javier arrived home after his meeting with Giovanni long after his family had gone to bed. He spent an hour roaming the house, absently touching everything he passed, and thought about what he would say to Laura the next day. He spent a long time slowly flipping through a photo album that always sat on the coffee table in the living room. As he turned the last page, he carefully set it back down and stared hopelessly into the dark fireplace in front of him.

After a restless night in bed next to Laura, Javier woke up earlier than usual and set about making the best breakfast he had ever cooked. When Laura came down the stairs forty-five minutes later, yawning and rubbing her eyes, she stopped in surprise at the feast that Javier had prepared.

Pancakes, waffles, scrambled eggs, bacon and sausages, a bowl full of mixed fruits, the cereal boxes were out, and there were pitchers of milk and two different kinds of fruit juices.

"Javier!" Laura gasped in surprise. "What is all this?"

Javier rushed over to her with a mug of coffee. "I just wanted to make a nice breakfast for my family today," he answered with a smile. Holding the coffee in one hand, he squeezed her with the other arm and gave her a kiss on the lips. "For you, my love," he said softly, handing her the coffee.

"What about the children?" Laura stared at the table in wonder. "And who will eat all of this food?"

Javier laughed and strode out of the room. "I'll go wake up the kids. Eat as much as you can. They say breakfast is the most important meal of the day."

He stopped by Billy's room first. Asleep, his mouth partially open and his hair tousled, he looked as if could be ten years old. Javier gazed at his son, the love plain to see on his face, and the regret for everything Billy had gone through written in his heart. Knowing this would probably be the last time in a long time that he would be able to see his son like this, Javier hesitated a moment longer. He tiptoed over to the bed and gently stroked Billy's hair.

"Wake up, Billy," he said softly. "Come eat breakfast."

"What?" Billy pushed his father's hand away. "What breakfast?"

"I made pancakes and eggs and waffles. Hurry up before it gets cold."

"Fine," Billy mumbled into his pillow. "Just two more minutes."

"Okay." Javier leaned over and kissed Billy on the back of his head. "I'll come get you after I wake up your sister."

Javier felt the same sense of longing and loss as he watched Jasmine sleep. Finally, knowing that time was running out, Javier sat on the edge of her bed and gently shook her awake. "Hey, baby. It's time to wake up."

"Daddy," Jasmine murmured sleepily as she rolled over and hugged her father. She then proceeded to climb into his lap and snuggled her chin into his collarbone.

Javier inhaled the scent of her hair and relished the feeling of closeness. A tear came to his eye when he realized that this may never happen again. Jasmine would soon get too old for this, and he would be…He couldn't imagine how she might see him in the future, but it was enough to make him doubt the path he had chosen.

Standing up with Jasmine clinging to him like a baby monkey, Javier carried her down the stairs and put her in her chair at the table. Without warning, Jasmine's eyes popped open and she gave a bright smile as she reached for the plate of pancakes.

"And Billy?" Laura asked with the hint of a grin.

"Let me check." Javier ran out of the kitchen and back up the stairs. "Billy!" he called out from the top of the stairs. "Let's go. Come eat breakfast."

"Coming!" Billy shouted drowsily.

Javier walked to the door of Billy's room and said sternly, "Now, Billy. We're going to eat breakfast as a family this morning." He watched Billy drag himself out of bed and listened to him complain all the way to the kitchen.

When Billy finally sat down at the table, he looked around and asked, "What's the special occasion?"

"Your father just wanted to surprise us," Laura answered, flashing Javier a quick smile.

"Whatever." Billy reached for the plate of waffles as Jasmine picked at her bacon and tore it into miniscule pieces, which she then placed upon her spoon.

"I know we don't normally do this," Javier began uncomfortably, "but I would like to say grace this morning."

Laura looked at her husband in surprise. "Really? Well, okay." She motioned to her children. "Stop eating for a second." Billy and Jasmine slowly lowered their food back to their plates and stared at their parents. "Okay. Ready," Laura said.

Javier cleared his throat nervously. "Um...alright. Can everyone hold hands?" He reached for Laura's and Billy's hands and watched as Jasmine did the same. When Laura closed her eyes and bowed her head, Billy and Jasmine followed suit. Javier, too, closed his eyes and prayed, "God. We haven't always been the most devout family, but in our hearts, I know that we believe in you and try to do right. Please bestow your blessing upon this family. Bless the food we eat, the house we live in, and please protect my family and guide them if ever they become lost. I know that the future won't always be bright, but I believe that with your guidance and support, that everything will be okay in the end. Please forgive us for our sins. Amen."

"Amen," Laura repeated. She opened her eyes and gave her husband a questioning look. He refused to make eye contact.

"Amen," Billy said. He stared at his dad thoughtfully for a second before turning his attention to his breakfast.

"Hey man!" Jasmine shouted as she laughed and picked up her spoon full of bacon bits.

Javier quickly glanced around the table at his family and knew in his heart that they were soon going to be lost to him forever. He slowly picked up his glass of orange juice and took a long sip. He was sure he would vomit if he tried to eat anything else.

Javier managed to avoid having Laura ask him questions the rest of the morning. After telling Billy to let his friends know that baseball practice would be cancelled, Javier spent the rest of the day tying up loose ends from his business life.

He went to his office at The School House and deleted all of the files on the computer. Realizing that it probably wouldn't be enough, he spent an hour trying to find a screwdriver, and then another hour learning how to remove the hard disk drives from his computer. Having finally accomplished that task, he just left the mess there for Vikram to clean up later.

Picking up a hammer that had been next to the screwdriver, Javier then took his anger out on the hard drives and smashed them on his desk into tiny pieces. Feeling slightly better, he picked up the pieces that looked important and took them with him. On his way to the bank, he stopped his car on the edge of a bridge and threw the chunks of hard drive into the water. Knowing that there had probably been no reason to do any of that, Javier still felt better and proceeded to the bank.

As soon as Javier walked through the door, he was escorted into the office of the senior vice-manager. Javier had called ahead and the paperwork was waiting for him. He signed the deed of the building over to Vikram and gave him the rights to the business. Upon the advice of the banker, Javier used all of his personal savings and bought T-bills under Laura's name, which she could then sell back for cash if she needed it.

Thanking the man for all of his help over the years, Javier suddenly felt an urgent need to leave the bank, and he nearly stumbled over a chair on his way out. At the entrance to the bank, he ran into Vikram. They stopped next to the revolving door.

Javier looked Vikram in the eye. He opened his mouth to say something, but whether it was "why?" or "traitor", Vikram would never know. With a shake of his head, Javier pushed against the revolving door and left Vikram behind.

Javier had arranged for Jenny to pick Jasmine up from school and take her to her horseback riding lesson. She had done it before, and it often made things easier for Laura and Javier if they were otherwise too busy with work.

This time, Javier needed to speak to Billy alone.

"Hey, Billy," Javier said, as Billy slid into the front seat. "How was school?"

"You won't believe what happened!" Billy snapped his seatbelt closed as Javier exited the school's parking lot.

"What?"

"Assaf got mugged today and he had his brand new laptop stolen."

"Really? What happened?" Javier was shocked. He had known Assaf since he and Billy were in kindergarten together, and he couldn't imagine something like that happening to the little boy he had known.

"It was on the way to school. He got jumped by a gang of dirty street kids."

"Is he okay?"

Billy thought about it for a second. "I guess. He's really upset about the laptop, and he's got a black eye. I don't think he would've wanted to practice today anyway."

"Billy," Javier said firmly. "I don't want you walking to or from school alone anymore. There's a lot of that kind of crime going around."

Billy shrugged his shoulders. "I'll be fine."

"I'm serious, Billy. Someone needs to fix that problem, but they probably won't. So be careful!"

Billy shrugged his shoulders again and bent down to tie his shoelace. "Alright. Whatever. So why did you cancel practice?"

Javier drove without thinking about where he was going as he tried to figure out how to explain things to his son.

Billy looked up when his father refused to answer. "Does this have anything to do with…with…Tom?"

You must show confidence, Javier told himself. But after trying to regain the proper demeanor, his body sagged as pulled into the parking lot of the playground. Javier stared at the kids hanging out on the equipment and thought that one of them seemed familiar.

"Dad?" Billy asked warily.

Javier turned off the car, exhaled slowly, and said, "Billy, we need to talk about some things before we go home."

"Like what?" Billy unlocked his seat belt and the sound of it snapping against the car punctuated the silence between them.

Javier wracked his mind for the best way to explain what was going to happen. "You remember those two men who were with us that night? Givoanni and Vikram?"

"Yeah. The scary one and the guy who works for you. What about them?"

"They…well, they have your knife."

Billy's eyes lit up. "That's great, right? They're on our side." He faltered as he studied his father's face. "Right?"

"Not anymore, no. They don't like the fact that I wanted to stop… selling boys. I told them about how I wanted to help them and start a school for them…"

"And they don't like that?"

"Giovanni sees it as a threat to his business. And Vikram, well…I don't know about him. He just doesn't get it."

"So what's going to happen?"

Javier closed his eyes and ran his hand nervously through his hair. "They called the police and told them where to find the body. And they are threatening to give the knife with your fingerprints on it to the police…"

Billy swallowed and stared speechlessly at his father.

"I told them that I will admit to the murder. And then they'll destroy the weapon."

"No, dad!" Javier could see tears filling Billy's eyes.

"Yes, Billy. I promised to keep you safe. You should never have been there in the first place."

"No," Billy denied weakly.

"This is the only way out of this." Javier took a deep breath and debated about how selfish he truly was. "I need a favor, Billy," Javier said, cringing inside as he said.

"Anything, Dad. What?"

"I think I can get a lesser punishment if I…" He paused, unwilling to go on.

"If you what? Dad, do what you have to do to fix this."

"If I tell them that Tom was trying to sexually abuse you."

Billy's lip curled up in disgust. After a few seconds, he asked dully, "And then what?"

"And then I would say that I was so angry that I killed him for trying to touch my son."

Billy looked down at his hands and started making triangles with his fingers. "And Mom?"

"Billy…" Javier struggled with how to phrase his thoughts. "I…yes. Your mom would have to know. Honestly, Billy, I am terrified of what will happen if she finds out I owned that bar. And so, yes…this is the easy way out for me."

"And so Tom was molesting me, you got angry and killed him, and Mom never needs to find out what you do for a living?" Billy continued to stare at his fingers as he considered everything his father had told him.

Javier chewed on his lip. "What are you thinking, Billy?"

Billy turned his gaze to the kids on the playground. Javier glanced at them and then did a double-take. That's Tavi, he thought.

"Okay," Billy finally said. "But I'm only agreeing because those two guys are pissed off that you wanted to change your bar." He looked at his dad in desperation. "That wasn't a lie, was it?"

Javier, who had been intently staring at Tavi, mentally brushed away the distraction and focused on his son once more. "No. You made me realize exactly what I've been doing all these years."

Billy's concern for his father was clear to see, but Javier thought he could also detect disappointment that his father wasn't the man he had hoped he would be. However, he simply nodded his head and said, "Okay. Let's tell Mom."

Javier quickly ruffled his son's hair in an affectionate gesture. He started the car and pulled out of the parking lot. Without another thought of Tavi, Javier headed home, knowing in his heart that he was still doing the wrong thing.

Chapter 9

After stealing Assaf's bag, the children split up. Byron and Tavi wanted to go eat, and the others went off to do whatever it was they did all day. Tavi was beginning to wonder what their lives actually consisted of, and what would happen to him.

Byron took his time, showing Tavi where he could get the cheapest breakfasts, where he could wash up if he needed to, and then showed him where the public library was since he knew how much Tavi enjoyed reading.

As they entered the library, Bryon instructed, "Make sure you clean up before you come here. Otherwise they won't let you in and they'll probably call security."

Tavi nodded his head as he looked around in awe. So many books. He had never imagined that there could be this many in one place. When he had imagined libraries before, he'd always thought of a place like his school. One room with a single shelf of used books on the wall. But this place was huge. Tavi couldn't imagine where all of these books had come from, or what they could possibly be about.

"Do you come here often?" Tavi asked softly.

Byron guided Tavi towards a table away from the entrance. "A few times a week," he said. "It's always air-conditioned, and the bathrooms and water fountains are nice. And the books help make the day pass by quicker."

Tavi nodded his head, still trying to assimilate everything. "How do I know what books are where?"

Byron pointed to a nearby computer. "Do you know how to use one?"

"Kind of." Tavi thought back to the ancient computer his school teacher had used, with its green and black monitor and the square black floppy disks. "My teacher used to let us practice typing letters on his."

"Cool. Let me show you how to use this one." Byron led Tavi to the nearest computer. "Okay, so...Tell me the name of a book that you like."

Tavi thought about the books in his bag and named his favorite one. He watched as Byron typed in the title, and then suddenly a list of books appeared on the screen. "You probably want this one." Byron moved the mouse and clicked on the first one listed. The information appeared on the screen, and Byron showed Tavi what everything meant. "Okay, so...It's in G47. If you look behind us, you can see that that's where the fiction section is." Byron clicked again. "Oh, look! It's the first book in a series of five."

"Wait..what?" Tavi asked.

"That book you like. There are four more after it in the same series."

Tavi felt like his mind was going to explode. "Shut up! Really? I thought that was the whole story and it was finished. You mean it continues?"

Byron laughed happily at Tavi's amazement and hopped down from the stool. "Come on," he said. "I'll show you where they are."

A few minutes later, Tavi sat at their table, holding the second book of the series uncertainly. Byron had already opened his own book and was flipping past the third page. He glanced up and saw Tavi still staring at the cover of the book. "What are you doing? Why don't you read it?"

Tavi slowly opened up the book to the first page. He looked around the library once more and said in wonder, "I can't believe that we can just read all of these books for free."

Byron just grinned at Tavi and turned his attention back to his book.

That evening, after they all met up again at the playground, the children headed towards Clarence's shop. They had been arguing among themselves for most of the day about how much a new laptop would be worth. Tavi soon grew bored with the discussion, and decided to bring up something that had been on his mind all day.

"Soooo," he said happily, "That plan that I had today...It worked out really well, huh?"

"Um...no," Pablo replied immediately.

"Not at all," Chloe said, as Kurt shook his head in agreement.

"What?" Tavi's self-esteem crashed to the ground. "Why not? I thought it went perfect?"

"Do you want to tell him, Byron?" Kyle asked.

Byron shrugged his shoulders and recited, "It took too long. The longer it takes, the more chance we have of getting caught. We shouldn't ever use knives. Do you know what happens if we kill someone by accident? It was too close to the school. The closer to the school, the more chance of being caught by parents or police. If the boy had called for help instead of running, then we would've been screwed."

"Is that it?" Tavi joked weakly.

"If this were a movie, then sure, things like that always work. But the best way to not get caught is to do it as quickly as possible, knock him down, grab his bag, and run. And if we do it in an area that we're familiar with AND if there's no one around, then it's even better. Your way might've gotten us someone faster, but it was a lot riskier. Our way takes longer, but we won't get caught."

Tavi's hopes were smashed. He'd been expecting praise all day from the other children. "So why did you even try it?" he grumbled.

Kyle laughed and gave Tavi a little shove. "Why not? It's fun to try something new every once in a while."

Chloe added, "And you were SO excited about your plan." Even Pablo was smiling at Tavi now, and he started to feel better.

"So, you guys are just kidding, right? It was an okay plan."

They all laughed and Byron answered for them, "No. It really was a terrible plan." He put his arm around Tavi's shoulders. "But it worked, and that's all that matters. Now we just have to see how much we get paid."

The bell above the door tinkled as they happily pushed each other into Clarence's store. A customer was paying for a bottle of water, and Tavi and his friends quieted down and quickly spread out through the store, browsing in different aisles. When they heard the bell ring signifying that the customer had left, they all hurried to the front of the store and watched proudly as Kurt pulled out the laptop from the bag they had stolen.

Clarence's reaction was unexpected. "Whoa!" he said, holding up his hands. "Where the hell did you guys get this?"

"Isn't it awesome?" Kurt asked excitedly. "How much will you give us for this?"

"Yeah. It's gotta be worth way more than a cell phone," Kyle added.

Clarence's face had gone slightly pale and he repeated, "Where did you guys get this?"

"From some boujie kid we jumped this morning," Pablo answered. "Why does it matter?" He looked around and said, "There was also a cell phone. Who has it?"

Kyle looked down at his feet and mumbled, "Um...me. But I think I dropped it?"
"What?!?" Byron, Kurt, and Pablo were visibly upset.

"I saw him drop it," Chloe said. "He gave it back to that kid." She shrugged. "Who cares? We already took his laptop. I think it was nice of Kyle."

Clarence looked around at the children in front of him and cleared his throat for attention. "Okay. I think there are some things you guys should know."

Kurt gave Clarence a wary look and muttered, "Fucking Candyman."

"What?" Kyle asked, giving Kurt a small nudge.

"You guys know I've been helping you out for the past year, right? You bring me what you steal, I give you some money for it. And then I resell those items and make money."

Everyone nodded their heads.

"Well, that isn't one hundred percent true." Clarence sipped at his tea and swallowed noisily. "I knew you guys needed some help, and so I agreed to give you money for what you found. But – for the most part – I always try to return the items to their owners. Sometimes they give me a reward and I'll split that money with you guys, but…" He shook his head and motioned at the laptop. "This is too much. I don't think you should do this anymore."

All of the children – excluding Tavi – stared at Clarence in anger and suspicion. "I can't believe you've been lying to us," Kyle said.

"I just wanted to help you," Clarence protested.

Kurt picked up the laptop and shoved it back into the bag. "Fine. We'll find someone else who will pay us for this. Thanks for everything, CLARENCE." Kurt slung the bag over his shoulder and marched out the door. The others watched him leave and then slowly followed him.

Tavi was the last one to leave. He rested his hand on the door and looked back at Clarence. He seemed so sad and lost that Tavi told him softly, "I'll talk to them. I understand what you were doing."

Clarence gave Tavi a sad smile. "Thanks, Tavi. Good luck," he said as the bell tinkled and closed silently behind Tavi.

Chapter 10

Billy walked past his mother without saying a word and ran upstairs to his room when they got home. Laura looked questioningly at Javier as he slowly stepped into the kitchen. The kitchen smelled like an Italian restaurant, and Javier inhaled deeply.

Laura put down the knife she had been using to chop vegetables for the salad. She wrapped her arms around Javier and said with a smile, "I decided you deserved to have your favorite meal since you made us such a special breakfast this morning." She leaned up to give him a kiss, but a look of concern crossed her face when Javier just gave her a distracted peck.

"What's wrong?"

Javier had never been so afraid in his life. He gazed into his wife's eyes, his mind in turmoil, and to his embarrassment, his eyes filled up with tears. He blinked and looked away quickly, and Laura's concern deepened.

"Javi...what's going on? Tell me."

"Sit down," he said quietly. As they both sat in their respective chairs, Laura reached across the table and grabbed both of Javier's hands. Javier stared at her wedding ring as she covered his hand with hers, and he slowly withdrew his hands and placed them in his lap.

I'm a liar, he thought. And a murderer. And I sell boys for money.

He squeezed his eyes shut as the disgust for what he was about to tell his wife threatened to overcome him.

I'm using my son's sexual abuse to help get me out of trouble.

"Tom Jackson," he managed to say.

"Oh, Javier. What about him?" He could tell by the sound of her voice that Laura was relieved and thought it was just a minor issue.

"He...Billy told me that..." Javier stopped knowing that he could still leave Billy out of it.

"Billy told you what?"

"Tom touched...I mean, he molested him. And maybe a couple of the other players on the team."

Laura put her hand to her mouth and her eyes widened in shock. "No," she whispered.

Javier nodded. "He's really embarrassed and ashamed about it, but he finally confided in me a couple of days ago."

"Oh my god." Laura was still speaking almost inaudibly. "What should we do? Do we call the police? Is Billy okay?" She answered her own question immediately. "Of course he's not okay. That was a stupid question."

"I should have told you."

"Yes," Laura agreed immediately. "You should have. Well, did Billy ask you not to?"

"Billy doesn't want anyone to know. He's afraid that it makes him gay and he feels disgusted by it."

"Oh, Javi." Laura reached for his hands again, but Javier had them clenched together on his lap under the table. "What can we do?"

Javier swallowed and lied, "I met with Tom last night. It was in a secluded place. I talked to him about Billy and he actually laughed."

Laura's hand was covering her mouth again. "What?!?"

"That fucker laughed when I asked him about Billy and he told me how cute he was." Javier's anger burst through his fear as he relived the emotions he had felt that night.

Laura made a steeple with her hands, and rested her head against it as she closed her eyes. "What did you do, Javier?"

"He just laughed about it," Javier tried to justify, the anger and frustration in his voice obvious.

A hint of a whisper. "What did you do?"

"I killed him." Laura inhaled sharply and tears dripped down from between her closed eyelids. "I killed him, Laura," Javier repeated. "He touched our son!"

They sat there quietly together for a couple of minutes. Javier didn't know what to say, and he was too afraid to move a muscle. Eventually, Laura sniffed loudly, wiped her eyes, and stared into Javier's eyes. "So what now?" she asked.

"Now…now I go down to the police station and confess to the murder of Tom Jackson."

"And what about our family? Who's going to help me deal with this?"

Javier reached for Laura's hands but she jerked them away. "I don't know," he replied. "I'm so sorry."

Laura stood up, and without looking at her husband, she left the kitchen and ran up the stairs to their bedroom.

Javier sat at the dinner table in the kitchen of his house, alone, and stared unseeingly at the flowers in the middle of the table. Without changing his expression, he pulled out his phone, quickly found a number, and dialed.

"This is Sergeant James Frost."

"Hey, James. This is Javier Lopez."

"Mr. Lopez! How can I help you?"

"Regarding that murdered man I called about yesterday…"

"Yep. I was just talking to one of our detectives. Apparently we have no leads with this one. We did get a hit from his fingerprints, though…"

"Tom Jackson, right?"

A pause. "That's right. How did you know?"

"I'm going to come to the station soon, and I'd like for you to be there. I need to confess to the killing of Tom Jackson."

Chapter 11

Vikram called Yuri early the next afternoon.

"Hey, Vikram."

"Yuri...I need you to tell all of the boys to meet in Bangarang at three today. Tell them to go through the back door and we'll meet them inside."

"Uh...You said Bangarang, right?"

"Yep. And as soon as you do that, come to the office. There are some things that we need to discuss."

"Okay. See you in about twenty minutes."

Vikram was sitting in Javier's chair and sifting through the mess on the desk when Yuri entered the office. "Sit down," Vikram motioned to one of the chairs.

Yuri looked curiously at the desk as he sat down. His eyes flicked around the office and then he calmly studied Vikram's face. When he didn't say anything, Vikram cleared his throat and said, "Umm..I thought you should be one of the first to know. Javier has been arrested for murder."

"Really?" Yuri asked in surprise.

"Yes. But before he went to jail, he signed over The School House to me, and so I am the new owner and manager."

Yuri's eyes returned to the mess on the desk. "Congratulations."

Picking up a trash can near his feet, Vikram awkwardly brushed the remaining pieces of the hard drive into it. Setting it down, he continued, "For now, Mr. Delvecchio from Bangarang will be a silent partner, but I'm the one who is in charge and running things."

He paused and waited for Yuri to respond. "I'm sure you'll do an amazing job," Yuri finally said.

Vikram smiled. "Thanks. And I want you to be my number two in charge. Javier and I both agreed that you have been a big help lately, and I think you'll enjoy it."

Flashing a true, but brief, smile, Yuri replied, "Really? That'd be awesome. Thank you!"

"Good," Vikram said, the relief evident on his face. Yuri wondered if he had been expecting him to say no. Vikram continued, "You'll get a much bigger salary, but your responsibilities will increase as well. I need to know that you'll always be able to support me."

"I will. I promise."

"Okay. There are a couple of things we need to discuss. Mr. Delvecchio and I both agree that things have been a bit lax around here lately. We need to make some changes."

Yuri nodded his head. "Like what?"

"The boys aren't motivated enough to find customers every night. We're going to change that."

"How?"

"Mr. Delvecchio will demonstrate a couple of methods in about twenty minutes. That's why I asked for our boys to meet us at Bangarang."

"Okay. That sounds like a good plan."

Vikram studied Yuri's face for a second before speaking again. "And we need to get Tavi back – as soon as possible. Let all of our contacts know, and then give them that photo we have of him."

"I think I probably know where to find him," Yuri said guardedly. "And then what?" He unconsciously rubbed his left arm where Vikram had broken it with a bat two years ago.

"We need to make an example of him."

Yuri nodded his head.

"We will bring him back here and kill him in front of the other boys," Vikram finished.

Yuri's mouth opened in shock. "What? Why? The first penalty is a broken arm," he protested.

"But how many boys would run away if the first penalty was death? This is a new era, Yuri. I need to know if you can handle it." Vikram gave Yuri a blank stare which didn't show any of the emotions that were warring inside of him.

For a brief second, Yuri's gaze flickered around the room before refocusing upon Vikram. "Okay," Yuri agreed softly. "I can handle it."

"I'm happy to hear it," Vikram said. He stood up and tossed Yuri a wad of cash held inside of a gold money clip. "And here is your first paycheck."

Yuri caught it easily and flicked through the money. "All of this is mine?"

Vikram walked around and put his arm across Yuri's shoulders. "If you do a good job, there's plenty more where that came from. But first we have to go give a demonstration."

There was a stark contrast between the boys of Bangarang and the ones from The School House. When Yuri and Vikram entered, the ones from their bar were clustered into small groups, chatting and laughing softly with each other. The boys from Bangarang stood in two orderly rows, eyes straight ahead, their faces devoid of any emotion.

Yuri began to feel uneasy. He walked over to the boys he knew and whispered for them to be quiet. He needn't have bothered as the thumping sounds of Giovanni Delvecchio descending the stairs were enough to silence every child in the bar.

He held out his arms and walked forward when he caught sight of Vikram. "Vikram! My friend and partner! Are we ready to begin?"

Vikram allowed himself to be hugged and kissed on both cheeks. Nodding his head, he said, "We are. Bruce. Apollo. Step forward." Two boys broke free from the cluster of boys and stepped forward nervously. They looked at each other before they each took another step. Yuri stepped behind them and nudged them towards Vikram and Giovanni.

Vikram raised his voice and said cheerfully, "First of all, I want you boys to know that Javier Lopez is gone. He has been arrested for murder." The boys from The School House looked at each other and smiled, and their little whispers carried around the room. The boys from Bangarang, however, still did not move a muscle.

"I want you to know that things will change a little bit with Javier gone." The boys' smiles slowly faded away as Vikram continued, "If you do not find a customer every single night, then you will be punished. If you can't find a customer for two nights in a row, then you will be severely punished." Apollo and Bruce looked at each other in fear. "Any boy who runs away will automatically be sentenced to death."

Giovanni stepped forward. "And one more thing that we do here which we're going to start doing at The School House." His cold gaze flicked from his boys in their orderly rows to the other boys who were still bunched together with sad expressions upon their faces. "We are instituting a short-time fee. Customers can buy you for only one hour if they want, and then you must come back to the bar, and you must find another customer...and another...and another. Those of you who don't will be punished."

He reached down and grabbed Apollo's and Bruce's arms. "Down to the basement!" he ordered.

The boys from Bangarang led the way, and everyone else followed at a slower pace. Yuri looked around the basement with a mixture of surprise and disgust. He had never imagined that places could be worse than The School House, but it was easy to see what some of the devices in the basement were used for.

"Who's first?" Giovanni asked, still holding onto the two boys' arms.

"Apollo," Vikram said, and even he looked uncomfortable. "He didn't find anyone last night." Giovanni thrust Apollo forward and two of his men grabbed the boy. Before he had time to struggle, he was strapped into a chair with a gag over his mouth.

Yuri stared at the scene in front of him. The small, ten year old boy, with the floppish hair and a happy laugh. He closed his eyes briefly and shoved all of his feelings deep into his heart. When he reopened them, one of the men was standing at the foot of the chair with a long lighter.

Vikram said softly, "If you don't find a customer to pay your bar fine, then this is what will happen to you that night." And with that, the man began burning the soles of Apollo's feet. His tiny body arched in pain and his muffled screams were plain to hear. After slowly burning each foot two times, Giovanni nodded to the man. He stepped back and unstrapped Apollo from the chair. Apollo sagged down, his eyes streaming with tears, and Yuri had never seen anyone look so scared and helpless. Steeling his heart once again, Yuri turned around and watched Giovanni drag Bruce to a small, round children's pool.

"Step in," he commanded.

Bruce...tall, chubby Bruce, who would often make the other children laugh with his jokes...shook his head in fear.

"Get in or I'll kill you," Giovanni warned softly.

Bruce stepped carefully into the pool. His entire body was shivering in terror.

"Sit down."

Bruce slowly sat down in the pool, resting his weight behind him on his arms. When nothing seemed to happen, his trembling eased up slightly.

Until Giovanni nodded at the man behind the pool.

The man dropped an electric wire in the pool. There were loud sparks and a high-pitched noise from Bruce as his whole body convulsed in shock.

After a couple of seconds, the man removed the wire. The whole room was silent as everyone watched Bruce twitch and moan while he lay in the water. After two minutes, Giovanni nodded his head once again, and the whole thing was repeated.

"That is what happens if you don't find anyone for two nights," he informed the children. "And after that, if you still don't find anyone, I'll just give you away for free for the entire night to as many men as I can." Giovanni glanced at Vikram with a smile. "I mean, we will do that."

Vikram gave a sick smile and tried to catch Yuri's gaze. Instead, Yuri turned and stared at Bruce, his face an emotionless mask as he watched the boy slowly stop twitching.

Chapter 12

After another long day spent at the library, Tavi and Byron were casually making their way to the playground as they discussed the series they were both reading.

"I still think the real bad guy is Titus," Byron insisted, referring to the name of the main character.

"That's stupid. Books are never like that. The good guy is the hero and the bad guy is always evil."

Byron scoffed. "And how many of these kinds of books have you read? You're up to...what...seven now?"

"Eight. But I'm sure that I'm right." Out of the corner of his eye, Tavi saw a police car pull up to the curb beside him. Without knowing why, he nudged Byron's arm and began walking quicker.

"What?" Byron glanced behind them and saw two officers climbing out of the front seat. Their eyes were glued to Tavi and Byron. "Oh, right. Turn at the next alley and run as fast as you can."

One of the officers called out, "Hey, you boys! Come back here. We have a couple of questions for you." Tavi glanced back and saw both men walking quickly behind them. As soon as they got to the corner of the building, Byron and Tavi broke into a sprint and ran down the alleyway.

"HEY!"

Tavi and Byron weaved in between the trash bags and crates that littered the alley. They could hear the sound of pursing footsteps behind them and Tavi realized that they probably couldn't outrun the men for long. "There," Byron panted, and they cut into the alleyway to their right, and then made the next left. There were two boys squatting against the wall of a building, and they stood up when Byron and Tavi noisily entered their alley.

"Where are you guys going in such a hurry?" the larger one asked. Tavi and Byron tried to go around them, but the boys moved quickly to block them, and all four bodies flew to the ground, arms and legs entangled as Tavi found himself lying on one of the boy's legs.

"Get off me!" the boy shouted and pushed and kicked until Tavi rolled off of him. Tavi looked over his shoulder and saw the two policemen entering the alleyway. Hopping to his feet, he knocked the other boy over, quickly pulled Byron up, and they both took off for the far end of the alley.

"Hey! Come back here!" The two boys slowly got to their feet and became aware of the approaching footsteps a moment too late. The smaller one grabbed his friend's arm and tried to run, but the policemen were upon them and swiftly wrapped their arms around the boys. As they kicked and shouted and struggled to get free, Tavi and Byron reached the end of the alley and turned around to watch.

One of the policemen skillfully handcuffed the boy he was holding and then helped the other officer handcuff his boy's hands behind his back. He nodded to his partner and said, "These will do. Let's drop them off with Victor and get paid." The man grabbed his boy by the upper arm and pulled him towards him. He looked behind him where Byron and Tavi were still standing, poised to run. "Next time, boys," he called with a laugh, and then he and his partner dragged the two boys towards the entrance of the alley.

Byron shook his head and let out a shaky breath. "What was that about? Why were they chasing us?"

"I don't know. But I don't think they cared about us. They just wanted to catch two boys." They both looked around carefully before jogging in the direction of the playground.

When they arrived, the other children were already hanging out on the playground equipment. Kyle was reclining on the bottom of the slide, Chloe and Kurt were perched on top of the jungle gym, and Pablo was gently swaying back and forth in one of the swings. The bag containing the laptop was resting on the ground near the jungle gym.

"You won't believe what just happened to us," Byron announced as he and Tavi approached. "We just got chased by a couple of cops."

Kyle sat up and Pablo put his feet on the ground to still his swing. "For doing what?" Kyle asked.

"Nothing," Byron claimed, and Tavi nodded his head in agreement. "They just started chasing us, and then we got lucky and they ran into two other boys. They said they were taking them somewhere and then the cops would get paid."

"Not this again," Pablo said. His face was filled with concern. "When I first got here, a couple of kids who were working there had been caught by cops on the street. The bars paid the cops a finder's fee, and that way the bars got extra boys."

"Did they stop doing it?" Tavi asked.

Pablo shrugged. "I guess. I haven't been bothered by any since that time with Yuri." The other children looked at each other and nodded in agreement.

"Well, I think we should…" Byron's voice trailed off as he stared at someone approaching them. "Who's this?" Everyone spun around and stared at the newcomer. Kurt and Chloe hastily slid down from the jungle gym and Kyle hopped to his feet.

"Hey, Tavi," the figure said. His voice changed slightly and there was a hint of emotion in it. "Hi, Pablo. Hey, Chloe. Long time, no see."

"Yuri?" Pablo asked in disbelief. Chloe walked forward a couple of steps to stand next to him.

"Hi," Yuri said again. He stopped about ten yards away from the jungle gym. His eyes roamed over the other children, pausing for a couple of moments on Tavi, before he looked at Pablo with a small smile. "It's good to see you again."

"Yuri!" Pablo took a step forward. The others had never heard him sound so excited. "I never got to say...I mean...well, Chloe and I haven't forgotten what you did for us."

Yuri's smiled turned down slightly at the corners, and he said softly, "Yeah. I know." Looking at Chloe, he said a bit louder, "Chloe, you're getting tall. Are these boys treating you okay?"

"Hey, Yuri," she replied shyly. "Yeah, they're nice."

Pablo seemed to be restraining himself from running over to Yuri. "So, what are you doing here? Are you here to..."

"I'm here for Tavi." Yuri's eyes flicked towards Tavi and Tavi felt as if someone had just punched him in the stomach. "Javier Lopez went to jail for murdering some guy, and so Vikram is in charge now." His nose wrinkled as if he had just smelled something distasteful. "And the owner of Bangarang. He's also in charge."

Kurt and Kyle walked over to stand beside Byron, who had already moved slightly in order to put himself between Yuri and Tavi. "You're not taking him," Kyle warned.

Yuri once again scanned the six children and gave them his small smile. "I know. I just came to warn him."

"What?" Tavi said, speaking for the first time.

"You've been sentenced to death. They've ordered me to take you back and then they're going to kill you in front of the other kids."

Hearing the word 'death' made goose bumps stand up on Tavi's arms. "Why? I thought that death was only if you ran a second time."

Yuri shrugged impassively. "New boss, new rules, I guess."

Tavi stared at Yuri, trying to read his expression. Without warning, images of Yuri from the rock quarry and from the hair salon came to mind. He spoke before he even knew what he was going to say. "You could come stay with us, Yuri. We'd have seven then. That'd be a..." He trailed off as Yuri shook his head.

"No...I can't. Vikram has made me his assistant. He's paying me a lot of money now." He pulled the money clip out from his pocket and waved it in the air. "He gave me this just for saying I would work for him."

"Oh! Do you want to buy a laptop?" Kurt snatched up Assaf's bag and hurried over to Yuri. "It's brand new, and we'll sell it to you for cheap."

Yuri raised his eyebrow questioningly at Pablo. "Who's this?"

"That's Kurt."

"I'm Kurt. You could have just asked me." He held out the bag to Yuri who ignored it and walked towards Tavi.

"I want to talk to Tavi for a second. How about we do it over there?" He pointed to the edge of the park.

Tavi opened his mouth to agree, when Pablo answered first, "How about you do it by the jungle gym, and we'll just make sure you guys don't go anywhere." Tavi wasn't the only one surprised by the change in Pablo's voice. He saw Kyle and Byron give each other wide-eyed glances.

Yuri smiled and said, "Okay." He approached the jungle gym and the others spread out around it, giving them a bit of privacy. "Hey, Tavi," he spoke quietly when he was only a few feet away.

"Why won't you join us?" Tavi asked, voicing aloud the question that kept echoing through his mind. "Remember when you saved my brother, John. Isn't that who you want to be? Not...this," he finished in despair.

Yuri's eyes went out of focus momentarily and Tavi thought that he was remembering John and the quarry. But then Yuri said, "You remember that boy I killed?"

Tavi's mind went blank for a second. "Um...oh, you mean Will?"

"I used to have nightmares about it. I could feel the knife going in him and I would wake up thinking that my hands were covered with blood." He paused and looked at his hands which he had splayed wide. Squeezing them into fists, he continued, "But lately, it doesn't seem to bother me that much."

"That doesn't mean you like it."

"No, I guess not," Yuri agreed. "But Tavi, there are some terrible things happening now. That guy from Bangarang…he wants to torture everyone worse than anything I've ever seen."

"But you can stop it, right?"

Yuri smiled again. "I'm just a sixteen year old boy who wants to make as much money as I can so that I can leave and never come back. So, no. I'm not going to stop it. And I'm not going to run away." He studied Tavi's face carefully. "What did I tell you when we first left the village?"

"Don't trust anyone," Tavi whispered.

Yuri reached into his pocket and quickly pulled something out. With a flicking noise, a long, sharp knife appeared in his hand. Tavi sensed the other children moving towards them, but he couldn't take his eyes away from Yuri's face. "I'm supposed to kill you, Tavi. But you remind me of…" He hesitated for a second before softly saying, "Me." He flicked the knife closed and stuck it back in his pocket. Putting his hands on Tavi's shoulders, he leaned his head in and murmured, "You're the only one who might understand. I don't know who I am anymore. I remember who I was, but I don't think that's me anymore."

"But it could be," Tavi replied softly.

Yuri stepped back, his eyes never leaving Tavi's. "Don't let it happen to you." He looked around at the other children who were only a few yards away. "Oh – and I think you can trust these friends. I know I would." He turned around and walked towards the swing set, brushing past Kurt on the way. Stopping suddenly, he said, "Let me see the laptop."

Kurt looked around uncertainly and then pulled the laptop out of the bag. Yuri flipped it over and read the list of components and specs that were written on the bottom. Handing it back to Kurt, he said, "I'll give you two hundred."

Kurt almost dropped the laptop in surprise as he tried to stuff it back into the bag. "Uh, what? Two hundred? Okay!" He shoved the bag into Yuri's arms, who slung it over one shoulder. Yuri nonchalantly pulled out his money clip, counted off a few bills, and handed them to Kurt. He gave a quick wave to the others and turned to leave the playground.

"Wait!" Tavi blurted out, running after Yuri.

Yuri turned around and waited patiently.

"What about me?"

"You? I'll tell them the same thing I told them about Pablo. That you've left the city and I'm sure you're never coming back." Yuri smiled one last time and then disappeared into the evening twilight in the park.

Tavi stared at the spot where Yuri had disappeared until Byron walked up and put his arm around his shoulders. "Don't worry," he said encouragingly. "We'll watch out for you."

Tavi tried to think of a response, but when he looked back at the small group of children who were quietly watching him, he wondered if that would be enough.

Chapter 13

Over the next few weeks, Tavi and Byron developed a routine which they were both happy with. They would wake up early and spend most days at the library. Sometimes they would help the others jump children who were on their way to or from school. The only problem with that was that they hadn't found anyone to sell their rapidly growing stash of stolen items, and Byron had refused to let them store anymore in his basement. As he correctly pointed out, it wouldn't be too difficult for the owners to discover by chance the items that were already stuffed behind the boiler.

The police were a growing concern. Pablo and Chloe had watched from a rooftop as three policemen chased down and captured two younger boys, while Kurt and Kyle had also been startled awake by the sound of a police car in their alley. The police lights had been flashing as the car cruised quietly down the alleyway. They spent most of their days after that trying to find a new place to sleep. When they had broached the possibility of sleeping on the roofs, both Chloe and Pablo had shaken their heads doubtfully and explained how a gang of six or seven boys had made them move three times in the last week.

The library, though, was a source of joy for Tavi. He was reading about two or three books a day, and had discovered to his pleasure a love for history. He had first read a biography about Genghis Khan, and after devouring everything he could find about the great conqueror, he had moved on to Alexander the Great and other famous leaders from history.

Another thing he loved about the library was that every Thursday afternoon, the library showed movies about nature, and for an hour each week, Tavi was transported into worlds he had never imagined existed.

For the third consecutive Thursday, Tavi and Byron sat down in the middle of the second row. He saw two familiar people in front of him and nudged Byron. "Look. Those boys are here again."

Byron nodded his head indifferently. He refused to be distracted as the National Geographic symbol appeared on the screen in front of them.

"I wonder what gang they're in," Tavi whispered.

Byron gave an exasperated sigh and replied, "They're probably just normal kids."

"They're not," Tavi argued. "I've seen them here during the day whenever we come in."

Byron looked at Tavi in frustration and hissed, "Shhhhh!."

As the movie began, the camera zoomed in on a pride of lions relaxing in the sun. The angle changed, and Tavi watched as a huge herd of wildebeests unknowingly trotted towards the lions.

I used to think I was a tiger, Tavi thought bitterly, but now I'm nothing more than a frightened buffalo.

His expectations were met a minute later when the six lions raced towards the wildebeests. A young calf that was just a few steps behind the rest of the herd was skillfully picked off by the lions. Suddenly, two of them jumped on it, and all three animals tumbled down into the water.

Tavi looked away, not wanting to see the baby wildebeest get eaten. Shouts of excitement made him look back, and he saw a crocodile trying to pull the calf into the water as the lions struggled to drag the calf back onto land, where the rest of the pride were waiting.

That's like us, Tavi thought, not looking away despite his dislike for what was happening to the calf. We're being attacked by the bars and their people on one side, and the police on the other. Feeling even more self-pitiful, he resigned himself to watching the rest of the movie, even though he knew that the only question remaining was who would kill the calf.

The lions won. And as the pride gathered around the calf to feast, Tavi realized that his fate was as inevitable as the calf's. He could enjoy his time in the library, but Pablo and Chloe had been on the streets for two years, and their lives hadn't improved at all.

There's no way out for me, he thought.

He refocused on the video when the whole room erupted in surprise. The herd of buffalo was coming back. Tavi shook his head and whispered to Byron, "They're too late. The baby is already dead."

"SHHHH!" Byron hissed, his eyes glued to the screen.

Tavi watched with growing bewilderment as the herd surrounded the lions, and then after a few seconds, one of the buffalo charged the lions.

The lions jumped off of the calf but stayed their ground.

As the calf struggled to its feet, three more wildebeests charged at the lions. Four of the lions quickly ran off, chased angrily by one of the bulls.

The two remaining lions laid back their ears and swiped their paws. Once again, another wildebeest charged, and this one caught one of the lions with its horns. It scooped the lion up and tossed her into the water. The other lion had seen enough and quickly ran away, chased by three wildebeests.

The baby calf stood still for a second, and then it slowly but surely walked into the herd, where it disappeared from the camera.

However, the lions could still be seen running from groups of angry wildebeests who refused to let this chance at revenge slip through their hooves.

But I'm a wildebeest now, Tavi thought with excitement. "I'm a wildebeest!" he murmured.

"Shut up, Tavi," Byron whispered as the video ended and the next one began.

Tavi quietly got up and went back to their table where he tried to organize his thoughts.

Byron returned after thirty minutes. He found Tavi doodling on a piece of paper, and as he sat down across from him, he asked, "Where'd you go? The second video was pretty cool. It was about penguins…"

"I have an idea," Tavi interrupted.

Byron smiled. "Another one?"

"No. I mean, really. But I need to see if you agree."

"Okay." Byron grew serious and gave Tavi his full attention. "What is it?"

"I used to say I was a tiger. But here in this city, I'm not a tiger or a lion. I'm like one of those wildebeests, who get hunted by the predator."

Byron nodded his head in agreement.

"But in that first video, the wildebeest won. Their instinct was to run, but they still won."

Byron looked at Tavi with a puzzled expression. "What do you mean?"

"Why do the lions normally win?" Tavi asked.

"Because they're the strongest."

"But they're not. Did you see how that one lion got tossed into the water? The lions ran away because they weren't the strongest."

Byron dropped his eyes to the table in front of him and thought about what Tavi was saying. "Okay. So why does that matter?"

Tavi's voice rose as his excitement got the better of him. "If there was only one wildebeest, then the lions would win. But if there are ten wildebeest and two lions.,."

"The lions usually still win," Byron finished for him.

"Not if the wildebeest don't run! What if instead of running, they…or we…fought back instead?"

"I don't know, Tavi. I don't think that would work."

Tavi sighed and tried to think of a better example. "Okay. Imagine there are two cops chasing us, right?"

Byron nodded.

"Our first instinct is to…what?" Tavi asked.

"Run."

"But what if there were suddenly eight or ten of us, and we didn't run or get separated. Instead, we surrounded the cops like the wildebeests did to the lions?"

Byron closed his eyes to imagine it. When he opened them, he had a huge grin on his face. "We need to find more people."

Tavi grinned back. "And then, if we had enough people, we could stay on the roofs with Pablo and Chloe."

Byron stood up and slung his bag over his shoulder. "We should go talk to the others about this. Do you have any ideas where we can find more kids?"

"I have a couple of ideas." Tavi's gaze roamed around the room and paused briefly on the two boys he had mentioned earlier. He studied them for a second and then followed Byron out of the library.

Chapter 14

"No way! No freaking way!" Pablo argued.

Chloe nodded her head. "Pablo's right. We don't need any new kids. We just got Tavi." She gave Tavi a quick smile. He ignored her and tried again.

"Listen, guys. Aren't you tired of having to move every night? You said that gang on the roofs only had five or six people in it. If we had nine or ten, then they would be outnumbered."

Kurt also shook his head in disagreement. "I don't know. It seems risky."

"Risky?" Tavi laughed. "And you and Kyle sleeping behind a dumpster in an alley isn't risky? What happens if three kids find you? They'll beat you up and take all of your stuff."

Kurt grinned. "Not all of it. Most of our stuff is in Byron's basement."

"Yeah, and that's another thing," Byron interjected. "Tavi and I have had to wait around the last two nights for them to leave the basement. The owners are starting to spend time down there."

Kyle gave Kurt a worried glance. "What about our stuff?"

"Everything is still there for now. But we need a better place. Somewhere more secure."

Tavi added, "And if we have more people with us, then no one will mess with us."

Everyone was silent for a few moments as they considered Tavi's idea. Finally, Chloe said, "Okay...so what's the plan?"

"I have a couple of friends who are still trapped in The Schoolhouse," Tavi said. "I think we should try to help them first."

Pablo refused. He admitted that Tavi's idea might have a couple of good points, but he didn't want to go anywhere near The School House.

"It's been over two years," Chloe said. "No one would recognize you."

Pablo just shook his head; his eyes wide with fear.

"Okay," Tavi said lightly. "We don't need you on the ground. But can you show us how you got to the roofs around there so that we can spy that way?"

Pablo cleared his throat nervously and replied, "Uh. Sure. Tonight?"

"Yeah. As soon as it's dark."

A couple of hours later, they were standing on top of a low building near The School House. Pablo had showed them how he climbed almost to the top of a nearby fence, and then leaning over, he hoisted himself onto the roof. The others quickly followed and looked around in amazement. This area of the city was mostly one story buildings, and they could see quite far in every direction.

"There's The School House," Pablo said, pointing to a nearby two story building.

"Okay. How do you move between buildings" Tavi asked.

Pablo led them over to the edge of the roof. A wide wooden plank lay between the two buildings. Tavi estimated that it was over eight feet long. He nudged it with his foot and was surprised to find it firmly attached.

"Who made this?"

Shrugging his shoulders, Pablo replied, "Who knows? They were here before me. And you know how there are so many twisty alleyways everywhere around here?"

Tavi nodded his head.

"Well, pretty much every building is connected. You just have to find the right path to get to where you want."

"And you won't help us?" Byron asked.

Pablo looked around at his friends. He suddenly looked ashamed and said, "Fine. I'll help you. Where do you want to go?"

Tavi described the location of the room where the boys stayed when they came back each day, and Pablo immediately headed across the plank. After ten minutes of what felt like constant backtracking, Pablo pointed to a building across from them.

"Is that it?"

Tavi squinted his eyes in the dim light and tried to see inside of the window from that angle. He had never known the lights to be turned off, but the room was completely dark.

"Maybe," he reluctantly admitted. "But it doesn't look right." He looked around at the others. "Can we come back here tomorrow during the day? I need you guys on the roofs checking to make sure that no one is ahead of me in the alleyways."

Byron reached into his pocket and pulled out a notebook. Flipping through the pages, he said, "Hmmm. Let me check our calendar. Tomorrow is…April, right? Yeah. We're free."

The other kids chuckled and laughed at Byron. Suddenly lightning filled the air and a crack of thunder exploded above their heads. "Holy shit!" Kurt yelled. "We have to get down!"

Pablo looked around wildly and then cringed as another bolt of lightning lit up the sky. Running across the nearest plank, he ran to the far side of the next building. Looking behind him, he nodded his head. As the others ran to catch up with him, Pablo put his hands on the edge of the roof and hopped down.

"What the…?" Kyle said as they ran to the edge. Looking down, they saw Pablo standing on a dumpster, his head only a few feet beneath them.

"Hurry up!" he commanded. "Chloe first!" Chloe quickly jumped down and the others followed. They hopped off of the dumpster and sprinted down the alleyway as the first large drops of rain began to fall.

"We need to find somewhere fast!" Byron shouted as they tried to keep up with Pablo. The rain began to pour down and more lightning and thunder filled the sky. Pablo was turning corners so quickly that Tavi was sure he didn't know where he was going.

Without warning, the end of the alley ahead of them widened up as the loudest boom of thunder erupted over their heads. Bursting into the street, Tavi looked around and realized with a racing heart that they had emerged from the alley that ran between Bangarang and The School House. Pablo, too, seemed to realize where he had led them and he froze in shock.

"Let's go!" Tavi screamed, pulling on his arm. As the rain pounded down, the children ran through the empty streets to the train station, knowing that it would be the only place where they could be safe from the fury of the storm.

Chapter 15

The monorail station was far from empty when Tavi and his friends ran up the stairs to escape the deluge that was falling upon them. Once they got to the top of the stairs, they looked around and quickly walked to an empty area near the ticket counter. Tavi glanced at the surprisingly large number of homeless men and women who were sitting or sleeping against the walls.

"Does this place get locked up at night?" he asked.

Kyle shook his head. "I don't think this part does. But the police come around two or three times a night and try to kick everyone out. Once they leave, though, most of these bums just come back inside."

Pablo and Kurt returned from the bathroom where they'd been using the hand dryer to dry their clothing. Looking a lot less wet than when they had entered, both of them sat down with smiles upon their faces. "You guys can go now," Kurt said. "It's empty."

Tavi hopped up with Byron and Kyle and the three of them crossed the main waiting area to the bathrooms. Carefully stepping around the men and women who were sprawled in his way, Tavi had a disturbing thought.

"What if this is us in twenty years?" he asked softly.

Kyle and Byron gazed at the sleeping bodies with fresh eyes, but neither one had a response. Suddenly, they heard a clatter behind them, and a boy about their age ran up the stairs alone. He looked around wildly, breathing heavily, but what he saw must have calmed him because he quickly relaxed and slipped into an empty spot under the ticket counter.

When they exited the bathroom, the boy was the first thing Tavi saw. He eyed him carefully, noticing that he seemed to be about the same age as himself. Without consulting Byron or Kyle, Tavi made a decision and headed straight towards him.

"Um…" Kyle said as he and Byron trailed behind Tavi.

The boy looked up in surprise as Tavi squatted on his heels a couple of feet in front of him. "Hey," Tavi said. The boy quickly checked around him, studied Kyle and Byron, and then slowly shifted his weight so that he would be ready to spring up if any trouble arose.

"Hey yourself," the boy responded. He had a slight, unfamiliar accent, and Tavi wondered where he had come from.

"Terrible weather, huh?" Tavi asked. He heard Byron snort in derision behind him as Kyle mumbled inaudibly to him.

"It's not too bad. I needed a shower and at least this was free." The boy examined Tavi and his friends again. "What do you want?"

Tavi opened his mouth to respond, but then closed it as nothing came to mind. "I don't know," he finally said. "Um…what's your name?"

"Malik. And yours?"

"Tavi. This is Byron and Kyle."

Malik continued to stare at Tavi, and raised one eyebrow questioningly. His light blue eyes stood out strikingly against his dark skin, and Tavi liked the intelligence he saw in Malik's intense gaze.

"Okay, listen. I think we need more people in our gang," Tavi admitted. "You're alone now, and I don't know how long you've been on the streets, and I know this sounds weird, but bad things keep happening. And I just think that if we can get more people watching out for each other, then we'll be...safer," he finished weakly.

Malik gave a short laugh. "And you want me to just come join you three right now?"

Tavi pointed to where the others were sitting and watching him with some anxiety. "And those three as well."

Malik slowly turned his gaze and looked at the others with a curious expression. He shrugged his shoulders and returned his attention to Tavi.

"Who are you with?" Tavi asked.

Malik grinned and just shook his head at Tavi. "This can't work. It doesn't work like this."

Tavi said seriously, "But we can try."

"Let's go, Tavi," Byron said.

Kyle agreed. "Yeah. This is just weird."

Tavi spoke hurriedly, "Listen. Tomorrow or the next day, if you want to come meet us and have a talk, we hang out at the playground in Winter's Park. We're usually there in the afternoon." Without planning on it, he held his hand out and said, "It was nice meeting you, Malik. Good luck if I don't see you again."

Malik looked at his hand in surprise, and then he slowly reached out and gripped it. "You too, Tavi." He smiled. "And I think we may see each other again."

Tavi smiled back, instinctively liking this boy. Suddenly, he felt a knee in his back, and Kyle said, "Come on, Tavi. I want to sit down."

"Fine." Tavi stood up and walked back to the others. When he sat down, he peeked over at Malik, only to see him strolling down the stairs into the rising mist.

"What was that all about?" Pablo asked irritably.

"Nothing," Tavi replied. Byron and Kyle laughed and took turns telling the story about how Tavi was hitting on another boy.

When they were finished, Chloe and Pablo exchanged glances. Tavi waited for them to tell him how stupid he was being, but neither one said a word. Kurt then piped up and wondered if any of the homeless people would be willing to buy their stolen goods. Everyone laughed at him and told him to go ask around, and while they were teasing and snickering, Byron made eye contact with Tavi. He gave him a small smile and a reassuring nod, and Tavi started feeling better about what he had done.

They soon left the station and made their separate ways home. Only Byron and Tavi were assured of having a dry night. Neither one mentioned Malik on the walk home, but both of them were wondering what the next day might bring.

Chapter 16

The next two days passed slowly for everyone. Even if they weren't sure that they agreed with Tavi about bringing in more kids, at least it had promised to be something new. But as the first day flowed into the second, the children found themselves growing excessively bored, waiting for someone who most likely wasn't going to show up.

After two full days of waiting, even Byron was showing his annoyance. "This is a waste of time," he complained. "Why do we all have to sit here anyways?"

"I didn't say you guys had to wait here too," Tavi protested.

"Yeah, but...whatever. I thought it'd be interesting. But I'm over it now. I want to do something else tomorrow."

"You guys want to help me go check out that room by The School House tomorrow afternoon?" Tavi asked. "Most of the boys should be back by then."

Everyone nodded their heads and agreed, except for Pablo, who still turned pale at the thought of going back. "How can you risk it?" he finally asked Tavi. "They'll kill you if they catch you."

Tavi laughed and nodded towards the rest of the group. "I trust these guys to keep me safe." He paused before adding, "I trust you, too."

Pablo let out an exasperated sigh. "Screw it. I'll come."

After the others had climbed up to the roof using the fence the following afternoon, Pablo warned everyone that it'd be easy for people to spot them and so they should be careful. Kurt laughed and asked, "What are they going to do? Fly up here and grab us?" The others laughed as well, but Pablo shot Tavi a look filled with dire warnings, and Tavi nodded his head.

"Yeah. But I'm the one who will be on the ground," he reminded them.

His friends sobered up at this thought.

"Hey, I was just joking," Kurt said contritely. "I'll be careful."

The others nodded their heads in agreement. "Okay," Tavi said, looking up at them. "Can you guys run ahead and see if anyone is in the alleys?"

Pablo began pointing towards different buildings, and telling who to run where. Glancing back at Tavi one last time, he promised, "Don't worry. We'll watch out for you."

Tavi jogged back into the alleyway and focused on Chloe who was the nearest person. Looking in all directions, she waved her hand for him to proceed.

He only had to stop and wait twice for the alleyways ahead of him to clear, and within five minutes, he was in front of the familiar room. Looking around cautiously, despite his friends' careful observations from above, Tavi quickly approached the door and tried to open it. The doorknob wouldn't turn and so Tavi banged on the door twice.

Complete silence. Tavi tried to peek in through the window, but the room was pitch black. Suddenly, Byron shouted out from behind him, "Hey!"

Tavi spun around and saw Byron pointing at an alleyway that was running parallel to the one Tavi was standing in. Without wasting any time, he ran back the way he had come, stopping only briefly to wait for his friends' assurances that the coast was clear.

Twenty minutes later, as they were walking back to the park together, Byron said, "By the way, that was Yuri that I saw."

Everyone stopped for a second and looked at him in surprise. "Did he see you?" Tavi asked.

Byron laughed. "He heard me, but I don't think he saw me." Shrugging his shoulders, he said, "Who cares? We didn't get caught. So, now what?"

They resumed walking as Tavi explained the tentative plan he had formulated in his mind and then let his friends help fill in the gaps.

Later that night, Tavi was hiding in the shadows across the street from The School House. Chloe, Kurt, and Kyle were nearby. Their job was to recognize and act upon any possible trouble that may occur. Tavi, meanwhile, only had eyes for the entrance to The School House.

"Why did Pablo say he has to wait with Byron?" Kurt whispered after a couple of hours.

Kyle replied, "He thinks it's best if none of us are alone anymore."

"Be quiet!" Chloe hissed.

Kurt began to point out that the people passing by and the traffic on a nearby road were louder than their voices, but Tavi suddenly whispered excitedly, "That's him!"

The others looked across the street and saw a husky boy walking hand in hand with an older man. When the man whispered in his ear, the boy laughed and gazed lovingly at the man.

"That's who we came to rescue?" Kurt asked doubtfully. "He looks quite happy to me."

"Shut up!" Tavi replied. "They probably gave him a pill or something." He looked at the others and noticed that they seemed to be as tense as he was. "You guys remember the plan?"

The others nodded their heads. They each picked up a short metal pipe from the ground beside them. Tavi and Byron had spent hours trying to find something resembling the image they had had in their minds before fortuitously stumbling across a plumbing store with all shapes and sizes of metal piping.

Following Tavi, they stayed in the shadows as they narrowed the gap between them and the couple in front of them. Tavi cursed when the man pointed at the line of yellow cabs waiting at the curb twenty meters in front of them. "He's getting a cab! We have to do it now!" Without looking to see if his friends were following, Tavi yelled and charged at the man who spun around in surprise.

"Anouram! I knew that was you!" Tavi shouted. "I'm going to kill you for what you did!" He closed to within striking distance and swung his pipe at the older man's arm. He cried out and tried to cover himself as Anouram stared at Tavi with a confused, wide-eyed gaze.

"Anouram!" Chloe shouted as well and swung her pipe at the man's knee. He screamed in pain and collapsed to the ground.

"That's him!" Kurt shouted. "That's Anouram!"

"It is," Kyle yelled back. "Let's take him!" Kyle bowled Anouram over despite the size difference and swung his pipe at the man. Kurt and Chloe were also beating on him, and the man soon lay bleeding on the ground, moaning in pain.

"Hey!" Tavi shouted at Kyle. When Kyle glanced at him, Tavi tossed him his pipe, and then bent down and helped Anouram up by his armpits. "Let's go," he ordered, grabbing Anouram's arm and pulling him along.

Kyle and Chloe instantly followed, but Kurt stopped to hit the man one more time in his ribs. Something caught his eye, and he bent down and yanked the man's wallet out of his back pocket. Slipping it into his own pocket, Kurt hurried after the others.

They ran for several blocks, with the other children helping Anouram along. When they were finally sure that they weren't being chased, Tavi let go of Anouram's arm and bent over, panting quickly. He glanced over at Anouram who was staring at them in fright.

"Hey, Anouram. It's me," Tavi said, slowly approaching him.

Anouram scrutinized Tavi with glassy, half-lidded eyes. After a few seconds, he leaned back and smiled. "Tavi?"

"Hey, man. How are you?"

"Hey, Tavi. I love you," Anouram said drunkenly and gave Tavi a lazy hug. When he stepped back, he looked at the other children and said, "What happened?"

"We...uh...rescued you," Tavi replied. He looked to see if any of the others had anything to say, but they were busy going through the man's wallet. "Anyway, you never have to go back."

Anouram stared at Tavi blearily for a few moments. He finally said, "Tavi, they're going to kill you."

"No, they won't," Tavi reassured him. "I have a plan." Without warning, Anouram's head and shoulders twitched and his eyes went out of focus for a second. "Are you okay?"

Anouram leaned heavily against the wall behind him. "Yeah," he mumbled. "I keep doing that ever since I was...I was...what's the word?"

Tavi shrugged his shoulders and shook his head as the others joined him.

"You know, when they put you in water and then..." Anouram shook his whole body for effect and made a hissing noise.

"They shocked you?" Kyle sounded appalled.

"Yeah, man. Twice." Anouram squatted down on his heels, still resting against the wall. His head dropped forward and Tavi reached forward to see if he was okay.

"Hey, you have to see this," Kurt insisted.

"Wait." Tavi reached for Anouram's head.

"No, really, Tavi. You have to see who this guy was," Chloe added.

Tavi grabbed the card that Kurt was holding out to him and walked towards the nearby streetlight. He squinted his eyes and examined the card carefully. He felt a sinking sensation in the pit of his stomach when he realized that the man was a Deputy of Security for the local government.

"Do you guys know what that means?" he asked, handing the card back to Kurt.

"No," Chloe replied. "But I don't think it's a good thing for us."

Tavi shoved the worries about the unknown behind him and walked over to help Anouram up. "At least our gang just grew by one," he said. "I hope Byron is still okay with letting him stay with us tonight."

"You did ask, right?" Kyle assisted Tavi in standing Anouram up, who immediately put his arms around the boys' shoulders and had to be dragged.

"Yeah, but I didn't know he would be like this." The five children slowly made their way through the darkened streets back to where Pablo and Byron were safely waiting for them.

Chapter 17

"What the hell happened last night?" Giovanni was shouting at Vikram when Yuri entered Vikram's office. He stood beside the closed door and watched with interest as Vikram groveled towards Giovanni.

"It wasn't my fault," Vikram insisted. "We've been following your suggestions and keeping most of the boys locked in their rooms at all times. And the customers like the new policy where they can just have the boys in one of the rooms inside of the bar." He glanced at Yuri for help. "Ask him. He'll tell you."

Giovanni didn't even turn around as Yuri nodded his head in agreement. "Then tell me what happened last night," Giovanni said in a low voice.

Vikram opened up a notebook and pushed it across the desk for Giovanni to study. "We have some customers who prefer to pay the extra price and take the boys home with them for the evening. On our busy nights, there are usually about ten or twelve boys who leave the premises. Mr. Swanson is one of those men who always pays extra."

Giovanni examined the notebook, flipping back a few pages and checking to see how many boys were bought each day. Seemingly satisfied with the information in front of him, he slid the notebook back and sat down across from Vikram. "Fine. Then what happened?"

"No one really knows. Witnesses said four children jumped out of the shadows and started beating Mr. Swanson with sticks or metal pipes or something like that. Mr. Swanson told me this morning that the children were angry at the boy, and that they threatened to take him away for something he did to them."

Giovanni picked up his briefcase and set it on the desk. Flipping it open, he pulled out that morning's newspaper. He tossed it across to Vikram. "Have you seen the front page? *Gangs of murderous children are roaming our streets.* Do you know how much damage it could've done to us and Mr. Swanson if the reporters had written that he was with one of our boys? Do you know how quickly we would get shut down?"

"I don't know what to tell you." Vikram looked towards Yuri in exasperation. "Do you have any ideas?"

Yuri approached the desk and stood off to the side. He stated, "I don't think that a gang of street kids would have any reason to be angry at Anouram. It doesn't make any sense. He's rarely on the streets."

"Then why would three boys and a girl attack him and his customer and then drag Anouram away?"

"Wait…you didn't mention before that there was a girl involved," Yuri said.

Giovanni rolled his eyes at Vikram. "Does it really matter?"

Yuri gave a small smile. "No. I guess not." He asked Vikram, "Do you want me to see if anyone knows anything?"

"Yeah."

Giovanni added, "And raise the bounty that we're giving out to five hundred talents for every street kid they bring us. The customers really like having a lot of fresh boys to choose from."

Yuri glanced at Vikram who nodded his head in agreement. "Yes, sir," Yuri said. "If that is all, then I will go see what I can find out about Anouram."

"Go," Giovanni dismissed him. Vikram just waved his hand and Yuri turned and strolled out of the room. As he closed the door behind him, Giovanni was saying, "You know? If we can turn the public against all of these street kids, then…"

"So, this is where you guys hang out?" Anouram asked Tavi. He was perched on top of the dome-like jungle gym and he kept looking around the playground nervously.

"Yep," Tavi answered as he and Byron tried to see who could swing the highest. They both leaped off of their swings at the same time, and Tavi laughed in dismay as Byron jumped a foot farther than him. "How do you do that?" he demanded.

Byron just smiled at Tavi and walked over to the monkey bars. He climbed up and sat on top of the ladder so that he could talk almost face to face with Anouram. "Sometimes," he said, answering Anouram's earlier question. "But Tavi and I also go to the library a lot to read books and watch movies."

"Really? That sounds fun. Can I go with you guys?"

"Sure," Tavi replied easily. He sat down at the end of the slide and leaned back against the warm metal, closing his eyes as the sun lit up his face. "And there are so many other things to see and explore."

Tavi couldn't see him looking around, but he heard the nervous tension in Anouram's voice. "Aren't you worried about getting caught? They really will kill you. And me too, I guess."

Tavi's stomach clenched in fear, but he kept his voice deliberately calm. "Just always be aware of who or what is around you, and try never to be alone. You'll be fine," he promised. "We'll watch out for you."

He heard a weird noise and opened his eyes as Byron said, "You okay, man? You just had a massive twitch."

"Yeah," Anouram said. "They're doing some crazy shit now if you don't find a customer every night. They're burning kids, shocking them, beating them, trying to drown then. Two kids have already died accidentally."

"Accidentally?" Tavi asked, closing his eyes again.

"Yeah. One kid got shocked for too long, and another one they drowned without meaning to."

Byron couldn't conceal the pity in his voice. "I'm sorry, man. I wish we could've saved you sooner. I mean, isn't it better being out here than inside there?"

"I guess. I just feel weird right now. Too much open space and time and I keep feeling like I'm going to see someone I know coming to take me back."

"Look! Here come Kurt and Kyle. Don't worry. If anyone comes, we've got your back."

Tavi sat up to greet his friends and was surprised when Kurt reached into his bag and pulled out some cell phones. He tossed them to the others with a grin on his face. "What's this?" Byron asked.

"I figure since we can't sell them then we might as well use them," Kurt said. "Kyle and I just bought sim cards at Clarence's and so you've each got about ten talents of calls on there. It's an early or late birthday present."

"Cool," Tavi said, touching the screen and turning his on. "What's your phone numbers?"

"Read off yours first and then we'll each call you. Our numbers should show up and then you can just save our names next to them."

"Sweet," Tavi said. He took a moment to figure out his way around the menu options and then he said, "Okay, my number is 91…"

"Oh, shit!!" Anouram shouted and rolled backwards off of the jungle gym. The others stared in shock as he landed on his back, and then they raced over to see if he was okay. He lay on his back, holding his head and moaning.

"What's wrong with you?" Tavi asked.

Anouram pointed behinds Tavi as a voice said, "Hi, guys."

Tavi spun around and felt a sinking sensation in his heart. "Hi, Yuri. Welcome back."

Yuri scanned the playground carefully before resting his gaze upon Anouram. "What were you guys thinking last night?"

"He's my friend," Tavi said simply.

"Do you know who the man was that you attacked?"

"Deputy of Security something," Kurt answered. "How's the laptop?"

Anouram slowly sat up, his eyes never leaving Yuri's face.

"It's actually pretty good. Anyway, I have to say nice job making people think that you wanted to hurt Anouram. However, Tavi, I've told them that you are gone. If you keep causing problems, then things may have to change."

Anouram grabbed Tavi's arm and yanked him close. He put his mouth next to Tavi's ear and whispered, "Yuri's bad, Tavi. He's helping Vikram and Giovanni. You can't trust him." Tavi kept his expression the same as he stared at Yuri.

"Anouram, it's not nice to tell secrets," Yuri chided.

Anouram gulped and stopped whispering. Yuri sat down in the swing and kicked back and forth until he was moving faster. "How far did you jump?" he asked Byron. "I was watching earlier, but I couldn't tell exactly where you landed."

Byron seemed to consider the question for a second, and then walked around to where the mark from his heel was still visible in the dirt. "Here," he said, scuffing a line with his foot. He stood there for a second before realizing that he was separated from the others, and then hurried back to stand near the jungle gym.

Everyone watched Yuri as he slowly climbed higher and higher. The entire swing set was soon shaking and creaking and then all of a sudden, Yuri was flying through the air. He easily cleared Byron's mark and landed about three feet past his line. He turned around with a small smile on his face, and Tavi had to restrain himself from cheering for him.

"Anouram, you should probably come back with me – now," Yuri said seriously. "If you stay gone for longer than a day, then there's going to be a death bounty on your head as well."

Tavi put his hand on Anouram's arm and replied, "He's not going anywhere. Just leave him alone, Yuri." Anouram looked at Tavi as if he were crazy for speaking like that to Yuri.

"Okay," Yuri responded. "But the next time I return, I won't be coming alone. And things won't go as nicely, I'm afraid."

"Is that a threat?" Tavi asked quietly.

"A threat?" someone said loudly from the bushes behind Yuri. Yuri spun around as two boys and a girl appeared as if by magic. "Who's threatening my new gang?"

"Who are you?" Yuri asked, stepping back a pace.

"Malik!" Tavi called out.

Malik nodded his head. "That's who I am. Yuri, right?" Yuri didn't respond as Malik continued, "Don't be threatening my friends with your scary talk. We've got each other's backs." He glanced over at Tavi and grinned. "Right, Tavi?"

Tavi laughed aloud and felt even happier when he saw that his friends were smiling as well.

"I apologize, Malik. And it won't happen again."

Malik stopped smiling and studied Yuri's expression. "What won't happen again?"

"Me apologizing." Yuri brushed past the boy who was standing next to Malik and headed towards the parking lot without a backwards glance. Malik followed him with his eyes until Yuri turned the far corner, and then he walked towards Tavi with a grin.

"Is this our big gang?" he asked.

"Don't worry. This is just the beginning," Tavi promised.

Malik eyed the others appraisingly and then glanced behind him to where Yuri had disappeared. Speaking softly, he warned, "That Yuri…he's a dangerous cat."

"He's not so bad," Tavi protested. "I knew him when I was young."

Malik shook his head and looked Tavi in the eye. "Trust me. You don't want to mess with him." Anouram nodded his head vigorously as Tavi remembered the words that Yuri had ingrained in him…Don't trust anybody.

Chapter 18

Malik's two friends, Sasha and Hector, didn't speak much. They were timid and skittish at first, but by the time Chloe and Pablo arrived an hour later, their bodies had relaxed and they were following the conversation with intelligent eyes and quick smiles.

"Hey," Pablo called out as he crossed the playground. Chloe strode beside him as their eyes swept across the children gathered on the equipment. Tavi hopped down from the monkey bars and walked a few steps in their direction.

"Hey. You guys remember Malik from the train station, right?" Tavi pointed at Malik, who nodded his head politely in their direction. "He brought a couple of friends – Sasha and Hector – and now we're just…" Tavi finished with a shrug.

"Hi," Chloe said. She gave Tavi a small smile as she passed him and then went over and sat near Sasha. Kurt jumped up and hurried over to stand next to Tavi, and Malik immediately followed.

"Pablo!" Kurt said excitedly, holding out a cell phone towards Pablo. "I got us some phones."

Pablo smiled as he accepted the phone from Kurt. "Cool." He turned his attention to Malik, who was now standing next to them. "What's your guys' stories?"

Malik hesitated for a second and glanced at his two friends. When he saw them in quiet conversation with Chloe, he relaxed and said, "I ran away from The Joy Luck Club a few weeks ago. Those two are twins. They don't really talk much. Their bar would sell them to customers as a package deal. I found them digging through a trashcan two weeks ago. They were starving and so scared, and I had to do something. They can't survive on their own out here."

"And that's why you need us?" Pablo asked.

Malik looked away and admitted, "Yes. I don't think I can make it alone either. What Tavi said made good sense. The more people you have, the less chance that someone will mess with you."

Kurt nodded his head in agreement and pointed at Pablo's phone. "Hey. You want to call me so that I can have your number?"

Pablo looked at Kurt in surprise and then burst out laughing. He smiled fondly at Kurt and said, "You're such an idiot." He looked at his phone and touched the screen. "Fine. What's your number?"

Later that afternoon, Byron and Tavi proudly led Anouram, Malik, Sasha, and Hector into the library. Anouram looked around excitedly, and Tavi remembered how he himself had felt the first time he had entered. Glancing back at the others, Tavi smiled at the wonder that was clearly written about their faces.

"Are there comic books?" Malik whispered to Byron.

"Yeah," Byron replied. "Come on. I'll show you guys where they are."

Tavi led Anouram to their usual spot as Byron and the others disappeared among the bookshelves. Leaning his head across the table, Anouram said softly, "I haven't read a book since I left home." He gazed around the room again, trying to absorb everything he saw. "I wonder if I can still read."

Tavi laughed quietly and stood up from the table. "Wait here," he commanded. "I'll be right back." Tavi hurried to the shelf he had first become intimately familiar with and pulled down the first book in the series. He slid the book across the table to Anouram as he sat back down. "Here. Read this."

Anouram stared at the cover of the book and then slowly flipped through the pages. Tavi watched expectantly and was disappointed when Anouram set the book down gently on the table. "What's wrong? You don't like it."

"No. It's fine," Anouram insisted. He swallowed hard and looked up at Tavi with fearful eyes. "We're going to die, aren't we?"

"What?" Tavi asked in surprise. "No! What are you talking about?"

Anouram opened his mouth to reply, but started chewing on his bottom lip as Byron returned with the other three. Anouram watched them spread out on the long table next to them and then whispered, "Yuri's going to come back and catch us." Tavi shook his head and Anouram insisted loudly, "He is! You were there when he killed Will!"

"Shhhh!" Byron shot them a warning glance.

"Fine. Yes, it's dangerous out here," Tavi admitted, "but would you rather be having sex with men for the rest of your life?" Anouram looked down and didn't respond as Tavi continued, "I have a plan. We just need a few more kids, and then I think we should be safer."

A spark of hope lit up Anouram's eyes. "Really?"

Tavi casually looked around the room and spotted the two familiar boys in the far corner. He nodded his head towards them and said, "Yes. And maybe those two will join us as well."

A few minutes later, Tavi left Anouram with his new book, and he and Byron nonchalantly approached the table where the two boys were sitting. The one who was facing them glanced up, nudged his friend's book, and then his friend turned around and stared at them.

"Hi," Tavi said. At this close of a distance, Tavi could tell that both boys were one or two years older than him. He wondered briefly if he was making a mistake.

"Hello," responded the boy who was sitting across from them. "What do you want?"

"Can we sit down for a second?"

"Why?"

Byron cleared his throat and said, "We have a proposition for you."

"What's that?" the boy asked.

"Um..." Byron glanced at Tavi. "A proposition...I mean, like an offer..."

The boy snickered aloud as his friend shook his head and turned back to his book. "I KNOW what a proposition is." He looked briefly at his friend before saying, "Fine. Sit. Hurry up."

Tavi and Byron sat on opposite sides of the table, keeping a couple of seats in between them and the two boys. The boy next to Tavi – the one who had done most of the talking – looked at them and said, "Well? Go on."

"Ummm..." Tavi's mind was blank.

He looked at Byron for help who murmured, "Movie."

"Right, okay...do you guys remember that movie we watched last week?"

The boy who was sitting next to Byron looked up from his book with a grin. "Yeah. That was awesome. I never knew that penguins..."

"Not that one," Tavi interrupted. "The other one about the lions and the wildebeests."

"And the crocodile!" the boy next to Tavi added.

"Yes! Okay. In that movie, who are you?"

"What do you mean?" the same boy asked.

"Do you see yourselves as the lions or the wildebeests or the crocodiles?"

The boys looked at each other with grins on their faces. The one next to Byron said, "We're the people with the cameras. We just watch everyone else fight each other." His friend nodded in agreement.

Byron stepped in. "Listen. We've been thinking that kids like us don't need to run away and be scared all the time if we can get a big enough group together. One wildebeest gets eaten by the lions, but twenty wildebeest can win if they don't run away."

"We're not scared all the time," the boy closest to Tavi denied.

"And you sleep safely at night?"

Again, the two boys looked at each other and grinned. "Yep." The boy next to Tavi flicked his gaze over towards Tavi's friends. "Is this why you two suddenly have four new friends?"

"We've got more friends than this," Tavi said indignantly.

Byron added, "Yeah. They just don't like the library."

Tavi was growing tired of the boys' secret glances and their mocking attitudes. He gave up all pretense and spoke from his heart, "Look…we just want to hang out and see if we get along. If we do, then maybe it could be better for all of us. We're not asking you to come join us right this second." He pointed to his friends across the room. "We just rescued that guy on the left from a bar last night, and the other three just visited us today for the first time."

Both boys studied Anouram and the others with renewed interest. Tavi continued, "And so…this is all new to us, too. We just think things can be better. And I don't want to die," he finished softly.

The two boys shared a silent conversation as Tavi looked at Byron and shook his head in defeat. Without warning, the boy next to Tavi said, "My name is Adam. His name is Mo; it's short for Mohammed. How about we talk again tomorrow? We get here around nine every morning."

"Really?" Tavi asked.

"Did you really rescue that boy over there last night?"

Tavi and Byron nodded their heads.

"Then, yes..really."

"Cool!" Tavi said excitedly. He stood up to go. "Oh – I'm Tavi. This is Byron. And that's Anouram, Malik, Hector, and Sasha."

Adam gave him a small smile. Turning his attention back to his book, he said, "We'll see you tomorrow, Tavi."

Tavi grinned at Byron, who laughed out loud when Tavi tripped over his chair. Feeling his face turn red with embarrassment, Tavi kept his eyes on the ground as he made his way back over to his friends.

Chapter 19

A few weeks after first meeting Adam and Mo, Tavi had just fallen asleep in the corner of the basement when the door opened loudly above him and a light shined down through the open doorway.

Someone took three steps down the stairs and flipped the light switch. Tavi reached over and shook Byron urgently as the man complained, "Honey! The light is broken again. Can you bring me another bulb?" Tavi stared wide-eyed at Byron in the faint light as the wife's muted response reached their ears.

"Because the hall closet is right next to you," the man replied.

Byron shook Anouram awake and hissed, "Get up. Someone's coming!" as they heard the wife again. The sound of footsteps somewhere above them warned them that she was bringing the bulb, while her husband remained standing on the stairs leading to the basement.

Scrambling up as quietly as they could, Tavi pointed at the box of stolen stuff that they'd been storing behind the boiler. Anouram picked it up too quickly and the items rattled around inside. They all froze in fear.

"Hey!" the man shouted into the basement. "Is someone there?"

Byron pushed Tavi towards the window. "Go!" he ordered. Tavi scooped up his bag and slung it over his shoulder.

"Hey! Who's there?!?" The boys tiptoed to the window, and as Tavi pulled it open with a slight screech, he saw the man take a step backwards into the kitchen. "Honey! I think someone's in the basement. Get my gun!"

Tavi said a quick prayer and stepped away from the window. "You guys hurry up and climb out," he said.

"What will you do?" Byron asked as Anouram thrust the box out of the window.

Tavi gave him a wild grin and said, "I'm gonna be a wildebeest."

He turned around and slowly approached the stairs. In a high-pitched voice, he said, "Mister. Heeeeelp me."

The man was clearly startled. He took another step back and called out, "Who is that?"

Glancing back, Tavi saw that Anouram was already outside and that Byron was climbing out of the window. He gave a long, high moan and shuffled slowly towards the stairs.

"Jonathan, who's down there?" the wife called out to her husband as she approached him.

Without waiting any longer, Tavi screamed as loud and as long as he could and ran up the stairs, his eyes and mouth open as wide as he could make them. The man, who was about three times the size of Tavi, screamed in fright as he tried to retreat up the stairs. He tripped over the top step and fell backwards into the kitchen as Tavi got halfway up the stairs.

"Close it!" the man screamed at his wife. The door slammed shut and Tavi heard the lock click as he stopped on the third step. His heart was beating wildly. He took a couple of seconds to control his breathing and then hurried back down the stairs.

Byron's head was sticking through the window. "You're insane, Tavi! Let's go."

"Did we forget anything?" Tavi asked. "I don't think we'll be able to come back." He ran past the window and into the corner, fumbling in his bag for a flashlight. After a couple of panicky moments, he finally found it and clicked it on, shining it wildly around the corner where they'd been sleeping.

"The blankets," Byron whispered. Tavi scooped up all of the blankets and threw them near the window. Two cell phones clattered to the floor and Tavi picked them up and put them in his pocket. Checking behind the boiler, he saw a small box which contained the jewelry they had stolen. Grabbing that as well, he ran back to the window, pushed everything through to Byron, and then climbed out himself.

"The cops will be coming," Byron warned. "We need to get out of here now." Tavi nodded his head as they picked everything up off the ground. Byron looked around quickly and pointed to a nearby alley. "This way," he said, leading the way. Anouram and Tavi quietly followed him, and within seconds, the street was empty and silent once again.

They spent the night sleeping fitfully in the playground. The morning seemed interminably long as they waited for their friends to arrive. The blankets were folded neatly and stacked on a nearby bench, while the box of stolen items was placed under the jungle gym. Finally, around noon, everyone started trickling in as Byron, Tavi, and Anouram took turns retelling the story.

"And so we need to find a new place to stay," Tavi concluded when everyone was there. Malik and the twins had taken to hanging out with the children every day, and Tavi felt sure that he could safely consider them part of the group. "And hopefully it'll be a place where we can stay for more than a couple of days." Byron nodded his head emphatically in agreement.

"Yeah, that sucks. We just got kicked out of our spot this morning by that group of boys," Chloe complained. She and Pablo sat on a bench together, both of them staring at the ground morosely.

"Wait a second. How many boys is it?" Byron asked.

Pablo shrugged. "Four or five. Why?"

Byron made an exaggerated show of counting the people around him. "...seven, eight, nine, ten. We have TEN people here." Tavi grinned and began nodding his head excitedly.

"You want us to fight them?" Kurt asked.

"I think we can make them move," Tavi said. Or ask them to join us, he thought, as he laughed out loud.

Kurt gave him a strange look. "So we're going to try and all sleep together now?"

Tavi looked around at the others who were all paying close attention to the conversation. "Do you and Kyle enjoy sleeping behind a dumpster?" Without waiting for a response, he asked Malik, "And do you guys feel safe at night? I think this could be our chance."

"What about Adam and Mo?" Byron asked. He and Tavi had gotten to know them quite well, and all of the children had stopped by the library at some point to meet them.

"Sure, why not?" Tavi felt giddy inside and couldn't stop smiling. "Do you think those boys will still be there?" he asked Chloe and Pablo.

Chloe nodded her head. "They were there an hour ago, so probably."

"Then let's go now," Tavi urged. "Byron and I will go to the library real fast and see if Adam and Mo want to come, and then we'll meet you there." The others agreed and picked up all of their possessions as Pablo explained to Tavi where to meet them. Still feeling buoyant that his plan was finally coming together, Tavi raced off in the direction of the library with yelling at him from behind to slow down.

It only took him a few seconds to convince Adam and Mo to come with them. They were sitting at their usual table and looked up in surprise when Tavi hurried over, with a winded Byron trailing far behind him.

"We need a big group to go scare some bullies who have been hassling our friends. You guys want to come?" Tavi asked.

Adam glanced at Mo who gave a non-committal shrug. "Sure. Let's go," Adam said. Leaving the books on the table, they stood up and followed Tavi out before Byron even had the chance to reach them.

Twenty minutes later, they were standing at the back of a five story building, staring up at a ladder that went all the way to the roof.

"You want us to climb THAT?" Adam asked doubtfully.

Chloe laughed and pulled herself onto the second rung. "We climb these things every day." She reached for a rung above her head, and within seconds, she was halfway up the building. Pablo gave Adam a challenging stare and immediately followed her.

"Those guys are crazy," Kurt whispered to Kyle as Tavi wiped his hands on his pants and slowly began climbing. He kept his eyes focused on the rungs above him and hoped that his friends were following behind him. Breathlessly, and after what felt like an hour, Tavi grabbed the top handle. Holding onto it tightly, he stepped up and could see the roof as his head popped over the edge.

"We told you not to come back," a boy the same size as Pablo was saying. There were four boys, two on each side of Pablo and Chloe, and they didn't look happy to see them. "We told you before – this roof and all roofs are ours." Tavi watched for a few seconds longer and then heaved himself up and onto the roof. He sat on the wall for a moment as everyone turned to stare at him, and then he hopped down and walked over to stand next to Pablo.

Two of the boys laughed. "Ohh, so you brought a friend to help you," the smallest boy said with a smirk. "I could beat him up all by myself."

Tavi had gotten a quick feel for the layout of the roof and he nudged Pablo and began backing up towards the wall of a small chimney that was fifteen meters from the edge of the roof. Ignoring the taunts and jeers of the boys, Tavi, Pablo, and Chloe slowly backed up until their backs were against the chimney and the four boys were facing them.

Thus, Tavi and his friends were the only ones to see Adam quietly climb over the edge of the roof, soon followed by Mo, Kyle, and Kurt. Tavi grinned when Anouram's head popped up and he could sense that Pablo had also relaxed and was smiling foolishly.

The boys' heckling and taunting grew more threatening until one of them finally shouted, "What are you idiots smiling about?"

"Us," Adam said, as Hector climbed onto the roof. The boys spun around and they each took a step backwards when they saw how outnumbered they were.

"Hey...we don't want any trouble," said the bigger one whom Tavi had seen speaking originally. Sasha pushed herself onto the ledge and jumped down with a smile on her face. Tavi had never seen her eyes sparkle so happily before.

"What do you mean you don't want trouble?" Pablo asked. The other boy reluctantly turned around and Pablo stepped towards him. "You've been chasing us and threatening us for almost a year. These are our roofs now."

The boy looked at his friends in fear. "What are we supposed to do?" he asked, almost whining. "There's enough space for all of us."

By this time, Tavi had walked away from the others and was looking around the huge area. Kyle joined him and they walked over to one of the planks which was connected to another building in the same way as the ones they had seen near The School House. Tavi looked around in bewilderment and murmured to Kyle, "This sucks. Why do they want to sleep up here? What happens when it rains?"

Kyle shrugged his shoulders and studied the roof. "Maybe they sleep over there." He pointed to an overhang near the chimney where two or three people could fit. "I agree, though. I don't want to move up here. I mean, there are no cops, but who wants to climb ladders every day?"

Tavi shared a look with Kyle and they walked back to where the others were arguing with the strange boys. Interrupting them, Tavi motioned to Kyle and said, "We don't like this place."

Everyone fell silent and looked at him in surprise. "What?" one of the other boys asked.

Kyle explained, "This place sucks. Why are you guys even fighting over this? What do you do when it rains?"

"We have ponchos," the boy replied, and Pablo and Chloe nodded their heads in agreement. By this time, the rest of their group had spread out and were making their own assessment about the roof.

"And doesn't it get tiring climbing the ladders every day?" Tavi asked.

Pablo glanced at his counterpart and said defensively, "It's good exercise." The other boys murmured agreement. "And we don't have to worry about cops," he added.

Tavi watched the interaction between Pablo and the other boys with interest. Making a snap decision, he asked the boy who seemed most like the leader, "What's your name?"

Pablo responded first. "His name is Ben."

Ben nodded his head once. "And you're Pablo." He gave Chloe a small smile. "And Chloe."

"Do you guys really like living up here?" Tavi asked. "I mean, really?"

Ben looked at his friends and then gazed around the rooftops of the nearest buildings. Above them, the sky gently rumbled and everyone looked up at the gray, overcast sky. The other boys reached into their bags and pulled out dark green ponchos. "Where else can we go? We'll get beaten up if we try to sleep anywhere on the streets. It's not safe down there, and there are only four of us."

This was the moment Tavi had been waiting for. He hoped he had judged everything correctly. "What about under that huge bridge?" He pointed off into the distance at the bridge that spanned the river.

"We tried," Ben admitted. "But we weren't big enough. We got kicked out after twenty minutes."

Tavi looked around at his friends who had rejoined them for the last part of the conversation. He raised one eyebrow questioningly at Pablo, who nodded after a couple of seconds. "What if you went there with us?"

"And then what?" Ben asked warily.

"And then we would have sixteen people. If we stay together and help each other, we might be too big for them to make us leave."

The sky rumbled again, and this time Pablo and Chloe pulled out their ponchos as well. The rest of the children glanced up at the sky and anxiously looked around for shelter. Kurt was the first one to head for the ladder, and the others quickly followed. Ben turned to watch them go and then asked, "When?"

"Now."

Chapter 20

The storm that had been threatening to break held off long enough for the children to run to the nearest train station. Ben pointed out storage lockers that Tavi had never noticed before, and they each rented one and stuffed most of their stuff into them. He showed them the key that he wore around his neck, and told them that if they remembered to pay one talent every week, then they could use it indefinitely.

Feeling less encumbered and freer from not having to worry about carrying their blankets and other possessions with him, Tavi looked around proudly as his large group crowded into the monorail car. His joy was tainted when he saw the looks of worry and disgust that some of the other passengers gave them, and he noticed that several people got up from their seats and walked to the adjacent car. He looked around, but it was clear that none of his friends had noticed or cared, and he tried to forget about it. However, it persisted in the back of his mind like a tiny, dark shadow, and he knew that he wouldn't be able to stop seeing their expressions in his mind.

Part of him wanted to get cleaned up and show those people that he wasn't just a dirty street rat. The other part of him wanted to go jump them and hurt them and steal all of their possessions. Fucking boujies, he thought scathingly.

"So, what's the plan?" Adam asked, interrupting Tavi's thoughts. Tavi explained to the people nearest to him how he hoped things would go, and then they discussed it and came to an agreement about how they would proceed.

An hour later, Tavi crept under the bridge and sat down against the pillar he had rested against before. Once again, he heard shouts of laughter and boys calling to each other loudly. He was surprised at how relaxed he felt, and he leaned his head back and closed his eyes, calmly waiting for something to happen.

"Hey, guy." The voice startled Tavi out of his reverie.

Looking up sleepily, Tavi saw the same boy who had confronted him the last time. "Hey, Jack."

Jack studied Tavi's face carefully. "Do I know you?"

"Do you?" Tavi looked to his left and saw two boys watching the exchange curiously. "How's Momo?"

Jack wrinkled his forehead in confusion. Comprehension quickly dawned and he chuckled loudly. "I remember you. You're that kid who ran away when we were fighting Momo's gang over you."

Tavi smiled. "That's me."

"Well, I don't know why you came back, but I appreciate it." He gave Tavi a charming grin. "Can we have your stuff now? It'd be easier than beating you up first."

Tavi slowly stood up. He looked around carefully and counted three boys with Jack, and four more sitting in the area where Jack had come from. He returned Jack's grin and said, "No!" He then sprinted towards the exit of the bridge. Tavi risked a quick glance back and saw that the boys were slow to react. However, with Jack in the lead, they soon raced after Tavi.

Tavi ran out from under the bridge and up the escarpment to his left. There were a few bushes in the way, and as soon as Tavi dodged around those, he saw his friends waiting for him. He stopped and spun around as his friends spread out to surround him.

Jack was the first one around the bushes. Before he could halt himself, he had almost collided with Tavi and had been grabbed by Pablo and Adam. He tried to call out a warning, but his three friends were too close behind. They managed to skid to a stop a few feet from where Tavi and his group were standing. Their eyes locked on Jack, who had already stopped struggling, and they looked ready to retreat.

"Wait," Tavi called out to them. He focused his attention on Jack. "I just wanted to talk."

Jack tried to shake free again as he said, "Talk about what?"

"About how we're moving under the bridge." Jack stopped wriggling again and gave Tavi a sullen look.

"We'll fight you," he promised. "We won't go that easily."

"I don't want you to go. I want us to live there together," Tavi replied. He nodded at Pablo. "Let him go."

Jack walked over to his friends as soon as he was free. They crowded against him and continuously swept their eyes over Tavi's group. It was as if they couldn't believe there were so many children. "I don't know if there's enough room," Jack began before Tavi cut him off.

"Shut up. It's huge under there. You guys can have your side. We'll have our side."

Jack smiled. "And we can join up and get rid of Momo."

"And Momo can have his side," Tavi added. Jack's smile vanished.

"Momo is a jackass."

"How many people does he have?"

"About nine or ten."

"And how many do you have?"

Jack hesitated. "About the same," he said slowly.

"And how many do we have if you and us add our numbers together?"

Jack quickly counted and grinned again. "A lot more than Momo."

Tavi sighed. "And how many would we have if we also added Momo's to our numbers?"

Raindrops began falling slowly upon them. Jack's three friends quickly ran back towards the bridge. Tavi looked Jack in the eye and said, "We're coming in now. We'll finish our talk once we get settled."

"Fine," Jack said. "But I'm not going to talk to Momo for you."

"No problem," Tavi replied as they began jogging towards the bridge. "I'll find him myself."

After they had set their stuff down, most of Tavi's group walked over to Jack's encampment to see how they had things set up. There was a metal barrel in the center where they threw their trash to be burned. A lot of the children had laid down tarps and had then placed their blankets on top so they could stay relatively clean.

Tavi studied the children and noted there were two girls and six boys, and that most of them seemed to be a couple of years younger than he was. He glanced at his friends and noticed that Kurt was carrying the box of items they hadn't been able to sell.

"Hey, Jack." Tavi walked over and asked discretely, "Do you know someone who will buy things?"

"Like what?"

"Cell phones, jewelry, laptops. Things like that."

"Sure. But if you want, I'll buy them from you for cheap. I'll give you a great deal." Jack's face stayed serious for a second before it broke into a grin. He had a charming smile that went well with his red hair and green eyes.

"Haha. I think we prefer to just meet your guy. Ours decided to stop buying from us."

"Sure. Jane can take you guys the next time she goes."

Tavi nodded his head and opened his mouth to speak when he heard someone shout his name.

He spun around and saw four older boys surrounding Byron, Anouram, Sasha, and Hector. "What the...?"

"You wanted to meet Momo?" Jack gave an ironic smile as the largest boy punched Anouram in the stomach. "There he is in all of his glory." He pulled Tavi's arm and began running towards the trouble. "Let's go!"

Tavi's friends were clearly beaten within the thirty seconds it took to sprint to their camp. Momo was already bent over and rummaging through their stuff by the time they reached the pillar.

"Momo!" Jack called, slowing to a stop. "Leave them alone."

Momo continued to dig through the items. "I don't think this is any of your business, Jack." He didn't even bother to turn around, but his friends had seen the large group that was following Jack and Tavi, and they slowly backed away and let Anouram and Byron go. As soon as he was free, Anouram ran over and kicked Momo in the ribs.

A normal person would have fallen over in pain. Momo, however, roared in anger and spun around, grabbing for Anouram. Anouram skipped backwards until he was standing in front of Tavi.

"Momo," Jack said again.

Momo glared at Jack. "I told you, Jack-off, this isn't...your...concern," he trailed off when he saw the large group of children who were spreading out to surround him.

"I think it is," Tavi said. "That's our stuff you're going through."

"Who are you?"

"I'm Tavi. We just moved in."

Momo flicked his gaze to Jack who nodded in agreement. Momo shook his head and said to Jack, "We should talk about this."

"I agree," Tavi said cheerfully. "How about we talk in Jack's camp? It's more comfortable than ours."

"We're not going there," Momo said immediately. "They'll just try to outnumber us and jump us if we go there."

Tavi and Jack and a few of their friends laughed. "Look around you," Byron said. "You can't be more outnumbered than this."

Momo glared at Byron and then looked around the circle. "Fine," he finally agreed. "We'll meet you there in ten minutes."

"Okay…what?" Momo asked after everyone had found a place to sit.

Tavi waited for Jack to speak since it was his place, but he just made a waving motion with his hand. "Go ahead. It's your idea."

"Okay." Tavi looked at Momo and said, "You guys are idiots."

Momo rolled his eyes and looked at Jack who just shrugged his shoulders. "And why is that?"

"Because Jack isn't the enemy." Tavi spread his arms out and looked around him. "Look how much space there is. What are you guys fighting about?"

"Because this is our bridge."

Tavi laughed in response. "You need all of this room for eight people?"

Momo gave a small smile and said grudgingly, "Maybe."

"Listen. We know the bars are paying people to grab street kids. A lot of us have seen cops doing it, and so we don't want to be sleeping out there."

One of Momo's friends nodded his head and said, "Yeah. A couple of cops took Tommy a few days ago. We ran when they started chasing us, but he was too slow."

"What'd you guys do to make them chase you?" Jack asked.

Momo snorted. "Nothing. We were just walking."

"Look…we're all poor and we're not going to hurt each other. And since the cops are trying to arrest us for doing nothing, well…we should start doing something."

"Like what?"

"The boujie kids. Jump them, sell their stuff, and get paid some money. And if we protect each other, then no one can touch us here. Not if we have more people than anyone else."

Momo sat quietly for a couple of minutes and stared at the ground. He looked up at Jack once and turned his attention back to his feet. "Okay," he said, finally meeting Tavi's gaze. "We'll give it a try."

Tavi grinned and held out his hand. Momo looked at for a second before shaking it cautiously. "Now you two shake hands," he told Jack and Momo. Both of the boys grimaced, but they held out their hands and briefly shook.

"One more thing," Tavi said when Momo stood up.

"What?" Momo said in exasperation as he sat back down.

"We need more people. I think we should welcome kids who come to the bridge, as long as they agree to help us."

Momo sneered. "Then who are we supposed to…"

"Boujies," Tavi interrupted. "Only boujies."

"Fine. Are we done?"

Tavi looked around at his friends who were looking at him with excitement in their eyes. When none of them said anything, Tavi stood up and said, "Yep. I guess so." The three groups separated and made their way back to their own camps.

When they had finally reached the spot where they were going to be sleeping, Byron whispered to Tavi, "That was awesome."

"Do you think it's going to work?"

Byron grinned. "I have no idea. But at least we're not out there," he said, pointing to the thunderstorm that was still pouring down.

Chapter 21

A few days later, Tavi was once again waiting in the shadows on the street where most of the bars were. This time, Jack and one of his friends had accompanied Kurt, Kyle, and Chloe. The living arrangements under the bridge had been going quite smoothly. Both Jack and Momo had their own fences to whom they sold their stolen items. When Jack found out how much Momo's was offering for the jewelry that Tavi's group had accumulated, he had immediately visited his man and told him that they were shifting all of their business to the other pawnshop. As a result, both pawnshop owners were in a price-raising war that was benefitting the children who used them.

The three groups hadn't been mingling much, but Jack had been intrigued by the tale Anouram told of being rescued by his friends, and he wanted to strike back at the bar owners as well. He had run away from The Fun Guy Ranch almost two years prior. He complained that he still had strange flashbacks from time to time due to all of the psychedelic mushrooms they had been forced to ingest. Apparently, many of the customers enjoyed watching the boys trip out on the mushrooms, and then they would rape them while they were out of their minds.

"So, what do we do?" Jack asked quietly, twisting his hands around the metal pipe he was holding. He hadn't taken his gaze off of the front door of The Fun Guy Ranch since they had arrived an hour earlier.

"You said that they let some children leave with the customers?"

"Yeah."

"Well, when we see one leaving, we'll wait until he's right in front of us, and then we'll run out quietly and beat him. Hopefully, Kyle and Chloe will be paying attention and they'll come at the same time."

"What about the other one?" Jack's friend, Yabu, asked.

"Who? Oh, you mean, Kurt?" Tavi laughed. "He's a great guy, but he's not really good at focusing on things."

They waited another twenty minutes before a likely prospect exited the bar. When they saw the boy who was holding hands with the man, Jack and Yabu cursed. "That kid can't be older than eight years old," Jack hissed.

"Let's get him!" Yabu said, already standing up with his pipe gripped in his hand.

"Wait!" Tavi cautioned, but it was too late. The man had glimpsed the movement and his eyes widened in surprised when he saw Yabu exiting from the shadows.

Tavi knew that they had screwed up. The man was already turning around and heading back towards the bar. He tried to pull the boy after him, but the boy dragged his feet and pointed away from the bar. The man tried to point at Yabu, who was quickly approaching with Jack and Tavi right behind him, but it was too late.

Without warning, the man collapsed to the ground, screaming in pain. The boy looked to his right, and Tavi saw Chloe swinging her pipe again and smashing it down on the man's arm. Kyle knelt down and said something to the boy who nodded quickly in response. They disappeared into the alleyway where Kurt, Kyle, and Chloe had been hiding.

"Pervert!" Chloe was saying in disgust as Tavi and Jack finally reached them. Yabu had hit the man on his back, and he was curled up into a ball, his screams having changed to high-pitched moans.

Chloe raised her pipe to hit the man on the head, but Tavi jumped over him and grabbed her arm. "No! That might kill him!"

Chloe looked beseechingly at Tavi. "Did you see how old that boy was?"

"No. I'm serious. If we kill him, then everyone will be after us." He looked at Yabu and Jack. "Let's go."

"What about his wallet?" Jack asked.

Tavi released Chloe's arm and they headed towards the darkness in front of them. "Take it."

Jack reached down and searched the man's pockets, and then he and Yabu quickly followed the others.

"That was fun!" Jack exclaimed as they approached the bridge half an hour later. "Can we do it again?"

"Sure." Tavi looked around for Kurt and Kyle since they had taken a different route back. He sighed in relief when he saw them with the boy in their encampment.

"Cool. I might take some of my guys and try it tomorrow."

Tavi gave him a look of caution. "Be careful. They'll catch us if we do it every night."

Jack thought about it for a second. "Yeah. You're right. We'll just jump some boujies then."

Tavi stopped to talk to Byron whom he hadn't seen all day, and then he made his way to where Kurt and Kyle were sitting on some old cinder blocks.

"Hey. How is he?"

Kyle looked at Tavi with concern. "Andy? He's okay, but…"

"But what?"

"He wants us to take him home."

Tavi was dumbfounded. "He wants to go back to the bar?"

"No. He wants to go home to his family."

Chapter 22

Tavi and Byron spent the entire day at the library. Andy remembered the name of his village, and when Adam had mentioned that he'd once spent a whole week looking at a book of maps in the library, Tavi decided to see if he could help.

"This is really cool," Tavi said, flipping through the atlas. The librarian had been happy to show them where the atlases were kept, and he and Byron had brought a few of them back to their table.

"Yep," Byron agreed. He pointed to the map he was looking at. "Look! There's our bridge. This book has a map for every neighborhood in the city."

"Cool." They continued studying their respective atlases for a few minutes until Tavi said, "Okay. I think I've found it. He said his village's name was Parksville?"

Byron nodded his head and looked up from the map he was studying.

"Well, then it's down here. And we..." He traced a line on the map. "...Are way up here. How is he supposed to get home from here?"

Byron shrugged and looked at his own atlas again. "I guess you could take him."

"Me? Why me?"

"Because you're the one who found his village. And you helped rescue him. I think it makes perfect sense." Byron gave Tavi a grin. "Or we can just tell him that we can't help him and good luck."

Tavi sighed. "Fine. But I don't even know how to do this."

Byron stood up and walked around the table. When he sat down next to Tavi, he pulled the atlas over and scrutinized it. "Okay. It's like a puzzle," he finally said as he reached for a nearby pencil and notecard. "The closest town to Parksville is Sudong. And then we look for the biggest place near Sudong, and it's Leawood. We keep going up, and the other important places are here, here, and here." He lightly circled three places on the map and then erased them after he had written them on the notecard.

"Okay. And now what?" Tavi asked.

"Now we go to the bus station."

Tavi remembered how in awe he had been the first time he had seen the Central Bus Terminal. Now it was just another dirty, crowded place in a city filled with dirty, crowded places. They patiently waited in the line for buying bus tickets. Tavi's stomach tingled with nervousness, but Byron just gave a winsome smile when they finally reached the window.

"Hi," Byron said. "My uncle is getting married next week and my parents told me that I have to go represent our family. Is there a bus that goes to Parksville?"

The woman studied a chart in front of her for a few seconds. "Um. No. I'm sorry."

Byron studied his notecard. "What about Sudong?"

"Yes," she said immediately. "It's ten talents for one way, or fifteen talents round-trip. When do you want to leave?"

"Wait. After I get there, will I be able to find a bus that goes to Parksville?"

"Is it near Sudong?"

"Yeah. Sudong is the closest town on the map. It looked like it was about fifty kilometers from there."

"Then I'm sure you should be able to. Sudong has its own bus station."

"Um…Could you call them and ask?" Byron pleaded. "It's really important and I'm going to be traveling by myself. I'm scared I'm going to get lost."

The man who was waiting in line behind them grumbled to his friend, but the woman gave Byron a reassuring smile and said, "Sure, honey. Just a second." She looked on the wall to her right, found a number, and then picked up the telephone and dialed. "Hi. This is Brenda at the Central Bus Terminal. I have a young boy who will be traveling alone. Do you have buses that go to Parksville?" A pause. "That's great. Does it leave from the same terminal that a bus from here would arrive at?" Another pause. "Okay. That's wonderful. Thank you for your help." She hung up the phone and smiled at Byron. "Yep. There's a bus that runs once a day to Parksville for two talents. Once you get off this bus, just go to the ticket window, and they'll be happy to help you."

"Awesome! Thank you so much for your help!" Byron looked at Tavi who was nodding happily.

"Do you want buy a ticket now, sweetie?" the woman asked.

"I have to tell my parents first," Byron replied. "We'll be back in a couple of days."

"Okay. Good luck!"

As they walked out of the bus station, Byron asked, "Do you want to do it? It's going to cost over thirty talents."

"For taking a little boy home to his family? I think it's a good deal," Tavi replied with a smile.

"Okay. Let's go talk to the others and see what they say." They passed a bus that was just departing for Penang, and Tavi realized that he had passed through that town when he was traveling with Vikram and Yuri.

I wonder if I could ever go back home, he thought as he stopped and watched the bus pull away.

"Are you okay?" Byron asked.

Tavi thrust the thoughts out of his head and gave Byron a small smile. "Yeah. I'm good. Let's go see if Andy still wants to go home."

Chapter 23

Tavi nervously boarded the bus. He hadn't been on one since he had arrived in the city and he felt apprehensive about being on one again. Andy was following close behind Tavi, his hand gripping the back of Tavi's shirt. Seeing an open seat near the rear of the bus, Tavi pointed to it and said, "Let's sit there."

Andy peeked out from behind Tavi and then ran past him to the seat. He clambered in and pressed his face against the window.

Tavi sat down next to him and put the bag filled with food and water under their seat. He leaned next to Andy and peered out of the window. "Look at all of those cars and people. It's so crazy out there."

"Do you think he followed us?" Andy asked softly, his forehead still pressed against the glass.

"Who?"

"Ronnie. He said he would kill us if we ran away."

Tavi felt his heart breaking to hear this eight year old boy talk about being killed. "No. I promise you that he has no idea where we are."

"Okay." Andy pulled his face away from the window and looked around the bus. "Are all of these people going to Parksville?"

Tavi shrugged. His experience with buses was probably the same as Andy's. "I don't think so. We have to stay on here for fifteen hours, and I think it stops at a lot of different places."

Andy pointed at the driver. "Is he going to drive us the whole way?"

"I think so." Tavi's stomach clenched in fear as a policeman boarded the bus. He bent over and spoke quickly to the driver, who nodded his head and motioned to the passengers. The policeman slowly made his way down the aisle, and Tavi couldn't look away as the man's eyes locked onto him. He glanced at a photo that he was carrying in his hand and then looked back at Tavi.

"Look at his gun!" Andy said. "I wonder if he ever shoots it."

The policeman stopped in front of their seat. "Excuse me, sir, but I need you to leave the bus with me."

Tavi swallowed and opened up his mouth to respond when a raspy voice from behind him said, "Me? Why?"

"A man matching your description robbed the currency exchange stand about forty minutes ago. I need you to come with me now." The policeman dropped his hand to his gun.

Tavi was frozen in fear, but Andy stood up on the seat next to him and said to the man behind them, "You're in trouble."

"Shut up, kid," the man replied. Tavi felt a hand touch the top of the seat near his head, and then the man was standing in the aisle. The policeman didn't even glance at Tavi as he escorted the man off of the bus.

"Holy shit. That was close," Tavi whispered.

"Where do you think they're going?" Andy asked, dropping back down to his seat.

Tavi felt the bus start and then the bus driver swung the door shut. "Probably to jail, Andy. That's what happens to people when they get caught doing bad things."

Andy remained silent for the next twenty minutes as the bus slowly made its way out of the city. Eventually, he said, "Ronnie didn't get caught."

"Not yet." Tavi smiled at Andy and put his arm around the boy's shoulders. "Not yet," he repeated. "But someday he might."

The bus ride seemed to last forever. Andy talked non-stop for the first six hours about anything that came to his mind. After their third rest stop, Andy curled up against Tavi and was soon fast asleep. Tavi, meanwhile, couldn't stop thinking about all of the boys like Andy who were still working at the bars, and he wondered how Andy's parents would respond to seeing their son again.

They arrived in Sudong at eleven o'clock at night. As they stumbled off of the bus, Tavi looked around and saw a deserted bus station, which was dark except for one small window through which a light was shining.

They were the only ones to disembark, and as soon as they exited the bus, the driver closed the doors behind them and drove off. Tavi turned around to ask him to wait, but he was too late. As they watched the bus pull away, Andy slipped his hand into Tavi's and said, "Where are we?"

"Sudong bus station." He saw movement through the lit window and said, "Let's go see if our bus is coming soon." He kept a firm grip on Andy's hand to keep him from wandering off and dragged him over to the ticket window. He knocked on it and waited for a response. When the shade was lifted, a bespectacled older man peered through the window. "Um…is the bus for Parksville coming soon?"

The man looked down in surprise. "Nope. Not until two tomorrow afternoon." He looked around and asked, "Where are your parents?"

"We're going home to meet them now," Tavi answered, thinking quickly. "We've been visiting our grandparents in…" His mind went blank as he tried to remember another name that Byron had written down. "In…um…Leawood."

"Ah, right," the man said, nodding his head in understanding. "That bus has the worst timetable." He studied Tavi and Andy for a second. "Do you boys need a place to sleep?"

Pervert! Tavi's mind shouted.

"Um...." Tavi looked down at Andy and watched him yawn with exhaustion. "Yeah," he finally said. "We do."

The man pointed. "I'll go unlock that door and you boys can come sleep in here."

Tavi was filled with apprehension but he didn't know what else they could do. He nodded his head and pulled Andy through the doorway after the man had unlocked it.

He led them through the office and to a small room in the rear of the building. When the light flicked on, Tavi stared in surprise at the bed that filled half of the room.

"Sometimes we have to work all-night shifts," the man explained. He smiled as Andy staggered sleepily into the room and crawled onto the bed. "But your bus was the final one for tonight, and so I'm going home ."

"What?" Tavi asked.

"I'm going to lock the office, but you boys can still use the bathroom." He pointed across the hall. "It's just right there. I'll leave a note for Marjorie. She'll be here at five in the morning, but I'll tell her to let you boys sleep."

"You're just going to leave us here?" Tavi asked in astonishment.

The man paused. "Is that okay? All the doors will be locked and so you should be safe."

"I mean, yeah. That's great. I just didn't understand."

The man gave Tavi a queer look. "Well, okay. Is there anything else you'll need before tomorrow morning?"

Tavi shook his head and set his bag on the floor just inside the room. "No, thank you." He looked up at the man and wished he could express how grateful he was, and how much this meant to him, and how sorry he was for thinking he was a pervert. "Thank you so much," he finally said.

The man smiled. "It's no problem. I have a couple of my own boys about your age. I hope that anyone would help out boys traveling on their own." He gazed at Andy for a few seconds, a kind smile upon his face. "Well, if that's all, then sweet dreams, and Marjorie will see you in the morning." The man turned and walked away.

"Thank you again," Tavi called out. He closed the door to the room and turned the lock in the doorknob. Feeling at peace with the world, Tavi took off his shoes, turned off the light, and gently nudged Andy over as he lay down beside him. Within seconds, Tavi was fast asleep. He felt safer than he could remember feeling in a long time.

Tavi stretched and yawned as he woke up, relishing the softness of the bed. As the memories from the previous night came back to him, he looked beside him but Andy was gone. The door was open a crack and the light coming through was just enough to see by.

"Andy?" Tavi called out in a low voice. When he didn't hear anything, he quickly got out of bed and put on his shoes, and then he crept out of the room. He stopped to listen. Suddenly, Andy's laughter filled the air and Tavi hurried in the direction of the office. When he got there, he found Andy happily eating a plate full of eggs and bacon and toast, and an older middle-aged woman singing a song to him. They didn't notice Tavi at first, and he smiled as the woman changed the lyrics to something about Andy, and Andy once again burst into laughter.

"Tavi!" Andy cried out happily. "Aunt Marjorie is funny!"

The woman looked at Tavi with a smile and Tavi felt a mixture of emotions as he realized that here was another good person. He was happy that people like her existed, but he was also angry that he had no one like that in his life. He returned her smile and said, "Hi. I'm Tavi."

"And I'm Marjorie." She stuck her hand out for Tavi to shake. "Please sit down. I'll make you what I made for Andy. He's on his second plate."

Andy grinned at Tavi with his mouth full and nodded his head happily. Tavi laughed out loud and replied, "Thank you. That'd be awesome."

The next few hours passed by quickly for Tavi. Marjorie was fun to be around, and she gave them a deck of cards and taught them new games, and when their bus for Parksville finally arrived, she gave them a bag full of snacks for the bus ride.

As the bus that would take them to Andy's village pulled away from the station, Andy said with contentment, "She was nice." Tavi just smiled and put his arm around Andy.

The ride took two hours, and Andy couldn't sit still the entire time. As the bus slowed down to a stop, Andy shouted, "I'm home!" and sprinted down the aisle. He impatiently waited for the bus to come to a complete stop, and he burst out of the bus as soon as the door opened. Tavi tried to catch up to him, but by the time he managed to step out of the bus, Andy was nearly fifty meters away and still running.

Tavi followed at a slower pace. He had noted where Andy had turned off of the main street, and as he approached the spot, a man and woman appeared. Andy was riding on the man's shoulders and beamed at Tavi. "Look, Tavi! It's my parents."

Tavi smiled back and studied his parents. They were looking at him curiously and Tavi couldn't tell if they were happy or not. The woman seemed to come to a decision and said, "Thank you for bringing our son home, Tavi. Would you like to come back to our house?"

Tavi followed them home and found a house that was nicer than the one his own family lived in. It was made from brick and had windows and electricity. A young boy ran out, followed by a puppy which was jumping around his feet, and Andy yelled, "John!"

The woman noticed Tavi's look of surprise. "What is it?"

"That's my younger brother's name too." They watched as Andy's father set him down on the ground, and then Andy and John began playing with the puppy.

His parents turned their attention to Tavi. They seemed younger than his own parents, and Tavi felt nervous about what he was about to tell them.

"So…what's wrong?" his mother asked.

Tavi thought about how to answer the question. Andy was still playing on the ground and Tavi wasn't sure if he was paying attention to them. "Andy wanted to come home and so I wanted to make sure he got home safely."

"And who are you?" the father asked. "Are you from his school?"

Tavi smiled bitterly. "No. I'm one of the people who rescued him from his school."

It took a while for Andy's parents to grasp what had been done to their son during the previous three months. At first, they refused to believe that Andy hadn't been at a school for gifted children, but Tavi had quickly convinced them by letting Andy talk about his life. At first, he had been embarrassed, and then he had been alarmed as both of his parents began crying, but by the time he got to the part about Tavi and his friends rescuing him and the day they had spent with Marjorie, his parents were listening quietly, their eyes flicking back and forth between Tavi and their son.

"Thank you, Tavi," his mother said, grabbing ahold of his hands. "We didn't have any idea…"

The father nodded in agreement. "But why did you save Andy? I mean, we are very grateful, but you didn't even know him."

"It was just chance," Tavi admitted. "And then he said he wanted to come home and so we decided to help."

Andy's parents were speechless. They were overjoyed to have their son home and safe, but Tavi could tell from the way they looked at Andy and at each other that they had no idea what to do about what Andy had experienced.

They invited him to stay that night; the next bus wouldn't arrive until the following morning. After a huge dinner, Andy's mother invited Tavi to go for a walk. "Listen…we want to pay you a reward for rescuing Andy."

"No. You don't have to do that," Tavi said immediately.

"They gave us five hundred talents when they took Andy." She shuddered and said, "We don't want any of that money. We still have about one hundred talents left. Please take it."

Tavi hesitated.

"If not for yourself, then maybe you can use it to save other children like Andy."

For a brief second, Tavi thought he was going to cry. He felt the tears welling up, but he didn't know why. "Okay," he finally said. "I'll take it. Thank you."

"No, Tavi. Thank you!" She grabbed him tight and gave him a hug. He instinctively flinched before allowing himself to relax and return it.

The next morning when he awoke, Andy was curled up beside him on the floor. He had moved from his bed in the middle of the night to sleep next to Tavi. When Andy's mother saw her son snuggled under Tavi's protective arm, she silently wiped away her tears and said a quick prayer of thanks.

Because of the disorganized bus schedule, it took Tavi almost two days to get home. When he finally walked under the bridge, Byron and the others who had helped rescue Andy ran over. "Did he get home safely?" Byron asked.

Tavi thought about his trip and nodded. "Yep." He looked around at his friends and the space behind them, and he thought about how many more children could fit in here. "We need to save as many kids as we can," he said seriously. The others nodded in silent agreement and walked back to their encampment where they began discussing their next step.

Chapter 24

"Yeah?"

"Hi. This is Dr. Niederman. We got the lab results back from the boy you brought in."

The man waited a brief moment before prompting, "And?"

"Um…" The doctor stammered in his uncertainty. "Are you the boy's legal guardian?"

"Listen, Doc." The man leaned back in his chair and raised his voice. "The boy is mine. I am responsible for him. Now tell me what's wrong!"

"He has HIV."

The man closed his eyes and cursed silently.

"It's why he's been sick lately," the doctor explained. "However, since you're his guardian, your insurance could help cover the treatment and medicine. There's a chance that…"

"No," the man interrupted. "We can't do that."

It was the doctor's turn to curse quietly, but his was directed towards the man he was speaking with. After a few seconds, he asked, "So you're just going to let him…" He trailed off into silence, took a deep breath, and tried again. "Are you at least going to tell him?"

"I don't think that's your concern."

"He is a seventeen year old boy who could still live a long and productive life!" the doctor retorted. "And what happens if he passes it onto your….customers?" He sneered and made the last word sound as contemptible as possible.

"As I said, it's not your concern," the man repeated. "But in order to ease your mind a bit, he doesn't do that anymore."

"This is the seventh boy that..." the doctor began.

"Again, thank you for letting me know," the man interrupted. "I'll make sure you get paid your usual fee." He hung up the phone and stared blankly at the ceiling, wishing that some things in life could be different.

After a few minutes, he sighed and reached for the phone. He closed his eyes when he heard a voice on the other end. "Yeah, Juan. It's me," the man said. "Can you do me a favor and let Yuri know that his test results came in? Apparently, he just has a flu that's been going around and the doctor says he should drink lots of juice and take some aspirin." Without waiting for a response, Vikram hung up the phone and resumed staring at a spot on the ceiling.

Chapter 25

Tavi and several of his friends strode into Jack's encampment early one morning. Jack was barely awake and was eating a donut that was left over from the previous day. He groaned when he saw the determined look upon Tavi's face.

"What do you want? Do you know what time it is?" Jack tottered over and collapsed into a nearby chair. He crammed the donut into his mouth and wrapped himself in a blanket.

"It's almost eight o'clock." Tavi motioned to the boy behind him. "And Ben had a great idea."

Jack looked at the people standing with Tavi. Besides his usual friends, there were four or five other ones whom Jack thought of as the outsiders of Tavi's group. "What is it?"

The blonde haired boy behind Tavi opened his mouth to respond, but Tavi spoke first. "I think Momo should be included in this as well."

"Oh my god! Then what are you even doing here? I'm not going into Momo's camp to wake him up. Stop bothering me!"

Tavi looked disconcerted. "I just thought you would want to know."

"Listen…go wake up Momo, bring him back here, and I'll be happy to talk. But you don't just come here with all of your friends and say, 'We have an idea that we can't tell you yet.'"

"Okay. I understand." Tavi shared a bemused look with a couple of his friends, and then they spread out and sat down around Jack's camp.

Jack stared at Tavi unhappily. "Are you serious?"

"We'll just wait for Momo to come to us."

Jack laughed. "Right. Momo's going to wake up early and…" He glanced to his right when he saw something move out of the corner of his eye. Slowly making their way to Jack's camp were Pablo, Adam, Anouram, and a couple of Ben's friends, and they were being followed by a complaining Momo who looked as if he had just been woken up. Jack shook his head and said half-jokingly to Tavi, "What's wrong with you guys?"

A few minutes later, everyone was seated in little groups around the camp. Two of Momo's friends had stumbled in a couple of minutes after he had arrived, and they were standing behind Momo, who was munching on a donut that Jack had given him. They shared a look of resignation when Tavi began speaking.

"Sorry for waking everyone up, but Ben has a great idea and we wanted to share it with you."

"It better be good," Momo warned. A few other children murmured in agreement.

Ben looked around nervously and said, "I don't know if it's good. We had that kid, Andy, a few days ago, and everyone felt happy that we had saved him." Jack nodded his head in agreement. Ben continued, "But we can't do that every day because they're going to realize what we're doing sooner or later."

"We already know this," Yabu complained.

"But there are still lots of kids out there who we can help. We were living on the roofs before Tavi asked us to join them because we were so scared of getting caught."

Malik added, "And Hector, Sasha, and I were digging in trashcans for food and sleeping in train stations and bathrooms every night. It was terrible. We didn't ever know what we would eat, or where we would sleep, or who would be chasing us."

Jack looked around at Tavi's friends who still outnumbered his and Momo's gangs in this meeting. "So that's how you got such a big group? I was wondering about that."

"Great story," Momo said, yawning noisily. "But why are we here?"

"I think we should send out groups of kids to go find others and bring them back here."

"What?" Momo asked.

Jack looked at Momo and nodded his head. "Yeah. Why?"

"We need more kids," Tavi said simply.

"Again…why?"

Tavi sighed. "We've talked about this. If we have more kids, then people can't mess with us, and we can just live our lives how we want…as long as we don't have to run away any more."

Momo smirked. "Unless it's the cops. And then I'm running faster that you've ever seen."

"No. That's where you're wrong. If two cops show up here…"

"We run," Momo said firmly.

"We fight back."

Jack sighed in exasperation. "Tavi, if we touch a cop, then we either go to jail or they will shoot us. "

Tavi looked at Adam for help, but he just smiled and shrugged his shoulders. "I wish you guys had seen that movie," Tavi said quietly. "Anyway, forget the cops. I want to send out groups of five kids to go find others and bring them back. We have lots of space and I think it would be better protection for us."

Momo rolled his eyes and stood up. "I'm not going to do that, but if you want to, I won't stop you." He looked at his two friends and said, "I'm going back to sleep. Let's go."

One of them followed him out of camp immediately, but the other boy hesitated for a second before choosing to sit down in the chair that Momo had just vacated. Momo turned around and said sharply, "Derek. Let's go!"

Derek, who was even bigger than Momo, shook his head and said, "Nah. I want to hear what they have to say. I'll come back in a while." Momo shot him a disappointed look, turned and whispered something to his friend, and then resumed walking back to his camp.

Jack eyed him curiously and then smiled. "Well, if this guy's doing it, then I'll do it as well. But I get to be in Derek's group." Derek grinned back and they waited for Tavi to continue.

"Okay. So, it's not something you have to do all day long. But if you can just go out occasionally in groups of five or six kids, and then find other kids who are alone. If there's just one or two of them, then only one or two of you approach them. If it becomes dangerous, then call for the others. You should outnumber almost everyone you meet."

"And what do we tell them when we find them?" a boy from Jack's camp asked.

"Tell them the truth. We live under the bridge, and we think it's safer to have large numbers. If they'll agree to protect us and help us, then we'll do the same." Children around the group began nodding their heads in understanding. "And then they can join our camp or your camp or sleep in the middle. I guess that doesn't really matter yet."

"And what about the kids in the bars?" Yabu asked.

Tavi opened his mouth to respond, but was suddenly struck with a memory of the two women who had tried to save him and his friends. He closed his eyes for a second and smiled as he thought of a plan. "My dream," he said as he opened his eyes, "is to go into a bar at night with at least thirty other kids." Everyone was listening to him quietly and there was an expectant hush in the air. Tavi reached down and picked up the pipe Jack had used the night they freed

Andy. "And each one of those kids is going to have one of these pipes."

"Yeah," a couple of boys murmured.

"And we're going to march into that bar, and we're going to beat the shit out of any adult who is there."

"Yeah!"

"And then we'll free every kid who is working there and we'll bring them back here and make an army!"

"Yeah!!!!"

"And then we'll do it again!"

The children erupted into cheers as Tavi looked around with fire in his eyes. Jack watched him with a huge grin on his face as Tavi's friends pounded him on the back. Jack leaned towards Yabu and said, "Even though I'm sure we're all going to get arrested, a part of me still wants to follow this crazy mofo."

Yabu nodded his head in agreement and they both raised their arms and cheered and laughed excitedly with the other children.

Chapter 26

Yuri met Vikram in his office and they leisurely made their way together towards Bangarang. It was clear that Vikram wasn't looking forward to his meeting with Giovanni, and he was walking the short distance as slowly as he possibly could.

"How are you feeling?" he asked.

Yuri looked up in surprise. "A little better. I have this cold that won't go away, but I'm fine." For an instant, Vikram's expression changed slightly, but it was gone before Yuri had a chance to understand it.

"Good. Just keep taking vitamins and I'm sure it will go away soon." He patted Yuri on the shoulder who flinched at the unexpected contact. Vikram quickly dropped his hand back down and they walked through the entrance of Bangarang.

Vikram continued to walk as slow as possible until even Yuri was getting annoyed with him. He began walking faster, forcing Vikram to catch up, and he led Vikram up the stairs to Giovanni's office.

As soon as he opened the door, Giovanni shouted, "It's about time you got here!" Seeing Yuri walk through the door, he said, "What are you doing here? Where's Vikram?"

Yuri stepped to the side so that Giovanni could see Vikram ascending the stairs. When he finally entered the office, Yuri shut the door behind him and followed Vikram to Giovanni's desk. They sat down in the two chairs that had been placed there.

Giovanni looked angrily at Vikram and then shot a concerned glance at Yuri. "How are you feeling, boy? Doing better?"

Yuri was too startled to answer for a second. "Yes, sir," he finally managed to stammer out. He didn't see Vikram shaking his head imperceptibly at Giovanni.

"Anyway," Giovanni said loudly. "I want to know what the fuck is going on."

Vikram cleared his throat nervously and said, "Well, our profits are about the same as a year ago, and…"

"Bullshit," Giovanni said. "Or they might be the same for the whole year, but I'll bet they've been down the last month or so."

Vikram glanced nervously at Yuri and muttered, "Well, it's not my fault."

"Not your fault?" Giovanni chuckled and repeated, "Not your fault?!? Since you took over for Javier, you have lost six boys, and four of them were in the last six weeks." He slammed his fist on the desk as Vikram opened up his mouth to protest. "Six boys! And I have had three boys run away in that time. Before you took over, neither one of our bars had lost any boys for almost two years. So how is it NOT YOUR FAULT?!?" he screamed, flecks of spittle landing on his desk.

"They aren't running away," Vikram denied. "They're being kidnapped."

"Right. Gangs of little kids are kidnapping them."

"Well, that's what the customers keep saying. And the police say that there are more children being mugged on their way to school."

Giovanni stared at Vikram and shook his head in disgust. He turned his attention to Yuri and asked, "What do you think the problem is?"

Yuri glanced at Vikram and said, "I think some of the street kids are organizing and trying to save their friends."

"And what can we do to stop them?"

"Stop letting the customers take the boys out of the bars. If they don't leave with them, then they'll probably stop getting attacked and beaten."

Giovanni took a sip of water from the bottle on his desk. He said in a low voice, "I want those boys back. And I want the ones who are doing it to be punished as well." He paused and waited for a response, but when no one said anything, he asked Yuri, "Do you know where they hang out?"

Yuri hesitated for a moment and Giovanni could tell that he was considering how to respond. Just as Giovanni was getting ready to shout again, Yuri said quietly, "I've heard that there's a group of kids who hang out under the Hangang Bridge."

"And this is where I'll find my missing boys?"

Yuri shrugged noncommittally.

Vikram looked at Yuri and said, "Could you go down there with Juan and bring them back?"

Yuri gave a small smile. "No. I think there are a lot of kids there. I wouldn't be able to go in there with even ten people."

"What is this city coming to?" Giovanni asked. "I don't understand why our customers should be scared of getting attacked, or why some of our people can't go take back what belongs to us." He sounded depressed about how unfair the world was becoming. Giovanni picked up a pen and began doodling on a notepad in front of him. After a few seconds of silence, he slammed it down and said, "I'm just going to ask some of our people on the force to go down and bring them back."

Vikram nodded his head. "Yeah. I think that's probably the best idea."

"I mean, they won't attack cops, will they?" Giovanni asked.

Vikram shook his head and said confidently, "No way. If we send three or four policemen down there, the kids will just run away and they can grab whoever they want.

Giovanni nodded in agreement. He glanced at Yuri who was staring thoughtfully at the pad of paper that Giovanni had been doodling on. He almost asked him for his opinion, but then reminded himself that Yuri was just a careless kid who had gotten HIV. Dismissing him from his mind, Giovanni picked up the phone and called one of his contacts on the police force.

Chapter 27

When Tavi returned from spending the afternoon at the library with Adam, he walked into a movie that Kurt was busy filming.

"Hey!" Kurt shouted as Tavi walked past two boys who were pretending that their metal pipes were swords. He pushed a button on the small video camera he was holding. "Cut. We have to start over. Tavi just ruined the scene."

Tavi laughed and looked at Adam in confusion. "Where'd you get that?" he asked Kurt, pointing at the camcorder.

Kurt held it up proudly. He admired it as he said, "It was in the bag that we took today from a boujie." He nodded at one of the boys who had been in the swordfight. "Bert got one too. We jumped two guys walking together today and they both had these camcorders."

Tavi smiled. "Nice. Maybe you'll become a famous director. And sorry for ruining your scene." He headed off towards his stuff.

"It's okay," Kurt replied. "They weren't being very convincing anyways."

"Hey!" Tavi heard one of the boys object, and then he tuned them out as they started bickering behind him. As he and Adam sat down in a couple of chairs in their encampment, he asked to the people sitting there, "Have you guys seen Byron? I wanted to talk to him about a book I read today."

Kyle shook his head. "He disappeared early this morning with a couple of new kids who came in last week, and maybe someone from Jack's camp."

Tavi nodded his head and looked around. He could scarcely believe how much things had changed in the previous two months. At first, the groups had remained separate and done everything with their own friends. But eventually, all three groups had started mixing and now instead of having three separate camps, there was a sprawl of mini-encampments throughout the whole area.

They had managed to save about fifteen children from the bars, and out of those, seven children had asked if they could go home. Tavi had taken two of them himself, while Chloe, Kyle, Derek, and Jack had taken the others. However, most of the bars had resorted to having men stationed at the entrances to their bars, and it was getting more and more difficult to rescue the children. A few nights earlier, Malik had gone with four other children, but as soon as they had left the safety of the shadows, ten men had come from every direction, intent on either hurting or capturing the children. They had been lucky that no one was caught that night.

Tavi studied the boy who was talking to Kyle. Ruffio. Kyle's group had found him two days ago and invited him to come back with them. The unofficial rule was that all new children had to join one of the three main encampments for at least two weeks, and then they could spread out and find their own place under the bridge. It was necessary to make sure that all of the children understood what they were hoping to do, and it was best if they would participate and help make things better for everyone else.

He looked around again and tried to count how many children there were now. At least sixty, he thought proudly. And with all of those children jumping boujies, they were collecting items faster than they could sell them. Feeling satisfied with how things were going, Tavi reached into his bag and pulled out a wrapped sausage that he had bought earlier.

"I wish we could get food around here," he complained to Kyle as he chewed his cold sausage. Kyle nodded his head in agreement. Suddenly, he wrinkled his forehead and appeared to think of something. "What is it?" Tavi asked.

Kyle smiled. "Nothing. Well, something. I just have to talk to Kurt about it."

Later that night, Tavi was sound asleep, wrapped up warmly in his blanket, when a nearby shout made him sit up in alarm, instantly alert. He looked around and saw Ruffio pointing towards the edge of the bridge.

"Hey!" he screamed again, jumping to his feet.

Tavi leapt up as well. "What? What is it?!?" All around him, children were struggling to their feet as they looked around in fear.

"I just saw three or four men grab some children who were sleeping over there." He continued pointing and Tavi glanced over and saw nothing there. "They just stood there and then..and then they just grabbed them."

Tavi quickly counted the number of friends who were standing and decided it wasn't enough. "Jack!" he yelled. "We have problems. Some kids just got taken!"

He only had to wait an instant before he heard, "Okay. We're coming!"

Tavi picked up the pipe that was lying next to his blankets. Most of his friends were already holding theirs - except for Kurt, who was busy videotaping everything with his new camera. Tavi threw an annoyed glance at him, but otherwise ignored him and ran through the camp. He heard Kyle behind him yelling at Kurt as Tavi ran out from under the bridge.

"Where'd they go?" he asked Ruffio. Without glancing around, he could tell that most of the kids who had been near them when the alarm was sounded were pressing close against them.

Ruffio looked around wildly for a second and then pointed up the embankment. "That way."

Tavi sprinted up the short hill, pausing for a moment to make sure everyone was following him. He did a double take when he saw the boy who was right behind him. "Hey, Momo," he said, as Momo stopped beside him, his eyes searching the area in front of them.

"There." Momo pointed at several figures who were making their way slowly about twenty meters away. "Let's get them." He took off after them and Tavi followed right behind, intent on catching them before they reached their cars.

Within seconds, Momo and Tavi were only a few feet away from the men. They had stopped and were facing the children, waiting for them to arrive. Three of the men were holding onto children that had just arrived within the last week, while the fourth man took a step towards Tavi and Momo. He was a policeman. "Hey, boys," he said, holding his hands out. "Go back. You don't want to get in trouble."

"Let them go," Momo ordered. Without looking back, Tavi heard the sound of pounding feet as the other children caught up to them.

The policeman raised his voice. "Listen, son. Don't give me any orders or you'll also be taking a ride with these boys." He looked overwhelmed by the number of children who were still appearing and glanced nervously at the other policemen. They had their hands full, though, as the three boys they were holding had started to struggle violently to get free.

Tavi smiled when he saw Derek lead a large group of children around to the other side of the men, effectively cutting them off from their cars. The one who had been speaking rested his hand on his gun, and it seemed to reassure him. "This is your last warning. You will disperse and return to your homes…NOW!"

The hum and buzz of unhappy voices filled the air. From somewhere close to Tavi, he heard Kyle whisper, "Hurry up, Kurt." Tavi took a quick count and guessed that there had to be more than forty children there, and most of them were holding metal pipes in their hands.

"Let them go," Tavi said loudly.

"These boys are criminals and so are you," the policeman shouted. He flicked the clasp that held his gun secure in his belt.

Tavi felt the anger around him rising. "We know you're taking them back to the bars. Just admit it!"

"Yeah!" "Admit it!" "Pigs!" The voices rang out in derision.

"Fine. We admit it," the policeman responded. "Now move." He half-drew his gun out of his belt. If he had thought it would scare them, he was completely wrong. The children pressed forward with their pipes held high.

Just then, one of the boys who were being held got loose and ran into the crowd. Seeing this, several boys jumped forward and pulled on the arms of the policemen who were still holding the other boys. Within seconds, they, too, were free.

The lead policeman pulled out his gun and aimed it at the crowd. "Step back!" he warned. Two of his fellow officers had also drawn their guns. "Those boys...or any three of you...are coming with us now. We will shoot you if you don't comply."

There was dead silence for an instant, until everyone heard Kurt mumble to himself, "How do I get more light on this....?" Suddenly, night turned into day as the powerful night light on the camcorder was turned on. Kurt resumed filming the police and said with a smile, "There. That's much better. Now we can see your faces and..." He paused as he played with the zoom button. "...your names, Officer Parker. And Officer Terriss." The other two police officers quickly covered up their badges with their hands.

Momo laughed loudly and a bunch of other children giggled. "You're going to shoot us on video?" he asked.

The policemen looked stunned. They slowly holstered their guns and looked around at the children who were still pressing close. Sensing that something bad could still happen, Tavi raised his voice and said, "Don't touch them." Several children looked at him defiantly. "Don't touch them," he repeated. "If we do, then all of the cops will be after us." Other children behind them started to whisper to them, and they slowly lowered their arms and stepped back.

"They will be anyways," the policeman threatened. "You have interfered with official police business."

Tavi felt a rush of anger. "You're trying to take us back to the bars so that we can be raped or killed." Momo put his hand on Tavi's shoulder to calm him down. Tavi tried to shake him off, but Momo squeezed even harder until Tavi's anger turned to pain. "Ow," he complained.

"Enough," Momo said in a low voice. He looked directly at the policemen and said, "All of this is on tape. Stay away from us."

"This isn't over," one of the policeman shouted as Momo and Tavi turned away. The children began walking back towards the bridge.

"Yes, it is," Tavi heard someone shout.

He was wrong. It was only just beginning.

Chapter 28

When they arrived back at camp, most of the children were too amped up on adrenaline to fall back asleep, and they sat in small groups talking quietly to one another. Kurt was the main attraction as pairs and groups of children kept coming over to watch the video he had shot. After the sixth viewing, Kyle asked, "What will you do when the battery runs out?"

"Uh...plug it in," Kurt answered as he gave Kyle a look of disdain.

"Uh...where?" Kyle asked, mimicking Kurt.

Kurt looked around and gave a weak smile. "I dunno. Somewhere."

"You can plug it in at the library," Tavi said. He was sitting in a chair on the far side of the barrel. "And we can probably get extra batteries in case one runs out."

Kurt nodded his head. "See. No problem," he said to Kyle.

"Do you know how to save the video?" Tavi asked. "It'd really suck if you erased it or recorded over it."

"Yeah, I think so."

One of the boys they had rescued that night, Zeke, hesitantly joined in the conversation. "I know how to save the video to a computer and then put it on a memory stick." He blushed in the flickering light of the fire when everyone turned to stare at him.

"Where'd you learn that?" Kyle asked.

"My bar used to video tape us with the customers and sometimes we had to help them upload the videos online."

"Cool. Is it easy to do?"

"Yep. Does the library have computers?"

Tavi nodded his head.

"Then yeah. It only takes a few minutes. We just have to get a memory stick."

"What's that?" Kurt asked.

"It's like a little rectangle thing about this big," Zeke said, spreading his finger and thumb apart. "And it has a small metal rectangle at one end."

"Ohh! I saw one of those today in the bag," Kurt said excitedly. He looked around wildly, "It's over…hmmm…I don't know where I put it."

"Relax. You can find it in the morning. Let's go to sleep," Kyle said.

Just then, Byron stumbled up and collapsed into a chair next to Tavi. "Hey guys," he said with a lazy voice. His eyes were half-closed and he reclined in his chair with a contented smile on his face.

"Byron! Where have you been all day?" Tavi asked. "I've been looking for you."

Byron turned his head slowly and looked at Tavi with bleary eyes. "Oh...me and some guys went off and hung out and stuff."

"Oh. Did you see what happened with the policemen?"

"Policemen…what?" Byron looked around their encampment.

Tavi shared a look of concern with Kyle and tried again. "Didn't you hear everyone get up and chase after them?"

"Oh, yeah. We heard that, but we were too…" Byron hesitated and obviously picked a different word. "We were too far away."

"Byron, did you do any drugs tonight?" Kyle asked hesitantly. Tavi looked at Kyle in surprise and then studied Byron's face.

To Tavi's distress, Byron appeared to feel guilty. "No, Kyle. Well, I mean, these guys they had some pills and so we took one today." A look of bliss crossed his face. "It was awesome. I can't remember feeling so good." Panic filled Tavi's chest as Byron continued. "And then tonight we smoked something, but that was just a little smoke. It's cool."

"Byron…" Tavi tried to keep his voice steady. "Please don't do any drugs. Remember what happened to Mac." He glanced at Kurt and Kyle and saw that they were as stunned as he was.

"Tavi, that won't happen to me," Byron said reassuringly. He tried unsuccessfully to focus his gaze on Tavi's face. "I love you, man. It was just one time."

"Do you promise?"

"I promise." Byron looked around the encampment and asked, "Does anyone have any snacks? I'm so hungry."

Tavi woke up early the next morning to go boujie hunting with Kurt, Bert, and another boy – Dog, whom he had never met before. Kurt and Bert acted like they were twins, while Dog was big, dumb, and happy, and Tavi enjoyed walking with them through the streets.

"I haven't done this for over two weeks," Tavi said. "I've been so busy taking those two kids home and going to the library that I feel like I'm out of practice."

Kurt laughed. "Just follow my lead. I'll teach you." The others chuckled at Kurt's joke and they pushed each other and ran through the streets until they got to a likely spot.

After waiting for twenty minutes, and then walking around for another fifteen, Tavi asked, "What's going on? Is today a holiday or something?"

Bert shook his head. "It's been like this for the last week or two. I think we've jumped so many boujies that most of them aren't walking to school anymore."

"What?" Tavi laughed at the absurdity of it. "How many kids have we been jumping?"

Kurt shrugged. "Well, if we have sixty kids, and together, they jump about fifteen boujies a day…"

"Probably more," Dog said, surprising everyone. "I like to do it twice a day when they go to school and come home."

Kurt counted on his fingers. "And so we've probably jumped three hundred kids in the last month. And that's just us. Who knows what the other street kids are doing."

Tavi had a sinking feeling in his stomach. "This isn't good," he said. "If we become too obvious then they might send the real police to stop us." The other three didn't respond, and Tavi had the feeling that they didn't really care about the consequences.

He glanced at his watch and saw that it was almost time for school to start. "Well, it's too late this morning to catch anyone. How about we try after school?" The others nodded their heads and agreed. "Okay. I'm going to go visit Clarence since we're so close to him. Do you want to come, Kurt?"

Kurt considered it for a second and then said, "Nah. I'm hungry. I want to go eat. But tell him hi for me." Tavi nodded his head, pleased to see that Kurt had forgiven Clarence for not buying their stuff anymore. Saying goodbye to the others, he went back the way they had come and headed for Clarence's.

"Tavi!" Clarence said with undisguised pleasure when Tavi entered his store. "It's been a while. How have you been?"

"Busy." Tavi leaned against the counter and began telling Clarence everything that had been happening during the three weeks since he had last visited. By the time he had finished, he was sitting next to Clarence on a stool behind the counter and they were eating a late breakfast, or a pre-lunch as Clarence liked to call it.

A few customers came in to the store, and Clarence had to deal with them. When they left, Clarence sat back down and was silent for a few minutes as he digested everything that Tavi had told him.

"First of all," he said when he finally spoke, "I want you to know how proud I am that you're helping those children. I don't know who else would spend two days on a bus making sure someone they didn't know got home safely."

Tavi shrugged off the praise. "Chloe and Kyle and others are doing it as well."

"Yes, but you did it first, right?" When Tavi didn't respond, Clarence continued, "And you need to be careful around those police. I can't believe they're getting paid to bring kids to the bars.

Tavi smiled and shrugged again. "It's life. It is what it is."

"Bullshit!" Clarence said vehemently. "It's wrong. Someone should do something about it."

"We're doing everything we can. I don't think there's anything more that we could do to help right now."

"I know, Tavi. I wasn't talking about you and your friends." Clarence stared at the counter in thought for a few moments. Without warning, he looked up with a grin. "Oh…guess what I found a couple of days ago?"

"What?"

Clarence reached under the counter and pulled out three books. "Remember these. You asked me to keep them for you and you even stopped by a few times to read them. I'm surprised you haven't asked for them since you've been free."

Tavi took the books from Clarence and flipped through them with a smile. "I actually read all three of these already."

Clarence took the books back from Tavi. "What? Where?"

Tavi pointed to the top one. "I read that one in the library because I wanted to see how it ended. And those two schoolbooks, well, we've collected a lot of them lately. A couple of friends and I finished each of them in about two weeks."

Clarence flipped through one of the books. "You studied algebra on your own and did the whole book in two weeks?"

Tavi smiled. "Yeah. We have a lot of free time."

Clarence studied Tavi in silence long enough for Tavi to start feeling uncomfortable. "What?"

Clarence just shook his head in admiration. "I'm just impressed with what you've done. I knew you liked to read, but…" He hesitated and chewed on his bottom lip for a second. "Do you want to go to school?"

Tavi gave a wistful smile that almost broke Clarence's heart. "That'd be amazing. But it's impossible."

"Are you sure? What if I sponsored you and did all of the paperwork?"

The excitement that Tavi felt when he heard those words flooded every nerve in his body. He tried his best to keep from smiling too broadly. "Really? You would do that?"

"Of course. I have an idea. How about we get you some clean clothes, and you can stop by my house and take a shower, and then we'll visit the school this afternoon?"

Tavi felt guilty about being uneasy when Clarence mentioned showering at his house, but he tried to swallow it and smiled as brightly as he could. "Sure. That sounds great."

When he left Clarence's house thirty minutes later, Tavi laughed at how stupid he had been. Clarence only lived a few minutes from the store, and so they had stopped off at a cheap clothing store, bought Tavi a new shirt and olive green pants, and then headed to Clarence's house. It consisted of one large room, which had a sofa, TV, bed, and coffee table, a small kitchen, and a tiny bathroom. After Clarence had let Tavi in, he had left to go get some lunch for them, and by the time Clarence got back, Tavi was already showered and dressed.

He savored the hot shower and inhaled the scent of the clean towel as he pressed it against his face. When he put on his brand new clothes, he couldn't imagine anything that could possibly feel any better at that moment.

The nearest school was only a ten minute walk from Clarence's house. Tavi was so thrilled that he couldn't stop hopping around and imagining what it would be like to go to a real school. As they entered the school, Tavi saw a couple of students pass by, and he recognized their uniforms from students he had beaten up. Hoping that none of them would recognize him now, Tavi walked close behind Clarence and tried not to be seen.

"Hi. I was wondering if we could speak with the principal for a few moments," Clarence said to the receptionist.

"Do you have an appointment?" Tavi peeked at her from behind Clarence and was amazed by how pretty she was. She had long brown hair and dark green eyes, and Tavi fell in love instantly.

"No. We don't. Will that be a problem?" Clarence asked hesitantly.

The receptionist gave him a bright smile and said, "It shouldn't be, sir. I'll see if she's free." Tavi stared at her perfectly shaped lips and her perfect white teeth, and he heaved a long sigh. He smelled the scent of flowers and as he inhaled deeply, he was sure that it was her.

After picking up a phone and speaking softly into it, the receptionist told Clarence that he and his son should have a seat and wait to be called.

Tavi was disappointed when – a short five minutes later – a tall middle-aged woman walked out from an interior room and came over to them. Clarence stood up quickly and Tavi immediately did the same.

"Hello, Mr...." The principal held out her hand.

Clarence took her hand and gently shook it as he said, "Rothschild. Clarence Rothschild. And this is Tavi."

"Hi, Tavi," she said, shaking his hand as well. "My name is Marcia Williams and I'm the principal here at Nall Hills. Let's speak in my office."

Tavi gave the receptionist a longing stare as they passed by her and entered the office beyond. Principal Williams sat down behind her desk, and Tavi and Clarence gently sat down in the two soft leather chairs across from her.

"So, how can I help you?" she asked. Tavi stared at the walls and couldn't imagine how one person could have so many awards and certificates.

"Well, we're interested in enrolling Tavi in your school."

"I see. Did you just move into the neighborhood?"

"Um, no. It's actually a long story," Clarence explained. "I've lived here for over thirty years, but Tavi has only been here for a year or so."

Principal Williams repeated, "I see. So you are Tavi's legal guardian now?"

"Um. Not exactly. But I would be willing to sponsor him."

Tavi felt his hopes being destroyed once again as he watched the principal's face. "I'm sorry, but it doesn't work like that. Only his parents or guardian can enroll him in school." She asked Tavi, "Where are your parents?"

He had no idea what he should say. Should he tell the truth? Should he say that they're dead? Finally, he just muttered, "I don't know."

"I see. Well…"

"What if I were to become Tavi's guardian?" Clarence asked quickly. "Then we could enroll him in this school."

"Yeeeesss," she answered slowly. "But who is Tavi's legal guardian now?"

Clarence gave Tavi a questioning glance and Tavi just shrugged and nodded because he already knew that it was hopeless. Clarence spoke bluntly, "Tavi lives on the streets. He was taken from his family and forced to work in one of the bars here. He ran away and that's how I met him."

Principal Williams's demeanor changed slightly. She pursed her lips and said, "To be honest, I don't think it'll be possible."

"Why not? Just because I was honest with you?" Clarence asked angrily.

"Of course not." She turned her attention to Tavi again. "I'm assuming you were born in a small village, right? Pretty far from here?"

Tavi nodded his head.

"And you don't have your birth certificate or any kind of paperwork that most people need to have if they live in this country, do you?"

Tavi didn't even bother to respond.

She looked at Clarence. "And so, I think it's a wonderful thing that you're trying to do, but to be honest, there is a legal term for children like Tavi. He is 'stateless'."

Clarence looked at Tavi and could see the pain in his eyes. He asked angrily, "And what does that mean?"

"Technically, he's not an official citizen of this country and so he can't go to school or get health insurance or a driver's license or anything like that."

"And you don't have any problem with that?!?"

"Look, Mr. Rothschild," she explained without emotion, "It is the law. Otherwise, we would have thousands of these village children entering our schools, and our classrooms are already too crowded as it is. I'm sorry, but my hands are tied."

Clarence rose to his feet and Tavi slowly followed. Tavi realized how stupid it was for him to waste time reading schoolbooks and pretending to study like a normal student. He would never be able to go to school and he would most likely never get off the streets. He turned around and walked out of the room without saying a word.

Principal Williams watched Tavi leave, and then she leaned forward and said in a confiding manner, "To be blunt, our students are at a much higher level than anything those village schools cover. Tavi wouldn't have belonged anyway. It would've been much too hard for him."

"I think you're a real bitch," Clarence replied. He stormed out, slamming the door behind him. He checked for Tavi in the reception area, and when he didn't see him there, he hurried outside. He looked anxiously in all directions, but there was no sign of Tavi.

Chapter 29

Tavi spent the next few days taking out his frustration on any boujie he could find. The afternoon after his visit to the school, Tavi had met up with Kurt, Bert, and Dog, and he had taken them back to Nall Hills.

"I want to hit this place hard for the next few days," he told them grimly.

"Why?" Kurt asked.

Bert added, "Yeah. Usually we move around so that we don't get caught."

Tavi clenched his jaw and there was a hint of a tear in the corner of his left eye. Blinking rapidly, he glanced around and simply said, "Please."

"Okay. Do you want us to tell the other kids?" When Tavi nodded silently, Kurt glanced at Bert with a questioning look on his face. They both shrugged at the same time and then turned their attention towards the school.

They had come up with a new plan to combat the lack of students on the street. Instead of trying to find the students, they would wait near the school and look for any student walking home. One person would start following the student, while the other three would run along a side street and get into position.

Tavi didn't bother pointing out that this was similar to the plan he had first devised when he had joined Kurt and his friends. The only thing he cared about at that moment was finding a boujie student to take his anger out on.

They only had to wait a few seconds before they saw two boys walking home. Since Bert was the smallest – and therefore looked the least intimidating – he would follow them and use his cell phone to let the others know where they were headed.

It worked like a charm.

Within five minutes, they had the two boys surrounded on a nearby residential street. Dog moved in and started punching robotically, quickly dropping one of the boys. Kurt went for the other one, but the boy turned and fought back, managing to land a punch across Kurt's jaw. Tavi tackled him and punched him twice in the head. He then stunned the boy by smashing the boy's head on the ground.

Usually, at this point, the fight would be over and they would quickly grab whatever they could and run. But Tavi didn't stop. "You think you're better than me?" he shouted and began slamming his right fist into the boy's face. Within seconds, his face was a bloody mess and his eyes were half-open but not moving.

"Hey!" Bert yelled. He tried to pull Tavi off of the boy, but Tavi shoved him down and punched the boy two more times. Suddenly, he was lifted in the air as Dog picked him up and threw him to the ground.

"Stop it, Tavi," he said. "Fight's done."

Tavi glared at Dog and then shifted his gaze to the boy he had beaten up. His expression didn't change. "Fine," he finally said. "But I want his clothes."

"What? Why?" Kurt asked.

"No one bothers boujies when they're wearing their uniforms," Tavi explained, still feeling the anger flow through him. "It'll be a good disguise to wear sometimes."

The others nodded their heads and agreed. They quickly stripped the pants and blazer off of both boys. "What about those shirts?" Bert asked. By this time, the other boy was kneeling next to the boy that Tavi had beaten up. He was gently shaking him and trying to wake him, but the boy just lay there unconscious. Tavi stared at him as the boy flashed them a dirty look.

"We don't have time," Kurt said, looking around carefully. "We have to get off this street now. So many people could see us." Just then a car turned onto the street. It slowed down as it passed them, and they could see a boy's face pressed against the window. He began talking agitatedly to the driver and pointing at them, and Kurt shouted, "We have go NOW!"

"You better run," said the boy who was still conscious. He continued to kneel by his friend as he said, "You guys think you're so tough, huh? Four on two? Someone should kill people like you. Fucking street rats."

With an inarticulate scream, Tavi stepped forward and kicked him in the face. "Kill us? I'll kill you!" He kicked the boy twice more in the face and the ribs before his three friends dragged him away. He continued to struggle and curse for a few seconds.

"Holy shit, Tavi! What is wrong with you?" Kurt yelled. "The cops are going to be coming right now. Let's go!" He slung one of the boy's backpacks over his shoulder and tugged on Tavi's arm. Tavi stumbled for a second until Dog grabbed his other arm and began running after Kurt and Bert.

"I'm fine," Tavi muttered, shaking him off and sprinting away. They could hear the sirens approaching, but within moments, they had made it into a nearby alleyway and vanished.

A few days later, Tavi and several of his friends were waiting near a bar far away from the street they usually hit. Three kids who had wandered into the bridge a couple of weeks earlier had asked why they only took boys from one bar street.

Kyle had looked at Tavi in confusion and asked, "What do you mean? It's where all of the bars are that we worked at."

The three boys had looked at each, puzzled, and then one of them exclaimed, "Ah. That makes sense. You're all in this part of the city because that's where your bars are. But there are at least two other huge areas that have those kinds of bars."

Jack, who had been listening surreptitiously a few feet away, asked what they were all thinking, "Where?!?"

They had spent half of the day reconnoitering the area, and they were confident that they would be able to escape. At the last second, Tavi suggested they wear the school uniforms they had collected from Nall Hills students.

"Why are we doing this?" Kyle asked unhappily, as he tried to find a blazer that fit. "I hate wearing these kinds of clothes."

Tavi shrugged. "Maybe they'll think some boujies did it for a school project or something."

Jack nodded his head in agreement. "At least they won't suspect us, right? I'm still waiting for the other bars to try to attack us, and so the less people who hate us, the better it is, I think."

At first, they had felt nervous walking through the streets wearing the uniforms. But soon, a confidence that none of them had felt for a long time infused them, and they strutted through the streets as if they belonged. No one gave them dirty glances. No on tracked them with their eyes. It was as if they were suddenly accepted by everyone around them and they could now be trusted. They even went into several stores they had been too intimidated to visit before, and the shopkeepers just smiled at them and spoke to them kindly.

"That was amazing!" Jack exclaimed as they approached the bar.

Tavi agreed. "I thought that people might treat us differently, but I didn't expect that." He grinned at Jack and they both said at the same time, "We gotta get more uniforms!" They laughed and gave each other little shoves as they walked down the street in the evening twilight.

Taking the boy was a simple matter. The street was longer than the one that their bar was located on, but there was more space between the bars, and so the street was filled with shadows. They had to let the first one pass by as there were too many people on the street at that moment. Tavi felt a twinge of guilt when he saw the young boy disappear around the corner with his customer and promised himself that he would come back for him.

He glanced around and saw a regretful look on Kyle's face. Kyle made eye contact with Tavi and gave a little nod. He whispered, "Next time. We'll come back for that kid." Tavi smiled in agreement.

Five minutes later, a fat, older man walked out of the bar. He was holding the hand of a young boy and Tavi squirmed for a second as something about the man reminded him of his first customer.

A couple of minutes later, the man was lying alone on the street, cradling his broken arm and weeping as blood dripped down his face from a gash on his forehead. Tavi hadn't been able to restrain himself and had smashed his pipe against the man's head. The others had stared at him in shock, and, to his chagrin, Chloe had reached over and taken his pipe away from him. Anger had quickly turned to embarrassment, and Tavi had just grabbed the boy's hand and followed Jack through the alleyways.

Chapter 30

The boy sat on the ground next to Tavi's chair. Like some of the children they had rescued, he seemed shell-shocked and continually looked around in fear. After a while, he picked up a stick and began drawing in the dirt at his feet.

"So, what's your name?" Tavi tried again. The boy had refused to speak since they grabbed him. He hadn't made eye contact with anyone yet and Tavi was unsure how to proceed.

"Are you hungry?" No response.

"Do you want to sleep?" Tavi thought he saw the boy's head move imperceptibly, but there was no change in his expression. Tavi sighed and asked impetuously, "Do you want to go home?"

The boy's stick stopped drawing lines in the dirt. Without looking up, the boy murmured, "Really?"

Finally, Tavi thought with relief. He gave a quick smile to Chloe who was sitting next to him and said, "Yes. If you want to go home to your family, we will take you."

Another longer pause. "Why?"

"Because it's the right thing to do. What's your name? How old are you?

At first Tavi didn't think the boy would answer either question. He was just getting ready to ask another question when the boy looked up warily and said, "Frederick. I'm nine."

Chloe leaned down and asked, "Do you know where your family lives?"

Frederick nodded. "Florencia."

Tavi sat back and thought about what he would have to do over the next couple of days to get Frederick home. No problem, he thought.

Everything did go smoothly. Tavi managed to find Frederick's village in the atlas without anyone's help. He had asked Byron if he wanted to help him, but Byron had just mumbled something in his sleep and then covered himself with his blanket.

He went to the bus station and found out that he would have to transfer buses twice and that the trip to the village would take fourteen hours, but Tavi had learned to bring books with him for the ride, and they helped make the time pass by faster. He had taken the next three books in a series he was reading from the library, carefully sliding his bag around the sensors so that they wouldn't beep when he walked out.

Tavi thought it was strange, though, that Frederick seemed to get more nervous as they approached his village. The other children he had taken home had become more and more excited the closer they got.

"Are you okay?" he asked Frederick when they were only a couple of kilometers away.

Frederick's blue eyes looked huge as he studied Tavi's face. Without answering, he just nodded his head and turned back to stare out of the window.

"You're going to see your parents soon!" Tavi tried make his voice sound excited, but Frederick was as still as a statue during the last five minutes of the bus ride to his village.

When the bus stopped at the edge of the village, Frederick heaved a worried sigh and trudged off of the bus. Tavi followed him, filled with trepidation.

Frederick waited for Tavi to join him outside of the bus, and then he slipped his hand into Tavi's and walked into his village. A couple of people watched them silently from darkened doorways, but Frederick didn't even see them. He continued staring at a small house ahead of them off to their right. "My brother and sister," he said so softly that Tavi leaned his head down.

"What did you say?"

"I want to make sure my brother and sister are okay."

Tavi had never walked through a village that was as silent as that one. The sun was beating down upon them as they walked down the dirt road, and the oppressive heat made it difficult for Tavi to breathe. Taking a deep breath and letting it out slowly, he said without conviction, "I'm sure they are."

Frederick's only response was to remove his sweaty palm from Tavi's hand, dry it on his pants, and then he grabbed ahold of it again as if it were a lifeline.

When they reached a tin shack at the edge of the road, Frederick stopped walking and said in a low voice, "My home." Tavi looked around the dirty yard which was filled with trash, and noted the graffiti painted on the walls of the shack and the fetid odor emanating from somewhere nearby.

Everything was dead silent. As they took two steps into the yard, Tavi thought he saw movement from inside of the house. Suddenly there were the sounds of a large smack and a child crying out, and he heard a woman screech, "Get back in your corner!"

Tavi stumbled for a second and his foot kicked a plastic bottle. He froze in fear as the bottle skittered over the gravel path and then a woman leaped into the doorway, brandishing a knife. "Who is it? What do you want?" she shrieked.

Tavi took a step back in alarm. The woman had stringy brown hair which was matted with filth. Her eyes were bloodshot and she had purple bags under each eye. He could see gaps in her mouth where her teeth should have been, and the odor he had smelled sharply increased.

The woman blinked as her eyes adjusted to the sunlight. "Who is that? Frederick, is that you?!?"

"Hi, mom," Frederick whispered.

"What the hell are you doing here? I sold you to that school." She looked at Tavi. "I'm not giving you the money back. I've spent it."

"I don't want any money," Tavi said after a moment's surprise. "I'm just helping Frederick get home safely. He escaped from the school."

"Escaped? Are they going to want the money back?"

"I doubt it." Tavi felt his anger rising. "But they were selling Frederick to men..."

"I don't care," Frederick's mother interrupted. "They bought him. They can do what they want."

"You don't care?" Tavi asked in disbelief.

"Fine. Welcome home, Frederick." She motioned for him to come closer. "I'll just sell you again and tell them not to let you run away."

Tavi put his hand on Frederick's arm and stepped forward. "Listen..."

"No, you listen, you little shit. Frederick is my son. I can do what I want with him." She motioned again for Frederick to come to her. "Thank you for returning him. Now go back to wherever you came from. Frederick! Get in the house!"

"Where are June and Jaime?" Frederick asked, not moving.

"Get in the house NOW!"

"Jaime!" Frederick shouted. "June! Come here!" Tavi saw something move behind the mother, but she took a step back and blocked the door.

She turned around and screamed, "Go back to your corners!" She raised her hand and swung it, and a young child started crying. Frederick's mother turned back towards Tavi and said, "Look what you've done. You're making everyone upset! Go away!"

Frederick looked up at Tavi with a hopeless expression and took a step towards his mom. Tavi grabbed him by the shoulder and pulled him back. "Fine. I'll buy them."

"What?" Frederick's mother snapped.

"I'll buy them. I'll give you one hundred talents for all three of your children."

"Ha! I can sell each one of them for one hundred talents. You're not going to rip me off."

Tavi reached into his pocket and pulled out the money. "Take this or I will come back and beat you to death and then take your children."

"You snot-nosed, little shit!"

"You can't sell the younger ones for another year or two anyways. Do really want to wait for the money?" Tavi asked, his fists clenched as he tried to control his fury. "Think how much drink you can buy with one hundred talents."

The woman considered it for a few moments. "Fine. Give me the money first." She held out her hand, still holding the knife in the other, but refused to move from the doorway.

Tavi studied her face and wondered if she was actually going to try and take the money, and then keep the children. He knew from the bus schedule that the bus he needed to catch would be coming within the next twenty minutes.

He looked around and pointed to a large leafy tree a hundred meters away. It was in the opposite direction from where the bus would be stopping. "There. I'll give you the money over there." Tavi showed her the money again and started walking towards the tree. He grabbed Frederick's hand and tugged him along. "Listen," he said softly. "When your mother comes this way, I want you to go into your house, get your brother and sister, and meet me where the bus dropped us off, okay?" Frederick nodded his head and let go of Tavi's hand. His mother took a couple of steps away from the doorway and looked at Frederick suspiciously.

"What's he doing?" she called out.

Tavi turned around and shrugged. "Can't he say hi to his brother and sister?"

She looked torn. Keeping one eye on her son, she started hobbling after Tavi. "I guess so," she mumbled.

Tavi glanced back only once. Frederick's mother was about twenty meters behind him and Frederick had disappeared into the house. When he got to the tree, he looked around curiously and decided that this village was a lot worse off than his own had been. When Frederick's mother finally arrived, Tavi saw Frederick disappearing with two small children around the corner of their house. She looked back quickly, but they were already gone.

"Hurry up! Give me my money!" Up close, she was even more hideous and reeked terribly. She was sweating in the hot sun and her shirt was sticking to her body. Tavi studied her face with a look of disgust. Faster than he would have thought possible, she reached up and slapped him across the face. "Who do you think you are to judge me?" she screamed.

Tavi held his hand to his face in surprise. He had so many questions he wanted to ask her, but he simply said, "Here. Go get it." He balled the money up in his hand and threw it behind him. He jumped back when she screeched in rage and tried to hit him again. Without looking back, Tavi ran past her and sprinted for the bus stop.

Frederick was waiting for him with his little brother and sister. His seven year old brother was a miniature version of Frederick, while his five year old sister had huge blue eyes that filled her face as she continued to stare at Tavi. Whether the look in her eyes was fear or confusion, Tavi couldn't tell, but neither of the siblings spoke a single word for the first eight hours that Tavi was with them.

They could hear their mother screaming and getting closer as they waited anxiously for the bus. When she was only two hundred meters away, Tavi searched on the ground and found a thick branch which he could swing with ease.

But he wouldn't need it. Frederick let out a shout of joy as the bus came around the bend in the road. As their mother's screams and threats filled the air, the four children boarded the bus, safe from at least one threat.

When Tavi finally made it home and stumbled under the bridge from exhaustion, Kyle and Jack laughed with surprise as the three children followed him to their encampment. "You leave with one kid and you come back with three?" Jack asked as Tavi collapsed into a chair. "Where'd you find them? And I thought you were taking that boy home. What's he doing here?"

Tavi shook his head as the three children sat down around his chair. Grinning weakly, he said, "I bought them. I guess they're mine." The looks on his friends' faces were worth the hundred talents, he thought. Well, almost.

Chapter 31

A couple of days later, Tavi was hanging out with Malik and Pablo in their encampment when he saw a group of children come in with two new ones. It was easy to spot the children who were just arriving. They often stopped and stared in astonishment at the huge area which looked like a miniature village filled with only children.

What had caught Tavi's attention, though, were the children who were leading the group. Or, to be more specific, one child in general. "Is that…?" Tavi asked, pointing at the approaching children.

"Yep," Pablo replied. "That's Momo."

"Really? I thought he didn't want to have anything to do with bringing kids here."

Malik explained, "I was here when it happened last week. Derek and Momo got into a huge argument because Momo wouldn't go to the bars with him that night. After Derek accused him of being a frightened girl and threatened to leave their camp, Momo agreed to go. I think this is the third one he's been on since then. He brought back two children last time as well."

Tavi listened to Malik in disbelief. He hopped up with a smile spread across his face and strode over to where Momo was talking to Derek.

Momo glanced around to see who was approaching, and when he saw Tavi's smile, his eyes lit up for a second.

"Hi, Momo," Tavi said.

"Tavi." His eyes danced with delight but his face remained as serious as ever.

"So, what have you been up to lately?"

And for a brief second, Momo's stern visage broke into a boyish grin. "Don't say a word," he warned. Tavi and Derek both laughed as Momo's face became serious again.

"I won't," Tavi promised. "I just wanted to say…" He grinned and patted Momo on the shoulder and then turned and walked away.

When he got back to camp, he saw Kurt and Pablo digging through a box, with several other boxes at their feet. "What are you guys doing?" he asked as he sat down next to Malik, who had a notepad and pencil ready to take notes.

They each pulled out several cell phones and sorted them into two separate piles. "Taking inventory," Kyle said, without stopping from what they were doing.

Tavi pulled one of the boxes closer to him and found it filled with watches, necklaces, and portable gaming systems. He whistled in surprise. "Whose stuff is this?"

"It's ours," Pablo replied.

"Ours?"

"Our group's stuff. Ben's. Malik's. Adam's. And a bunch of other people."

"Why aren't we selling it? I thought that was the whole point."

Pablo looked up in exasperation. "Because there are too many of us trying to sell stuff right now. We all agreed to split the money when we sell stuff, but it's not working very well."

"Hmmm. Well, good luck doing inventory. I'm going over to Jack's camp."

Kyle stopped counting and looked up as well. "So you're not going to help us?"

Tavi grinned. "I have an idea!"

"I hate it when you say that," Pablo grumbled. He counted the piles of phones in front of him. "Seventeen smart phones and twelve normal ones," Tavi heard him say as he walked away.

When he got to Jack's camp, he didn't see him anywhere. Looking around, he noticed that there were a lot of unfamiliar faces. He greeted several children that he recognized and walked over to talk to Yabu.

"Hey, Tavi," he said, eating from a can of ravioli. "What's up?"

"Have you seen Jack around?"

"He's gone. He's taking a kid home to his family." Yabu scraped the bottom of the can with his plastic spoon and then tossed them both into a nearby trash bag. "I heard about that last kid you took. It sounded rough."

"Yeah. I didn't know what to do. I couldn't just leave them there for the mom to beat on every day and then sell them to a bar or something."

Yabu nodded. "I hear you. I just don't know if I would've had the balls to buy three kids from their own mother."

Tavi gave Yabu a bitter smile. "It's a shitty world we live in."

"Cheers to that," Yabu said, holding up the can of coke he was drinking. After he took a long draught, he asked, "So, did you just come over here to chat?"

"No. I was wondering if you guys are able to sell everything you take from the boujies."

Yabu laughed and pointed under the chairs. Most of them had medium-sized boxes under them. "There's where we keep our stuff if you ever need anything. The guy we use has been really picky lately. We're not selling shit anymore."

"Yeah, neither are we. I think it's time we tried using other guys."

Yabu looked around the underworld of the bridge. "There are a lot of kids here now," he said, not responding to what Tavi said.

"I know. There's probably close to a hundred people by now."

"And we're all trying to sell the same stuff."

Tavi nodded. "That's why I have a plan."

"What is it?"

"First, we find other pawnshops and people who will buy our stuff."

"I heard you before. I guess that could work, but it's going to be a hassle walking all over the place to different guys, only to have them say they don't want any more stuff."

"And then we invite all of them here, and we make them come to us."

Yabu looked confused and raised his eyebrow at Tavi. "What?"

"Okay. Here's what I was thinking. We make a flyer or something on a piece of paper and hand it out to a bunch of pawnshops. And then we tell them that we're having an open market on Saturday morning. And then we can all have our stuff out, and they can come around and buy what they want."

"Would that work?" Yabu asked doubtfully.

"I think so. We should all agree on prices before they come, or maybe a small range of prices. And then we can see how many come the first week and decide from there."

Yabu nodded. "Today is…Tuesday, right?" When Tavi nodded, Yabu said, "Let's go talk to Momo's people and see what they say. And then when Jack gets back tomorrow, we can have almost everything planned out."

"Cool! Let me see if Kyle and Pablo want to come."

Tavi turned to leave, but Yabu said, "Hold up. I'll come with you." He called to two of his friends. "Sarah. Mickey. We need to go have a council meeting." The two kids hopped up and joined Tavi and Yabu.

"Is that what we're calling them now – council meetings?" Tavi teased.

"It's what they are," Yabu replied seriously. Tavi thought about it for a second and the smile slipped from his face when he realized that Yabu was correct.

After a long meeting at Momo's which eventually included about thirty children, it was agreed that they would print out flyers in the library the next day, find the addresses for all of the pawnshops in the city, and then groups of children would go to every single one and invite the owners to an open market on Saturday. Pablo and Kyle were discussing it animatedly as they walked back to their camp.

"This will be awesome if it works," Kyle said. "I bet we'll be able to sell everything that we've got."

Pablo agreed. "I was thinking we could start stealing stuff and selling it as well. If we don't get caught, we could sell TV's and things like that."

Kyle looked at Tavi and rolled his eyes. "Ummm…I don't know about that. We can discuss it later."

Tavi smiled. He was excited that people liked his idea, and he was really hoping it would work. "I wonder…" he trailed off when he saw Byron standing about twenty feet away. It was difficult to see him in the darkness, but he was standing in the open space next to the bridge, and a sliver of a streetlight from above was shining down upon him. Tavi pointed at him. "Look – there's Byron."

The three of them adjusted their path and headed straight for him. Byron was just staring at the ground by his feet and jumped in surprised when he heard them approaching. "Oh! Hey, guys! How are things?"

"Hi."

"Hey, Byron."

"Hey. What are you doing out here?" Tavi asked.

Byron shrugged. It was difficult to see his expression, but Tavi thought that he seemed uncomfortable. "Just thinking."

"About what?" Kyle asked.

Byron looked around nervously and then pulled something out of his pocket. He held out his hand, and they all gasped at the large wad of money that was resting in his palm. "Where'd you get that?" Kyle asked in awe.

Byron grinned nervously and shoved the money back into his pocket. "We've been…uh…selling those pills and stuff to boujie kids."

"Who's 'we'?"

"Me, Rory, Janice, and Hugo."

"What's wrong with you?" Tavi asked softly. "I thought you promised you wouldn't do that anymore."

Byron laughed nervously and reached into his pocket. He pulled out a pack of cigarettes and quickly put one into his mouth. Tavi watched in shock as Byron lit it and inhaled deeply. "When did you start smoking?" Pablo asked.

"I don't know. A while ago. Geez, you guys are acting like my parents."

"Most of us were forced to do different kinds of drugs," Kyle retorted. "We know what it's like."

"Man…you guys….I'm not doing anything really bad. We just take a pill every now and then and smoke sometimes."

"The pill makes you feel amazing, doesn't it?" Tavi asked knowingly.

Byron smiled and took a drag from his cigarette. "It does. There's nothing that feels that good."

Tavi, Kyle, and Pablo looked at each other in concern. Tavi looked back at Byron and tried to see the best friend with whom he had spent hours at the library and exploring the city. "Byron, please don't do this."

Byron shook his head in annoyance. "You think this is any worse than jumping boujies and stealing all of their stuff? At least I'm not ruining their lives like you guys do."

"It's not the same thing," Kyle said.

Byron shrugged. "Either we're both wrong or we're both right. Which one do you want it to be?"

"Forget it," Tavi said. He turned around and began walking back towards their camp. "Good luck with your new friends."

"Thanks," Byron replied, and Tavi could hear a trace of bitterness in his voice. "And Tavi, you're a great friend." Tavi looked back and tried to think of something to say, but Byron was already walking away, headed up the embankment to the top of the bridge.

Chapter 32

Almost every child helped prepare for the arrival of the pawnshop owners in some way. Several helped design the flyers on the computer at the library. Most of the children spent the next two days delivering them to all of the pawnshops in the city. It had been a bit of an organizational nightmare until Momo had just grabbed the list of addresses from Tavi, ripped it into strips, and handed a couple of pieces of paper to each child, each with the address of a different pawnshop.

A couple of children had even gone to the trouble of making welcome signs, and writing on the sidewalk in chalk, with arrows pointing the customers in the right direction.

Everyone woke up early on Saturday morning in anticipation of their first customer. They didn't have much to do, and soon the children were just sitting around their individual stands, disagreeing with each other about whether anyone would show up.

Tavi anxiously checked his watch for the twentieth time that morning when he heard someone approaching loudly from around the corner of the bridge. With a smile upon his face, he turned in expectation and broke out laughing when Kurt and Kyle stumbled in with metal boxes strapped against their chests.

"What are you guys doing?" Chloe exclaimed.

"HOT SAUSAGE! GET YOUR HOT SAUSAGE!" Kyle shouted as he gave Chloe a grin.

Kurt joined in. "WHO'S HUNGRY? DID YOU MISS BREAKFAST? HOT SAUSAGES!"

Half of the children sitting around Tavi scrambled over to buy something. Tavi decided to wait until the line got shorter, but the shouts of joy and the sound of running feet echoing under the bridge motivated him to jump up and rush to the end of Kyle's line. Within seconds, there were thirty children pushing and shoving behind him.

When Tavi finally got to the front of the line, he shook his head in admiration as Kyle tried to keep a serious demeanor. "Hello, sir. What would you like today?"

"Two sausages, please."

"And would you like a bun or ketchup or mustard?"

Tavi laughed. "Are you serious? Of course."

Kyle refused to break character. "That will be an extra ten cents for each bun."

"Okay."

Handing Tavi his two sausages, Kyle said, "Your total today is one talent and twenty cents."

"That's ten cents more than what most of the stands charge," Tavi argued, as he shifted both sausages to one hand and dug in his pocket with the other.

"Yeah. But they're far away and their sausages are usually cold."

"Fine." Tavi handed Kyle the money with a smile. "But I think you're a crook!"

Kyle laughed and whispered, "We're all crooks." Raising his voice, he said, "And a good day to you, sir. I hope you enjoy your sausages."

Tavi returned to his seat and savored the hot food. Pablo made eye contact with him while he was chewing and nodded his head approvingly. After swallowing loudly, he said, "These are really good."

Tavi just nodded his head in agreement. His mouth was too full to speak, and he was too hungry to stop eating.

That was the only excitement for the next four hours. The waiting was hard on them, and from time to time, there'd be pockets of children arguing and cursing, with the sound of trinkets and cell phones being scooped up, and then small groups of children would angrily march out from under the bridge, complaining about the wasted time.

The first man showed up around noon. As soon as he cautiously made his way under the bridge, all of the children stood up straight and stopped talking. He stopped at Jack's stand first and was soon offering to buy several objects. The other children watched in envy as the man handed over some cash to Jack, who then put the items that the man had bought into a plastic bag.

Tavi smiled at a memory when he saw the bags. The previous night, someone had piped up that most stores put things in bags when you bought them, and after a frantic search, they had realized that no one had any. And so at midnight, about forty children had raced to the nearest all-night store and bought up their whole supply of plastic bags.

The man left Jack's encampment, hesitated briefly, and then turned and walked even deeper into the underworld of the bridge. Tavi could see the children perk up and they all smiled brightly as the man approached them.

Without warning, three men appeared on Tavi's side of the bridge. They stopped near Tavi's camp and gazed around in wonder. One of them saw Tavi and his friends staring at him and said, "We were all wondering if this was real." He turned to the man next to him. "You want to go tell the others that it's not some kind of joke?"

"The others?" Tavi asked.

The man laughed as he stepped forward to look at their stuff. "There are about thirty pawnshop owners standing around nervously up on the bridge. They were afraid they were going to get mugged if they came down."

Kurt, who had been standing behind Tavi, half ran and half stumbled to the foot of the embankment and began shouting, "SAUSAGES! HOT SAUSAGES!" Within minutes, there was a stream of pawnshop owners flowing under the bridge.

The first Saturday ended up being a huge success. During the following week, a few people stopped by to buy things. Most of them were college students who had somehow heard that they could buy cheap electronics under the bridge. After a quick discussion, a few of the stands opened for business and the children raised their prices as demand soared.

The second Saturday was even better. There were less pawnshop owners, but there were a lot of normal people who had come for the amazing bargains which they had heard could be found there. Kurt and Kyle had to hire a couple of their friends to make several trips to the store as they kept running out of food. Finally, Kurt hired one of the newer children to sell his sausages for him, and he got out his video camera and filmed everything.

That night, Pablo made a show of opening each box and turning it upside down to show that it was empty, and then he threw them all against the wall behind their camp. They crowded around Kurt and watched some funny moments that he had recorded that day, and then they watched the video he had been editing on a laptop that he had stolen from a boujie.

Tavi was really impressed with the video. It was a documentary of their lives on the streets. It included the video of police trying to snatch the three boys and Kurt had even filmed Momo and Derek and a few others as they helped rescue a child from a customer.

"When did you do that?" Tavi asked.

"Last week. I told them what I wanted and they said I could come. They were going to the other bar street, and so we went early and figured out how to get on the roofs. And then I just waited and filmed." He shrugged and smiled. "They did all of the work. I just sat there and pointed my camera."

"I notice they're not beating up the customer too bad," Kyle said.

"Yeah. We thought it would look better if we didn't come across as too violent."

"Look better to who?" Chloe asked.

Kurt shrugged again. "I don't know." He turned to Tavi. "Are you going to the library tomorrow? There's another book on video editing that I want to read. There's this special effect that I'm trying to do where…"

Knowing that Kurt could talk for hours about everything he had been learning about video editing, Tavi interrupted him and said, "Yep. You want to go in the morning?"

"Sure." Kurt leaned over and powered down his laptop. "I need to charge this anyways. The battery runs down too quickly."

As he leaned back in his chair and closed his eyes, Tavi smiled in contentment and let his friends' conversation wash over and surround him like a warm blanket. He felt like things were finally going the right direction.

Chapter 33

A few evenings later, they were sitting around their encampment as they watched Kurt film his new project. There was a large crowd of children since this was the only entertainment happening at the time.

"Okay, so…Kyle. What do YOU want to be when you grow up?" Kurt asked in his best announcer voice.

Kyle shifted nervously in his chair when he felt everyone watching him. He gave a weak smile and said, "A businessman."

Kurt pushed a button on the camera and held it at his side. "What's wrong with you? I need attitude and excitement and pizzazz!" He shook his head disappointingly at Kyle. "Can we do it again?"

"Fine. Let's do it."

Kurt lifted the camera up and started recording again. "Aaaaand Kyle. What do YOU want to be when you grow up?"

"I want to be a BUSINESSMAN!" Kyle shouted, jumping to his feet. He waved his arms and danced around as he chanted, "Businessman, businessman, I want to be a businessMAN! Businessman, businessman, I want to be a businessMAN!" Within moments, everyone was chanting along with Kyle. Kurt let it go on for forty more seconds before he pushed a button on his camera.

"Cut." He turned and faced Chloe. Without warning, he quickly pointed the camera at her and said, "Chloe. What do YOU want to be when you grow up?"

Chloe, who had been talking to Sasha, looked around in surprise and blushed when she saw the camera. She squirmed nervously and pleaded, "Come on, Kurt. I don't want to do this."

"Just answer the question."

Chloe looked everywhere except at the camera. She glanced at Sasha and they both began giggling. Kurt let out a loud sigh and Chloe finally said, "Fine. I want to be a doctor."

"Interesting choice. Why?"

Losing all traces of nervousness, Chloe looked directly into the camera, "I want to help people. I'm not very strong, but I enjoy helping my friends when they hurt themselves. I've been reading first aid books at the library, and…" She shrugged and looked away.

Kurt turned the camera around and spoke into it. "Well, you heard it here first. If you have a cut or a booboo, then Chloe is the pretty nurse you want to come and see." He ducked as Chloe threw her empty water bottle at him. Flipping the camera around, he aimed it at Sasha. "And here we have Sasha. She doesn't really like to talk, and so we're not expecting much, but let's give it a shot. Sasha, what would you like to be when you grow up?"

Sasha looked around calmly and then stared directly into the camera. "I want to be a singer," she said with confidence. She stood up as Kurt said, "Well, that's interesting. Why…?"

Sasha cut him off as she began singing in a loud voice. "Amazing Grace, how sweet the sound…" She sang beautifully. Everyone stared at her and listened in complete silence as she sang the entire song. When she was finished, there was a brief instant when the underworld of the bridge echoed with her last note ringing in the air, and then all of the children erupted into cheers. Half of them jumped up and gave Sasha a standing ovation. She turned bright red and sank back into her seat, hiding her face in her hands.

Kurt had stepped back to film all of the children applauding and cheering, and he was the first one to notice the disturbance in the crowd. "Hey!" he shouted, but no one paid him any attention. "HEY!" he tried again, pointing at some children who were frantically pushing their way through the crowd.

Momo, who was standing across from Kurt, quickly saw what he was pointing at and shouted, "SHUT UP!" It was like turning off a switch. Everyone froze and stared at Momo in silence, except for the children pushing through the crowd. "Let them through," he ordered, pointing at them.

It was Ben and three of his friends. They were breathing heavily and their eyes were wide with panic. "They just grabbed two kids!" Ben said urgently. Kurt took a couple of steps backwards and unobtrusively continued filming.

Tavi jumped up from his chair. "Where?" he asked, reaching down to grab his pipe.

"It's too late," one of Ben's friends said. "They're already gone."

Momo stepped forward. "Start from the beginning," he commanded softly.

Ben took two measured breaths and described what happened. "We went and saw a movie today because some people had never seen one before. When we were walking back, we were like two minutes away from here, and suddenly four policemen just stepped out of nowhere. And then three cars pulled up. It's like they were waiting for us."

"Or waiting for any kid to walk by there," Kyle murmured to Tavi.

"We didn't want to run, but there were seven of them and only six of us," he explained, clearly hoping that they would understand. When Momo nodded his head, Ben continued, "I don't know what happened. Two of them came after me and I managed to dodge them. When I got far enough away, I looked back and they had caught two of us."

"Where's Hector?" Sasha suddenly said loudly. Her voice echoed throughout the underworld just as her song had a few minutes before. "He said he was going to see a movie today."

Ben shook his head, as tears welled up from his eyes. "They took him. Him and Zeke."

"What?" Sasha screamed. "You left my brother?!?!"

Ben looked around in fear and confusion. "We couldn't…" he began before one of his friends interrupted.

"There were too many of them. We didn't have a choice."

Sasha stared at him defiantly for a second before she broke down, sobbing into Chloe's shoulder. Tavi shared a look of worry with Momo and he knew that things were going to start getting worse.

The next morning, Tavi and a few people from his camp headed over to Jack's encampment so that they could decide what to do. They ran into Momo and a few of his friends on the short walk over, and the two groups merged into one as they strode to the council.

Jack didn't have enough spare chairs for everyone, and he apologized profusely for it, but the ones without chairs just waved him off and sat down with no complaint.

"How's his sister doing? Sasha, right?" Jack asked without any preamble.

"Not good," Chloe replied. "And it's his twin sister." Jack frowned sympathetically as Kyle added, "I think Kurt's taking it just as hard." He motioned to the edge of the group from where Kurt was filming them. "Zeke has been his little production assistant for the last month or two. It's like he just lost his little brother.

Everyone glanced over at Kurt, but he remained focused on his camera and refused to look up.

"So, what should we do?" Tavi asked.

Jack cleared his throat uncomfortably. "First of all, I know that this isn't what we're here to talk about, but it's about your friend, Byron."

Tavi and his friends exchanged worried glances. "What about him?"

"He and his friends were trying to sell pills around here today. When I woke up this morning, I caught him trying to convince a couple of eight year olds that it would make them feel amazing." He shook his head in disgust. "They're only eight and we just saved them from the bars a couple of weeks ago. What is he thinking?"

Tavi sat there stunned, unable to think of a reply. Derek added, "Yeah. We caught them doing the same thing around our camp yesterday. Momo and I told them to go away and not to come back, but I think they're just going to wait until we're not around."

Pablo responded in a low voice, "We already tried talking to him. What do you want us to do?"

Jack looked him in the eye. "I think we all need to tell him together that either they stop doing it or they have to leave."

Tavi felt the need to defend Byron. "I'm sure he doesn't realize that it's dangerous or that we don't want him doing it. He'll stop. I'm sure of it."

"And if he doesn't?" Momo asked.

"Then I guess he has to leave."

"And what if he comes back?" Jack asked softly.

Derek stood up and looked around the council as he explained, "Yeah. Stealing from boujies isn't the best thing we could do, but if the cops hear that we're selling drugs down here, then they will come down here and destroy us. I saw one of Byron's friends selling some weed to a couple of those college students. We don't need that."

Tavi shook his head, not wanting to believe what they were saying. "Fine. What do we do if they don't listen and they come back?"

"We have to treat them like an enemy then," Momo said. "And attack."

Tavi looked at his friends for help. Pablo, Chloe, Kurt, and Kyle had all known Byron for longer than Tavi had, but none of them would make eye contact with him at that moment. He realized that they agreed with what the others were saying.

"Fine. Let's do it after this meeting then. All of us together."

Jack nodded. "I'm sorry about that. About what happened last night…"

"We need to be more careful," Momo said.

"How? They had seven policemen with them."

Momo shrugged. "Then we go out in groups of fifteen. Or if we are out rescuing a kid from the bars, we have a larger group waiting to meet us as soon as we get away."

Jack looked around and waited for someone to respond. When no one said anything, he rebutted, "I don't think people will want to walk around in such large groups. It'll make us stand out too much. We'll look like scary gangs of children."

Momo shrugged as Derek answered for him, "Then people can take that risk if they don't want to. We can't fight back directly. All we can do is try to stay safe."

Tavi watched as the people around him discussed the problem, but he couldn't stay focused on it. He kept thinking about Byron and imagining how he would respond. He stared at the ground in front of him for the next few minutes, unaware of anything that was going on around him. It was only when Kyle nudged him that he came back to the present and listened as Jack said, "Okay. Let's tell everyone that if they want to be safe, then they should go out in larger groups. Otherwise, we can't guarantee their safety when they leave here." Everyone nodded and murmured in agreement. As people stood up to leave, Tavi caught a glimpse of Byron and two of his new friends as they came down the embankment on Jack's side of the bridge. He hoped in vain that no one else would notice them.

"There he is," Momo said, and everyone turned to watch Byron enter. "Let's go talk to him."

Tavi trailed behind Jack's and Momo's groups as they walked over to confront Byron. He could tell that Jack was looking around for him, but Tavi slid behind Derek and remained invisible. He stepped back out when he heard Jack say, "Hey…um…Byron. Can we talk to you for a second?"

The familiar voice that Tavi knew and loved replied, "What? All of you?" Tavi took another step to his right and was able to look between the people in front of him and see Byron's face.

"Yeah. Uh…It's about the drugs you're selling…"

Byron sighed and exchanged annoyed glances with his friends. "What about it?"

"You were trying to sell to some eight year olds today!"

Byron shrugged indifferently. "Fine. We won't do that anymore. Are you guys happy?" His eyes roamed the small crowd in front of him, and for a couple of heartbeats, his eyes locked onto Tavi's. Tavi couldn't breathe until Byron's eyes flicked towards Momo, who had just stepped forward.

"No. We're not happy. Either stop selling or leave."

Byron laughed in surprise. "What? You can't tell me to do that."

"We can," Jack replied. "We all agree."

"All of you?" Byron raised his voice slightly. "Even Tavi and Pablo and…Chloe, are you back there? And Kurt and Kyle? I don't think they would agree to this."

Tavi felt as if a huge weight were pressing down on him. He knew that it had to be him to respond. Byron was his best friend. He was the one who had let Tavi live with him. He was the one who had introduced him to the library, shown him where to get food, helped him learn about how to live on the streets. He was the one…who was trying to sell drugs to eight year olds. "Yes," Tavi said clearly. "We all agree." He could still see Byron through the spaces in the crowd, and for a second, Byron's unconcerned demeanor cracked, and Tavi could read the sadness and disappointment upon his face.

Please choose the right path, Tavi thought, staring hard at Byron.

Byron's face became a mask of indifference once more and he stared at Tavi as he gave a small, bitter smile. "Fine."

"Fine, what?" Momo asked.

"Fine. We'll leave. Can we grab our stuff first?"

Jack nodded. The crowd split apart as Byron and his friends strode towards their different encampments and quickly packed up anything they had left there. Without looking back, Byron and his friends walked out from under the bridge, never to return.

Chapter 34

The next several days passed without incident. No one saw Byron or his friends, and the police left the children alone. A couple of groups of kids claimed to have seen a police car slowly following them, but they both ran away immediately and nothing ever came of it.

One evening, Kyle suggested to Tavi that they go back and try to rescue that one boy they had let pass by the night they took Frederick. Tavi instantly agreed and asked around to see if anyone wanted to go rescue kids that night. Kurt volunteered to film it, and several others jumped at the chance, and within twenty minutes, they were ready to go.

As they were leaving the bridge, Momo jogged over, carrying his metal pipe. When he caught up with them, Tavi asked, "What's up?"

"I heard you were going to go save a kid tonight. I thought you could use an extra hand."

Tavi nodded. "Good. I've never done one of these with you before."

"You're not going to have another group meet us there?"

"Nah. I don't think there's anything to worry about. I think those cops taking Hector and Zeke was just a random, unlucky incident."

"Really?" Momo asked doubtfully.

"Sure. Nothing else has really happened since then."

Momo didn't respond and they hurried to catch up with the others. Once they were in position, they sat and waited for hours.

"This sucks," Kyle finally whispered. "I don't think they're letting them take kids out of the bar tonight."

"Maybe they're just waiting. We usually hit them earlier than this," Chloe suggested.

Another hour passed, and just when they were ready to give up and go home, a thin man with a bushy mustache stepped out from the bar. He had his arm around a young boy, and he was being escorted by two burly men.

"Shit," Momo whispered.

"Is that the same kid?" Kyle asked uncertainly, studying the little blonde haired child.

Tavi shook his head. "No. The kid we saw was black." He shrugged his shoulders. "Oh well. If we let this kid pass, then we'll have to come back for him next time."

Chloe interrupted, "But what about those men?"

Momo spoke from the shadows. "We wait for them to pass by and then we run up behind them as silently as we can. We hit them both in the knees, take out the customer, grab the boy, and run." The other five children nodded their heads in agreement.

Kurt whispered, "Hey, Momo. I wasn't able to see you on the camera. Could you step forward about six inches and say it again?"

Momo reached out and hit Kurt lightly on his forehead. "Videotape this!" Momo balanced on his toes and then with exaggerated strides, bounded silently after the three men. The other children were right behind him, and before they knew what was happening, both bodyguards were on the ground in pain, and the customer was getting hit across the back.

Tavi grabbed the boy's hand and pulled him along as he sprinted into the street. Without looking back, he ran around the corner to his right, ran straight for about fifty meters, and then cut into an alleyway to his right. Still holding the boy's hand tightly, he waited for his friends to arrive.

"You okay?" he asked the boy.

The boy nodded his head. "That was cool," he said. Tavi smiled, but was starting to worry that his friends weren't showing up.

He tugged on the boy's hand and said, "We have to keep moving. We'll go this way. It's the quickest way home." They walked for fifteen minutes through the alleyways until they had to cross a busy street. Again, Tavi glanced behind him to see if his friends were coming, but they were still nowhere to be seen. He waited until he saw the crosswalk turn green, and then he said, "Let's go. We have to hurry up and cross the street."

Once they got to the other side, Tavi looked around in confusion. He didn't recognize any of the stores and wondered if he had taken the wrong route. He knew in which direction the bridge lay and without hesitating any longer, he began walking.

After a couple of minutes, he began to feel antsy about being so exposed on a main street. He noticed an alleyway up ahead that he would use to cut over to a less busy street when suddenly, out of the corner of his eye, he sensed a car pulling to a stop at the curb. The doors opened, and he heard someone say, "We found them."

Tavi gripped the boy's hand as tight as he could and shouted, "Run!" He glanced back and saw two policemen hop out of their car and give chase. He had a good lead when they entered the alleyway, but the boy kept stumbling and wasn't able to keep up. Tavi was half-dragging and half-carrying the boy and the policemen easily caught up to them when they were only halfway down the alley.

"You can't escape, kid. We both ran track in high school," said the nearest police officer. "Just let Bobby go and put your hands against the wall." Tavi stood there defeated. His shoulders were slouched and he stared angrily at the ground, still gripping the boy's hand.

"Your name's Bobby?" he asked. The second policeman walked behind them and put his hands on their shoulders as he tried to separate them.

"Yeah," the boy said quietly. He squeezed Tavi's hand even tighter as the policeman attempted to pull their arms apart. Tavi couldn't stop thinking about what was going to happen to him. He was going to die.

"Let go!" the policeman demanded crossly.

"Man, did you guys get lost or what!"

Tavi spun around and saw Kyle, Chloe, and another friend approaching from their right. "Kyle!" Tavi shouted happily. The nearest policeman grabbed Tavi and Bobby and yanked them towards him as the other police officer stepped closer to them.

"Stay back! You are interfering with…"

"Official police business," interrupted a voice from nearby. "We've heard that one before." Tavi looked behind him and saw Momo with two other kids walking towards them as Kurt filmed everything from the entrance to the alleyway.

"You again," one of the policemen said to Momo. "And that stupid kid with the camera."

"Leave us the fuck alone!" Momo warned. He approached to within ten feet as Kyle's group rapidly closed from the other side. They all had their metal pipes out.

"Let them go," the policeman said to his buddy. He stepped back and said softly to Momo, "We're going to get you." He looked at Kurt who was slowly walking towards them. "And that little asshole with his camera." He tried to walk around Momo and the other two, but Momo stepped in front of him.

"Kurt! Hurry up and get behind us." Kurt realized the danger he'd be in if he was at the end of the alley by himself, and sprinted to where Momo was. When he was safely behind Momo, he turned his camera back on, and Momo said, "Now you may go."

The other officer clenched his fists. "You little punk…"

"Oh! You're Officer Terriss, aren't you?" Kurt said loudly. "And your friend is Officer Watson." He looked up from the camera and smiled at the officers. "I think it's always good to know each other's names."

"Let's go," Officer Terriss said to his partner. They strolled down the alleyway and turned the corner without looking back.

"Where were you guys?" Tavi asked.

"Where were you?" Kyle retorted. "We said to cross the street, turn right, and then meet at the end of the first alley. Even Kurt was able to find us."

Kurt nodded his head as he put away his camera. "It's true."

Tavi gave an embarrassed grin as they began walking home. "Um…sorry. I thought it was go right, turn right in the next alley, and then cross the street later on. At least it all worked out."

Momo gave him a serious look. "Yeah. Except for those cops."

"Well…" Tavi shrugged his shoulders. "At least nothing bad happened. Thanks for saving us."

"You're welcome," Momo said stiffly. The others laughed and imitated his stern way of speaking the rest of the way home. By the time they got to the bridge, even Momo had a smile on his face.

Two days later, Tavi took Bobby to the bus station. He had been so excited when they told him that he could go home, and after his last experience with Frederick, Tavi wanted to enjoy a happy reunion again.

They had gotten to the station early and after Tavi bought their tickets, he realized that they still had an hour wait. He looked around for a place to sit and led Bobby over to an empty bench. After thirty minutes, Tavi felt his right leg falling asleep and he stood up to get the blood flowing again. He casually looked around as he wiggled his leg and almost collapsed in shock when he saw Yuri standing close behind him.

"Hello, Tavi," Yuri said in a low voice.

Tavi looked around and saw a couple of men staring at him. They each took a step forward when they saw him notice them.

"Hey, Yuri," Tavi said, unable to keep the panic out of his voice. "What are you doing here?"

"We've heard that you sometimes take the boys home who you steal from the bars. We got lucky and one of our people saw you here today. They called us and here we are."

Tavi swallowed and looked around again. He saw two more men spread out near Yuri.

"Do you know much trouble you're causing? A lot of customers are staying away because of what you and your friends are doing." Yuri raised his arm to cough into it and was overcome for a few seconds by the severity of it. Spitting a wad of phlegm on the floor, he added, "And some of the boys are getting rebellious and trying to fight back."

"Really?" Tavi asked with interest.

"Well, they were. And then we caught Hector and Zeke and now the other boys have realized what happens to boys who run away."

Tavi looked around again. The men were slowly moving closer. "What did you do to them?" he asked, not wanting to hear the answer.

Yuri shrugged. "Broken arms. Broken feet. Burns. Oh…and they both have to be dressed as girls – at all times."

Tavi looked at Yuri in disgust. "What is wrong with you?"

Yuri bent over as he was wracked by another fit of coughing. "You know I have to take you back. And Bobby's bar wants him back as well."

"Yuri…please…"

Yuri glanced at the men around them. They were still too far away to hear what was being said. "Tavi, it's out of my hands. These men won't do what I say. And I've tried to protect Zeke and Hector. Because of me, they weren't killed. But there's not much that I can do."

"And what will you do when they try to kill me?"

"I would do what I could, but that would be out of my hands too."

For the second time in two days, Tavi felt trapped. He wanted to ask Yuri to come with him again and to help him escape, but as he looked at the men who had them surrounded and he saw the look of resignation on Yuri's face, he knew that he had no chance.

"Hi Yuri."

Tavi looked around in surprise and found Pablo and Kyle emerging from the crowded station. Yuri's face was a blank mask as he glanced at his men. "Pablo. Kyle. It won't work. We have too many men."

"We will see," Kyle said. He whispered to Tavi, "Run, now!"

Tavi hesitated for only a moment and then he dashed away from Yuri. Pablo and Kyle were right behind him and the three of them had Bobby in between them. There was violent movement on both sides of Tavi, and he realized that he had overlooked a couple of Yuri's men. Six of them had them surrounded and they rudely shoved their way through the crowds until they were only a few feet away.

"What now?" Tavi asked Kyle. Kyle pointed towards the stairs that led to the upper waiting area, and Tavi was surprised to see Kurt standing there, filming the whole thing. Kurt waved his hand and Tavi raised his hand uncertainly. "That's it?"

"Watch," Kyle said, as the men reached out to grab them.

Suddenly, people throughout the station started shouting and cursing. The first one he saw was Momo. Tavi looked around wildly, and children appeared from every direction. Without warning, they swarmed towards the men and attacked them with metal pipes. Tavi learned later that eighteen children had volunteered to escort him and Bobby to the bus station to make sure that nothing happened to them, but he'd been unaware that anyone had followed them.

Two of the men dropped to the ground in pain as soon as they were hit. The other four turned and started fighting back, and screams filled the air as the crowd of people fled from the fight. Within moments, the only people in the center of the terminal were the children and the men. Tavi turned and searched for Yuri. He hadn't moved.

Clasping Bobby's hand, Tavi walked towards Yuri as if he were in a dream. The sounds of fighting faded and he studied Yuri's face. He looked thinner than Tavi had ever seen him, and his face had an unhealthy pallor. He approached to within two paces of him.

Yuri gave him a small smile. "I didn't expect this."

"Neither did I." They stared at each other for several moments. Finally, Tavi said, "Please come with us. You could do so much good."

Yuri let his eyes wander over the battle, where five out of the six men were lying on the ground unconscious. "I can't," he said. "I gave Vikram my word."

"But you're doing terrible things!"

"I'm doing my best to make them not as terrible." He looked around and saw people talking on their cell phones. "You need to get out of here, Tavi. The police will be here soon."

Tavi's friends had had the same thought. Momo ran over and pulled Tavi away, and they ran out through the rear exit of the police station. Tavi glanced back as he ran through the doorway only to discover that Yuri had already vanished. The six men lay alone in the center of the room, unconscious and bleeding profusely.

Chapter 35

Laura checked the traffic in front of her and realized that she wouldn't be able to escape from this traffic jam anytime soon. The cars were inching forward every few minutes and the line of cars was bumper to bumper for as far as she could see.

Annoyed, she watched the cars going in the other direction zoom past her, and she wished for the hundredth time in as many days that she didn't have to work to this hour every day. It was just another thing she could blame on her husband.

She thought about her visit to the prison the previous Sunday and worried again about the future. Javier had lost a lot of his bulk and seemed to be aging quickly. His once black beard was now streaked with gray and each time she saw him, she was dismayed at how quickly he was deteriorating in prison.

As soon as he had walked into the room assigned to them, he looked around and asked hopefully, "Did Billy and Jasmine come?"

Laura had busied herself with unpacking the lunch she had brought and shook her head. "No. Billy has a baseball game and Jasmine has a riding lesson."

"Riding lesson? She could've skipped it."

Laura had just shrugged. The truth was that Billy was home watching television and neither of the children wanted to visit their father in prison anymore. She was tired of arguing with them about it. Jasmine always ended up crying and complaining about the smell at the prison, and Billy would scream at her that he didn't want to have anything to do with their father. She had been trying to be understanding and treat him with compassion ever since she had learned about what Tom had done to him, but it was getting more and more difficult. She was more sure than ever that she would probably have to force Billy to go and talk with a professional psychologist about what had happened to him.

It was just another thing that she had to discuss with Javier.

Both of them had just picked at their lunches as she shared his family's life with him. His eyes had sparkled with pride when he heard about Jasmine winning her riding competition. He had been disappointed that Billy wasn't a starting pitcher anymore, but Laura hadn't had the heart to tell him that Billy seemed to have lost all interest in baseball. She wasn't sure if it was just a teenager phase or if it was related to what he had gone through, but it was just one more thing that she didn't know how to handle.

"There are some things we need to talk about."

"Like what?"

"First of all, money. We've been cutting back, but still, with the house payments, and the cars, and the school fees, and everything else, my salary isn't enough to cover everything."

"What about the money I set aside for you in the bank? Haven't you talked to my accountant?"

"Yes," Laura said slowly. "We've used part of that money already, but...where did it come from? Why didn't I know about this money that you were setting aside?"

Javier shrugged. "It was just an emergency fund that I set up. I put money in there each week and it grew into that."

"Well, it's not enough. Jenny says that Jasmine is getting too big for Puppy and that she needs a new horse."

"She's been saying that for months."

Laura sighed. "And Jasmine has been growing for months. I don't think you realize how tall she is getting."

"That's because you never bring her to visit!" Javier retorted.

She doesn't want to come, Laura's mind shouted. Instead, she said, "Fine. I'll change her lessons for next week. But for now, what should we do about a new horse? I can't afford it."

"Just use the money I left in the bank."

The anger that was always simmering inside of Laura these days exploded. "That money is almost fucking gone! Stop talking about the money you left in the bank."

Javier froze and stared at his wife warily. "Fine. Do you have any suggestions?"

"I want to sell the land that you bought where we keep Puppy."

"What? No!"

"It's so much land and we have it just so Jasmine can ride her horse around it four times a week? It's a huge waste of money."

"Then what will Jasmine do?" Javier asked angrily.

"She can take lessons like other kids do."

"Well, I don't agree with this decision."

Laura snapped back, "Then you shouldn't have killed that man." She raised her hand to her mouth in shock and watched as Javier's expression changed from surprise to hurt. "I'm so sorry," she whispered. "I didn't mean it." She reached across the table to hold his hands but he stood up from the table and took a step back.

His voice was cold and his face showed no emotion. "Is there anything else you wanted to discuss today?"

"Javier..." Laura said, her heart breaking as tears rolled down her face.

His face relaxed and she could see how sad he truly was. He stepped around the table and she threw herself into his arms. They clung to each other, afraid to let go, and Laura's mind went blank as she inhaled his scent and felt secure once again in her husband's strong embrace.

After an endless amount of time, Javier whispered, "I am so sorry, Laura. Just do whatever you think is best for our family."

She felt the tears falling from her eyes and she pressed her face into his chest. "Please come back to us. We really need you."

She didn't know how long they stayed like that, but all too soon, there was a knock on the door and Javier had to leave her again.

Laura felt miserable remembering it and she honked her horn in frustration. All around her, other cars sang out in agreement and the sound of their horns filled the air. To her surprise, the line of cars immediately moved forward. She shifted her car into first gear and lightly stepped on the gas. After ten feet, they stopped moving again. Laura looked to her left and right and saw the same red sports car and the same green SUV that had been right beside her for the past thirty minutes.

Noticing that day's newspaper on the floor of her car, she reached down to pick it up. The amount of excitement that she felt at having a newspaper to read made Laura laugh aloud. She made a tsking sound as she read the headline, "Teen Gang Attacks Bus Station," and the sub-headline which said, "Angry teens leave six men unconscious." The article reported that a huge gang of teenagers had invaded the Central Bus Terminal and then randomly attacked and robbed six innocent men. She thought about how Billy had mentioned that a few of his friends had gotten mugged by groups of children and she hoped that the police would do something about them soon. She studied the photo of the bus station which showed a number of children surrounding each man and she shook her head and tsked again in disapproval.

She moved on to the next story, and by the time she finished the paper, she had managed to advance half a mile and could see the end of the traffic jam ahead. Tossing the paper into the back of her car, she concentrated on the traffic ahead of her and idly wondered what they should have for dinner.

As Laura walked through the kitchen door, she stopped in surprised when she saw a woman's purse sitting on her kitchen table. She followed the sounds coming from the television and found Jasmine and Jenny sitting on the sofa watching a cartoon.

"Hi, Mommy," Jasmine said, her attention focused on the show she was watching.

"Oh, hey, Laura," Jenny said, standing up to greet her.

"Hi, Jenny. Is there anything wrong?"

"No. But Billy wasn't home yet and I didn't want to leave Jasmine alone and so I decided to wait with her."

"Thank you," Laura said with smile. "I really appreciate it. I'm sorry for the trouble. I guess Billy got held up at school or something."

"It was no trouble," Jenny reassured her. She followed Laura into the kitchen, and as she picked up her purse, Jenny asked, "Have you thought any more about what we talked about before? About getting a new horse for Jasmine?" Laura hesitated and Jenny said quickly, "There's no rush. I mean, I know that things must be difficult for you now. It would just be a shame if Jasmine had to give up riding. She's so talented."

"Well…" Laura considered telling her about her plan to get rid of the property and have Jasmine attend a riding academy, but that would mean that Jenny would lose her position and Laura didn't want to deal with that at the moment. "I spoke with Javier a couple of days ago and we discussed several options. I'll let you know as soon as we make up our minds."

"Cool," Jenny exclaimed. Laura walked with her to the front door and Jenny called out, "Bye, Jasmine. See you Thursday!"

"Bye, Ms. Jenny!"

"Again, thank you so much for everything you've done. If you didn't pick Jasmine up at school twice a week, I don't know how I would be able to manage."

"It's my pleasure." Jenny smiled and walked out the front door. "Have a great evening!"

"You too." Laura watched her jog towards her car and then she headed into the kitchen to make dinner. "How's ravioli sound for dinner?" Laura asked as she passed by the living room.

"Yummy!"

Laura laughed and took a quick detour to give Jasmine a kiss on her head. "How was school today?"

Jasmine moved her head so that she could see the television. "Good."

"Fine. Enjoy your show. We'll eat when Billy gets home." Just then, the front door slammed open and shut and she hurried to the foyer. "Billy?" she called out.

She heard a grunt in response and peeked around the corner. Billy was leaning on his arm against the wall and was slowly kicking off his shoes. Feeling a sense of relief, she stepped forward and asked, "Why were you late today?"

Billy turned to face her and she gasped in surprise. It was his bloody lip that held her attention, but she also noticed the ripped t-shirt and the bruise that was forming beside his left eye. His shirt and face were covered in dirt. But she couldn't stop staring at the fresh blood that was trickling down from his lip.

"What happened?!?"

Billy dropped his head and muttered, "I got jumped by a bunch of kids. They took my bag and my blazer and everything I had in my pockets. I tried to fight back but there were too many of them."

"Oh, Billy!" Laura rushed forward and wrapped her arms around her son, but he just stood there stiffly as if she wasn't even there. "I thought you weren't going to walk home alone anymore. I thought we agreed that…"

"I wasn't alone!" Billy shouted. "I was with Abu and Crixus. There were like twelve kids. They just appeared out of nowhere and surrounded us." He looked up at his mother with tears in his eyes. "They took my phone. And they just kept hitting me and calling me 'boujie'."

"Come on," Laura said and led him towards the kitchen. "Let's clean your face off and put some ice on your eye." Laura felt a cold anger building up inside of her. She thought of the article she had read about the innocent men who had been beaten and robbed, and she swore to herself that she would do everything in her power to make the authorities deal with this gang that had attacked her little boy.

Chapter 36

Tavi sat uncomfortably in his chair, his gaze flicking from Bobby, who was doing a video interview with Kurt, to June and Jaime, who were sitting on either side of him, waiting for him to continue. His responsibilities were becoming overwhelming and he didn't know if he would be able to find the right solutions.

"You can't stop now!" Kyle exclaimed from ten feet away.

Tavi hadn't known that anyone else was listening. A second later, he jumped in surprise when Momo spoke directly behind him. "Yeah. Finish reading the book. I've never heard this story before."

"Where did you come from?" Tavi asked, turning his head to look at Momo. June leaped out of her chair with a big smile on her face and clambered into Momo's lap.

"I've been here since you read the part where they went into the woods," Momo said, giving June a squeeze. "And now we all want you to finish, right?" he asked June, who nodded her head emphatically.

Tavi laughed. "When did you two become so close?"

Momo smiled, looking content for the first time since Tavi had met him. "I've been helping Chloe watch them when you guys are gone." He shrugged and squeezed June tight until she giggled and gasped for help. "She reminds me of my little sister," he said fondly. His face grew stern and he relaxed his grip on June. "Now finish reading the story!"

Glancing around nervously at the large group of kids now listening, Tavi finished the story with as much pizzazz as he could.

Later that night as Tavi sat around the fire with Kyle, Pablo, and Kurt, he finally voiced the thoughts that had been weighing on his mind for the last two weeks. "What am I going to do with them?" he asked softly. "We can't take care of little kids. We can barely take care of ourselves."

Pablo glanced over to where June and Jaime were snuggled up against Frederick. He shook his head in concern. "I don't know. But we have to do something."

"Oh!" Kyle yelped loudly. He quickly covered his mouth with his hand and looked around guiltily. Seeing that no one was disturbed, he whispered, "We saw Pastor Mike today. He's actually heard about you, Tavi, and wants to meet you."

Kurt nodded his head in agreement. "Yeah. He couldn't stop asking if we knew you."

Tavi shrugged. "What does that have to do with June and Jaime?"

"He has a pretty big church," Kyle replied quietly. "Maybe he will know of a place where they can go or someone who will take them in. To be honest, an orphanage would probably be better for them than growing up under this bridge."

Tavi stared at the fire and tried to grab ahold of the thoughts that were whirling through his brain. He felt like there was something on the tip of brain that he couldn't remember, but Pablo broke his concentration and said, "I think it's worth a try. I haven't been back since I went there with Yuri. It'd be nice to see Pastor Mike again."

"Okay," Tavi conceded. "Tomorrow morning, then?"

"Yeah." Kyle said. Pablo and Kurt stood up and made their way to their bedding. Kyle's face softened as he stared at the two young children again, and he said, "I'm sure Chloe won't mind watching them while we're gone."

Tavi nodded his head in exhaustion and climbed into the blankets that were right behind his chair. His eyes closed as soon as his head touched the ground. "Good night, guys," he murmured.

"Good night!"

The next morning, after making sure that Chloe was ready to watch June and Jaime, the four boys set off to meet Pastor Mike. They went to the nearest train station, and after only a couple of stops, they got off and headed to the church.

"You can see it from here," Kurt said as they walked down the steps from the station. He pointed at a cross that was slightly sticking up from the surrounding buildings a few blocks away. "See?"

Tavi nodded his head and looked around. "I've been in this area plenty of times, but I'd forgotten that your Pastor Mike lived around here too."

"Yeah. It was always a good place to run to if you needed some help or anything like that." Pablo pointed to a spot across from the street from them in the direction they were heading. "That's where the police grabbed me and Yuri."

The others quietly studied the street. "That's pretty close to the church," Kyle said. "Too bad you didn't have the chance to run there."

"Yep," Pablo agreed. He cleared his throat and changed the subject. "Does Pastor Mike still have that annoying, whiny assistant? What was his name – Qbert?"

"Yah. Cuthbert," Kurt replied. "He's a douchebag. You should see the look on his face whenever we walk in."

Kyle laughed and added, "His face wrinkles up and he acts like we're the dirtiest people he's ever seen."

"That's him," Pablo said with a smile. "Man, I did not like guy."

"Is he really that bad?" Tavi asked.

Kurt shrugged. "He's just a douchebag. You'll see when we get there."

They walked for a few more minutes before turning down a small, deserted alley. Kurt and Kyle walked boldly up to a wooden door and pressed a small button which Tavi would never have noticed. The door itself was so old and filthy that it blended in with the surrounding bricks and would have normally been unnoticeable.

While they waited for someone to open the door, Kyle explained, "This is the back door which the kids use. The front of the church is huge, but we're not supposed to go there unless it's an emergency." He was interrupted by the sound of a lock being released, and then the door swung open quietly on well-oiled hinges.

Tavi stared at the man who had opened the door. He didn't at all resemble the image that Tavi had created in his mind for Pastor Mike. This man was in his early twenties, and he was very pallid and overweight and his skin had a slight sheen to it. The pale blue eyes flicked from face to face without emotion and finally came to rest upon Kyle.

"What do you want?" he said in surprisingly high-pitched voice.

"We're here to see Pastor Mike," Kyle replied. Tavi could tell by the tone of his voice that Kyle was trying to control his irritation.

"You saw him yesterday."

"Come on, Cuthbert," Kurt said as Kyle bit his lip in anger. "He asked us to come back. He wanted to meet our friend."

Cuthbert turned his gaze to Tavi and Pablo. His forehead wrinkled in confusion as he stared at Pablo. "Wait. Aren't you…?"

"Pablo. You don't remember me?"

Cuthbert's eyes widened in surprise. "I heard that you had left the city." He flashed a smile at Pablo which didn't reach his eyes. "Welcome back." He looked at Kurt and Kyle. "I guess you can come in. Pastor Mike may have a couple of minutes he can spare for…" His nose wrinkled in disgust and the tone of his voice changed as he said, "….you boys."

Kurt shot a glance at Tavi and whispered so that only he could hear. "You see – douchebag."

Cuthbert stepped back and allowed the boys to enter the narrow hallway beyond him. After Tavi stepped through the door, Cuthbert pulled it shut and locked it with his key. Tavi noticed Kurt and Kyle giving each other strange looks as Cuthbert walked past them so that he could lead them further into the church.

"What?" Tavi whispered to Kurt.

Kurt shrugged. "He never locks the door. It's just weird."

The boys followed Cuthbert through several dim hallways until they entered a brightly lit waiting room. There were closed doors on the other three walls, but Cuthbert just led them into the center of the room and had them wait there while he disappeared through the door on their left.

"Can't we sit down?" Pablo asked, pointing to the chairs that were spread throughout the room.

Kurt and Kyle glanced at each other and shook their heads. "No. Cuthbert doesn't like it," Kyle said.

Tavi looked at Pablo and snorted derisively. "Who cares what Cuthbert likes? These look comfortable and I'm tired." Tavi walked over to the fattest, largest chair and plopped down into it. Pablo immediately sat down in the chair nearest him, and Kurt and Kyle slowly followed their lead. Tavi picked up a magazine from the table next to his chair and began flipping through it. "You see? Isn't this better?" he asked.

Kurt and Kyle nodded nervously and glanced at the door that Cuthbert had disappeared through while Pablo closed his eyes and leaned his head back against his chair. The only sounds for the next ten minutes were the occasional flipping of a page from Tavi's magazine and the ticking of the clock on the wall.

Finally, the door opened up and Cuthbert walked out. Kurt and Kyle quickly slid off of their chairs and stood next to them. Pablo opened his left eye, saw that it was only Cuthbert, and then lazily closed it again. Tavi glanced up but then turned his attention back to his magazine.

"What did I tell you about sitting on the furniture?!?" Cuthbert hissed at Kurt and Kyle. "This is the last time I'm going to let you in."

"We tried telling them," Kurt argued. "You try to make Pablo and Tavi do something."

"It's not my job to control your friends," Cuthbert replied. "And besides..." He trailed off and looked hard at Kurt. "Did you say Tavi?"

"Yeah." Kurt point at Tavi. "That's him."

Tavi felt a sinking sensation in the pit of his stomach when Cuthbert looked at him again. He waited for him to say something, but Cuthbert just gave a small smile and turned his attention back to Kurt and Kyle. "Anyway, let's go. Pastor Mike will see you now." Tavi and Pablo hopped down from their chairs and followed them through the door. He didn't know why, but every nerve in his body was screaming that he was in danger, and he walked cautiously behind the others, trying to stay as far away from Cuthbert as possible.

Cuthbert led them through another smaller waiting room where a huge desk dominated the room. A door on the far side of the room led into an office, and Tavi could see a man sitting at a desk. Cuthbert looked back before they reached the office and warned quietly, "He only has a few minutes to spare for you. Make sure you don't wear him out." Without waiting for a response, he spun around and walked through the door.

"Pastor Mike," Cuthbert said respectfully as the boys filed into the room. He motioned towards Kurt and Kyle with a frown on his face. "These two are back again." He then glanced at Tavi and Pablo and his eyes glimmered with an emotion Tavi couldn't understand. "And they brought a couple of friends."

Pastor Mike looked up with a smile. "Kurt! Kyle!" As he stood up and hurried around the desk to greet them, Tavi realized he had never met anyone who seemed so….good, was the only word he could think of to describe Pastor Mike. He was in his late thirties, and his bright, intelligent eyes and huge smile filled the room with his spirit. He warmly shook Kurt and Kyle's hands in greeting, and Tavi could see why they enjoyed visiting him. The man seemed to radiate happiness and comfortableness and Tavi was anxious to make a good impression.

"And this is…" Cuthbert said as he motioned towards Pablo.

"Pablo!" Pastor Mike shook Pablo's outstretched hand and pulled him in for a hug. "It's been so long. I always wondered what happened to you and Chloe and Yuri and why you guys never came back."

Pablo was at a loss for words. "I…um…I'm sorry."

Pastor Mike laughed as he stepped back, holding Pablo by his shoulders. "Don't apologize. I'm just happy to see that you're alright. How are Chloe and Yuri?"

"Chloe is good. She's actually back at our place right now. Yuri is…" Pablo glanced at Tavi for help. "Um….Yuri…"

"Yuri got caught again," Tavi said quietly.

Pastor Mike turned his attention to Tavi and studied him carefully. "Well, I am truly sorry to hear that. If you know where he was taken, maybe there's something I could do to help." When Tavi just shrugged his shoulders, Pastor Mike held out his hand and said, "My name is Pastor Mike. Some people might call me P. Mike. And you are…?"

Tavi reached out and shook his hand firmly. "I'm Tavi."

Without letting go of his hand, Pastor Mike put his other hand on Tavi's elbow and practically dragged him over to Cuthbert. "Cuthbert, have I mentioned Tavi to you before?"

Cuthbert gave Pastor Mike a charming smile. "No, sir. Not yet!"

"I have heard so many good things about what this boy and his friends are trying to do that I asked Kurt and Kyle if I could meet him." He let go of Tavi's hand and put his arm around his shoulders. "If every person in our church tried to do a tenth of what these children are doing, then we would be able to solve so many of the problems that are plaguing our city."

"That's wonderful," Cuthbert said, his grin becoming more forced. "I'd love to hear more, but I need to go make some phone calls and do some work. Your next appointment is in twenty minutes, and so…"

"Could you call them and see if we can push it back a bit?" Pastor Mike asked. "There's a lot that we need to talk about."

"Uh…yeah. I'll do my best." Cuthbert gave Tavi one last glance and then backed out of the office, shutting the door behind him.

"Have a seat, boys," Pastor Mike commanded. "Do you want anything to drink?"

"Coke," Kurt and Kyle said in unison. Pablo and Tavi nodded in agreement as they sat down on a nearby sofa.

"Okay." Pastor Mike went behind his desk and opened up a mini-refrigerator. He pulled out four cokes and set them on his desk. "Kurt, Kyle. Could you guys slide your chairs over to where Pablo and Tavi are sitting? And I'll bring my chair around and we can all sit there."

They spent the next hour talking about their lives with Pastor Mike. Tavi had never met an adult who was so skilled at getting people to talk, and he and the others were constantly cutting each other off as they tried to tell all of the stories that kept popping up from their subconscious minds. After a short lull where the four boys just sat quietly together, caught up in the maelstrom of memories they had evoked, Pastor Mike cleared his throat and said softly, "You boys have no idea how amazing you are."

The boys looked up at him, their eyes shining with emotion, as he continued. "I will do everything I can to help you. I knew it was bad out there, but…" Pastor Mike shrugged as if confused. "Besides Kurt and Kyle, half of the boys don't return more than once or twice. But now that you tell me how many children there are out there who are lost and alone right now, I have to wonder what's happening to them. I always believed that they found help, but as Pablo explained about Yuri, maybe all of those boys aren't getting help. Maybe they're…"

Tavi jumped up and shouted, "That's it!" Everyone stared at him as if he had lost his mind, and Pastor Mike froze with his mouth hanging open. "That's what's been bothering me this whole time." Tavi turned to Pablo. "When you and Yuri got caught, how did the police know exactly where you were?!?"

"What?" Pablo asked.

"You always said that you guys left here, and then you were walking on the street, and the police almost immediately showed up. But how did they know who you were and where you would be?"

"We were just unlucky."

"No. There's no way. The cops who are working for The School House just randomly find you on the street? It's impossible. Someone told them."

The other boys glanced at Pastor Mike. "Who? Me?" He asked in surprise.

Tavi shook his head. "No. I don't believe it's you. But what about the other boys who never came back? What if someone turned them in as well?"

"Who?" Pastor Mike said, but Tavi could see the realization on his face. He shook his head. "No. Cuthbert wouldn't do that. He's been here for almost ten years."

"Did you ever mention my name to him?" Tavi asked.

Pastor Mike shook his head. "No. I don't think so. Why?"

"Because he knew me." Tavi looked at the others and they nodded their head in agreement.

"Yeah," Kurt said. "As soon as I mentioned Tavi's name, he acted like he knew who he was."

Pastor Mike contemplated what Tavi and Kurt had said before standing up and walking over to the door. "We'll see what Cuthbert has to say," he said. He opened up the door and looked into the foyer. He turned back to the boys and said, "That's odd. He's not here."

Kyle leaned his head over and whispered something to Kurt. He nodded in reply and they stood up and walked towards the door. "We'll be back. We just want to check something." Before Pastor Mike could say a word, they both sprinted past him and out the far door.

Pastor Mike shook his head and walked back over to Pablo and Tavi. Sitting down, he said, "I really think you might have jumped to the wrong conclusion. Cuthbert is a good boy."

Tavi shrugged in response. Pablo jerked as if he had just thought of something and said in a low voice, "You haven't told him about June and Jaime yet."

"Ah, right." Tavi explained to Pastor Mike about how he had bought two young children from their mother, and how he was worried that they wouldn't be able to take care of them. After he finished, Pastor Mike sat back in his chair, clearly stunned by what Tavi had told him. "I don't know if I can condone this," he began.

"I had to!" Tavi protested. "If I had left them there, then they would've been beaten and sold...or maybe even dead. No one else cared about them."

"Sometimes we have to trust that God has a plan and that he will do what's necessary."

"What if God is the one who sent Tavi to rescue them?" Pablo asked quietly.

Pastor Mike stared at Pablo, the indecision clear upon his face. After a couple of seconds, he smiled and said, "You're right. Maybe God is using Tavi as his instrument right now."

"I don't care about that," Tavi interrupted. "I need help. I can't take care of two little kids."

Pastor Mike closed his eyes briefly and Tavi wondered if he was saying a prayer. When he opened them, Tavi saw that he had tears in the corners of his eyes. "My wife will probably be surprised, but we've been trying to have children for a while without success. I think we should foster them and raise them until I can find a better solution for them. How about if my wife and I come to the bridge this evening to get them?"

Tavi stared at Pastor Mike in surprise. "Are you serious?"

He nodded his head. "Yes. I wish I could do more, but I believe that this is the right thing for me to do."

He was interrupted by Cuthbert peeking around the edge of the doorway. "Oh….you're still here," Cuthbert said in a disappointed voice.

"Cuthbert, could you come here for a second?" Pastor Mike asked.

"Sure." Cuthbert shuffled over to where they were sitting. "Yes?"

"Have you ever called anyone about any of the boys who have visited here?"

Cuthbert's mouth opened in surprise and the guilt was obvious to everyone. "I…uh…no."

"Oh, Cuthbert," Pastor Mike said sadly.

"I swear, I haven't…" Cuthbert tried to explain but was interrupted by the sound of running feet.

Kurt and Kyle burst through the doorway. "There are two cop cars out front and one out back!" Kyle shouted as Kurt stood breathing heavily next to him. "Tavi was right."

Cuthbert swallowed and stood up straighter. "Yes. I did it. But only they're just filthy animals. They shouldn't be coming here. They shouldn't be allowed to talk to you. You have so many better people who need your help. These things…"

"Cuthbert! Shut your mouth!" Pastor Mike's voice was like a whip. "Do you know how much pain and sorrow you have caused?"

Cuthbert shrugged his shoulders and said clearly, "They don't deserve any better."

"Then get out! And don't ever return. You don't belong here."

Cuthbert's righteous expression crumbled into shock and sadness. "What? This is my home."

"Not any longer. Leave. Now! And may God have mercy on your soul."

Cuthbert opened his mouth to argue, but his gaze fell upon Tavi and Pablo who were standing next to Pastor Mike. He sneered and said, "Fine. With filth like this around, why would I want to stay?" Without another word, he spun on his heels and strode out of the room.

Pastor Mike looked at Tavi and his friends. "Boys…I'm so sorry. I had no idea…"

"It's okay," Pablo said. He was the only one among them who had the right to forgive him. "You didn't know."

"But how are we going to get out of here?" Kurt asked. "If they're watching the front and back doors, and Cuthbert will probably tell them that we're in here…"

"The bell tower," Pastor Mike said instantly.

"What?" Kyle asked.

"The bell tower. Use it to climb to the roof and then you'll see some walkways connecting to other buildings. Use those to get far enough away and then you should be able to find a building with a ladder."

"Those walkways are on the church too?" Pablo asked.

Pastor Mike laughed. "They should be. Who do you think put all of them up there?"

"The church? But why?"

"That, my friends, is a story for another day. I'll show you where the tower is and then I'll go have a chat with the police who are parked in front of my church."

As Tavi and his friends disappeared up the ladder, Pastor Mike reminded them, "Don't forget. My wife and I will come by the bridge this evening to meet June and Jaime."

Their affirmative responses rang through the stone tower and Pastor Mike spun around and stalked towards the front of the church, where he intended to put the fear of God into some men who had volunteered to serve and protect.

Later the same day, Tavi was sitting with June and Jaime and holding Kurt's camcorder so that they could watch some of the funnier videos that the children had recorded. He was just getting ready to show them one of the dancing contests when Chloe ran into their encampment.

"Tavi!" she cried out as she ran to his side. Tavi set the camera down on a nearby chair and stared at Chloe with a growing sense of fear. He had never seen her look so rattled before.

"What is it?"

Tears streamed down her face as she whispered, "It's Byron."

"What? What happened?"

Chloe shook her head in pain and squeezed her eyes shut. "He's been arrested for selling drugs at one of the boujie schools. His friends said he's going to be locked up in juvie until he's eighteen." Tavi glanced over at Jack's camp and saw two of Byron's drug buddies surrounded by a group of kids as they retold the story. He reached over and awkwardly patted Chloe on the back, hesitating in surprise when she buried her face against his shoulder. He gently wrapped his arm around and held her close as she sobbed against him.

He looked down and saw June and Jaime watching with wide eyes. "It's okay," he said, trying to soothe them. "Things will get better." He realized that he wasn't sure if he was trying to reassure them or himself.

When Pastor Mike and his wife came by to pick up June and Jaime, a somber mood had settled over the entire underworld. His wife squatted down next to them and began speaking softly while Pastor Mike took a few steps away from Tavi's camp and studied the children and their lives.

"Is it always like this?" he asked in a hushed voice when Tavi walked over to stand next to him.

"No. We got some bad news today about one of our friends and I think everyone has realized that it could happen to them."

"Do you want to talk about it?"

Tavi shook his head. "No. Not right now." He heard a disruption behind him and grimaced when he saw Jaime crying while his older brother held him. Frederick rocked him back and forth and whispered in his ear as June sprinted away towards Momo's encampment with a defiant scream.

After an hour of good-byes and promises to see each other soon, June and Jaime left the underworld with their new foster family. As they watched them disappear up the embankment, Momo said softly to Tavi, "At least they'll have a chance at a normal life."

Tavi swallowed the lump in his throat and just nodded his head. His gaze met Frederick's and Tavi saw the sorrow in his eyes. He sat next to him and patted him gently on the back as they silently watched the twilight fade into darkness.

Chapter 37

A few days after meeting Pastor Mike, Tavi was walking back to the bridge after successfully escorting Bobby home when several children he knew sprinted past him as if running for their lives. Tavi instinctively started running and glanced behind him to see if anyone was chasing them. All he saw was Derek lumbering after him, cradling his left arm against his chest.

Tavi slowed down and waited for him to catch up. "Why are you guys running? What's wrong with your arm?"

Derek continued to run as fast as he was able, breathing heavily with every step. "We got jumped," he panted. "And my arm is broken."

Tavi stumbled in surprise for a second. Regaining his balance, he asked, "Did everybody make it?"

"No. Momo and Olaf were taken."

This time Tavi stopped and stared behind him. His first instinct was to run back and save Momo from wherever he was, but he knew that if Derek was running away, then it must have been impossible. Sighing, Tavi turned to follow Derek and ran the rest of the way back to the bridge with a heavy heart.

Twenty minutes later, a large crowd of children were gathered around Momo's camp. One of Derek's friends had a first aid kit open and was trying to wrap his arm, but Derek kept flinching in pain. Finally, he roared, "Fuck! Go away!

It's broken." He gently lifted his arm by the elbow and rested it against his chest, hissing in agony.

"What happened?" Tavi asked.

"We were doing the same as always. We were waiting across from Bangarang and then these men just came at us from everywhere. There were at least ten of them. The alleyways were blocked off and they grabbed three of us right away." Derek shook his head in disbelief. "It was like they were waiting for us. But Momo and I freed two of the kids and they ran off. Someone hit my arm with a bat and Momo shoved me and told me to run. The last thing I saw was him trying to save Olaf and then getting beaten by a bunch of grown men." He grew silent at the thought of it. After a few seconds, he said, "And then they started chasing us, but we lost them around the night markets."

"Was Kurt filming you guys?" Kyle asked worriedly. He looked around the underworld and sighed with relief when he saw Kurt filming a couple of kids dancing in Jack's camp.

"No."

"You have to let a doctor fix your arm," Tavi said.

Derek snorted. "Yeah. That'll really work. What kind of a hospital is going to treat a street rat?"

Tavi didn't reply. He knew that Derek was probably right. He stuck his hand in his pocket and unconsciously rubbed his cell phone with his thumb. An idea came to him and he pulled it out and searched through the phone book. When he found Clarence's number, he pressed *call* and stepped away from the other kids.

"What about Momo?" he heard someone ask before Clarence answered.

"Hello?"

"Hi, Clarence. It's Tavi."

"Hey, what's up? Is everything okay?"

"Not really…no. One of my friends got attacked today and he's got a broken arm."

"What?!? That's terrible. Is there anything I can do to help?"

Tavi hesitated. "Um…could you pretend that he's your son and take him to the hospital? I don't know how else we can get it fixed." He held his breath as he waited for Clarence to respond.

He answered almost immediately. "Of course. Where are you guys now?"

"The Hangang Bridge."

"Okay. Let me think…There's a hospital pretty close to where you are. Just go down to Woodson Road and head towards my store. You should see it on your right."

"Really? That's awesome. When can you meet us?"

"Can you guys be there in twenty minutes?"

Tavi glanced at Derek who was listening numbly to everyone talk about Momo. "Yeah. Derek will be glad to get out of here, I think."

"Okay. See you soon."

Tavi shoved his phone back into his pocket and walked up to Derek. Leaning down, he said quietly, "I have a friend who will pretend to be your dad at the hospital. Let's go meet him."

Derek shook his head and looked up in surprise. "Are you serious?"

"Yeah. Come on." Derek stood up awkwardly and explained to everyone where they were going and then he followed Tavi up the embankment to the road.

They walked in silence for the first ten minutes until Derek muttered in a choked-up voice, "We're never going to see them again."

Tavi looked at Derek and turned away quickly when he saw the tears streaming down his face. "You don't know that."

"You didn't see them beating on Momo. And half of those men were cops."

"What? You didn't say that before."

Derek shrugged. "I forgot to mention it. But they're not going to let him go. Trust me."

Tavi didn't know what to say and just trudged beside Derek in silence. When they arrived at the hospital, Clarence was already there. He looked up at the dark-haired boy who towered over him. "This is my son?" he teased with a doubtful expression on his face.

"You're the only one we could call," Tavi said, and something in his voice made Clarence look at them carefully.

"Okay," he said quietly. "Let's do this."

It was much simpler than Tavi had anticipated. Once Clarence filled out the papers and gave them his insurance card, everyone treated them respectfully and the doctor managed to set the broken bones and put a cast on his arm within two hours. As they walked out of the hospital, Tavi said, "Thank you so much, Clarence. Without you…"

"Yeah," Derek added. "You really saved me."

"It was nothing," Clarence said. "Tavi, if anyone ever needs anything like this again, please let me know. I have a couple of friends who I'm sure would be willing to help out as well."

Tavi nodded his head gratefully. "Okay. Again, thank you, Clarence. I'll stop by the store soon."

"Good luck, boys."

"Bye."

As they walked back to the bridge, they only spoke once. "So you don't think we'll see Momo again?" Tavi asked.

Derek was silent for so long that Tavi assumed he wasn't going to answer. "I don't think we'll see him alive," he finally said softly.

They walked the rest of the way to the bridge in silence; each of them alone with their thoughts.

The following day, not many children ventured away from the bridge. Momo had been larger than life and if he could be caught, then the common feeling was that none of them were safe. Tavi and Pablo went for a walk near their old bar. They knew that it was a stupid thing to do, but they were hoping against all odds to catch a glimpse of Momo, and maybe they would find a way to save him.

The streets felt oddly deserted and after wandering around for an hour, they headed back to the bridge. Tavi was overwhelmed by a sense of unease, and the longer they stayed out, the stronger it grew. At one point on the walk home, he found himself walking faster and faster, and then without meaning to, he was soon running as if he were being chased by something. He could see Pablo out of the corner of his eye, and it seemed that he felt the same way.

As they approached the bridge, Pablo suddenly grabbed Tavi's arm and pulled him to a halt. A police car was parked at the edge of the bridge and two officers were climbing into the car. As it drove away, they heard a scream of pure terror.

They sprinted down the embankment on Jack's side of the bridge. When they got to the bottom, there was a huge crowd of children gathered around something. Everywhere he looked, Tavi saw children crying and gasping and covering their faces with their hands. He and Pablo shoved their way through the crowd and stared at the sight before them.

A boy's naked body was lying in the dirt. The face was so badly bruised and beaten as to almost be unrecognizable, but Tavi knew that it was Momo. He couldn't look away and his mind started chanting everything he saw... *bruised face, missing ear, broken arm, missing fingers, shattered knees, burned feet. Bruised face, missing ear, broken arm, missing fingers, shattered knees, burned fee. Bruised face, missing ear, broken arm...*

Tavi finally managed to tear his gaze away and he looked around wildly at the hysterical children. He collapsed to his knees in front of Momo's body and gently touched it with his hands. For an instant, he raised his palms and stared at the blood on his fingertips before burying his face in his hands and letting out an inarticulate scream. The weeping and moans of children filled the air, as Kurt stepped back and silently continued filming the spectacle before him.

Chapter 38

Laura rose nervously to her feet as the door swung open.

"Councilwoman Walsh," she said, extending her hand. "Thank you so much for meeting with me."

"Please – call me Rachel." They briefly shook hands and Rachel motioned for Laura to follow her into her office. "Joan has spoken so highly about you so often that I feel like I've known you for years."

"Well, you know how Joan exaggerates," Laura said with a laugh. She glanced around the spacious office as Rachel led her over to a comfortable sofa near the desk. She was surprised when Rachel grabbed a couple of glasses and filled them herself with water from a nearby pitcher. Rachel handed the glass to Laura and sat beside her on the sofa.

"Before we get into what brought you here, I just want to say how truly sorry I am about what happened with your husband." Laura opened her mouth to reply, but Rachel continued, "I know that you prefer to keep it as quiet as possible, but I remembered hearing about it when it happened, and when you made an appointment with my secretary, I was curious and looked at the official records."

Laura hesitated, unsure of how to respond. "Um…thank you. I mean, it's been tough, but we're managing okay."

Rachel shook her head and her eyes flashed with anger. "To be honest, if anyone ever hurt my son…well, I can't condone what your husband did, but I do understand why he did it. I can't understand anyone who would hurt children in that way." She studied Laura's face and asked softly, "Are things okay with you and your husband?"

To her surprise, Laura felt tears spring to her eyes. She hadn't expected her meeting with the councilwoman to start like this. She quickly blinked them away and replied, "I don't know. He seems like a completely different man these days. I guess it's a blessing that he only received four years for voluntary manslaughter, but when you're actually living those four years day after day with two children, it seems like a lifetime."

Rachel reached over and grabbed Laura's hands. "I'm sorry. Please let me know if there's anything I can ever do to help."

"Actually, that's why I came here today." Laura picked up her glass and took a long sip of water. Setting her glass back down, she said, "It's about my son, Billy."

"The one who…?"

Laura nodded. "Yes. He's been struggling a bit, which I think is only natural, what with all that's happened in his life over the last year. However, a couple of weeks ago, he was walking home from school with a couple of friends and they were attacked by a large group of street kids."

"Is he okay?"

"He wasn't hurt too badly, but all of his stuff was stolen. And this isn't the first time it's happened. Quite a few of his other friends have been attacked as well over the last six months or so. Something has to be done about this."

Rachel was silent for a few seconds as she thought about how to respond. "I understand that no one likes to see their child attacked," she began cautiously, "but I'm not sure if this is something the city should get involved in. Children have scuffles and fights all the time. It's just a part of growing up, I think."

Laura bristled. "This isn't something typical that happens to all children."

"I know it may seem that way, but…"

"Did you not see what happened at the bus station two weeks ago?"

Rachel tilted her head and shook it in negation. "I don't think so. What happened?"

Laura reached into her purse and pulled out a folded up newspaper. She handed it to Rachel and said, "Here. It's the article at the bottom of the page."

Laura watched in silence as Rachel quickly read through the article. When she was finished, she handed the newspaper back to Laura and said, "And you think it's connected?"

"I do. But what finally convinced me was a conversation I overheard between a couple of our summer interns."

"And that was?"

"They were talking about how a large group of street kids is living under the Hangang Bridge and selling electronics and jewelry for really cheap prices. I think if you connect the dots, then it's clear that these children are becoming a menace to our society."

After only a couple of seconds, Rachel said, "Okay."

Laura looked startled. "I'm sorry. What do you mean by 'okay'?"

"I agree with you that there's probably a connection. I will go check it out tomorrow."

"You're just going to go to the bridge and see what's there?" Laura asked.

"Well, yeah. I don't think this is something for the police to deal with. I just want to see what's happening down there and then I'll make a decision."

"I see. Could you let me know what you find out?"

"Of course. I'll have my assistant call you and arrange a meeting after I've learned more. How does that sound?" Rachel asked, rising to her feet.

Laura stood up as well. "I think that sounds fine. Thank you. I look forward to hearing from you." As they walked out of the office and through the large waiting area, Laura wished that she could let Rachel know how much she had eased her mind, and how relieved Laura was after having had a chance to speak with her. When they reached the hallway, Laura held out her hand and simply said, "Thank you so much, Councilwoman Walsh."

Rachel beamed and shook her hand. She watched Laura walk away for a couple of seconds before turning around and heading back into her office.

Chapter 39

The next day, Tavi was sitting by himself in his encampment, staring blankly at the ground in front of him, when he heard someone give a short scream. He jumped to his feet in alarm and saw a woman tumbling down the embankment on his side of the bridge. He was by her side in an instant, and he knelt down and gently touched her shoulder.

"Are you okay, ma'am?" he asked.

Rachel moaned in pain and pushed herself off of the ground. Tavi awkwardly grabbed her arm and helped her stand up. "Stupid heels," Rachel muttered. She leaned her weight on Tavi's shoulder as she bent down and slipped off her shoes. She stuffed them into the large purse she was carrying and tentatively stood up straight, wincing slightly as her left ankle throbbed in pain.

"Thanks," she said. She gazed down at Tavi who was only a few inches shorter than her. "What's your name?"

"Tavi." He tried to stare boldly into her eyes but glanced away after a few seconds. After all of the pain and sorrow he had suffered over the last couple of weeks, he had lost his self-confidence and could barely make eye contact with his friends. After they had found Momo's body, the children had argued about what to do with it. They couldn't leave the corpse where it was, but any suggestions to report the murder were quickly shot down when it was pointed out that they would most likely be blamed for Momo's death.

The arguing lasted for hours. When it was clear that nothing was going to be decided, Tavi and Derek had quietly slipped away, grabbed the children who had known Momo the best, and silently made their way to his body in the dark. Someone had covered it with a blanket. The dim light muted the outline of the body as the children stood in the shadows and quietly said whatever prayers they could remember from their childhoods. When their murmuring subsided, the children gently wrapped the blanket completely around Momo. Struggling mightily, they each gripped an edge of the blanket tightly in their hands and carried and dragged Momo's body to the river's edge. Jack and Tavi, who were in the lead, kept pulling and walking as they waded deeper into the river. When their feet finally lost touch with the bottom, they swam back and pushed the body away from them towards the center of the river. It had already sunk a few inches below the surface of the water, and after pushing it hard one last time with their feet, they slowly swam back to shore.

Within the next few days, another four children had been taken and more and more children were slipping away from the underworld in the hopes that they could find a safer place where they wouldn't be tainted by association with the kids who were living under the Hangang Bridge.

This was the atmosphere Rachel was exposed to when she first discovered the underworld, and she was less than impressed with what she saw.

"Is this all of you?" she asked in confusion as she followed Tavi to his encampment.

Tavi looked around and shrugged. There was a group of kids in Jack's camp, probably watching a movie on one of the laptops they had stolen. Derek and a few of his friends were lounging around their camp. Pablo and the rest of Tavi's friends were out getting food and had gone to check on June and Jaime with Frederick. The rest of the underworld did look a bit empty, but Tavi knew that a lot of the kids were just out doing stuff, and so he replied, "No. Some of our friends are out doing stuff."

"I see," Rachel said. She watched Tavi flop down in one of the chairs which were scattered everywhere throughout their camp. "Can I sit down?" she asked.

Tavi shrugged again. "Sure." He watched as she carefully brushed off a chair before gently lowering herself into it. "What do you want?" he asked her.

"Well, my name is Rachel Walsh, and I am a councilwoman for the city. I just wanted to talk to someone and ask a few questions."

Tavi looked around for anyone else who could talk to her. Sighing audibly, he said, "Do you work with the police?"

"What? No. Well, we both work for the city, but I don't work for the police department. Why?" She gave a small smile and her eyes glinted craftily. "Have you done anything that the police might be interested in?"

Tavi couldn't help himself. He laughed out loud at her lack of subtlety. "No," he said, quickly growing serious again. "But we're having some problems with them."

"Like what?"

They're kidnapping us and they killed Momo, he wanted to shout. But instead he just shook his head and mumbled, "Nothing."

"I see," she said again. "Well, do you mind if I ask you some questions?"

A shrug.

Rachel reached into her purse and pulled out a newspaper. She handed it to Tavi who casually scanned it. "What?" he asked.

"Oh!" Rachel put her hand to her mouth, the chagrin on her face obvious. "I'm sorry. Can you...well, if you can't read, then I can..."

Tavi laughed again and quickly read the headline aloud. "'Teen Gang Attacks Bus Station.' Yes, I can read. Why?"

"Because I've heard that the kids in the article came from this bridge." She hesitated when she noticed that all of Tavi's attention was focused on the article. He finished it quickly – far quicker than she would have expected – and crumpled the newspaper up and tossed it to the ground.

"That's bullshit!" he exclaimed.

"What is?"

"Those men they talk about – the innocent men – they fucking work for those bars and they were there to catch us."

"What bars? Catch who?"

Tavi stared at Rachel in amazement. "What do you mean 'what bars'? The ones where they sell kids for sex!"

Rachel's heart skipped a beat as she inhaled sharply. She raised her hand and said, "Wait a second. I feel like we're not talking about the same thing even though we're speaking the same language. Let me start over. So you WERE part of that teen gang that attacked the people at the bus station?"

Tavi shook his head scornfully. "Who are you again?"

"Like I said – my name is Rachel Walsh and I'm a city councilwoman."

"Then, excuse me, Ms. Walsh, but how can you be so stupid?"

Rachel stared at Tavi for a second in surprise before her face reddened with anger and she stood up. "I came here to find out what's going on…" she began before Tavi interrupted her.

"Then why don't you understand? I was there to help take one of the boys that we had rescued back to his hometown and those men were there to catch me and to take me and him back to the bars where they would kill me. My friends showed up to stop them. If it wasn't for them, I'd be dead right now."

Rachel slowly sat back down, her eyes never leaving Tavi's face. "What bars are you talking about?" she asked again.

Tavi's green eyes glowed with anger. "You're a city councilwoman? Doesn't that mean you run the city? How can you not know about this?"

Rachel said quietly, "Then explain it to me."

Tavi stared at her thoughtfully for a second but was distracted by a group of five children entering the underworld. They called out greetings as they passed by and Tavi noticed the questioning glances they threw at Ms. Walsh. "All of us," Tavi began, pointing to the children in the underworld, "all of the children you see here were kidnapped from their homes and forced to work in bars in this city." Rachel scrutinized the children she could see through a new perspective as Tavi continued. "We had to have sex with different men every night, and the only way to get free was to escape. But if we get caught now, then we will either be beaten or killed." He faltered for a second as he thought about Momo. Staring at the ground, he said softly, "I know for a fact that there is a death sentence on me."

Rachel stared at him uncertainly. "That can't be possible. I'm sure I would know if this was true."

"They killed Momo," Tavi said, almost inaudibly.

"Who was that?" Rachel asked just as quietly.

Tavi looked up and wiped the tears from his eyes. He nodded his head in the direction of Momo's camp. "He was their leader. But they got him and now none of us are safe." He looked at Rachel for a brief second. Her heart broke as the tears streamed down his face amidst the hopelessness and fear. "It's all my fault. It was my idea to join up and rescue the other kids. And now I don't know what to do anymore. I don't want any more of my friends to die." He lowered his head and buried his face in his hands.

Rachel studied him as he silently sobbed in front of her, and as she glanced around the underworld, she realized that he was probably telling the truth. Unsure of what to say next, she was on the verge of rising to her feet when she heard footsteps right behind her.

"Tavi!" A boy about Tavi's age ran past her. He pulled a chair close to Tavi and sat down and wrapped his arm around Tavi's shoulders.

"What did you do?" Rachel stood up and turned around. A group of children had materialized behind her and she noticed that most of them were holding metal pipes in their hands. A young blonde girl with a dirty face repeated, "What did you do to Tavi?"

The boy next to her put his hand on her shoulder and said, "Relax, Chloe. I don't think she's a threat." Rachel realized the boy was actually a couple of inches taller than herself, and she decided he must be one of the older ones. Looking at the rest of the children, she marveled at how young they looked and wondered why they were living under a bridge.

"It's okay," Tavi said, looking up. His face was damp with tears and flushed with emotion. "It's fine, Chloe, Pablo. She's just asking questions."

Some of the children relaxed and gave her cautious smiles, but still more eyed her suspiciously as they made their way to the chairs.

"How are June and Jaime doing, Frederick?" Tavi asked.

One of the boys, a small, fragile looking child with brown hair and huge blue eyes, gave Tavi a brilliant smile and replied, "They're so happy. They have their own rooms and lots of toys." A wistful expression slipped across his face as he said, "It looks like a great place to live. Pastor Mike is really taking care of them."

"Who's Pastor Mike?" Rachel asked abruptly. She hadn't planned on speaking but something compelled her to find out more information.

Rachel noticed how the other children deferred to Tavi and glanced at him before responding. Tavi glanced around at most of the children and she could see a silent conversation happening around her. She tried to follow his gaze, but she couldn't tell who the leaders were or who would decide if she got an answer. After several seconds, Tavi finally said, "He's someone who tries to help kids like us. He adopted Frederick's younger brother and sister because they were too small to stay here."

"Why were they here?" she asked Frederick.

"Tavi bought them," he said with a grin and the other children giggled as if it were an inside joke.

"You what?" she asked Tavi in disbelief.

Tavi sighed. "What do you want?" he asked.

Rachel again studied the children who were sitting around her. They didn't look like violent criminals or druggies or how she imagined gang members would look. They looked like dirty, hungry children who didn't have homes. She searched her heart and thought about why she had wanted to work for the city, and why she was under this bridge in the first place, and then she thought about her own child, Alex, who was the same age as some of these children. "I want to understand what's really happening in my city," she said honestly.

Tavi stared at her for a few moments. His eyes roamed over her face and then he shifted his gaze to the boy sitting on her left. "Kurt, can you give her copies of the videos from when the police first came, the video from the bus station, one of the trips we made to the bars, and the night we found Momo?" He choked up on the last word, but no one else seemed to notice.

Kurt nodded his head and slipped off his backpack. After zipping it open, he pulled out a relatively brand-new, high-tech laptop. He flipped it open and as it powered up, took a memory stick out of a pouch in the backpack, and plugged it into the laptop. Within a few seconds, he had transferred the necessary files and was putting away his laptop. He handed the memory stick to Rachel and said, "Could you give it back when you're done? We don't have enough of them."

Rachel took it from him and carefully slid it into an inside pocket of her purse. "Where did you get that laptop? It looks pretty new."

Kurt smiled and pointed at a group of children who were approaching. "It was a gift from Jack. My old one was too slow and they needed another camera, so I swapped him one of my video cameras and my old laptop for this."

Rachel's brow wrinkled in confusion. "Um…Wait. You mean…?"

Tavi interrupted her before she could ask any more questions. "If you want to talk some more, we will be here for a few more days. Afterwards, we might be gone." The children sitting around them nodded their heads. The group of children who had just arrived with Jack stood behind Tavi and also murmured in agreement.

"Really? Why?"

Tavi shook his head and pointed to her purse. "It's on the videos. If you really want to help, then I'll talk to you again. But it has to be soon."

"Okay. Should I just come back here?"

To her surprise, Tavi pulled a cell phone out of his pocket. "If you want to meet, call me." He read off his number to her and she punched it into her phone. When she was done, all of the children seemed to stand up at the same time and she realized that her meeting was finished.

She stood up and took her shoes out of her purse. The broken heel had snapped completely off and she clumsily put them on and tried to stand normally. Before she could leave, though, one of the boys said, "Wait. Can you give me your shoe for a second?"

"Why?" Rachel bent over to take off her shoe. "Which one?"

"It doesn't matter," he said. He reached out and took the shoe with the broken heel from her. He slipped between the chairs and knelt down in front of a box in the middle of their camp. After a couple of moments, he returned with a pair of sneakers. "Here," he said, handing them to her, along with her shoe. "These should be the same size."

Rachel held up the shoes and studied them. They looked like an almost brand new pair of women's sneakers. "Where did you...?" She paused, knowing that she wouldn't get an answer. "Are you sure you want to give these to me? I know they're quite expensive."

The boy shrugged. "We have too much stuff right now. If we leave, we can't take it all with us anyway."

Rachel sat back down and quickly slid on the sneakers. She sighed in relief at how much more comfortable they were than her heels. When she stood up, the silent children were just staring at her, waiting for her to leave. Suddenly feeling awkward, Rachel slipped her purse over her shoulder and said to Tavi, "I'll watch these videos tonight."

Tavi nodded his head. "Okay."

"Well," Rachel looked around at the crowd of homeless children. "It was....um...nice meeting you."

A couple of children to her left snickered and Rachel flushed in the dim light. She felt better when Tavi said, "I hope we can talk again." Giving him a warm smile, she turned and headed towards the bright afternoon light. When she reached the edge of the bridge, she turned around for one final look, but the dark underworld had been shielded from her by the light from the beautiful afternoon sky.

Chapter 40

As the dawn slowly changed from a dark pink horizon to a brilliant blue sky, Tavi sat on a large rock near the river and watched the tendrils of fog covering the water fade away until only a few wisps remained.

"Coffee?" a voice behind him asked quietly.

Tavi slid over to make room on the rock as Jack sat down next to him. He handed a mug of coffee to Tavi and they sipped in silence, alone in their thoughts, as they communed with the river in front of them, the skies above them, and the wakening city around them. Amidst their lives of noise and filth and action, Tavi and Jack had discovered this sanctuary a month earlier, as a place and time where they could find the momentary peace needed to reflect upon their lives and the incessant problems they faced.

Besides lifting their arms to raise the mugs to their mouths, they remained like statues for the next twenty minutes. Finally, Tavi set his empty mug down between them and said softly, "Thanks. I'll make it tomorrow."

Jack imperceptibly nodded his head and continued staring at the river. He nudged Tavi with his knee and nodded towards a mother duck swimming with several ducklings near the edge of the bank fifty yards downstream. "Look," he whispered. "They're back."

Tavi stared at them eagerly, hoping that they would swim in their direction like they had the previous day. He was fascinated by how cute they were and he wished he could hold one and play with it. But on this day, the mother duck continued swimming away from them and Tavi and Jack each let out a sigh of disappointment when they disappeared amongst a clump of reeds on the far side of the river.

"Do you trust that woman?" Jack asked unexpectedly.

"Who? The one who was here yesterday?"

"Yeah."

Tavi shrugged. "I guess so. She seems to care."

Jack nodded his head, but didn't reply. After a couple of minutes, he glanced back into the underworld and studied it carefully. "You know," he said, turning around to gaze at the river again, "we only have about a hundred kids left."

Tavi nodded. "I know."

"So, what's the plan?"

Tavi shook his head and stood up, his eyes focused on the ground. He picked up a rock and tried skimming it across the river. After the third skip, it hit a wake and flew high into the air before it crashed and sank beneath the water. "We've lost," Tavi said, staring at the disappearing ripples. "No matter what we do, they're just going to keep taking kids or killing us."

Jack watched in silence as Tavi picked up another rock and threw it across the water. This one almost made it across to the other side, and they were both unintentionally holding their breath in excitement as they watched it near the other bank. Jack exhaled and snickered at his own disappointment when it sank ten feet from the opposite side. He stood up and started searching for the perfect rock.

"Do you remember that movie you told us about?" Jack asked, picking up several rocks and tossing them aside after inspecting each one.

"Which one?" Tavi threw another rock into the water.

"The one about the lions and the wildebeests."

A long pause. "Yeah."

"And what happened when the lions jumped on the baby wildebeest and tried to kill it?"

Tavi threw another rock hard into the river. This one only skipped twice before sinking. "The wildebeests came back."

At the edge of the shore, underneath an inch of water, Jack saw it. The perfect skipper. He leaned over carefully to avoid getting his shoes wet and grabbed it. Running his fingers over the edge, he knew it would make it. "And do you remember what you promised us?"

Tavi finally stopped looking for rocks and looked at Jack. "No. What?"

"You said you would lead an army into the bars and we would free every single kid there."

Tavi stared at Jack and the corner of his mouth twitched up. "And?"

"It's time. Before too many more kids leave, we all go at the same time, we go in with our pipes, and we free every single kid we can find."

"And then?"

Jack bent low and threw the rock as hard as he could at an angle across the river. Even before it left his hand, he could feel the perfectness of the rock as it rolled along his finger and flew spinning across the surface of the river. He smiled with pride as it skipped twelve...fourteen...seventeen times before landing on the far shore. "And then we run for our lives. But if we stay here, they're just going to pick us off anyway. If we're going to get caught, let's go out with a bang."

For the first time since Momo had died, Tavi grinned. His eyes sparkled and his white teeth flashed in the sunlight. "Yes!" He excitedly stepped towards Jack and awkwardly hugged him and punched him on the shoulder. "Let's do it! Today."

Jack smiled and bent to pick up his mugs. "Welcome back, Tavi," he said, as they excitedly hurried into the underworld to wake the other children.

That afternoon, Tavi walked with Pablo, Kurt, Kyle, Frederick, Sasha and Chloe through the alleyways as they approached rear entrance of The School House. Ten other small groups were taking their own routes to the meeting points as the children did their best to blend in. Half of them were wearing school uniforms, but the rest of the children were wearing their old clothes. Pablo had pointed out that most of the children they rescued would need clothes to wear, and so Yabu had collected all of the extra clothing which the children had stolen and was waiting near Pastor Mike's church with a couple of his friends.

The plan was to enter the bar through the front and back, quickly disable any adults, free the children, and then meet Yabu and his friends. Tavi gazed down at the shoes he had retrieved from his storage locker in the train station and wiggled his toes comfortably, smiling at the toes that protruded from several holes in the shoes.

Tavi looked up and realized that they were near a familiar alley. "Wait," he said. After looking around the corner to his left cautiously, he quickly led them to a padlocked door with a red circle spray-painted on it. Tavi swung at the padlock with his pipe. "We have to open this," he said. He pounded on it ineffectively two more times before Pablo nudged him aside.

"Let me try," he said. Grunting with effort, Pablo smashed the pipe into the padlock three times before it broke. Tavi looked around anxiously because of the noise and saw a couple of old men peeping out from their doorways.

"Go back inside," he shouted at them as Pablo pulled off the broken padlock and opened the door. The familiar smell of sweat and dirty bodies and fear filled his nose and for a second, Tavi was overwhelmed with the feelings that were associated with it. He leaned weakly against the door as the others entered the room.

"Hey," he heard Pablo say softly.

"How many are there?" Tavi asked.

"Six," Kyle replied.

Tavi took several breaths of fresh air and continued looking in both directions for danger. He heard his friends softly murmuring inside of the room, and within moments, they hurried out with six young boys trailing behind them. Tavi gazed at them with a mixture of pity and envy and wondered if he had looked so small and lost when he had first arrived there. At least they won't have to go through what we did, he thought.

"They can't come with us," Pablo said. "Who wants to take them to Yabu?"

"I will," Frederick said quickly. He had confided to Tavi earlier that he didn't want to fight men who were twice his size, and Tavi didn't blame him for volunteering to escort these children.

Pablo nodded. "Okay. Anybody else?" He looked at Sasha. "Do you want to help him, Sasha?"

Sasha bit her lip and her eyes welled up with tears. "I want to save Hector."

Kyle knelt down in front of Sasha and said softly, "I promise you that I will find your brother. But Frederick will need help taking these kids to Yabu."

Sasha studied Kyle's face as she wiped her eyes. "Okay," she said. "But you promised!"

Kyle nodded. "I promise. If he is anywhere in this building, I'll bring him to you."

"Okay."

"Do you know where to go?" Pablo asked Frederick.

"I do," Sasha said. "Let's go."

The six boys had been blinking their eyes in the afternoon sunlight and following the conversation with confusion on their faces. When Sasha ordered them to follow her, they jumped in surprise and quickly ran after her. Frederick followed behind and within seconds, they had turned the far corner and vanished from sight.

The five children looked at each other with smiles on their faces. Tavi was surprised to find that he didn't feel any nervousness or fear. He just felt ready, and he could tell that his friends felt the same. "Let's do this," he said.

The others grinned and silently followed him as they ran down the alley towards The School House.

Three other groups met them at the back door within a minute of them arriving. Tavi remembered back to when the two women had tried to save them, and he vowed that none of the customers would escape through the back door this time. Tavi pulled out his phone and called Jack.

"Are you guys ready?" he asked as soon as Jack answered.

"Yep. You?"

"Yep. Let's do it in one minute."

"Okay."

Tavi closed his cell phone and slid it into his pocket. Checking one last time to make sure that everyone was ready, Tavi gripped his pipe tightly in his left hand and reached out to open the back door.

He froze when his phone vibrated in his pocket. He exchanged a worried glance with Kyle and quickly held it up to his ear.

"What?"

"Is this Tavi?" a woman's voice asked.

Tavi's mind went blank and he could barely manage to say yes.

"Hi. I met you yesterday. This is Councilwoman Walsh and…"

"I'll call you back!" Tavi closed the phone without waiting for a response and jammed it into his pocket. He shook his head in disbelief at Kyle and said, "It was that woman."

Kyle opened his mouth to respond, but shouting from inside the bar made him freeze. Tavi looked behind him as he yanked the door open and shouted, "Any man you see is an enemy. Take them all down!"

He ran into the dimly lit hallway, the adrenaline pounding in his head, and the next thing he knew he was entering the main bar area. He looked around wildly and quickly recognized the setting. Only five boys were working and there were three regular customers visiting. Juan was behind the bar, and what should have been a calm, relaxing afternoon was demolished as Jack led twenty-five children through the front door.

When Tavi and his friends burst through the curtain which blocked off the rear hallway, two of the customers were running directly towards them while a third customer was on the ground, bleeding and unconscious.

Tavi knew that he would be trampled if he hesitated and so he ran to the right and stopped next to a boy sitting at the bar who looked vaguely familiar. He was looking around in shock and Tavi put his hand on his arm.

"It's okay. We're here to save you."

"What?" the boy stammered, as children continued to flow into the bar. The two men who had been running for the rear exit were quickly clubbed and beaten unconscious and a small group of children ran around the bar and began hitting Juan with their pipes. Tavi opened his mouth to tell them to stop, but then realized that Juan had been a part of the business as well.

"We're getting you out of here," Tavi said. "We're getting all of you out."

"But they'll kill us," the boy said. His eyes widened in recognition and he said, "You're Tavi!"

Tavi grabbed him by the shoulders and said, "Where are the others? The only way to be safe is if we all leave together. What's your name?"

"They're upstairs. I'll show you. My name is Julius."

"Ok." Tavi looked back and saw Jack approaching with his horde following him. "I think we can handle anyone who's upstairs," Tavi said. "Do you want to take your group and go save the kids at Bangarang?"

Jack glanced around and saw how tightly packed the children were. "Sure," he said. He turned around and shouted at the kids behind him, and within seconds, they were running out of The School House.

"Is Yuri here?" Tavi asked Julius urgently.

Julius flinched at the name and shook his head. "No. I haven't seen him."

Tavi turned and spoke to the children nearest him. The ones at the back of the group were gripping their pipes tightly, anxious to do something. "The kids are upstairs. Julius is going to show us. Four children go into each room together because we don't know who might be waiting."

Tavi motioned to Julius and he led them up the stairs. Instead of entering Vikram's office, though, they went down a hallway that Tavi had never noticed. It led to the back of the second floor and it was lined with doors on both sides.

"All of these?" Tavi asked.

Julius nodded his head. "Yeah. But we need to get to the kids in the last room. That's where the bad things happen." Tavi felt a chill run down his spine at Julius's words, but he stopped for a brief second to open up the nearest door on his right. He unbolted the latch and slowly opened the door. The light from the hallway lit up just enough of the room for Tavi to see four boys sleeping on the floor. They looked up blearily as Tavi stepped back and followed Julius down the hallway.

The door at the end of the hallway was directly in front of him, and it was the only one with a padlock. The padlock hung open from a ring beside the door, and Tavi wondered why it was unlocked.

Julius hurried to the door, but Tavi caught up with him just as he was reaching for the doorknob. He grabbed Julius's shoulder and pulled him back, silently shaking his head at him. Tavi pointed to the padlock and then glanced behind him, relieved to see his friends were still with him. Beyond them, the hallway was slowly filling with confused children, who were being herded gently towards the stairs by their rescuers.

Tavi turned around and slowly reached out his hand. Grasping the doorknob firmly, he glanced at his friends and saw that they were ready. Taking a deep breath, Tavi turned the doorknob and flung the door open. He sprinted into the room with his friends right behind him. When he thought about that moment later, he thanked god that he didn't freeze up from the scene that barraged his senses.

He ran directly at the man who was holding a bamboo stick, a primeval scream escaping from his lips as he swung his metal pipe. Kyle was right beside him, and as the man swung his stick at Tavi's head, both of their pipes smashed into the man's knees. He cried out in agony and his stick lightly glanced off of Tavi's head as he collapsed to the ground.

Tavi spun around, looking for the other man. He was waving his blowtorch at Pablo and Chloe as he reached behind him towards a nearby table with his free hand. Seeing the knife that he was reaching for, Tavi ran towards him, the same primitive scream escaping from his mouth. The man turned around in surprise and, in that instant, Chloe and Pablo started swinging their pipes, knocking the man down and beating him bloody as he lay on the floor in front of them.

Tavi looked around the room wildly, his eyes never resting on anything for more than a couple of milliseconds. He saw the cages with the children in them, Kurt filming with his video camera, the boy on the table who was crying out, covered in burns, the baby pool, the hooks, the blood on the floor and the table, the man being beaten by Pablo and Chloe.

"Stop!" Tavi roared at them. He pointed to the sobbing child whose feet were still red from the blowtorch. "Help him." Tavi hurried over and unstrapped the other boy who was tied face-down on the table. His back and legs were covered with old and fresh bruises, and as Tavi gently tried to help him up, he moaned and opened his eyes.

"Tavi?" the boy asked weakly.

Tavi almost dropped him in surprise. "Zeke?" he asked, barely recognizing him as the boy who had helped Kurt with his videotaping and had been taken from them a few weeks earlier. His bloodshot eyes were bruised as well, and his face was etched with dried blood.

"Thank you," Zeke whispered. Tavi struggled to ease him off of the table and looked around for Kyle. He saw him kneeling in front of one of the cages which were about three feet tall.

"Kyle!" Tavi called to him.

Kyle shook his head and continued staring into the cage. When Tavi called his name again, Kurt hurried over instead, his video camera stored away, and helped Tavi ease Zeke to the floor. "Can you take him?" Tavi asked. "I have to free these other kids." Kurt nodded his head and Tavi ran to one of the nearby cages. He peeked inside but couldn't tell if the boy was sleeping or dead.

"Tavi?"

Tavi spun around. He'd never heard Kyle sound so scared and hesitant.

"TAVI! COME HERE!"

Tavi jumped and ran over to Kyle. He squatted beside him. "What?!?"

"Look in the cage."

Tavi peered into the cage and shrunk back in surprise. Inside was a young girl, with short hair, a short skirt, and a lot of make-up. "What? Who is that?"

"Hi," the girl said in a high voice. "Who's your friend? He's really cute."

"Tavi…" Kyle whispered urgently.

The girl smiled, her overly made-up face making her look like a caricature. Tavi noticed that one of her front teeth was missing and wondered if it had been knocked out.

"If you guys let me out, I promise I'll be really nice to you."

Tavi felt a wave of disgust go through him.

"Tavi!" Kyle hissed.

"What?!?" Tavi snapped back.

"That's…" Kyle closed his eyes and shook his head. "Ask him what his name is."

"It's not a…" Tavi looked at the girl. "What's your name?"

The girl giggled unnaturally. "Sasha."

Overcome with horror, Tavi skittered back a couple of steps. "That's Hector," he hissed.

The girl's eyes widened in fright. "No!" she screamed. "There is no Hector. I'm Sasha. Sasha! Please let me out. I'll be a good girl."

"Oh my god," Tavi said to Kyle. "What do we do?"

Kyle looked at Tavi and swallowed. "I promised Sasha I'd bring her brother back. I'll do it. You go help the others."

Tavi flashed a glance at Hector and shuddered slightly. "Are you sure? Will he be okay? What…?"

"I got it," Kyle said, speaking with more composure than before. "I'll take care of it. Go check the other cages. There may be worse things."

Tavi grimaced and hopped up. A few more children had entered the room, and together, they carefully searched the other cages. By the time they left fifteen minutes later, they had rescued twelve more children, and left behind the three bodies of the children they hadn't arrived in time to save.

Chapter 41

"We can't let them get away with it! I want to kill them all! Vikram, look at me! What are we going to do?!?"

Vikram reluctantly raised his gaze from the floor in front of him and studied Giovanni. He had been ranting and spitting for the previous half hour, and his rage seemed to have reached its apex. His head was wrapped in a bandage where he had been clubbed above the ear, and the doctor had just finished wrapping his left arm and securing it in a sling around his neck. Giovanni picked up his glass and gulped down the rest of the whiskey and then stared at Vikram with bloodshot eyes.

"Answer me! What are we going to do?"

Vikram shook his head and shrugged his shoulders. "I don't know. Get them back?"

Giovanni leaned across the desk and rested his weight on his good hand. His face was inches from Vikram. "Get them back? Get them back?!? I lost over seventy boys today and The School House lost around fifty? How do you propose we get them back?" Flecks of spittle covered Vikram's face and he brushed them off as he scooted his chair back a few inches.

"We can call our friends in the police department and have them start looking for them. I don't know what else we can do."

Giovanni's lip curled up in disgust as he gazed at Vikram. He stood up and started pacing behind his desk.

"I'll tell you what else we can do. We're going to offer one hundred talents for every dead street kid anyone can bring us. We're going to put the word out to everyone on the streets. Any of our runways they catch or any of the street kids they catch who broke in here and did…" Giovanni touched the bandage on his head, and his voice rose to its previous level. "THIS TO ME, then we'll give them one hundred talents for each dead body they bring us."

Vikram shook his head. Inside, a voice was shouting that it was madness, but he controlled himself and said cautiously, "I'm not sure if that's the best idea. What if they start killing innocent kids?"

Giovanni spun around and stalked towards Vikram, who leaped out of his seat in surprise. Only his self-respect kept him from running across the room. Giovanni stuck his nose in Vikram's face and said, "I don't give a FUCK! And where were you when this happened? Why weren't you in your office to stop them?!?"

"I already explained that to you." Vikram silently cursed himself for his quavering voice. "I decided to take Yuri to the doctor and get some more tests. I was hoping that…"

"And where is your little AIDS boy?!? Shouldn't he be here helping us?"

Vikram took a couple of steps back. He sensed Giovanni was losing control of himself again. "He disappeared after the doctor told him about why he's been sick. Anyway, about these kids…"

Giovanni interrupted him in a low voice, filled with warnings and promises. "We do this my way, Vikram, or you will regret it. Send everything we have after these kids. No one can come into my house and do this to me. No one!"

Vikram wiped his forehead with a trembling hand and tried to calm his racing heart. Giovanni walked back to his desk and stared at him from across the room. Finally, Vikram nodded his head and said weakly, "Okay. I'll make the calls."

"Now," Giovanni commanded, sitting down at his desk.

Vikram nodded his head again and hurriedly left the office. He stumbled at the entranceway, but regained his balance and ran down the stairs towards safety.

Chapter 42

Rachel waited all evening for Tavi to call her back. She stayed late at the office, rewatching the videos again and again, and when she couldn't stand to look at them one more time, she took a taxi home to her empty house, her mind awash with the images she had seen.

When she arrived home, she dropped her purse by the front door, kicked off her shoes, and collapsed on the sofa in a daze. On the floor in front of her was a small splotch of light shining in from a nearby window, and she focused her gaze upon it as she thought about the videos the children had given her.

The incident at the bus station was the one she had watched first. Interested in seeing if Tavi's version of the events matched up with the story he had told her, she had watched with interest, quickly followed by shock, as Tavi's conversation with another boy was interrupted by a group of men surrounding them. It was clear to see from the overhead viewpoint how the men had intentionally made their way to Tavi's position, and during the second viewing, the children who had positioned themselves around the bus station were equally noticeable.

The speed and ferocity with which the children had descended upon the men were startling to watch, but if Tavi was speaking the truth about the men intending to kill him, which she still doubted, then Rachel could understand why they had reacted so violently.

She skipped past the video which was simply marked "Momo". She remembered Tavi mentioning his name, but she had no idea who he was and decided that she would save it for last. She clicked on the one that said "School House – 6" and watched in horror as Tavi ran at the head of a pack of children who attacked and beat a man without any provocation. As far as she could see, the man was walking down the street with a boy, most likely his son, and the next thing she knew, the man was lying on the street, unconscious and bloody, as one of the children searched his pockets and the rest of them grabbed his son and disappeared down a darkened alleyway.

The violence and animal-like viciousness of these young children shocked her, and she couldn't understand why they had allowed her to see it. This video was a perfect example of what everyone knew street children to be – brutally cruel thieves. She replayed the video a second and third time, pausing to study the expressions of the children as they attacked the man, and by the time she finished watching, she was shaking her head in disappointment.

Oh, Tavi. I had hoped you and your friends were different than this.

Realizing that Laura Lopez was correct in her assessment of the situation, Rachel clicked on the third one, already knowing that it would just show Tavi and his friends doing something wrong which they thought was probably justified. The date on this video was a couple of months earlier than the previous one, and it was clear that the cameraman wasn't as experienced.

The video opened up with the cameraman running in the dark and after a couple of nauseating seconds, Rachel was tempted to turn it off. However, she realized that this video must be important for some reason, and so she let it continue. Her eyes widened in surprise as the conversation became clearer, and when the light from the camera finally lit up the night, she wasn't surprised to see the policemen standing there, surrounded by children, with their guns pointed at the crowd.

When it finally ended, she stared at the dark screen of her computer in confusion for a few seconds, unsure of what she had just witnessed. She slowly picked up a nearby pen, pulled her notepad to her, and replayed the video. She kept her eyes focused on the paper and paused the video after each sentence as she quickly scribbled down what she had heard. When she was finished, she leaned back and reread the conversation between the children and the policemen.

"What do they mean 'any three boys' are going with them? And why are they taking them to bars?" Rachel mumbled aloud.

Okay, she thought. What if Tavi was telling the truth about the sex bars? And these policemen are taking children to them? If the second video was shot after this one, then maybe the man's son who they took with them was…

Rachel quickly clicked on the second video again and watched it from a new perspective. Instead of seeing a man innocently walking down the street with his son, she saw a customer strolling towards a taxi with a boy whom he had just bought for sex. And instead of feeling horror as she watched Tavi and his friends attack the man and take the boy, she felt awed that these children were willing to take on adults in order to save each other. She thought about her own son, Alex, who was spending the week with his father, and wondered how he would have acted if he'd been in these children's situation. In her heart, she doubted that he would have done anything.

Lost in thought, she idly clicked on the video titled "Momo". The ear-shattering screams made her jump in her chair, and she stared at the screen, sickened by what she saw. The cameraman had been interviewing a little boy about what he wanted for his birthday, when suddenly – almost directly behind him – something fell from the sky and thudded against the ground.

The cameraman was one of the first ones to stand up, but he wasn't able to videotape the object before the screams started. As some children knelt down and others stepped back, the crowd parted and she could see the beaten corpse of a young, naked teenager. The screams and moans drowned out almost everything else, but she could hear the name 'Momo' being repeated again and again. When she saw Tavi push his way through the crowd, she covered her mouth and willed him to turn away…to run back…to not look at his friend's dead body. She began weeping as the anguish crossed Tavi's face, and when he knelt beside Momo's body and gently touched it with his fingers, she buried her face in her hands, unable to watch as Tavi screamed and broke down in front of her.

Her secretary, Kristy, raced through the door without knocking and listened in horror as the screams abruptly cut off. "Councilwoman Walsh! Is everything okay?!?"

Rachel took a deep breath and wiped her eyes. She looked up and gave Kristy a weak smile. "I'm fine. I was just watching something a constituent shared with me."

Kristy stared at her, obviously not believing her. "Is there anything I can do? Do you need anything?"

"No. Thank you, but I'm okay." She thought for a second. "Actually, could you call Laura Lopez and see if she has time to stop by tomorrow?"

"Of course. What time?"

"Find out when she can make it, and then arrange my schedule accordingly."

"Yes, Councilwoman." Kristy gave her one last concerned glance before backing out of the office and shutting the door tightly behind her.

Rachel stood up and looked out of her office window at the city around her. She had believed that she knew everything about this city and the people who lived here, but now she wondered if she were only seeing the sunlight reflecting off of a beautiful pond, while the cold darkness hid beneath it, lying in wait for its next victim.

Steeling herself, Rachel sat back at her computer and began watching the videos again, going through them and taking note of anything that might help her find the truth.

After the umpteenth viewing, she had decided that everything that Tavi had told her had been the truth, and that the city, the people of this city, and especially she herself owed Tavi and the other children something for what had been done to them. Ignorance, she told herself, is no excuse when people are hurting and raping children. Even worse is that the people who are doing these monstrous acts are barely attempting to conceal what they're doing, and still no one notices or tries to stop them.

Rachel had decided then and there to help Tavi in any way she could. Based on the videos and the children she had seen at the bridge, she estimated that there were probably around sixty or seventy children who were living like Tavi and she was going to figure out a way to help them.

And now, sitting on her comfortable sofa in her air-conditioned house, Rachel wondered again why Tavi wasn't calling her back, and so she called him for the seventh time that day. The first time, he had rudely hung up on her, and his phone had been turned off the other five times. When it started ringing, Rachel's heart beat a little faster, and she felt a surge of joy when Tavi answered.

"Hello?"

She slowly released the breath she had been holding and tried to speak calmly. "Hi, Tavi. This is Councilwoman Walsh."

"Oh...hi." She could hear voices in the background and wondered if he was at a party.

"Is this is a bad time?"

"No." The voices faded away and she could hear him clearly. "We just had some issues today and we're still trying to deal with them. I'm sorry I didn't call you back."

"It's okay. I watched the videos you gave me..."

A long pause. "And?"

"I believe you are probably telling the truth."

Tavi laughed harshly. "Of course I am!"

"And I want to try and help you. Can you meet tomorrow? I have a lot of questions I need to ask you."

Tavi took so long to respond that Rachel looked at her phone to make sure it was still connected. "I…uh…meet when? Why?"

Rachel quickly thought about her schedule for the next day. A meeting in the morning, Laura Lopez at three-thirty, a couple of other things during the day. "How about I buy you lunch at noon?"

"Okay. Can we meet near Market Street Station? It's easiest for me to get there."

"You don't want to meet near the bridge?"

Another long pause. Rachel wondered if every question she was asking was the wrong one. "We don't live there anymore."

"What? I just saw all of you there yesterday."

"Tomorrow…Come to Market Street Station and I'll call you and let you know where to meet."

"Okay. But wouldn't it be easier to just…?"

"Good-bye, Ms. Walsh."

Rachel hung up her phone and dropped it onto the sofa next to her. What a strange boy, she thought.

The next day at noon, Rachel stood next to the train station where she had had the taxi drop her off. She waited impatiently for Tavi to call her and constantly checked her phone to see if the sound was turned off. After ten minutes, she irritably opened the phone book in her phone when someone touched her elbow lightly.

"Hi."

Rachel looked around in surprise and saw Tavi standing beside her. She put her phone back in her purse as she studied his face. His eyes were bloodshot with dark circles under them, and he looked filthier than he had when she had first met him.

"Everything okay?"

He nodded his head as his eyes nervously scanned the street. "Yep. Can we eat at Burger King?"

"Sure." Rachel looked around and tried to spot one, but Tavi was already walking away.

"This way," he said, looking back at her over his shoulder. Rachel hurried after him and realized that he hadn't been looking at her. Again, he was checking the street and alleyways as if searching for something.

"What do you keep looking for? Is someone after you?"

Tavi snorted and said softly, "Yeah. The whole world."

"What?"

"Nothing." He pointed ahead of them and she saw the Burger King sign. "There it is."

Rachel ran through the list of questions in her mind that she wanted to ask him as they entered the restaurant. When it was their turn to order, Tavi said, "What can I order?"

"Anything you like. The city is paying for this."

Tavi gave her a quizzical look and then gazed at the menu. "Really?" he asked doubtfully. She nodded her head, and he told the cashier, "Can I have a double cheeseburger set and a chicken sandwich for here, and ten double cheeseburgers and ten chicken sandwiches to go? And no mayonnaise on any of the sandwiches."

The cashier noted Rachel's look of surprise and glanced at her for confirmation. She could sense Tavi grinning at her from the corner of her eye, and so she quickly nodded her head and gave her own order. After she paid with her credit card, they sat down at a nearby table and waited for their order to be ready.

"Did you think I would say no?" Rachel asked.

Tavi grinned. "I just wanted to see if you would keep your word."

Rachel laughed. "Well, I hope that I have proved to be a little trustworthy."

"A little bit."

"Good. Then I was hoping I could ask you some questions."

"What did you think of the videos?"

"I thought they were terrible and frightening. Oh…" Rachel dug through her purse and pulled out the memory stick she had been given. "Please give this back to your friend and tell him thank you."

Tavi took it from her with a smile. "Thanks. Kurt will be happy to have this back. He's been worried about it ever since we gave it to you."

"Good." Rachel returned his smile and tried to decide which question to ask first when Tavi suddenly hopped up from the table. "Where are you…?"

"Our order's ready. I'll bring it back." He returned a minute later with two giant bags and a tray filled with food. He set everything down and walked off of again. "Do you want ketchup?" he called out to her. She nodded her head, and he came back with large cup of ketchup and two straws. After setting these down, he turned and began to walk away again.

"Where are you going now?" Rachel asked in exasperation.

Tavi held up his hands. "I want to wash my hands." He raised his eyebrow at her. "You should probably wash yours too."

Rachel smiled and shook her head in amusement as she followed Tavi to the bathrooms. When she returned, he was already sitting down and halfway finished with his chicken burger.

"Sorry for starting without you," he apologized, "but I haven't eaten since lunch yesterday."

"Why not?"

Tavi just shrugged and stuffed a few fries into his mouth.

After eating in companionable silence for ten minutes, Rachel ate her last French fry, dabbed at her mouth with her napkin, and watched Tavi as he finished wiping up the last of the ketchup with his fries. "Do you want anything else?" she asked.

Tavi shook his head. "No, thank you."

"Okay." She couldn't decide which question she should start with and so she asked him the easiest one. "Can you just tell me about yourself and how you came to be here?" He gazed at her with a guarded expression. "Oh..." She pulled a voice recorder from her purse. "Do you mind if I record this?"

Tavi swallowed and studied his empty tray. He took a deep breath and began softly, "Okay. I was born in a small village far from away from here. On my thirteenth birthday..." For the next hour, Tavi explained to her about how Vikram and Yuri had lied and bought him from his family, about Mac and Will, about having sex with different men, about how he escaped and joined other children on the street, about Byron and what happened to him, about rescuing children and trying to take them back to their homes, and about how the police were trying to catch them now.

Rachel did her best to keep her face an emotionless mask. Her eyes constantly flicked to the recorder to make sure it was still on. She didn't want to believe some of the things that he was telling her, but she didn't doubt that he was telling the truth. The men, the drugs, the sex, the police, the murders...It seemed impossible that one child could have witnessed so much. When he finally talked about Momo and trailed off into silence, Rachel wanted to hug him and tell him that everything would be okay, and that he had done everything he could, and that he could rest now, but she knew that it might be a lie.

She waited for him to begin speaking again, but it was clear that he had decided to end his story. "What about the school children?" she asked softly.

"Who?" Tavi looked at her with a confused look upon his face.

"Lately, some of the school children have been attacked by gangs of children..." She paused when she saw his grin.

"Oh…you mean boujies. Yeah. That's where we got most of our stuff."

"But that's stealing," Rachel criticized.

Tavi's grin disappeared. "Riiiight…but we don't have families or homes or money or food. What are we supposed to do?"

It was Rachel's turn to shrug her shoulders. She knew – just like everyone knew – that stealing was wrong. But Tavi had a point. What did she expect him and his friends to do if they had no families or homes?

"And fuck them!" Tavi said, with more vehemence than anything he had said so far. "They won't let me go to school. They said that I'm not allowed to."

"Wait…what? You didn't tell me that."

Tavi sighed. "This man we know – Clarence – he tries to help us out when he can. He offered to sponsor me and support me so that I could go to school, but the principal at Nall Hills said that I'm…" Tavi paused and spat the next word with hatred. "…stateless, and that I can't attend."

Rachel's eyes widened in shock. That was the same school that Alex attended. While she believed most of Tavi's story so far, she was positive that he had misunderstood the principal. She made a mental note to speak with Principal Williams at the first possible chance.

"That sounds…irrational," Rachel said, trying to find the correct word. "Do you mind if I speak with Clarence? He could probably give me some more insight into this."

"Sure." Tavi explained to Rachel how to find Clarence's store and what he looked like.

Rachel glanced at her watch and was surprised to see that it was almost three. Knowing that she had to meet Laura soon and make a decision about what to tell her, Rachel vacillated between leaving right then or asking one more question. She noted the look of frustration which Tavi still wore and wanted to leave on a happy note. Remembering something she had heard when she was at the bridge, she said, "Tell me about Pastor Mike. What's the deal with him?"

Tavi's gaze turned blank as he studied her face. She felt that he could see what she was thinking, but then his face relaxed and was split by a huge grin. "I've only met him twice, but he is such a good person." Ten minutes later, Rachel was running late, but she had another story to check out and the address for Pastor Mike.

She walked with Tavi out of Burger King and again noted how his eyes carefully studied the buildings and alleyways around them before he stepped outside. When she shifted to walk towards the station, she noticed that he had moved away from her. "Aren't you coming this way?" she asked.

"Nope." He clutched the bags of burgers tightly in his left hand and gripped the strap of his backpack with the other. "My friends are this way."

"Okay." Rachel thought about her meeting with Laura. "Oh – do you mind if I show those videos you gave me to a few people?"

"Who?" Tavi asked, instantly suspicious.

Rachel smiled to reassure him, but inside she felt dejected that he didn't trust her. "Some people who may be able to help you and your friends. Please…trust me."

Tavi nodded his head and said, "Okay. I do." He looked her in the eye and gave a shy smile. "Thank you for lunch, Ms. Walsh."

"You're welcome," Rachel replied. "And thank you for the conversation. I'll call you in a day or two."

Tavi smiled and nodded his head again, took a quick glance around, and darted into the alleyway next to Burger King. Rachel rushed forward, curious to see where he was going, but by the time she reached the alleyway, it was completely empty. Praying that Tavi could take care of himself, Rachel turned around and hurried back to the station, hoping she wouldn't be too late for her meeting with Laura Lopez.

Chapter 42

"Can I watch them one more time…from the beginning?" Laura asked.

Rachel silently clicked on the first video and let Laura watch them for a third time. Even Rachel, who had seen each one at least a dozen times, was still moved and shocked by the story told in the videos. Rachel got up to refill their water glasses and she waited until the final video was finished playing before she sat down across from Laura at her desk.

"So, what did you think?" Rachel asked.

Laura gratefully took the glass of water that Rachel handed her and shook her head in bewilderment. Her eyes were still glassy with emotion. "So these children are the ones who attacked Billy and his friends and stole their stuff?"

Rachel nodded. "They are. The boy I met had no problem admitting it. As he pointed out, without a family or home or any type of support system available to them, they don't really have many choices for getting money to feed themselves."

"I guess." Laura's eyes went out of focus for a second before she met Rachel's gaze again. "But you didn't see Billy. For something like that to happen to him, after what he has already been through… How can we condone the fact that our children are getting mugged and beaten up just because they are lucky enough to have a family?" Rachel opened her mouth to respond, but Laura continued. "Granted, these videos do help put a human face on these street gangs, but..." She trailed off and shook her head. "I don't know what you should do about it."

Rachel nodded her head in agreement. "I don't think it's a problem with a simple solution. If some members of the police force really are kidnapping these children and selling them to child sex bars – and, unfortunately, I do believe Tavi – then we can't just ask them to arrest these children. But the truth is that we, as a society, are letting these children slip through the cracks and we owe it to them to try and help...which doesn't mean punishing them and locking them away."

"Honestly, I don't know what to say," Laura said helplessly. "I didn't expect this meeting to go this way. Before I saw those videos, I thought those street kids were just violent, mindless thugs, but..." Laura shrugged. "But if they're children who have been taken from their homes, sold to men for sex, and then escaped and made their way to the streets, then that changes things. And yet, they can't keep attacking children who have normal lives."

"I have an idea that's forming in the back of my mind," Rachel said. "I want to talk to a few more people about this, but I think we may be able to help them."

Laura nodded. "Good."

"I was wondering if I could ask you for a favor, though. I'm aware that your law firm sometimes deals with human rights issues. Could you find out anything you can about statelessness and how it would affect children like this? Tavi was talking about how he wanted to attend school, but the principal claimed that he was stateless and wasn't allowed to. I'm not sure if it's one hundred percent correct, but if it is, I'd like to know what can be done about it."

Laura had pulled out a small notepad and was jotting down notes quickly. "Sure. I'll look into it when I get to work tomorrow morning." She put the notepad back into her purse and glanced at her watch. She made a slight sound of disappointment and said, "I'm sorry to cut this meeting short, but I have to pick up my daughter at her riding lesson."

Rachel stood up. "Of course. I understand." She came around her desk and together they walked towards the door. "Where does she take lessons at? I tried to have Alex take them when he was younger, but I couldn't find a good place in this city."

Laura smiled bitterly. "Javier actually bought a huge tract of land right outside of the city before he went away. It's perfect for riding lessons, but it's so much land and it's so costly that I'm hoping to sell it. Unfortunately, I haven't had a single interested buyer.

"I'm sorry."

"It's okay. But if you know anyone who wants to buy a beautiful piece of land outside of the city, please don't hesitate to give them my number."

Rachel rested her hand on Laura's shoulder compassionately. "I'm sure things will work out. In the meantime, find out what you can about laws regarding statelessness, and I'll be in contact with you soon."

"Alright. I'll talk to you soon," Laura said. She put her sunglasses on and walked out of the door.

Rachel watched her walk away and tried to catch hold of the idea that was tickling the back of her mind. Shaking her head in irritation, she spun around and said to her secretary, Kristy, "Please call Nall Hills and arrange a meeting with the principal for early tomorrow morning. And then find the number for Our Family's Ministry, call Pastor Mike, and see if he can meet with me after I finish speaking with Principal Williams."

"Yes, Councilwoman," Kristy responded.

"After you do that, you can go home for the day. I have to go find a man named Clarence right now and see what he has to say."

"Do you need me to help you with that at all?"

"No, thank you. From what I've heard, he sounds like a good man. I should be okay." Rachel hurried into her office, grabbed her purse, and walked back out. Kristy was already on the phone calling Nall Hills, and so Rachel just waved to her as she walked out. As she waited for the elevator, she recalled the directions Tavi had given her to find Clarence's store. Hoping she had remembered them correctly and she wouldn't have to skip through the recording to find them, she impatiently pressed the lit down button for the elevator. She was surprised to discover how excited she was for her upcoming meetings. The allure of being a councilwoman had slowly faded over the past year, but she once again felt like she could make a difference in her city, beyond the usual meetings about budgets, and meetings with people who wanted favors, and meetings with bureaucrats who were mainly interested in saving their own jobs by doing as little work as possible.

The park was nearby, and as the taxi dropped her off, she looked around curiously, trying to match this place with the park from Tavi's stories. As she walked past it, she saw an older teenager sitting disconsolately on one of the swings. Rachel stared at him closely, wondering if she had seen him the day she visited the bridge. Beyond a vague resemblance to Tavi, she decided that she had never seen him before, and she quickly walked past Yuri without giving him another thought.

The store was easy to find and Rachel glanced at the neon sign with the strange writing as she opened the door to the store. A bell on the door tinkled and a short, stocky man with bushy red hair came out from the backroom.

"Welcome," he said, giving her a friendly smile as he walked behind the counter. "Is there anything I can help you find?"

Rachel stopped next to the counter and looked around. Remembering a comment Tavi had made, she said, "I was wondering about your sign out front. What language is that?"

The man looked up at her curiously. "It means 'hello' in Nepalese. I lived there for a couple of years when I was in the Peace Corps. Is that all you needed?"

Rachel laughed. "No. I'm sorry. I was just curious because…Well, are you Clarence Rothschild?"

"Maybe. Who are you?"

Rachel pulled out a business card and handed it to him. "My name is Rachel Walsh, and I am a city councilwoman."

The man accepted it and quickly glanced at it. "Okay. How may I help you?"

"Well, it's about Tavi…"

As soon as she mentioned his name, the man's eyes widened in alarm. "What about him? Is everything okay?"

"I think so. I've met him a couple of times, and I'm hoping that I will be able to help him out somehow. He mentioned you today while he was telling me about his life. You are Clarence, right?"

Clarence nodded and held out his hand. "It's nice to meet you, ma'am," he said politely, firmly shaking her hand.

"It's nice to meet you, too. I was wondering if you could tell me about Tavi…maybe how you met him, what you know about him, things like that."

"Why?"

"Because he and his friends might be in trouble soon. Did you know that they're mugging and robbing other children?"

Clarence scratched the back of his head awkwardly. "Yes," he said slowly, "but I was hoping that they weren't doing it as much anymore."

"And did you know that men from their sex bars are trying to catch them and bring them back?"

Clarence's eyes flashed with anger. "Isn't that your fault? Those bars are a scourge on this earth. I have no idea why you – the city – let them operate. They should be shut down and their owners locked away."

"I agree. To be honest, I had no idea that they even existed in this city."

Clarence snorted derisively. "If you didn't know about those, don't you wonder how much else you're clueless about?"

Rachel opened her mouth to respond but then realized that he was probably right. She thought about the stories Tavi had told her and nodded her head in agreement. "I do now. And so I want to make things better."

"How? How can you do that?"

"Well, off the top of my head, help Tavi and his friends somehow, and then get those bars shut down."

Clarence stared at her thoughtfully. "What exactly did Tavi tell you about me?"

"He mentioned how you tried to get him into a school around here. I wanted to hear your side of it."

Clarence shook his head and said, "That fucking bitch. She said that Tavi was stateless and that village kids weren't as smart as her students."

"What? Are you sure?"

"What do you mean 'am I sure'?!? Of course I'm sure! She said that kids like Tavi don't really have any rights and village kids were different from city kids."

Rachel sighed. "And this was Principal Williams at Nall Hills?"

"Yeah. How'd you know?"

"Tavi told me."

"Ah...right. But, yeah...after she said that, Tavi just disappeared and I didn't see him for quite some time. And this was after he had taught himself algebra and God knows what else, and then that...that...woman just shit on his dreams of going to school."

"When did Tavi study algebra?"

Clarence hesitated before continuing. "I guess he and his friends were using the books they stole from the other children to teach themselves."

"That doesn't seem very likely, though, does it?"

"You're saying that they're too stupid to do that?"

"No, but…"

"If you were living on the streets, and you couldn't go home, and you knew that you would be homeless forever unless you did everything in your power to change things, what would you do? Some kids sell drugs. Some kids sell their bodies – again. But some of them are actually trying to get back into society, and then the system blocks them off and says, 'Nice try, but you don't belong.' It's bullshit!"

Rachel was silent for a couple of moments. "You're right. I was jumping to conclusions. What can you tell me about these kids?"

And for the next thirty minutes, Clarence told her about the first street kids he had ever met and how his life had changed since then. He finished with the story about helping Derek get admitted to the hospital, and when he was done speaking, Rachel stared at him with open admiration.

Clarence shifted uneasily and demanded, "What?"

Rachel smiled. "I just wish there were more people like you who were willing to help."

He snorted in disdain. "There are plenty. I have a lot of friends who do what they can. You guys just don't ask or try to find us."

Rachel nodded her head again, accepting another lesson in a day full of lessons learned. "I may need you and your friends to help out sometime soon."

"All you have to do is ask."

"Well, I'm really glad I got a chance to talk to you," Rachel said, holding out her hand. "I'll be in contact with you soon."

"Okay." Clarence shook her hand and came around the counter. "And tell Tavi to come visit me. I get worried when I don't see or hear from him every few days."

"I will." Rachel walked to the door and pushed it open. The bell tinkled above. "Good-night, Mr. Rothschild."

"Good-night, ma'am," Clarence said, gently closing the door behind her.

Chapter 43

Tavi lay on his stomach and peered over the edge of the roof at the two police cars which were silently pulling into the alleyway below. The four policemen eased their doors shut, and two of them entered the building through the front door, while the other two ran around to the side where the ladder was. Tavi and the other children, who were watching from four stories above, leaped up and quickly moved to the other edge of the roof. A quick peek showed that the two policemen were already standing at the foot of the ladder, but they seemed hesitant about climbing it in the dark.

Tavi shared a discouraged look with Kyle as they ran back to the twenty children sleeping close together in the middle of the roof.

"Hey!" Tavi whispered, as the children who were already awake began picking up their bags. "They've found us! We gotta go now!"

Most of the older children immediately jumped up, and Tavi wondered if they had even been able to sleep at all. The younger children, though, so exhausted from the constant moving and stress over the last couple of days, just curled up into little balls as they squeezed their eyes tightly shut.

"This way," Pablo hissed, pointing towards a nearby roof. He looked at Tavi and put his hands on his hips as he waited impatiently.

"Just go! We'll follow right behind!" Tavi rushed over to the nearest child and gently shook him awake. Chloe, Kyle, and a couple of the other children joined him while the rest followed Pablo across the nearest plank.

"We can't keep running," Kyle whispered, as he woke Hector up and then turned around so that he could climb onto this back. "We just...can't." He stood with a grunt and walked as quickly as he could in the direction Pablo had led the others.

"I know," Tavi said, so softly that no one else could hear him. He had been in contact with the other groups since they had split up, and he knew that several of them had had disastrous run-ins with men who were working for Giovanni and Vikram. So far, his group had managed to stay just ahead of the police, but each day, their window of escape grew narrower and narrower.

As soon as the young boy's arms locked around his throat, Tavi stood up and hobbled as fast as possible after Chloe, who was just crossing the plank. He took one last glance behind him to make sure that everyone had made it, and then he, too, was across the plank and running for his life.

By the time the policemen reached the roof a couple of minutes later, the children were already six buildings away and getting further with each passing second. Two of the men made as if to follow the children, but one of the others shook his head and said, "Don't bother. There's no direct path between all of these buildings. By the time we figured out how to get there, they'd be long gone." He shrugged and turned back towards the door. "As long the reward is high enough, we'll have enough informants on the roofs with their binoculars searching. We'll get them soon enough."

"How many are in this group?" one of the others asked.

"Supposedly about thirty or thirty-five."

"Nice! That'd be more than three thousand talents."

"Tomorrow," their leader said. "We'll catch them tomorrow." He led his men down the stairs back to their cars and thought about how he would spend his share of the reward money.

Chapter 44

Rachel strode into her office, her mind abuzz with ideas after her meetings with Principal Williams and Pastor Mike. Kristy looked up from the computer and said with a smile, "Good morning, Councilwoman."

"Good morning, Kristy. Could you please call and check if Laura Lopez will be available to talk in about forty-five minutes?"

"Yes, ma'am."

Instead of going into her office, Rachel walked through a doorway into one of the adjoining rooms. Here, two of her assistants and one intern worked in an office about the same size as the foyer where Kristy sat. Only Tina, the summer intern, was at her desk, and she guiltily set her phone down on her desk as Rachel walked in.

"Tina!"

"Yes, Councilwoman?"

"Where are Brett and Jeremy?"

"I think they went out for coffee."

"Already? Why didn't just one of you go? Well, tell them to come to my office when they get back. You, too. We have something important that needs to get done as soon as possible."

"Um…" Tina twisted her long blonde hair around her finger. "Do you want me to just call them on their cell phones and tell them to come back now?"

Rachel smiled. "Sure. Thanks. Be in my office in five minutes." She turned around and walked towards her own office and smiled again when she heard Tina warning Brett that Rachel was angry and that they had better return immediately.

As she sat down at her desk, she wondered again what she had ever done to make Tina so afraid of her. God knows that Brett and Jeremy didn't fear her. Setting that thought aside, Rachel thought about the meetings she had had that morning.

The one with Principal Williams was unfortunately predictable. Once she had found out why Rachel was visiting, Principal Williams's demeanor had changed instantly and she had spoken at length about how she agreed with statelessness and the separation of students with good genes from those students who were born to "inbred, dirty, village monkeys". Her vitriol on the subject had stunned Rachel, and after a couple of bland comments, Rachel had quickly excused herself and hurried out of the school.

The meeting with Pastor Mike had been much more refreshing. He had been playing with his wife and two children in the playground near the church when she had arrived. Upon introducing herself, his wife had taken the children to get a snack, leaving Rachel alone with Pastor Mike. They had sat at a nearby picnic table and watched a young mother push her infant daughter in a swing as they talked.

"Your children are beautiful," Rachel said.

Pastor Mike beamed and Rachel felt herself smiling in response. "They are, aren't they? And they're so smart too, especially considering what their life must have been like before."

"Tavi mentioned something about that. Can you tell me what you know?"

Pastor Mike shrugged. "I'm sure Tavi knows more than I do. But, supposedly, Tavi and his friends had rescued this boy, Frederick, from one of the bars and Tavi offered to take him home to his family. After they arrived, the mother threatened to sell Frederick back into slavery, as well as his brother and sister when they were old enough. It sounds like their mother needs a lot of help. According to what Tavi saw – and what little Frederick will say about the matter – their mother was always drunk and would beat the children for no reason." He trailed off and stared blankly at the table, lost in thought. After a couple of seconds, he looked up and his eyes were glowing with anger. "When I hold them and see them flinch if I move too fast, or when I watch them smile tentatively about things that would make most children laugh out loud, I feel this rage that I have never experienced, even though I know that she should be forgiven and prayed for."

Rachel studied his face and softly asked, "So do you think Tavi did the right thing?"

"When he took them from their mother?"

Rachel nodded.

"Yes," he answered slowly. He glanced at the baby squealing with joy as her mother pushed her higher. "I mean, yes. I do. Something had to be done. But he bought them, just like all of these other children, and so we are in a tough situation right now. We can't legally adopt them, unless the state intervenes with the mother and then lets us keep them. I'm not even sure if they could go to an orphanage right now, since they don't officially belong here. And to be honest, I don't want to give them up. They have changed so much in the short time that we have had them, and I love them as if they were truly mine." He shook his head. "Something needs to change."

"I know. When I think of all of those kids living on the street with nowhere to go, and not being able to have normal lives, I feel so frustrated at how powerless I am to make their lives better. But I'm not sure what we can do."

"They need a place where they can go and be safe – like a sanctuary – where they can live and study and learn how to exist in society again, while we fight this legal loophole that prevents us from truly helping them."

"Couldn't your church do something?"

"We have been in touch with a couple of international organizations, and it's an issue that my congregation seems to be rallying around, but...honestly, I don't know what the next step is. I have people who are willing to help, but now we just need to direct their energy and time and money in the right direction."

Rachel nodded thoughtfully. The vague outline of a plan was coming together in her mind, and she thought she knew how it could end, but she wasn't sure how to get there. "Would you be willing to work together to change this? Not as a church project or necessarily a city project, but just something so that we can help these kids."

"Of course," Pastor Mike said without any hesitation.

Rachel smiled with relief and was about to ask about his congregation when Pastor Mike suddenly said, "Oh! Have you seen Tavi or his friends recently?"

"I saw Tavi yesterday. Why?"

"Four children came through the front door of the church yesterday. They looked as if they were running for their lives, but they refused to talk about it for a few hours. Eventually, though, one of them told us how all of the kids from under the bridge had attacked a couple of the bars and freed all of the other children there."

"What? When did this happen?"

"A few days ago. And now they're all running for their lives. These kids were lucky – relatively speaking. A couple that I know was visiting the church at the same time, and they've agreed to let the boys stay with them for a few days. After that, though, I don't know what will happen."

Rachel sighed, trying to imagine what these children's lives must be like. "Okay. Let me go make some calls and I'll try to figure something out."

Pastor Mike stood up with her and held out his hand. "It was nice meeting you, Councilwoman. And trust in God. I believe that all of this is happening for a reason."

"I hope so," Rachel replied softly, shaking his hand firmly. "I'll be in touch."

As she waited impatiently for her staffers to arrive, she wondered if the plan she had devised, made from hopes and wishes, could be successfully implemented within a few short days. After another ten minutes, Tina scuttled into the room, followed by Jeremy and Brett as they lazily strolled over to the two most comfortable chairs in the office.

Rachel despised them. They had gone to the best schools, their families had connections with important people throughout the entire city, and she knew that they had only accepted this job so that it would appear on their resume as their entry point into a life of politics. They were both handsome, wealthy, intelligent men in their mid-twenties, and they believed that the world was made for them to rule and have fun.

Well, this time you're going to have to do some work, she thought.

Brett took a sip of his coffee and said, "What's up?" Tina sat nervously in an uncomfortable chair near Rachel's desk with her pen poised above her note pad. Rachel turned her computer monitor around and closed the blinds behind her. Jeremy whispered something to Brett, who laughed louder than necessary.

"What's so funny?" Rachel asked.

Brett just smiled and shook his head while Jeremy said, "Nothing. Just a thought that popped into my head."

"Tell me," Rachel said, trying hard to smile naturally. "Maybe I'll think it's funny, too."

Brett gave Jeremy a warning glance, but Jeremy grinned broadly and said, "I thought it'd be funny if you turned it around and you had accidently left some porn site open." He gave a short laugh. "Well, it was funnier the first time around."

"I'm sure it was." She sat behind her computer and pushed play, and then flipped the light switch by her desk. "Please pay attention. I have an assignment for you that relates to these videos."

Rachel watched their faces as the videos played. Tina seemed to be the most disturbed by what she was seeing and constantly pressed the bridge of her glasses as if they were slipping off of her nose. Brett and Jeremy, however, exchanged whispered comments the entire time, and the only time they seemed perturbed was when Tavi and Momo were standing up to the police. When the videos ended, she turned the light back on and said, "So, what do you guys think?"

Tina opened her mouth to respond, but Brett said first, "About what? A bunch of homeless kids killing each other and attacking the police? I think they should all be locked up." Jeremy nodded his head in agreement.

Rachel felt a stab of disappointment. "And you, Tina?"

Tina glanced nervously at the two men. "Um…who were those kids?"

"Most of them are children who were kidnapped and then sold as sex slaves to men. The kids in the videos are some of the ones who have escaped."

"Eww. Really?" Jeremy asked, a look of disgust crossing his face.

"What do you mean 'eww'?" Rachel asked.

"They had sex with men? So they're like little child prostitutes?"

"They didn't want to do that, Jeremy. They were forced to!" Rachel snapped.

Brett had a similar look of distaste on his face. "I don't know about that. No one could force me to have sex with a man."

Jeremy laughed. "You can't force someone who's willing."

"Shut up," Brett said, pushing Jeremy and laughing along.

Rachel stood up and raised her voice. "I don't care if you agree or disagree, but we are having a fundraiser one week from today, and you will make sure that all of the right people are there. I want the wealthiest ones who are always the most willing to donate to a cause. I want people who have children of their own. Basically, I want you to find anyone who will give us money to attend."

"One week?" Jeremy said in disbelief.

"Yes. So, you better get started. I know that you think you're guaranteed a better position when you leave in a month, but if you screw this up, I will find some way to make sure it goes on your record."

Jeremy opened his mouth to argue, but Brett touched him on the arm and shook his head. "Fine. We can do this. Anything else?"

"Try to reserve one of the hotel ballrooms first and tell them it's for me. I know you don't believe me, but this is urgent."

Jeremy and Brett stood up. "Okay," Brett said, following Jeremy out of the room. Tina watched them leave and then stood up hesitantly, obviously unsure about what to do.

"Tina, could you...?" Rachel began before Tina interrupted her.

"Councilwoman Walsh, I just wanted to say how incredibly moving I thought those videos were. I'll do my best to make sure that Brett and Jeremy do what they should. If they don't, then you can depend on me."

Rachel smiled. "Thanks, Tina."

Tina continued in a softer voice, "My family didn't have much money growing up, and so...if it was bad for us, I can't imagine what those kids are going through."

Rachel walked around the desk and placed her hand on Tina's arm. "Thank you, Tina. You've done a really good job so far during your internship. If you want to come back after you have graduated, I'll make sure to write a recommendation for you."

Tina gave a huge smile and practically glowed. Rachel had never seen her so animated. "Thank you,

Councilwoman! I promise I won't let you down." She rushed out of the office, and Rachel went back to her desk to get ready for her call with Laura.

She had just gotten off of the phone with Pastor Mike when Kristy buzzed her and said, "Laura Lopez is on line one." Rachel took a deep breath and picked up the phone.

"Hi, Laura. Thanks for making time for me."

"It's no problem. If you're calling about the statelessness, my co-worker is still looking into it."

"No. That's fine. I was actually calling about the property that you mentioned you were interested in selling."

"What about it? Do you know someone who might be interested in purchasing it?"

Rachel smiled at the eagerness in Laura's voice. "Yes. Me."

Chapter 45

By the end of the following day, Rachel knew she had made a huge mistake. Everything seemed to be going wrong, and she had no idea what she could do to turn things around. Tina was the only one of her three assistants who was trying her best, but she didn't have the connections or the charisma of the other two, and her talents were best used with organizing and taking care of the little details.

Brett had a more lackadaisical attitude, but he was still making an effort – albeit, a rather unimpressive one – and was slowly spreading the word about the fundraiser. Jeremy, on the other hand, was still not working and was doing his best to distract Brett and Tina. She had finally sent him home in the late afternoon and told him that he should consider himself fired and that he couldn't use her as a reference, unless he wanted his future employers to know what a lazy shit he truly was. His only response was a smile as he calmly said, "My father will hear about this," and then he collected his things and sauntered out of the office.

Brett's look of envy which followed Jeremy as he walked through the doorway did little to stir hope in Rachel.

She had no idea what had inspired her to promise Laura that she would be able to either lease or buy her land from her. She had gotten so excited when speaking with Pastor Mike that she had been positive that she would easily have enough money with his help and the money from the fundraiser. But if the fundraiser was a complete failure, then everything would collapse like a house of cards balanced upon only one card.

Tavi wasn't answering his phone. The mayor's office hadn't responded to her call about corrupt police officers. Alex was coming home in two days.

Not knowing what else she could do at the moment, Rachel opened up a bottle of wine, quickly drank it – and a second one – while feeling sorry for herself, and then stumbled up the stairs and soon passed out in her bed.

She woke up late, took several ibuprofen with a glass of water for breakfast, and walked into her office an hour late. "Any messages?" she asked Kristy, wincing slightly at the dull pain throbbing above her ears.

Kristy picked up a couple of pieces of paper, but glanced at Rachel in concern before reading them aloud. "Good morning, Councilwoman. Are you feeling okay?"

"No. I'm not. Messages?"

"Well, um…Judge O'Neal called – twice."

Rachel closed her eyes and pinched the bridge of her nose until it hurt. "Great. I wonder what the Chief Justice of our state Supreme Court wants to talk to me about."

"I think it's probably about Jeremy," Kristy said helpfully.

"I know. I was being facetious." Rachel had met Supreme Court Chief Justice Thomas O'Neal only once before, and that had been on Jeremy's first day of work when his father had come with him to promise that Jeremy would live up to his family's name. Since then, Jeremy had been nothing but trouble, but Rachel was confident that that wasn't what his father wanted to hear.

"I'll call him back later. Anything else?"

"The mayor called as well."

Rachel looked at Kristy quizzically. "You mean someone from the mayor's office called, right?"

"No, ma'am. The mayor himself called twenty minutes ago."

"And what did you tell him?"

"I said that you were out meeting with your constituents and that you would be back soon. He wanted me to tell you that he will be calling back at two this afternoon and that you should be here to accept his call."

Rachel sighed. "Tell me, since you keep up with this kind of stuff…are the mayor and the Chief Justice acquaintances?"

"Yes, ma'am. They've been really good friends for years."

"Great. There goes my career." Rachel shook her head despondently and headed towards her staff's office. She hoped they had accomplished more than she had so far that day.

Tina was on the phone, alone in the room, and was pleading in a high, wispy voice, "You really should come. These children are…um…so poor and homeless. And we're going to show a video…Yes, I understand…So, I can put you as a 'maybe'?" Tina drew a line on her paper. "Okay. Thank you. I will put you down as 'maybe you don't care now, but you will next week.' Thank you for your time!" She hung up the phone and slumped on her desk, burying her head in her arms.

"Where's Brett?" Rachel asked.

Tina leaped up in shock. "Councilwoman! I didn't see you. How are you today?"

"Brett?"

Tina shook her head and collapsed back into her chair. "He didn't show up for work today."

Rachel could only nod her head. "Okay. Please keep up your hard work."

"Ma'am, are you…okay?"

"Yep!" Rachel gave Tina her brightest smile. "Everything's perfect! How are you doing?"

"Well…I haven't really been able to convince many people to come," Tina answered slowly.

"That's okay. As long as you do your best, I'm sure it'll work out. How many confirmations do you have so far?"

"One?"

Oh my god, Rachel thought. Flashing her professional smile again, Rachel said, "That's great. The first one is always the hardest. Keep it up! I'll check on you again in a few hours." She spun around without waiting for a response and rushed to her office, being careful not to slam the door behind her.

The morning passed in a blur. She attended a couple of meetings and before she knew it, it was already noon and everyone was heading out for lunch. Rachel walked back to her empty office and sat in her chair. She swiveled around and stared out of the window, trying to figure out how everything had gone so wrong in the last twenty-four hours. Without even thinking about it, she pulled out her phone and called Tavi. She almost dropped it in surprise when he answered on the first ring.

"Yeah?"

"Tavi! It's Rachel Walsh. I've been trying to get ahold of you."

"Sorry. My phone battery died and I was only able to charge it now in the library."

"Oh. I see. I should have realized that it'd be hard for you guys to…well, how are you? I met with Pastor Mike. He told me about how you and your friends attacked those two bars."

"Yep." Rachel had been expecting him to sound happy or proud, but the only emotion she could detect was weariness. "We did. And now we can't stop running."

"I want you to know that I have an idea to help you." Rachel frowned as she said it, knowing that her idea was probably not going to work.

"Well, that sounds great. I hope it works," Tavi responded unenthusiastically.

"Would it be possible to get more of the videos that you guys have shot? I'm going to be showing them to some people and hopefully they'll want to help change things as well."

"Ummm...wait a second." Tavi mumbled to someone in the background and Rachel listened for a few seconds to the angry mutters. His voice suddenly became much clearer as he said, "Just do it! Hello? Ms. Walsh?"

"I'm still here."

"Yeah. We can do it. Can I give them to you tomorrow?"

Rachel calculated quickly. Tomorrow...We'll only have three or four days to go through them and pick out the best ones before setting up for the fundraiser. On the other hand, there's only one person attending so far. "Yes. That'll be fine. Do you want to meet at the same place?"

"Actually, we decided to see how things were on the other side of the city. Can we meet outside of Asok Station?"

"Sure. Is one o'clock okay?"

"Yep. I'll see you tomorrow."

"Bye, Tavi." She listened to him hang up and then she rested her head on her desk, her disappointment and the wine hangover effectively sapping all of her energy.

Rachel woke up with a start as someone knocked on her door. She blinked her eyes rapidly and then opened them as wide as she could, trying to look more awake. She saw the small puddle of drool on her desk and quickly wiped her face and ran her fingers through her hair. Wondering why Kristy hadn't buzzed her, she snatched some tissue from the box on her desk and hurriedly wiped up the drool.

"Yes?" she called out, dropping the tissue into the wastebasket by her chair.

The door opened slowly and Jeremy stepped in. Rachel did her best to hide her disdain as he turned to shut the door firmly behind him, and then he walked forward and stopped in front of her desk.

"Hi, Councilwoman," he said. She couldn't read the expression on his face, but she had never seen him acting so uneasy before.

"Hello, Jeremy. What can I do for you? I'm having a busy day, what with only having Tina here to do all of the work."

To her surprise, Jeremy looked down in chagrin. "I spoke with my father when I got home yesterday."

Here it comes, Rachel thought. This is the moment my career ends. "And?"

"After I told him how you fired me, he made me describe the videos you showed us and what you had asked us to do."

"And?"

"He was really displeased."

Rachel swallowed. "And?"

A long pause. "And I owe you an apology."

Rachel's heart stopped beating for a second. "What?"

Jeremy let out a deep breath and Rachel was astonished by the emotion in his eyes. "He said I was an embarrassment to him and that I've been acting like a spoiled child, and if I didn't figure things out, then he himself would guarantee that I would never work in politics."

Rachel snorted. "And that's it? You're apologizing because your father threatened you?" She shook her head and said, "Go away, Jeremy."

Jeremy spoke quickly, "And then he made me volunteer at a soup kitchen last night and he told me I have to live there for a week so that I can understand what those people are going through." Rachel raised her eyebrows in surprise and Jeremy added, "And Brett, as well."

"And that's it?"

"No. The reason Brett was late this morning is because we were volunteering at an orphanage. We played with the kids and helped them with their homework, and then when most of them went to school, we stayed there and spoke with the volunteers who usually work there." Jeremy swallowed and looked Rachel in the eye. "I am sorry for what I said and did yesterday. I know that me spending half a day with these people who have to spend their whole lives like this isn't much, but I understand a bit more about why you want to help them. If it's possible, I was hoping you could let me have one more chance?"

Rachel kept her face passive, but inside she was shouting with joy. A motivated Jeremy – if there was such a thing – could be the miracle she needed. After pretending to think about it for a few seconds, Rachel said, "Okay. You have one more chance."

Jeremy grinned, his blue eyes lighting up his entire face. "Thank you…so much! Brett's going to apologize, too, but he wanted to get started on calling people."

"Okay. Tell him to come in here when he gets the chance." Jeremy nodded his head and turned to leave, but Rachel stopped him to ask him another question. "Do you know why your father called earlier? I haven't had a chance to speak with him yet."

"Ahh, yeah. He wants to help you organize it. He was calling his friends last night and explaining to them about these kids and the sex bars and the shady policemen, and I think a lot of them are really fired up about this."

Rachel could only nod her head and close her mouth which had dropped open in surprise, and watched as Jeremy rushed out of her office so that he could get to work.

Chapter 46

With the full weight of the mayor's office behind her, and the connections that Jeremy's father brought with him, the preparation for the fundraiser exceeded all of Rachel's expectations. Both men had volunteered to speak and people were suddenly lining up to pay a thousand talents per plate. Within the next three days, the fundraiser was sold out and Rachel and her staffers could focus on how they wanted to present everything.

Tavi had shown up for their meeting the following day, but he had insisted that he had to leave and only stayed a few minutes. Before he left, though, he had given her four memory sticks and asked her to keep them safe. Over the next few days, her mind kept replaying their brief conversation and she wondered if there was anything more she could have done.

He had been unwilling to meet her in the open near Asok Station. Instead, he had called her on the phone and directed her to a nearby alleyway. When she had finally seen him, Rachel had nearly dropped her phone in shock. Tavi had looked so thin and exhausted that she couldn't imagine how he was able to stay on his feet.

"Tavi," she exclaimed, unable to hide her concern. "Is everything okay?"

He shook his head wearily. "No." He closed his eyes and rested his body against the bricked wall of the building. "They have men all over the roofs and so we had to split up, and now a lot of us are on our own."

"Is there anything I can do?"

Tavi gave a bitter laugh and looked at her through slitted eyes. "Not unless you can find all of us homes and make these men stop chasing us."

"Soon. You just have to give me a little time. I've arranged a fundraiser for next…"

Tavi interrupted her. "Time?" he scoffed. He held out his hand to her. There were four memory sticks resting on his palm. "Here. Take these. I don't think we have much time left."

Rachel took the memory sticks from Tavi and put them in her pocket. "Listen, Tavi. Maybe we can…" She trailed off as he shook his head and pushed himself away from the wall.

"I gotta go," he said, looking carefully in both directions. "There was a store owner who looked at me funny when I passed him earlier. If he called anyone, then they're going to be here soon."

"Tavi, I don't think…"

He gave her a sad smile. "You don't understand, Ms. Walsh. Good luck with your fundraiser!" Glancing one last time in both directions, he turned around and sprinted away from her. As she watched him run away, her phone rang, startling her, and she quickly pulled it out of her purse.

"Hello?"

"Hi, this is Jeremy."

"Yes?" Regardless of his new change in attitude, Rachel still didn't like him very much.

"I wanted to let you know that we got the Cowells and the Chungs."

"That's great! Excellent work."

"When will you be back? My dad is sending over someone to help organize the fundraiser, and they'll be here in an hour or so."

"Soon. I just talked to..." Rachel felt a chill go through her as two policemen entered the alleyway. "I'll call you back," she said quickly, hanging up the phone.

"Excuse me, ma'am," said the nearest policeman. He was a well-built man in his late twenties with blond hair. Rachel flicked her eyes to the nametag on his chest – Terriss. "Did you see a boy anywhere around here? About fourteen or fifteen years old. His clothes were probably a bit dirty and ragged."

Rachel's mind froze. She recognized this policeman from one of Tavi's videos. "Um...no. I don't think so. Did he do something wrong?"

Officer Terriss glanced at his partner. "We got a call that this boy has been selling drugs to children. It's best if we catch him as soon as possible." He reached into his pocket and pulled out a card which he handed to Rachel. "If you do happen to see him, could you give me a call? He's about 69 inches tall, brown hair, green eyes. We think his name is Tavi."

Rachel took his card and studied it. "Sure. No problem."

"Thank you. Have a great day, ma'am." Both officers flashed her charming smiles as they walked past her and began jogging in the same direction as Tavi had gone. She watched them until they turned the corner, and then she carefully put the card into her pocket and hurried out of the alleyway.

When she returned to her office, Jeremy was standing near Kristy's desk, laughing with a man who was about the same age as him and Brett. She hesitated for a brief moment, unsure of what to do, and Jeremy noticed her in that instant as she stood frozen in the doorway to her own office.

"Councilwoman Walsh! This is the guy I was telling you about! Martin Bushell." They both started walking towards her and Rachel unfroze and smiled politely as she held out her hand.

"It's nice to meet you," she said.

"You, too," Martin replied, shaking her hand. He spoke with a British accent and Rachel wondered what he was doing working for the city. "I've heard a lot about you through Jeremy."

Jeremy gave a slight smirk and added, "We met each other when I went to Oxford for a year. I actually helped get him a job with my dad."

"Well, hindered is probably a better word," Martin replied dryly.

"So, you two should meet now and start going over everything," Jeremy told Rachel. "My dad has already talked to Martin about his ideas for the fundraiser, and I think you'll like them. How about…?"

"I have a better idea," Rachel interrupted. She hadn't been able to stop touching the memory sticks in her pocket since she had entered the office. All she wanted to do was to watch them and figure out how to use them to help Tavi and his friends. "You meet with Martin and then after you guys have a rough outline, give it to me, and I will let you know what I think."

"But…my dad said that…"

"Jeremy, for the love of God, stop mentioning your dad! It's time for you to grow up and do good work because it's what you want to do, and not because it's what your dad told you to do." Jeremy looked at her sullenly as she added, "I am putting you in charge of this. I trust you to do your best. What more could you ask for?"

Jeremy glanced at Martin, who had focused his attention on a nearby painting. He looked back at Rachel and nodded his head imperceptibly. "Okay. We'll do our best. Let's go, Martin."

Martin grinned at Rachel as he followed Jeremy towards the staffer's room. Letting out a long sigh, Rachel followed them and stopped at the doorway. Brett was busy talking on the phone while Tina was reading a list and typing information into her computer without once looking at the keyboard.

"Tina," Rachel said softly, hoping not to startle her.

It didn't work. Tina leaped up from her chair in surprise and stammered, "Councilwoman! I didn't know you were here."

"Could you come to my office? I have a job for you."

"Sure." Tina hurriedly walked out from behind her desk and followed Rachel to her office. Once there, Rachel turned and handed the four memory sticks to Tina.

"Can you do me a favor?"

"Sure. What?"

"Put all of these videos on my computer in a folder on my desktop. And then I want you to go through each one carefully, write a summary about what it's about, and if there are any policemen in the videos, please write down their names if possible."

"Yes, ma'am. When do you want this done by?"

"It's extremely urgent. So, the sooner, the better."

When Rachel returned from getting coffee twenty minutes later, Tina was back at her own desk, staring intently at her computer with her headphones on and a pen in her hand. Rachel watched her for a few seconds, pleased with how seriously Tina was taking notes, and then she went back to her own office to watch what she could.

There was no rhyme or reason to how the videos were organized. They appeared to be shot at different times, and while some of them showed the children rescuing others as they exited the sex bars, a lot of the videos were just brief windows into the daily lives of these children.

In a few of them, the cameraperson crept around in the early morning light and showed how peaceful and young the children appeared while they slept. A couple of the videos just showed Tavi and another boy staring at the river while the fog slowly disappeared as the sun rose into the sky.

More than a few videos were interviews with various children, and while a lot of them were silly and intentionally goofy, a fair number of them were heartbreaking as the children spoke about how they had come to be there, or about their future hopes and dreams. Rachel watched the video of Sasha singing three times, and each time she wept as Sasha realized that her brother had been taken.

A couple of hours later, Rachel was taken by surprise at a solemn video which showed Sasha's brother, Hector, dressed as a girl, as Sasha stood weeping next to him and tried to convince him that he really was Hector. They couldn't have been more than ten years old.

Soon after that, Jeremy and Martin came into her office, excited about their plans for the fundraiser. Rachel sent Jeremy back to the phones to continue calling prospective donors and she ordered Martin to take copies of the memory sticks and to watch them that night. Only after he had watched them would she then discuss and agree to what he had planned.

Rachel watched the videos for four hours straight, and by the end, she was so emotionally disheveled that she numbly turned off her computer and stumbled out of her office. She didn't even notice that Tina was still at her computer, diligently taking notes on each video that she watched. Rachel took a taxi home, happy that her son, Alex, wasn't due back until the following day, and was asleep within minutes of getting home.

The next morning when Rachel arrived at work, she glanced into her staffers' office and was surprised to see Tina sleeping at her desk. She debated about whether she should wake her up, but decided that it would be best to let her sleep. They were going to have a busy day.

When Rachel sat down at her desk, she was surprised to find her computer already on. Atop her desk in front of the keyboard was a short stack of papers. Rachel gave the top sheet a casual glance and her hand froze in the act of setting it to the side. She read the first few entries in detail and then flipped through the following pages. Someone – most likely Tina – had given each video clip a number and a thorough summary. The ones where police officers were videotaped were highlighted in yellow, and the bottom sheet of paper had a list of all of the names that Tina had been able to find.

Rachel's eyes were drawn to her computer, and she used the mouse to click open a new folder which was on her desktop. Inside of it, Tina had renamed all of her videos so that they corresponded to the list on her desk and had made a separate folder where she had categorized the videos by their content – personal stories, rescuing kids, police, etc. Rachel clicked on the folder marked "Police" and studied the list of names on the sheet in front of her. She pulled out a pen and began watching each clip carefully.

By the time Martin walked through her office door two hours later, Rachel had verified that Tina had been able to list all of the policemen possible. Rachel made added notations next to each name, concerning what they did, how many times they appeared, and how confident she was that they should be punished. She had just finished typing a summary of the folder and its contents when Martin entered with a distraught expression upon his face.

"Hi, Martin," Rachel said. "Did you watch the videos?"

He sat down at the chair in front of her desk. "That's some messed up shit. I'm glad we don't have these kinds of problems in the UK."

Rachel smiled knowingly. "That's what I used to think."

"But to answer your question, yes, I watched the videos."

"Good. I want to show some of them at the fundraiser. I think it'll be extremely helpful to put some faces and personalities to these kids if these people are going to be donating money."

"I agree. Especially the video of that little girl singing and her brother who got taken." Rachel nodded in agreement as Martin asked, "But what about the police? We should definitely show a video or two about what they've been doing, but I don't think we can until…"

Rachel interrupted him and said, "I'm going to speak with the mayor about them today. With the kind of proof we have right now, we can at least suspend these officers who are shown in the videos. I'll get the mayor's permission to show the videos after we decide which ones will be the most effecting."

"Smashing. We agree on that. Let me show you what else we'd like to do…"

The following day, around the same time that Rachel was picking up Alex from the airport, seventeen police officers were arrested on a variety of charges and the mayor gave his approval for Rachel to use parts from the incriminating videos at the fundraiser. The next morning, it was the leading story in all of the local newspapers, and Rachel was elated about all of the extra attention this was bringing to her cause. She and the mayor discussed raiding The School House and Bangarang, the two bars which were featured the most often in the videos, but they decided to wait a couple of days so that it, too, would be the day's leading story. The mayor also suggested that the police take statements from several of the children which would assist them in getting warrants.

Rachel tried calling Tavi twice that day, but both times, his phone was turned off and she wasn't even able to leave a message. She lay in bed that night, tossing and turning, and worried about the following day. The fundraiser would be in the evening, and she was hoping to speak with Tavi before then. She had already told Alex that he was going, and even though he seemed unhappy about it now, Rachel was sure that it was just jetlag and that he would be eager to be there once he saw what was happening.

Around three o'clock, she finally felt herself drifting off to sleep when her phone vibrated loudly on her bedside table, snapping her out of her doze. She snatched it up and pressed it to her ear. "Hello?"

"Ms. Walsh?" Tavi whispered.

"Tavi, what's wrong?"

"Me and a couple of friends are near your office building downtown. Is there any way we can stay there for tonight?"

Rachel leaned over and flicked on the bedside lamp. The light seemed to help her focus her thoughts better. "My office? How do you know where it is? And what are you doing up at this time? It's past 3am."

"We thought we were hidden, but these men came into our alley and started looking behind all of the dumpsters. We all got away except for Kyle! And now they're still looking for us!!"

"Who? Who's Kyle?"

"Jesus…Yes or no? If not, then we need to find somewhere else tonight."

Rachel shook her head. "I'm sorry, Tavi, but I can't let you in tonight. If you still need a place tomorrow night, I guess you and your friends can stay in my office. I'll tell the security guard to let you up."

"Okay." A moment of silence, and then she heard him ask doubtfully, "Really?"

"Yes, Tavi. I promise. If you need a safe place – a sanctuary – tomorrow night, tell the security guard and he'll let you and your friends into my office."

She could barely hear him whisper, "Okay. Thanks."

"Tavi, are you sure that someone's chasing you right now? We arrested all of the policemen today."

"Not all of them. Good night."

She heard a click and stared at her phone in confusion as she set it on the bed. With the fundraiser ready to go and the corrupt policemen neutralized, Rachel wondered what else could be bothering Tavi and his friends. She mused about it as she closed her eyes in the dark, but she drifted off to sleep before she could come up with a suitable answer.

Chapter 47

Tavi's eyes slowly opened as he raised his chin from his chest. He blinked a couple of times before suddenly looking around in a panic. The light which managed to slip through the cracks of the boarded up window was just enough to make out the motionless bodies of the other children curled up on the floor around him. Pablo and Chloe were the closest to the door. Kurt, who had been hysterical after Kyle had been taken, was lying a few feet away from Malik. Sasha and Hector were lying closest to the window, and he gazed in silence at the dust particles as they trickled through the sunbeam and landed upon their clasped hands.

He thought back to the previous night with loathing and shame at how they had run in fear from the three men who had surprised them in the alleyway. None of the children had been fully asleep, but the sound of the men's voices and laughter in the silence of the night had been so startling that Tavi had leaped up and sprinted for the end of the alleyway. Without looking back, he had turned the corner and continued running, only stopping after he had gone three blocks. The rest of the children were about a hundred yards behind him, except for one who was lagging behind. When the nearest ones had finally caught up to him, Tavi had done a quick headcount and realized that two of them were missing. As soon as Kurt arrived with tears streaming down his face, Tavi knew who was missing.

"They took him!" Kurt shouted as the rest of the children stood with their hands on their hips, breathing heavily.

Tavi closed his eyes and asked what needed to be asked. "Who?"

"Kyle! And there were only three of them! What did you run for?!?"

When Tavi didn't respond, Kurt dropped his bag and tackled him. As he punched Tavi's body and cried in rage, Tavi just lay there, refusing to protect himself. He didn't even realize the others had pulled Kurt off of him until Malik was helping him to his feet.

"I got scared," he finally admitted.

Kurt shook himself free from Pablo and Chloe. "Do you know what they're going to do to him?!?"

Tavi swallowed as he fought back his own tears. He shook his head in defeat and whispered, "I know. I'm sorry." He tried to think about what else to say when Malik stepped between them and pointed in the direction they had come from.

"Look!" Two men had cautiously turned the corner and were walking in their direction. "Let's go!"

Everyone had quickly picked up their bags and followed Malik away from the men. At one point, they passed Rachel Walsh's office building, which Tavi had looked up online recently, but when he had called her, she told him that she couldn't help them. It was then that Pablo and Malik had ripped off a couple of boards covering a door to an abandoned room. Pablo had hurried everyone inside, and then after picking up the boards from the ground, he had followed them and locked the door behind him.

Tavi looked around with worry and pondered about what they could do next. He couldn't stop thinking about Kyle and every instinct told him to do anything possible to save his friend, but he had no idea where to begin. And a small voice inside of his head was already asking if Kyle might already be dead.

Seven children left, Tavi thought, as he counted the sleeping bodies. That's all that we have left. How can we possibly survive?

An image of Jack laughing crossed his mind and Tavi wondered how his group was doing. When they had split up after raiding Bangarang and The Schoolhouse, they had agreed that smaller groups would have a better chance of not getting caught. Tavi had spoken to Jack briefly since then, but he unexpectedly longed to hear his voice. He stood up and quietly walked into the bathroom, gently easing the door shut behind him.

"Hello?" Jack answered softly after the first ring.

"Hey, Jack. It's Tavi."

"Hold on a second." After thirty seconds, Jack spoke again in a more normal voice. "Hey, Tavi! How are you guys doing?"

"Bad. They got Kyle last night."

There was a long moment of shocked silence. "Shit," Jack breathed. "I'm so sorry."

"Yeah. What about you?"

"Running. Yesterday was okay, but there were guys chasing us before that. We're actually sleeping in Vetinari Station now, but a crazy homeless man tried to attack us last night, so we need to find a new place soon."

"Lucky you. We've been chased every day. We just broke into a boarded up home last night, but we can't stay here. We'll be trapped if anyone comes." Tavi paused and thought about his talk with Rachel the previous night. "I may have a safe place to stay tonight. You can probably come, too."

"Really? Where?"

"Long story, but it's in that councilwoman's office. She offered it to me."

"We might need it. Thanks." Jack was silent for a couple of seconds before saying, "Have you spoken to Derek or Anouram or Ben or anyone?"

"Nope. We saw Adam and Mo at the library a couple of days ago. I think we may go back and spend today there. Have you talked to the others?"

"Yeah. Derek's group is nearby. The others are around. Same story for all of us. No place to sleep and kids keep getting taken every day."

"Well, if you talk to them, tell them they can stay in the councilwoman's office tonight if they need to. I'll send you a text with the address after I look it up at the library."

"Cool. Thanks, Tavi. Ah, shit!"

"What?"

"A security guard is coming over. We gotta go. I'll probably see you tonight. Be safe!"

"Good luck! Bye." Tavi listened for a response, but Jack had already hung up to deal with his own problems.

Tavi exited the bathroom and found Chloe peeking out through one of the cracks in the window. She didn't turn around as he walked up and stood behind her.

"You see anything?" he whispered.

She shook her head. "What are we going to do, Tavi? What about Kyle?"

"I don't know. Today, we go back to the library. Tonight, we go to that councilwoman's office. Maybe Jack and Derek and the others will show up and we can talk about it."

Out of the corner of his eye, he saw her swallow and close her eyes. "I can't do this anymore," she said almost inaudibly.

Me neither, Tavi thought, as he put his arm around her shoulders and pulled her towards him. They stood in silence by the window, alone in their own thoughts, until Sasha murmured and woke up behind them. Within minutes, the rest of the children were awake, yawning and stretching in the shadowy room.

There was no discussion about where they were going to spend the day. As soon as Tavi mentioned the library, all of the children nodded their heads wearily in agreement as they each stared at the floor in front of their feet. Tavi casually tried to sit next to Kurt, but as soon as he slid down next to him, Kurt hopped up and said in a voice devoid of any emotion, "Let's go."

They spent the day at the library, only leaving in pairs to get food. Tavi quietly explained to the others about Rachel's offer to let them stay at her office. The only dissenter was Kurt, who didn't trust Rachel and then hissed angrily that it was Tavi's fault that Kyle was gone, but Chloe had grabbed his arm and pulled him away from the table, and the rest of the children murmured their assent and went back to their own niches in the library which they had picked out. A few other children showed up throughout the day, including Ben, Mohammed, and Anouram, and Tavi handed them a map he had printed from the computer and told them to come after seven if they had nowhere else to go. They all accepted the offer gratefully, and from their exhausted demeanors, Tavi had no doubt that most of them would show up as well.

For the first time, he wondered how big Rachel's office was and how many kids were actually going to show up. Mentally shrugging his shoulders, he decided he didn't care. If they could truly have a safe place for just one night, then that was all he could ask for.

Tavi and his friends stayed at the library until it closed, and then they stopped by a nearby food stand to eat dinner. Tavi saw a look of pain cross Kurt's face when they passed the sausage truck, and he swore to himself that somehow he would help get Kyle back. As soon as they finished eating, Tavi led them through the alleys until they were only a block away from Rachel's office. Glancing back to make sure that everyone was still together, he hesitated in surprise when he saw four children approaching Pablo, who was bringing up the rear.

He hurried back and reached Pablo at the same time as the children.

"Hey," one of the boys called out. The three boys who were with him smiled uncertainly. They all looked painfully thin and dirty.

"Hi," Pablo said, as Tavi nodded his head.

The boy who had spoken stepped forward. "Um…We know Anouram. I'm Fred. He said that there was a place around here where we could sleep tonight."

"Ah!" Tavi said, recognition flashing across his face. "I know you! Anouram saved you about three weeks ago. You were only at the bridge for a few days." Tavi nodded his head at the other three boys. "Who are they?"

"They were at Bangarang. When we split up after saving them, they had nowhere else to go. I didn't really know anyone, so…" He shrugged, not seeing the need to explain any further.

Tavi felt a sinking feeling in his gut. He glanced at Pablo and saw a similar look upon his face. How many of these kinds of kids were out on the streets? Recently freed from The School House and Bangarang, they had no money or experience on the streets. Shaking the thought from his head, Tavi tried to focus on the present and said, "Yeah. For sure. Come with us. After we get upstairs, we will figure out a way to help these guys."

Fred nodded his head and looked back at the three boys whose faces were split wide with smiles. Tavi smiled back and turned to lead them towards Rachel's office. He paused when Pablo asked, "Have you guys eaten yet?" Tavi glanced back and saw Fred shake his head.

"Um…no. We haven't really eaten anything for two or three days."

Pablo put his hand in his pocket and Tavi knew that he was counting his money. "Okay," Pablo replied. "I'll go get some food and bring it up." He looked at Tavi, his eyes filled with pity. "What floor did you say it was? Fifth?"

"Fourth."

"Okay. I'll be up in a while." He looked at Chloe who had come back with the rest of their group. "You want to go with me?"

"Sure," she said.

Pablo nodded his head and said to Tavi, "Don't worry. We'll be up soon."

Tavi nodded his head and watched them walk away. He looked around at the other children and said, "Let's go."

When they reached the front of the building, Tavi paused for a moment as a sliver of doubt consumed him. He stared at the clean marble in front of him and saw the security guard through the revolving door. Taking a deep breath, Tavi marched confidently through the door, leading his friends inside.

The security guard looked up from the newspaper he was reading. "Can I help you?" he asked suspiciously, his eyes wandering over the large group of kids in front of him.

Tavi cleared his throat. "Umm…Councilwoman Walsh said that we could stay here in office tonight." He cleared his throat again. "Um…my name is Tavi." For a brief moment, he was sure the security guard was going to reject him and force him and his friends to leave. He stared intently into the man's eyes and relaxed when he saw the smile which reached his mouth an instant later.

"Sure," he said. "I was told to expect you. Let me show you where her office is." He ran his eyes over the group of kids again and said, "Is this all of you or should I expect more?"

Tavi bit his lip indecisively. "I know that there are at least two more children coming soon," he said hesitantly, "but there may be more to follow."

"Okay," the security guard said. "I was just asking because I was wondering if those kids outside were with you or if you were having trouble with them or…"

Tavi spun around and gasped when he saw the large group of children huddled on the sidewalk in front of the building. He pushed through his friends and hurried through the revolving door. There were at least forty children milling around anxiously on the sidewalk and Tavi smiled in relief when Jack emerged from the crowd.

"Hey!" Tavi shouted.

"Hey, yourself!" Jack gave Tavi a quick hug and stepped back to look at him.

"Is this everyone?" Tavi asked.

Jack shook his head. "No. Derek's not here yet, and neither is Yabu or a few other kids. Is this cool? Are we allowed to go up?"

"Yeah. I think," Tavi added. "Let's go ask the guard." Tavi led Jack into the building and studied the guard as they approached him. His face was impassive. Tavi looked at Jack before asking, "They're with us. Is that okay?"

The security guard smiled at Tavi reassuringly. "I was told to give sanctuary to any kid tonight who knows Tavi…which is you. If you say it's okay, then it's okay."

Tavi told Jack, "Okay. Bring them in. And let Derek and everyone else know that it's cool." Jack nodded his head and went back outside as Tavi and his friends followed the security guard into the elevator. When they got out on the fourth floor, Tavi felt a load of pressure fall from his shoulders as he felt safe and secure for the first time in a long time. The security guard waved his card in front of a scanner next to a door, punched in a code, and the door clicked. He pushed it open and led the children into the room. When he switched on the light, Sasha gasped in surprise at the size of the rooms.

"We have plenty of room!" she whispered to Tavi excitedly. Tavi smiled back and was about to reply when the security guard interrupted him.

"Okay, so I'm going to leave this door unlocked. Please don't destroy anything or try to go into any of the other offices on this floor. The councilwoman is doing you and your friends a huge favor and so try to be respectful."

Tavi and his friends murmured in agreement. The security guard turned to leave, but stopped and asked in a surprisingly hesitant voice, "Do you mind if I ask what's going on? Why do you guys need this place?"

Tavi shared glances with all of his friends, except for Kurt who was staring at the floor. Sasha gave him a sad smile and shifted her gaze to Hector, who was still wearing a dress and insisting that he was a girl. Tavi returned her smile and with a shake of his head replied, "I can't even explain it. We pissed off the wrong people and now they're after all of us."

"All of who?"

Tavi motioned to the children around him. "Us. The street kids. The runaways from the sex bars." He saw the man's eyes widen in shock and realized that he could never explain who they were. "Us," he finished simply, with a shrug of his shoulders.

The security guard gave a slight nod and said, "Okay. I'll be downstairs if you have any problems. Let me know if you need anything."

"Thank you," Tavi said. The security guard turned and walked down the hall. As Tavi's friends spread out through the office to explore, the elevator dinged and the sound of children's voices filled the hallway.

Chapter 48

The sound of the elevator doors sliding open yanked Tavi from the darkness and soundlessness of sleep, and he listened in a daze as the footsteps got closer and closer. He let out a sigh and was struggling to open his eyes when a woman's voice said softly, "Tavi?"

Instinct trumped confusion, and Tavi grabbed his bag and leaped to his feet. His eyes flew open as he looked for a way to escape, and the first thing he saw was a giant boujie kid wearing a suit. Tavi flinched in surprise, but when he flicked his gaze to the boy's companion and saw that it was Rachel, he felt the adrenaline leave as quickly as it had come, and he gave a weary sigh as he dropped his bag on the floor beside him.

"Tavi, what are you doing out here? I told you that you could use my office if you needed a safe place to sleep." She paused and Tavi heard the tone of her voice change. "Did the security guard not let you in?"

Tavi thought about everything the security guard had done for them that night, including bringing blankets which he had found somewhere when he noticed how young some of the children were. "No, Ms. Walsh," he insisted. An image of the security guard wrapping one of the young boys in a blanket flashed through his mind. He smiled involuntarily and said, "He was really nice to us."

"But then why are you out here? Wait..us? So you brought some friends too?"

Tavi bit his lip, unsure about how to reply. He was positive that she had told him that he could bring friends with him when they had spoken on the phone the previous night. He wasn't sure if he should remind her of what she had said, but before he could respond, she added impatiently, "What is it? I told you, you don't have to keep watch out here. You can all sleep safely in my office for tonight. There's plenty of room."

"I know, Ms. Walsh." Tavi swallowed before continuing. "You know how you said I could tell a couple of my friends about this? If they haven't been able to sleep either because they were worried about danger that..." Tavi paused and struggled to find the words. "You told me we could have a safe place. A sanctuary, you said." He shrugged and opened up his hands. "Well, the ones who needed it the most came."

Rachel reached for the door handle, and Tavi reached out instinctively, not wanting her to disturb the children. It had taken them about four hours to finally get settled down and sleeping comfortably beside each other. He just wanted them to be able to sleep well for at least one night. "Quietly," he cautioned, turning the handle and trying to push the door open. It stopped after only a couple of inches. He leaned his shoulder into the door and continued to gently push it open, knowing that there were children lying right beside it.

The large boujie kid, whom Tavi had decided was her son, used his weight to knock Tavi aside and said, "Let me do it!" He shoved at the door and Tavi heard someone shout in pain.

"HEY!" Tavi wished he had been carrying his metal pipe with him so that he could quickly end this situation. Instead, he just grabbed the boy's arm and warned, "Be careful!"

"Let go of me!" The boy shoved Tavi aside and looked at his mom. In a whiny voice, he asked, "What are his friends doing in there? Selling drugs?"

Tavi glared at the boy and shifted his gaze to Rachel. He had already told her about Byron. She knew how he and the others felt about drugs. He waited for her to say something to her son in his defense.

Instead, she said, "Tavi – I have to see."

Tavi felt like his heart was being ripped out. He had trusted Rachel and believed that she would stand up for him and his friends, and now it took just one fat boujie kid to turn her against him. He couldn't bear to look at her any longer, and so he dropped his eyes to the floor. Shaking his head in disappointment, he mumbled, "Fine."

He watched as she gently opened the door and heard as she stepped on one of the children – probably Jack – who was lying closest to the door. He slid in beside her to make sure that the children wouldn't be alarmed when she woke them up, and waited as she tried to turn on the light switch.

When the lights flickered on, Tavi felt his heart break when he saw again how many children had needed a place to stay for the night. He glanced up at Rachel and again felt the disappointment and grief that she hadn't understood and would probably just make everyone leave again. The idea of forcing all of these children to go back to the streets and knowing that he couldn't protect them any longer overwhelmed him, and Tavi felt tears coming to his eyes.

"What is this?" Rachel asked. Tavi thought she sounded angry and he could barely think of how to answer her question.

"You told me that I could bring my friends who couldn't sleep safely at night. They also had a couple of friends. I guess word got around." He shrugged, wishing that he could explain to her that he must have misunderstood her offer, and wanting to ask her if maybe she could still help them. Instead, all he could say was, "I'm sorry."

To his surprise, she wrapped her arms around him and gave him a hug. He hadn't been embraced with such love and compassion since he had last seen his mother, and his arms unconsciously went around her and held tight to Rachel as he felt Alex push in beside them. Tavi buried his face in Rachel's blouse and let out a sob of relief as she continued to hold him tight. For a brief moment, Tavi felt completely safe and secure.

After a few moments, Tavi felt Rachel's grip relaxing and he stepped back and hurriedly wiped his eyes. Her eyes looked haunted as she cast a final glance over the children sleeping in her office, and then she stepped back and flicked the lights off. She gently eased the door shut as she and Alex followed Tavi into the hallway. Tavi dropped his bag and met her gaze.

"What?" he asked.

Rachel minutely shook her head and said softly, "I didn't know."

Tavi shrugged in response and sat down against the opposite wall. Rachel's son was still staring at him as if Tavi were from another world, but Tavi realized almost immediately that it was true – neither Rachel nor her son had any idea what kind of life Tavi and his friends had to live every day.

Rachel wrinkled her brow and said, "You can't sleep here."

Tavi looked around curiously. "Why not?"

"Because…you don't want to sleep on the floor. You can come home with us and sleep in Alex's room. He has two beds." Both Tavi and Rachel saw Alex's body tense in hostility. "Or you can sleep on the sofa," she quickly added.

Tavi shook his head. "No. I want to stay with my friends."

Rachel studied him for a moment. He noticed a change in her expression as she glanced at her son, and for a moment, it seemed as if she were disappointed that the boy was hers. "Okay," she finally said. "But I'll come here early tomorrow and we will figure out what to do next."

"What time should I make everyone leave by?"

Rachel hesitated before responding. "Is it still dangerous out there?"

Tavi nodded his head. "I think so."

"Then...you and your friends can stay here if you need to. We will just work around you."

"Really?"

"Sure. It should only be for a couple of days, I think."

"Okay. Thank you."

Rachel nodded her head and turned to walk away. Her son reacted immediately and hurried to the elevator. "Good-night, Tavi," Rachel said. "Sleep tight."

Tavi replied, "Good-night, Ms. Walsh," and curled up on his side, with his head resting on his bag. Within seconds, he was fast asleep.

The next day, Tavi was woken up by two men shouting at the children to get out of their office. He leaped to his feet, unsure of what he could do as frightened children hurried through the doorway. But before his mind could clear away the cobwebs of sleep and decide upon an action, Rachel was hurrying down the hallway, yelling at the men.

"Jeremy! Brett! Leave them alone! I said they could stay!"

Both men spun around, and one of them said, "What are you talking about? There's no room for them." His face wrinkled up into a sneer. "And the smell..."

"Jeremy!" Rachel was nearly screaming as she reached them. "What's wrong with you? How's this any different than staying at the soup kitchen or working at the orphanage?"

Jeremy replied, "That's done. After the fundraiser last night, my dad told me and Brett that he was proud of us and we'd done a good job." The man next to Jeremy nodded his head in agreement.

"And so what? It was all a show?!?" Rachel asked disbelievingly.

"Well, no," Jeremy said.

"It's just that this is too much," Brett said, motioning to the children around them. "Look how many of them there are. And they smell like…"

"Get out!" Rachel said. "Just leave. We'll talk about this when it's all over."

Both men shrugged their shoulders and, without saying a word, strolled to the elevators and disappeared.

Rachel shook her head in exasperation and let out a long sigh. Raising her voice so that all of the children could hear her, she announced, "I promised Tavi that this could be a sanctuary, and that is what it will be. If you want to, you can stay here today."

Murmurs of surprise filled the air as Rachel asked Tavi, "Do you think any of these children would be willing to make police statements against their former bar owners?"

Tavi nodded his head. "Probably. I would, but the only one that I knew is already in jail."

"Good!" Rachel said vehemently. "I'm glad that at least a few of them have already been caught and punished!"

The rest of the day was a blur for Tavi. Children filled the hallway as they tried to stay out of everyone's way. The policemen arrived soon after Rachel did. Tavi helped Rachel find the children who had worked at specific sex bars and were willing to speak to the police. Later in the afternoon, the mayor showed up with enough food for all of the children, and he made a big display of sitting down with the children and eating lunch with them for the television cameras which had followed him in. At one point, Rachel pointed Tavi out to the mayor, who came over and began complimenting him and asking him questions. Tavi tried to respond, but when a reporter hurried over with a television camera right behind him, Tavi felt himself blushing and couldn't give a coherent response.

The mayor, seeing how nervous Tavi was, gave him a wink and said, "I hope you enjoy your new place." Tavi and Jack exchanged confused glances as the mayor wandered away, still followed by the cameraman.

Soon after that, the largest television that Tavi had ever seen was wheeled down the hallway and set up inside of Rachel's office. She asked everyone to sit down quietly because there was something important for them to see. When the television was turned on, children started calling out requests for television shows and movies that they wanted to watch. But after two commercials, the words on the screen froze Tavi's blood.

"Child Sex Slaves"

Tavi watched in fear as the anchorman began talking about their situation. He gasped when they showed the policemen being arrested, but the biggest shock was when the television showed The School House and Tavi recognized Vikram being led out in handcuffs. The camera then panned over to Bangarang and Tavi saw a large man being forcibly carried out by three policemen. Following behind them was a small boy with a blanket wrapped around him, as he gingerly hobbled beside a policewoman.

"That's Kyle!" Kurt shouted from across the room. He jumped up and looked in Tavi's direction. "Tavi! That's Kyle! He's okay!" Kurt started pushing his way past the other children as he rushed for the door. Tavi and Pablo stood up and made their way through the crowd. By the time they reached the door, Chloe was waiting for them, along with Rachel.

"Where is he?" Kurt demanded from a few feet behind them. "Where's Kyle?"

"He's okay," Rachel reassured him. "I just asked. They took him to a hospital. If you want, someone can take you guys to visit him."

Kurt looked at the others and his face split into a huge grin as tears glistened in his eyes. He reached out and grabbed his friends, and they gave each other a long hug as they all softly murmured words of relief to one another.

Chapter 49

"Do you mind if we start building here as soon as possible?" Rachel asked as she looked from the barn to the forest. "You will receive the money within a few weeks."

Laura shook her head. "No. I've seen the news for the last couple of days. Your office looks pretty crowded."

Rachel laughed. "You have no idea." She looked at the others. "Anyone have any idea how long it'll take to get things set up and built here?"

"To build what you need? A few months, at least," Pastor Mike said.

"I have an idea," Jenny offered. She had wandered over when Laura, Rachel, and Pastor Mike had arrived to look at the property and had been tagging along behind them quietly.

"What is it?" Laura asked.

"Why not just get tents and blankets and cooking stoves? It's probably better than anything else they've got. And they'll be safe here."

"What about running water?" Rachel asked.

"The barn has water running to it. There are several faucets inside and outside."

The others looked at each other and nodded their heads, knowing that her suggestion was better than any alternative.

"And so after you build their living quarters…" Laura began.

"The barn and horses can stay here just like we agreed," Rachel said.

"And I have a lot of people in my congregation who have volunteered to help out here and take care of the children," Pastor Mike added. "I also have several teachers in my congregation who have volunteered to teach the children until we get the statelessness issue dealt with."

"And so that's it?" Rachel asked in a voice full of wonder. "We've done it?"

Pastor Mike nodded his head, his face beaming with joy. "I think so. The only thing we have left to do is…"

"Tell the children," Rachel finished for him.

Chapter 50

When the first bus arrived, Rachel and Pastor Mike were standing in front of the barn, ready to greet them. The children hadn't been told where they were going. Rachel had announced that they had another place where the children could stay indefinitely if they wanted to, and all of the children had agreed to come along.

Tavi was one of the first ones off of the bus, and his look of confusion was mirrored on the faces of the other children as they debarked from the bus.

"Where are we?" he asked.

Rachel and Pastor Mike stepped forward in greeting and pointed to the tents. "Have you guys ever been camping?" she asked.

The children silently shook their heads.

"Well, for the next few months, you will be sleeping in those tents. They have blankets and pillows and clean clothes for everyone. After that…" Pastor Mike pointed to the land where they had decided to build the dormitories. "You will be sleeping in buildings, made for you, and this is where you will live."

The children's faces relaxed as they looked around in wonder and stared at the trees and the tents. A gasp arose from the crowd when Jasmine exited the barn on her horse, Puppy. Miss Jenny followed her on the new horse they had just bought for Jasmine. She had wanted the new children to see both horses and had hoped it would spark their excitement. Their enthusiastic response was more than she had dreamed possible.

Tavi wrenched his gaze away from the horses and looked at Rachel with a gaze so full of hope and fear that it broke her heart. "And then what?" he asked softly.

"And then," Rachel raised her voice, and the other children were immediately quiet as they focused their attention upon her. "And then," she repeated, "you will work here. You will help keep it clean. You will help cook. You will help raise crops. You will help take care of the horses. This will be your house and your responsibility. And," she paused for brief moment, "you will go to school here and study."

It was as if something cracked inside of Tavi's soul as tears gushed from his eyes. Rachel had never thought that happiness could be a physical sensation, but as she stepped forward and wrapped her arms around Tavi, the happiness of the children overwhelmed her and almost knocked her from her feet as they realized that they had finally found a home.

Chapter 51

From the edge of the alleyway, he watched as the teenager stepped off of the bus, radiating confidence and health. The teenager hesitated for a second and glanced in all directions as if sensing danger, before relaxing and heading straight towards where Yuri was hidden.

Yuri muffled his persistent cough with his hand and stepped back a few feet as he waited for Tavi to pass by. He knew that Tavi was still trying to save other street kids, and he had secretly watched him disembark from the same bus every Friday for the last two months, but this was the day when it was finally time to end everything.

Sliding his hand into his right pocket, Yuri felt a sense of comfort as he caressed the item with his thumb, and he grasped it tightly in anticipation of meeting Tavi for the last time. He peeked around the corner. Tavi was only fifteen feet away, still cautiously eyeing his surroundings as he walked down the street. Timing it perfectly, Yuri stepped out from the alleyway directly in front of Tavi, grabbed him by his shirt with his left hand, and dragged him as deep as he could into the alley.

The shock on his face was palpable. He shoved Yuri back with both hands and Yuri felt the strength in Tavi's healthy body. He stumbled backwards a few steps as Tavi stared at him with wide eyes, his body poised to run.

Recognition flashed across his face and Tavi's jaw dropped slightly as he gazed at Yuri. "Yuri? Is that really you?"

Yuri coughed again and pulled the hood of his sweatshirt away from his head. "Hi, Tavi," he said in a raspy voice. He studied Tavi's face and felt a mixture of emotions when he saw how vigorous and happy he looked. Envy. Anger. Pride. That should have been him, and yet...

"Finally! I've been searching all over for you for the last nine months! I didn't know what happened to you after I..."

"After you helped destroy The School House," Yuri finished for him.

Tavi nodded, his gaze growing slightly wary, and he took a step back. He ran his eyes over Yuri's body and they narrowed slightly at Yuri's right hand which was still shoved into his pocket. "I didn't know what had happened to you. I hoped you were okay."

Yuri thought about his last nine months. He had gotten a cheap room which he could easily afford from the money Vikram had been paying for him. After visits to a couple of doctors who had only confirmed what Yuri already knew, he had resigned himself to the fact that he was going to get sick and die soon. He rarely left his house, only leaving to buy food or books, and he was barely eating anything at all. He had spent a lot of time reflecting upon his life and everything he had done, and he had become obsessed with finding Tavi and tying up the loose ends before he finally died in ignominy in the small, inexpensive room where he was waiting for his life to come to an end.

"I left a few days before the police came. No one ever came looking for me."

Tavi grinned in relief. "Good! That means you can come with us. Yuri! You won't believe what's..." Tavi trailed off when he saw Yuri shaking his head.

"I'm just here to send a message." Yuri tightened his grip in his pocket. He hoped he was doing the right thing.

Tavi's eyes flicked to Yuri's pocket again. "Send a message to who?"

Suddenly, without warning, Yuri slid his hand out of his pocket and jammed it into Tavi's chest. Tavi's eyes widened in alarm, but he had no chance to react.

"My mom." Yuri relaxed his grip on the envelope he had been squeezing as Tavi reached up and took it from him. "Could you give this to her? It has the rest of my money and a letter explaining to her what happened to me."

"What? Why don't you give it to her yourself?"

Yuri's body heaved as he coughed deeply. "I'm dying, Tavi. I've got the HIV."

Tavi scrutinized Yuri in silence, and Yuri felt himself cringing under his gaze. He flipped his hood up and felt secure as it drooped over his forehead. Finally, Tavi shook his head and said, "No."

Yuri's mouth opened in surprise. He had imagined this conversation numerous times, but it had never gone like this. "No? Why not?"

"Because I don't think you're dying yet."

Yuri gave a bitter laugh. He held out his arms and threw the hood away from his face again. "Look at me! What do you see?"

"You look like you're starving."

"That's the HIV!"

Tavi sighed and took a step towards Yuri. "Yuri, please come with me."

"What? No! I'm dying! Do you know the things I've done?!?"

Tavi shook his head. "There are about ten kids with HIV at our home right now. With the right medicine and the right food, they can live a long life – and so can you." Tavi's eyes lit up, and he smiled as he said, "I've been studying it in biology class. Yuri, you won't believe what we're doing there. We actually have real teachers! I'm going to graduate in six months!"

Yuri's mind was a maelstrom of emotions. He listened to Tavi speak excitedly, watched his eyes glow with passion, and yet he couldn't understand him. Why didn't Tavi hate him? It was Yuri's fault that Tavi had ended up here. Yuri had killed his friend, beaten other children, and done so many terrible things that…that…he should be dead. He shook his head again and interrupted Tavi's stories about his new home. "Stop! What's wrong with you?"

Tavi looked at him, confused. "What?"

"Why do you keep asking me to come with you? Don't you know who I am? Don't you know what I've DONE?!? And yet every time, you just say, 'Yuri, come with me.' Why?!?"

Tavi answered softly, "Because it's not your fault."

"It is! I did those things!"

"You survived, Yuri. But I know you. You saved my brother. You saved Pablo and Chloe. You even tried to help kids when Vikram was in charge."

Yuri shook his head in denial.

"Whatever you did wrong," Tavi continued, "would never have happened if you hadn't gone to The School House in the first place."

"What about you? You didn't do those things," Yuri responded harshly.

Tavi's gaze drifted away from Yuri and he stared blankly at the wall with a small smile on his face. "I had friends that I could trust," he said, looking Yuri in the eye.

For the last couple of years, Yuri had only ever thought about the things he had done since he had started helping out Vikram and Javier. He now tried to cast his memories back to when he had just been another boy being sold to customers, but his mind refused and kept veering away. One stray memory slipped through; just a brief emotion at most. But Yuri suddenly remembered how alone and afraid he had been, and how he had been forced to lock away every aspect of himself which wasn't hard enough or strong enough to survive.

"Don't trust anyone," he reminded Tavi with a small smile. Tavi responded with a similar smile, and Yuri finally admitted, "I'm glad I was wrong."

"Please come back with me, Yuri," Tavi pleaded softly.

"I can't."

"It's a chance to put all of this stuff behind us and be who we might've been."

Yuri shook his head again. He stared at the ground and mumbled, "I can't. I'm afraid."

"Of what?" Tavi asked gently.

"What if they hate me for what I've done? What if I die?" Tears streamed down his face. "I don't want to die, Tavi. It's not fair!"

"We have doctors, Yuri. And teachers. And food. And beds. And horses! Come, Yuri."

Yuri imperceptibly shook his head.

"And after you feel a little better, we can go see our families together. I think it's time for me to finally go see mine."

Yuri swallowed and looked up, just in time to see a look of fear in Tavi's eyes as well. "What is it?"

"I don't want to go back alone. I don't know what to tell my family." He met Yuri's gaze and said one last time, "Please come with me."

Yuri hesitated for just a moment before nodding his head. Tavi's face broke into a grin as they turned and made their way back towards the bus station.

A Couple of Years Later...

The man was one of the most recent volunteers at the children's home. He showed up every morning at nine, and every day, he volunteered to do to the filthiest jobs that needed to be done. As he carried the buckets of waste from the outhouses to the nearby compost pile, he relished the feeling of the sun shining upon him as he used muscles that had remained dormant for far too long. After dumping out the last bucket, he went to a nearby shed and took down a pitchfork. Gripping it tightly in his hands, he stepped onto the large compost pile and began shoveling the manure around. He lost track of the time as he concentrated on doing it perfectly, and he was eventually distracted out of his reverie by the sound of nearby laughter.

He looked behind him and saw two teenaged boys walking towards the barn. He squinted his eyes against the sunlight, and his heart began beating swiftly in recognition. Hesitating for a moment, he willed his legs to move, and he stumbled off of the compost pile and directly towards the two boys.

They glanced at him in surprise when he was only a few feet away, and they both tensed up when they saw him staring at them while holding his pitchfork in front of him.

"What do you want?" the older one asked, as they each took a step back.

The man looked down at his pitchfork and his manure-covered boots and realized how deranged he must look. He tossed the pitchfork to the side and studied the boys' faces. Their eyes had followed the pitchfork as it landed in the grass, and now both boys were gazing quizzically at his face.

"Wait a second," the younger teenager said. "Aren't you…?"

The man fell to his knees, overcome with emotion. His son still refused to talk to him. His daughter treated him as if he were a stranger. And Laura…his wife had told him the previous week that she couldn't be with him anymore. For four years, he had thought about the boys he had sold for sex, how he had destroyed each of their lives, and he couldn't stop wondering about what had become of them. He hadn't been sure if he would know any of the boys at this home, but he had hoped that maybe…just maybe…he might get the chance to apologize. And now that he finally had that chance, the only thing he could do was weep as he said, "Yuri, Tavi, it's me, Javier…"

Yuri's eyes widened in shock for a brief moment before a murderous look of rage swept across his face. His lip curled up in the hint of a snarl and Javier flinched back instinctively. Tavi rested his hand on Yuri's arm and gently held him back. Javier tried to smile at Tavi, but he froze when he saw the loathing on Tavi's face.

An eternity passed in the span of five heartbeats. Without saying a word, Yuri and Tavi turned away and walked towards their dormitory, leaving Javier alone on the grass, his heart breaking in agony, as he watched the forgiveness he had so desperately sought walk away from him without even a backwards glance.

Epilogue

(Today)

Amy surreptitiously studies the other girls in the room as they wait for the casting agents to reappear. Of the twenty girls in the room, she is forced to admit that at least six of them are probably more beautiful than her. She had always been the prettiest girl in her class in Omaha, but since arriving in New York City, she's started to feel doubts about herself for the first time in her life. Everyone had always told her that she should be a model or an actress, and when she won the modeling competition at Westroads Mall, she just assumed that it was the first step of a long and successful modeling career.

But the never-ending job offers, which her new agent promised would be falling at her feet once she came to New York City, turned out to be daily cattle calls with hundreds of models all competing for the same shoot. Her dreams of glamorous parties and dating famous people quickly came to a crashing halt and she was forced to find part-time work at a call center, asking people if they were happy with their health insurance, and then trying to convince them to give her their social security numbers over the phone.

She had finally managed to land a couple of modeling gigs, but she could tell that her agent had lost all interest in her. The only reason her agent had sent her today was because the model request was for wholesome, Midwestern girls between the ages of eighteen and twenty, with blond hair and blue eyes. This was the first casting call Amy had attended where they had asked her to strip completely naked, but the money at stake was too high, and so she had swallowed her misgivings and slowly disrobed in front of the two women as they stood to either side of her. She had frozen for a second when she noticed the flashing light of the web-camera that was aimed at her, but she was so overwhelmed by the situation that she just forced her mind to go blank as the women took her clothes from her.

A middle-aged dark-skinned man enters the foyer where they are waiting and walks through the room without looking around. The secretary sitting behind the desk gives him a respectful nod as he passes, but he ignores her and barges into the casting room. When he closes the door behind him, Amy makes eye contact with a girl sitting across from her and they both shrug their shoulders in confusion.

A couple of minutes later, the two women exit the room. One of them announces, "Will numbers 2, 3, 6, 9, 12, 15, and 18 please come with us? The rest of you, thank you for coming, but unfortunately you're not what we're looking for." As the other girls gather their things and stand up, Amy feels her heart pounding in her breast as she looks at the number pinned to her shirt – 15. She swallows nervously and joins the group of girls who are entering the room.

"Thank you for coming," the man begins, speaking with a slight accent. Amy stares at his mustache as she listens to him speak, and she wonders if he is the person who had been watching on the camera. "We would like to offer you all a year-long modeling contract in either Saudi Arabia or Japan. It will pay between one hundred and one hundred fifty thousand dollars, depending on how well you do your job. And if you enjoy it there, you can resign for a second year." He studies the girls for a second and asks, "Does anyone have any questions?"

The girl next to Amy raises her hand. "When does this begin?"

"You will fly out this Saturday – in five days. If you cannot do it, please leave now. Otherwise, Annika and Annette will give you all of the information you need."

Amy looks around and can see a couple of the girls wavering, but after a few seconds of silent debating, all of the girls choose to stay. Amy feels a flutter of excitement in her stomach as she leaves the room to meet with the two women. This is her chance – international modeling experience! She swears to herself that she will do anything she can so that she can return home as a success. She doesn't even notice the four men who pass her in the hallway as they enter the office she has just recently departed.

It is unfortunate that she can't hear the conversation.

"I'll give you fifty thousand for number fifteen."

"What happened to the girls you bought six months ago?"

"One of them has died. And one of them is a drug-addled whore."

"That seems to happen a lot to the girls you buy." The other men laugh. "Okay. Fifty thousand. Her name is…"

"I don't care. She's just a whore. I'll have the money wired to you."

The men quickly conclude their business as the two professions that are as old as civilization, slavery and prostitution, continue their insidious spread throughout the world.

...And that's it. The end.

Well, not really, but I think if I were to follow Amy's story, it would be more of the same tragic occurrences. And, to be honest, there were a couple of places in the first Boys for Sale novel where – after putting it off for a day or two – I had to grit my teeth and silently apologize to Tavi as I wrote about him being raped and abused. I discovered that writing is not always enjoyable or cathartic.

And so, what's next? I wish I knew. When I first learned about this, I realized that I'm not much of a public speaker, and I'm not really a rah-rah type of person usually, but maybe...I could write a story and try to help other people learn about what's happening...

And maybe you are a good public speaker...or you have friends who might need to learn about this...or you're a lawyer or a teacher or a voter or a...I don't know. But maybe if enough people become aware of what's happening, then we could do something.

But even I'm copping out here. It's easy for me to say, "I wrote a book. I did what I could!" But that would be a lie. I could still go and volunteer during my free time. I could donate money to try to help. I could go to these organizations or the churches that are combatting this problem and say, "I'm here! What can I do?"

And so maybe my next step can be your next step as well – swallowing that nervous feeling and asking strangers what I could do to help...while also saying, "By the way, there are a couple of books you should read. Go to Amazon and search for Boys for Sale..."

A note from the author:

A last bit of truth – I need your help. I love writing and sharing ideas and stories, but it's so difficult to spread my stories very far. If you were entertained by this story or enjoyed it, please write a review on Amazon. The feedback and support mean more than you know.

Text copyright © 2013 Marc Finks
All Rights Reserved

This book is licensed for your personal enjoyment only. This book may not be re-sold or given away to other people. If you would like to share this book with another person, please purchase an additional copy for each person. If you're reading this book and did not purchase it, or it was not purchased for your use only, then please purchase your own copy. Thank you for respecting the hard work of this author.

This book is a work of fiction. The names, characters, places, and incidents are products of the author's imagination or have been used fictitiously and are not to be construed as real. Any resemblance to persons, living or dead, actual events, locales, or organizations is entirely coincidental.

All rights are reserved. No part of this book may be used or reproduced in any manner whatsoever without written permission from the author.

About Me:

Between studying for my Master's degree in Education and teaching really smart students in Seoul, South Korea, I've discovered that when I do have a little bit of time off, my happy place is a small, mostly deserted island in Thailand (Ko Jum), and I find that living in a bungalow for a few weeks right on the beach is the perfect place for me to focus without any distractions. Also, since the only thing there is a small restaurant, a beach, and a dirt road leading to a village which is five miles away, there's not much to do besides swim, read, and write.

My first attempt at writing and finishing a book became T.A.G., The Assassination Game, a 600 page novel. It was based on something I wished was real, but I was tired of reading books with protagonists who were all good, and antagonists who were clearly bad. Personally, I liked the story, but I think my dad gave me the most honest feedback when he said, "I didn't really find any of the four main characters to be likable." Apparently I went too far to the extreme, but hopefully after a bit of editing, it'll appear on Amazon someday.

After that I wrote a book based on the idea 'what if imaginary friends weren't so imaginary?' However, that was all hand-written in two notepads, and it's still unfinished. Usually, when my vacation ends, I stop writing since there are too many other distractions in life - unfortunately. Hopefully, that one, too, will be finished someday.

Boys For Sale, and it's follow-up novel, Redemption, were inspired by a speech given by David Batstone in Seoul in January of 2011. I was shocked by how many children are bought and sold as sex slaves and the things that happen to them...and I was moved by how much some people give in order to save these children. One of his anecdotes led me to the character of Tavi, and as I imagined what he had to go through to get to where I met him in my mind, the story just seemed to write itself...

One last reminder…

When you turn the page, you should be given the opportunity to rate this book and share your thoughts on Facebook and Twitter. If you believe the book is worth sharing, would you take a few seconds to let your friends and family know about it? And if you have a few minutes and a few words to say, it'd be great if you could leave a review on my Amazon page. If it turns out to make a difference in someone's life, they'll be forever grateful to you. As will I.

All the best…and thank you for reading my novel.

Marc Finks

Printed in Great Britain
by Amazon